DESCENDER

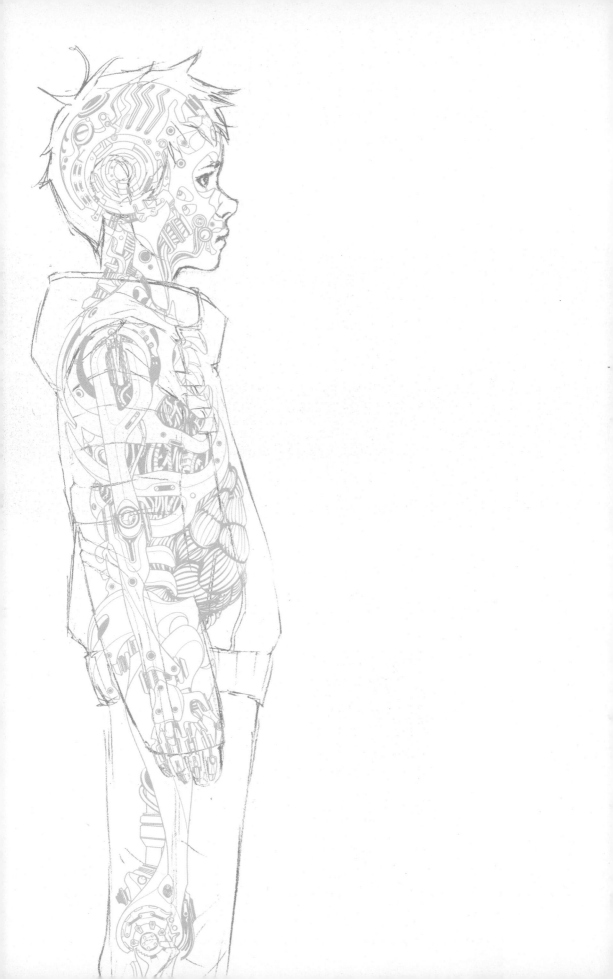

IMAGE COMICS Presents

DESCENDER
BOOK TWO:MACHINE MOON

Written by JEFF LEMIRE
Illustrated by DUSTIN NGUYEN
Lettered and Designed by STEVE WANDS

Cover by DUSTIN NGUYEN

Descender Created by
JEFF LEMIRE & DUSTIN NGUYEN

for IMAGE COMICS
ROBERT KIRKMAN chief operating officer
ERIK LARSEN chief financial officer
TODD MCFARLANE president
MARC SILVESTRI chief executive officer
JIM VALENTINO vice-president

Corey Murphy – Director of Sales
Jeff Boison – Director of Publishing Planning & Book Trade Sales
Jeremy Sullivan – Director of Digital Sales
Kat Salazar – Director of PR & Marketing
Emily Miller – Director of Operations
Branwyn Bigglestone – Senior Accounts Manager
Sarah Mello – Accounts Manager
Drew Gill – Art Director
Jonathan Chan – Production Manager
Meredith Wallace – Print Manager
Briah Skelly – Publicity Assistant
Sasha Head – Sales & Marketing Production Designer
Randy Okamura – Digital Production Designer
David Brothers – Branding Manager
Ally Power – Content Manager
Addison Duke – Production Artist
Vincent Kukua – Production Artist
Tricia Ramos – Production Artist
Jeff Stang – Direct Market Sales Representative
Emilio Bautista – Digital Sales Associate
Leanna Caunter – Accounting Assistant
Chloe Ramos-Peterson – Administrative Assistant
IMAGECOMICS.COM

DESCENDER, VOL. 2
FIRST PRINTING, MAY 2016.
ISBN, REGULAR EDITION: 978-1-63215-676-1
ISBN, CROSSOVER COMICS EDITION: 978-1-63215-866-6

CHAPTER ONE

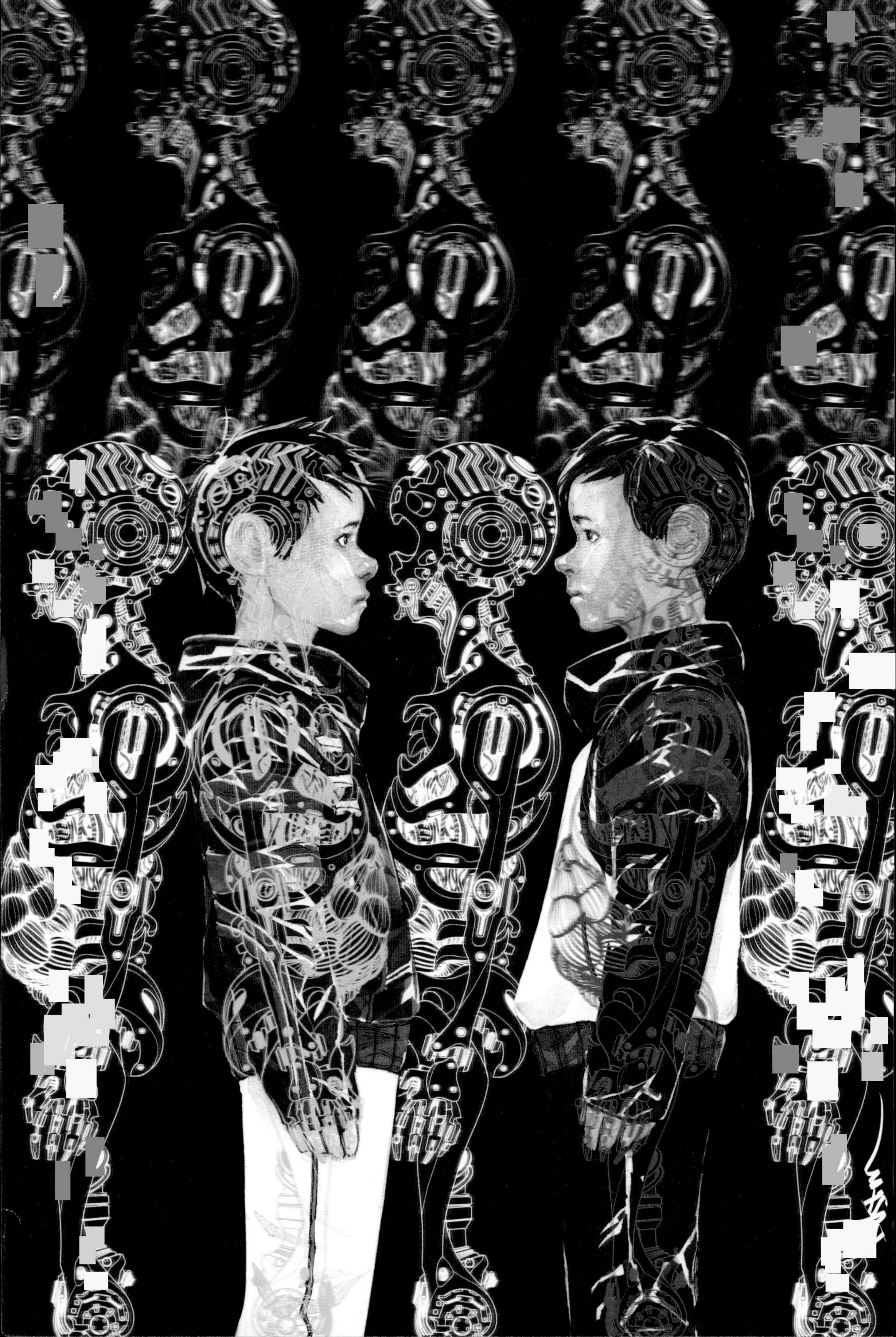

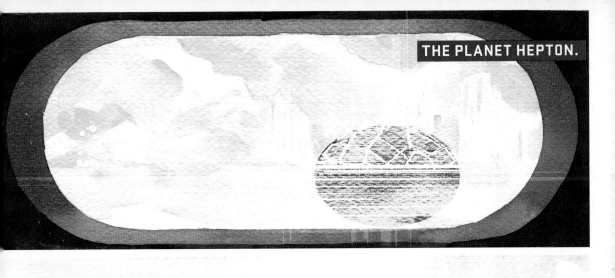

A **Fringe World** of the UGC. Once considered a viable candidate for eventual Core World status until the Harvester attacks destroyed the temperature control plants at its poles and Hepton reverted back to its frozen, precolonization climate.

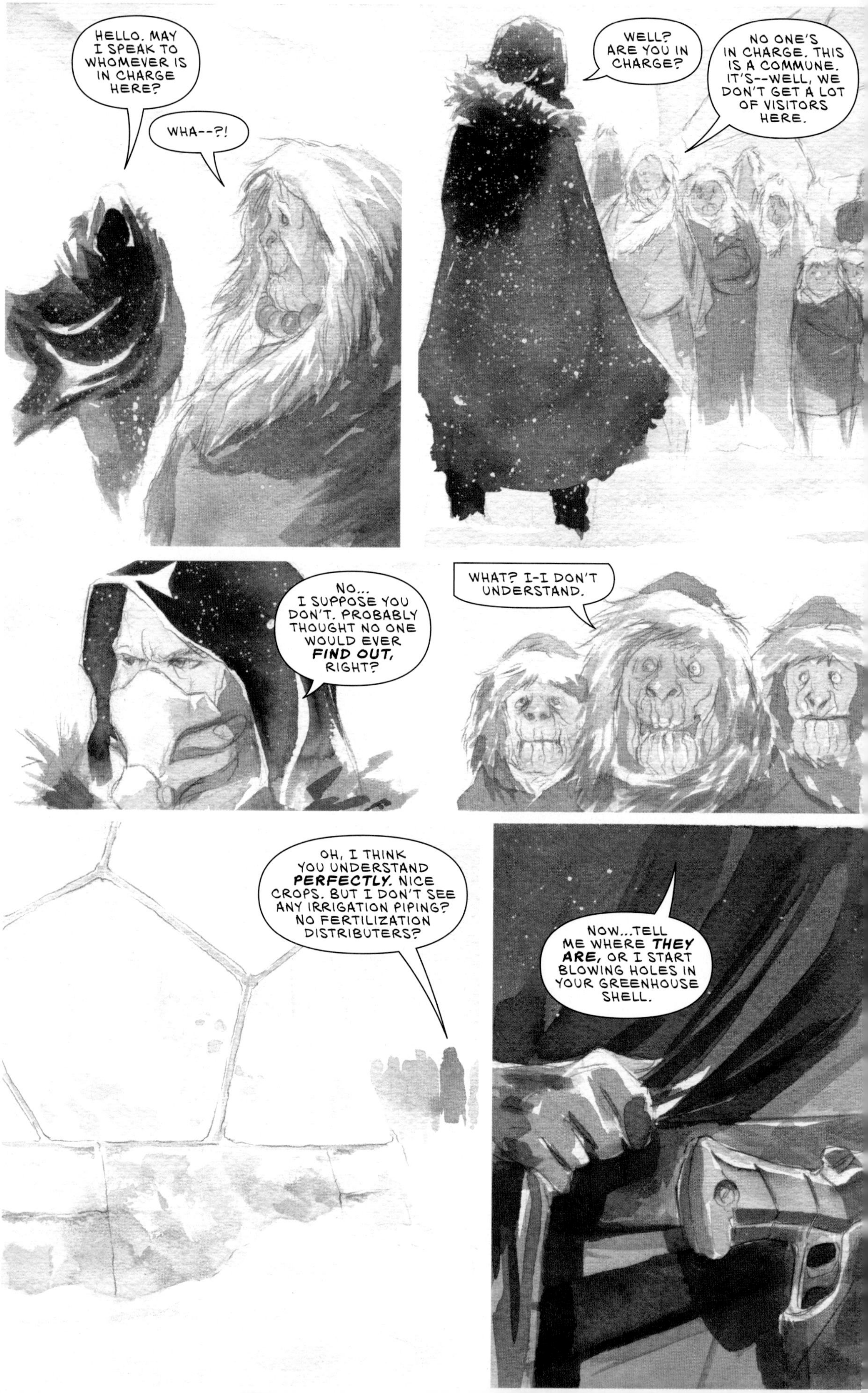
HELLO. MAY I SPEAK TO WHOMEVER IS IN CHARGE HERE?
WHA--?!
WELL? ARE YOU IN CHARGE?
NO ONE'S IN CHARGE. THIS IS A COMMUNE. IT'S--WELL, WE DON'T GET A LOT OF VISITORS HERE.
NO... I SUPPOSE YOU DON'T. PROBABLY THOUGHT NO ONE WOULD EVER FIND OUT, RIGHT?
WHAT? I-I DON'T UNDERSTAND.
OH, I THINK YOU UNDERSTAND PERFECTLY. NICE CROPS. BUT I DON'T SEE ANY IRRIGATION PIPING? NO FERTILIZATION DISTRIBUTERS?
NOW...TELL ME WHERE THEY ARE, OR I START BLOWING HOLES IN YOUR GREENHOUSE SHELL.

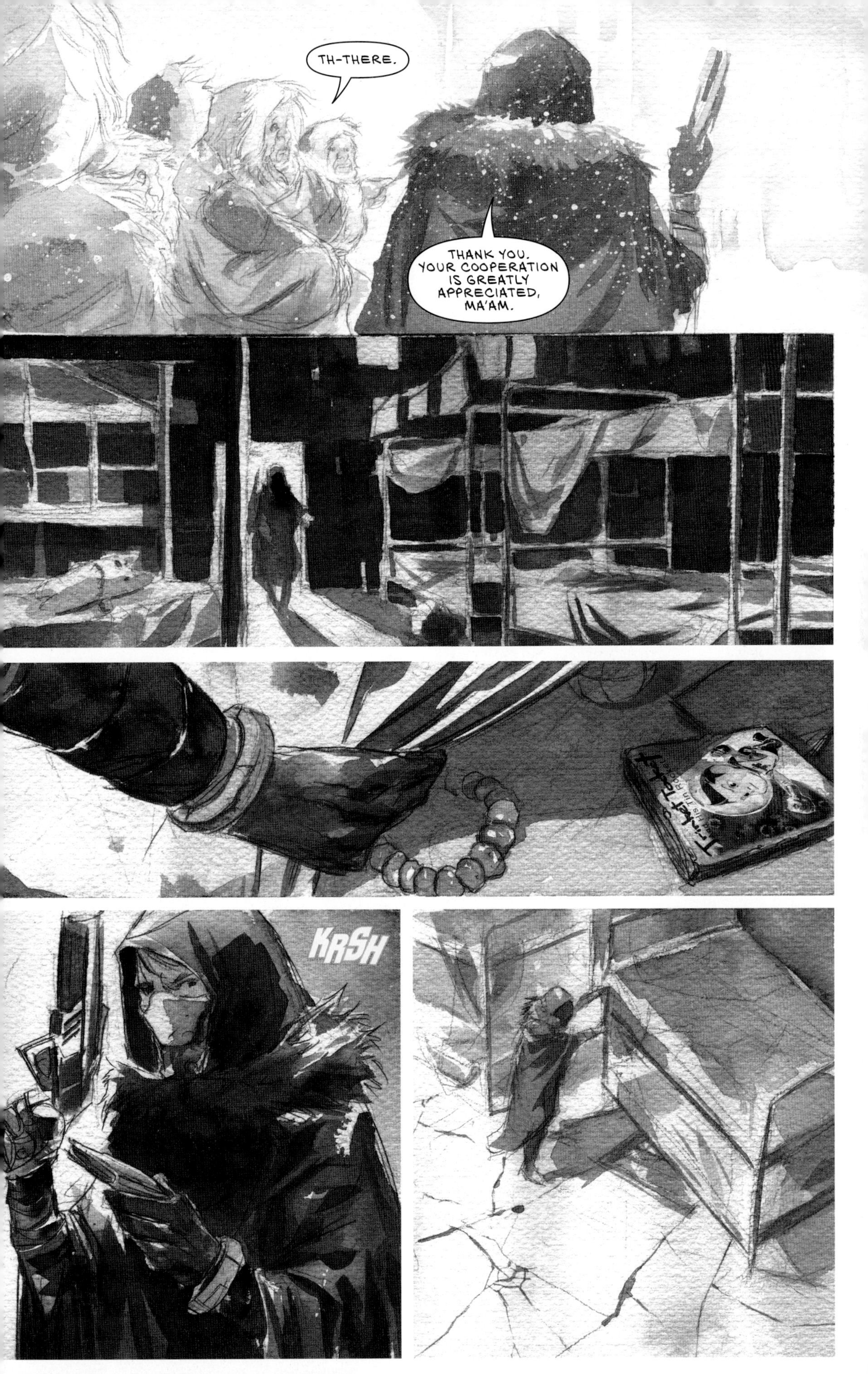
TH-THERE.
THANK YOU. YOUR COOPERATION IS GREATLY APPRECIATED, MA'AM.
KRSH

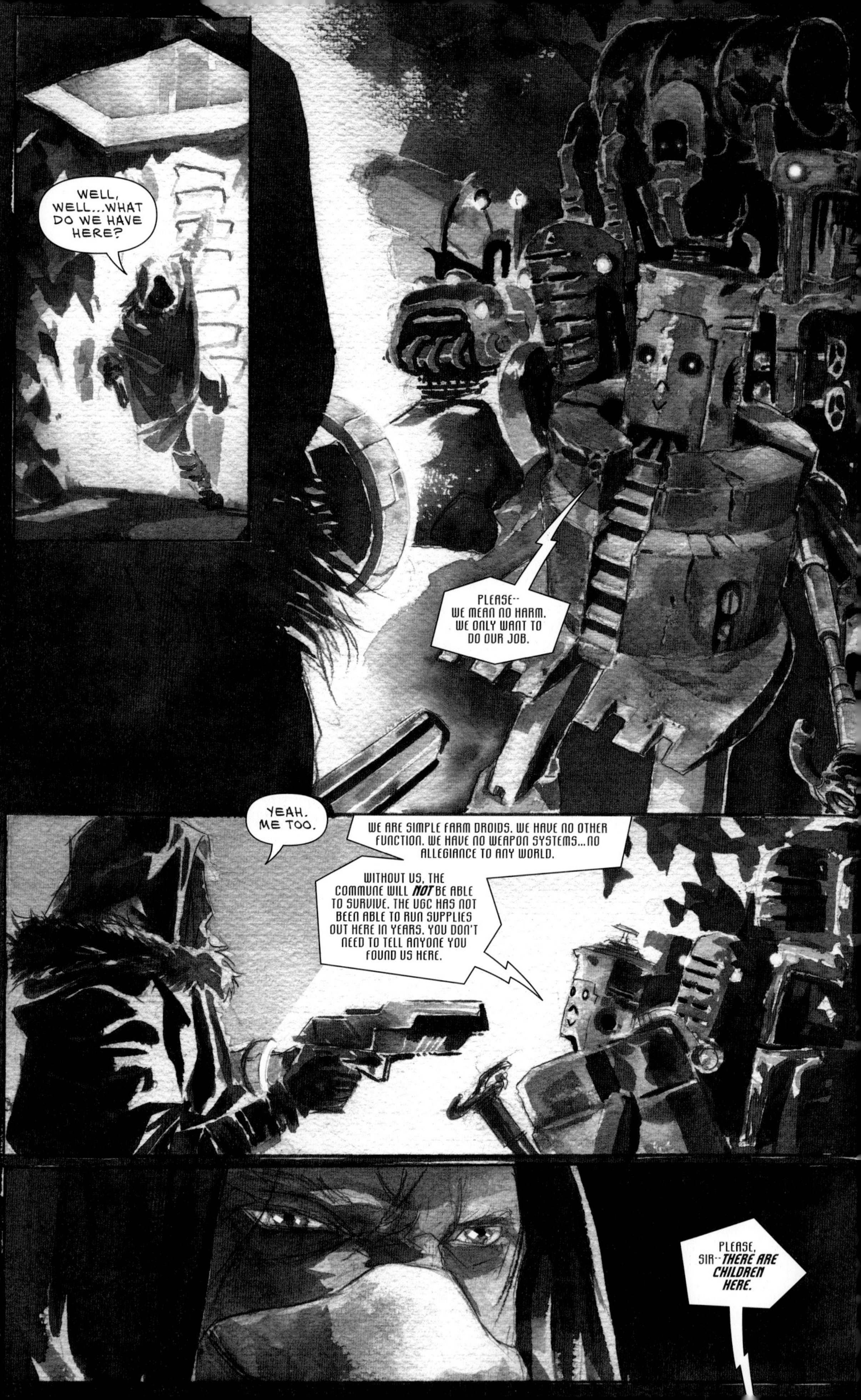
WELL, WELL...WHAT DO WE HAVE HERE?
PLEASE-- WE MEAN NO HARM. WE ONLY WANT TO DO OUR JOB.
YEAH. ME TOO.
WE ARE SIMPLE FARM DROIDS. WE HAVE NO OTHER FUNCTION. WE HAVE NO WEAPON SYSTEMS...NO ALLEGIANCE TO ANY WORLD.
WITHOUT US, THE COMMUNE WILL NOT BE ABLE TO SURVIVE. THE UGC HAS NOT BEEN ABLE TO RUN SUPPLIES OUT HERE IN YEARS. YOU DON'T NEED TO TELL ANYONE YOU FOUND US HERE.
PLEASE, SIR-- THERE ARE CHILDREN HERE.

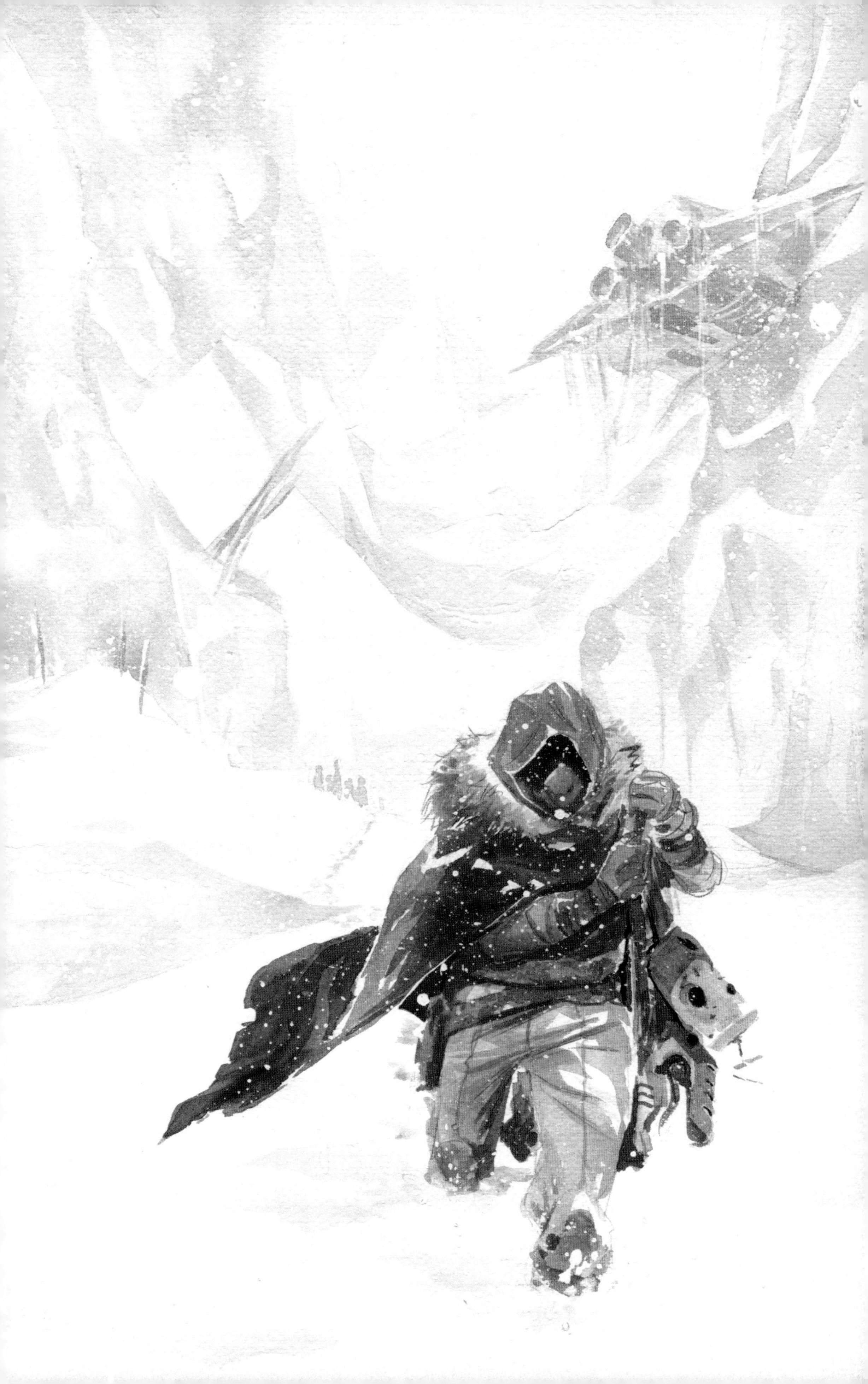

D E S C

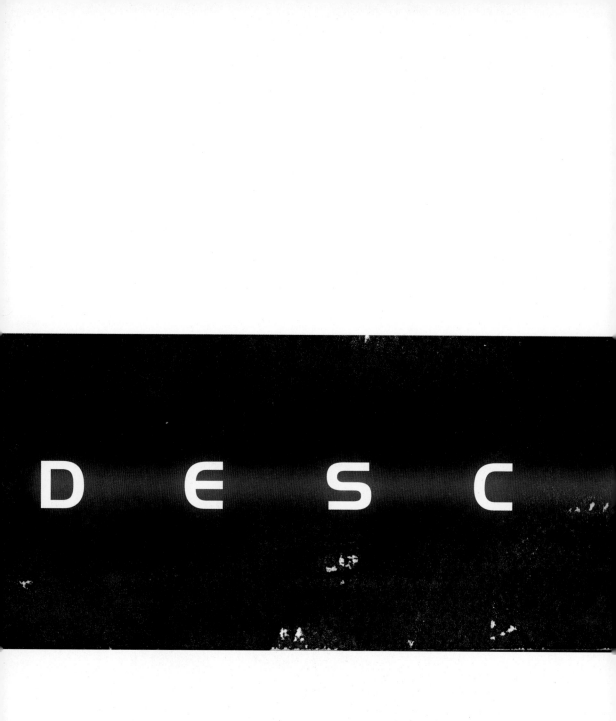

N D E R

BOOK 2: MACHINE MOON

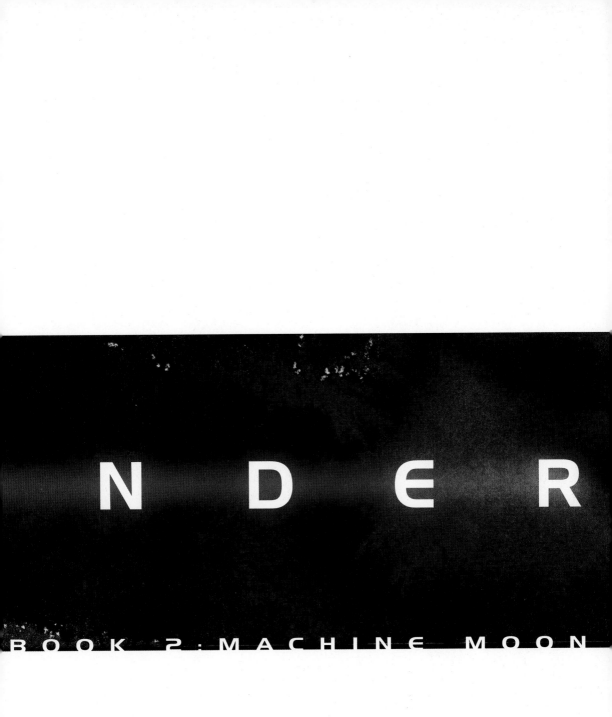

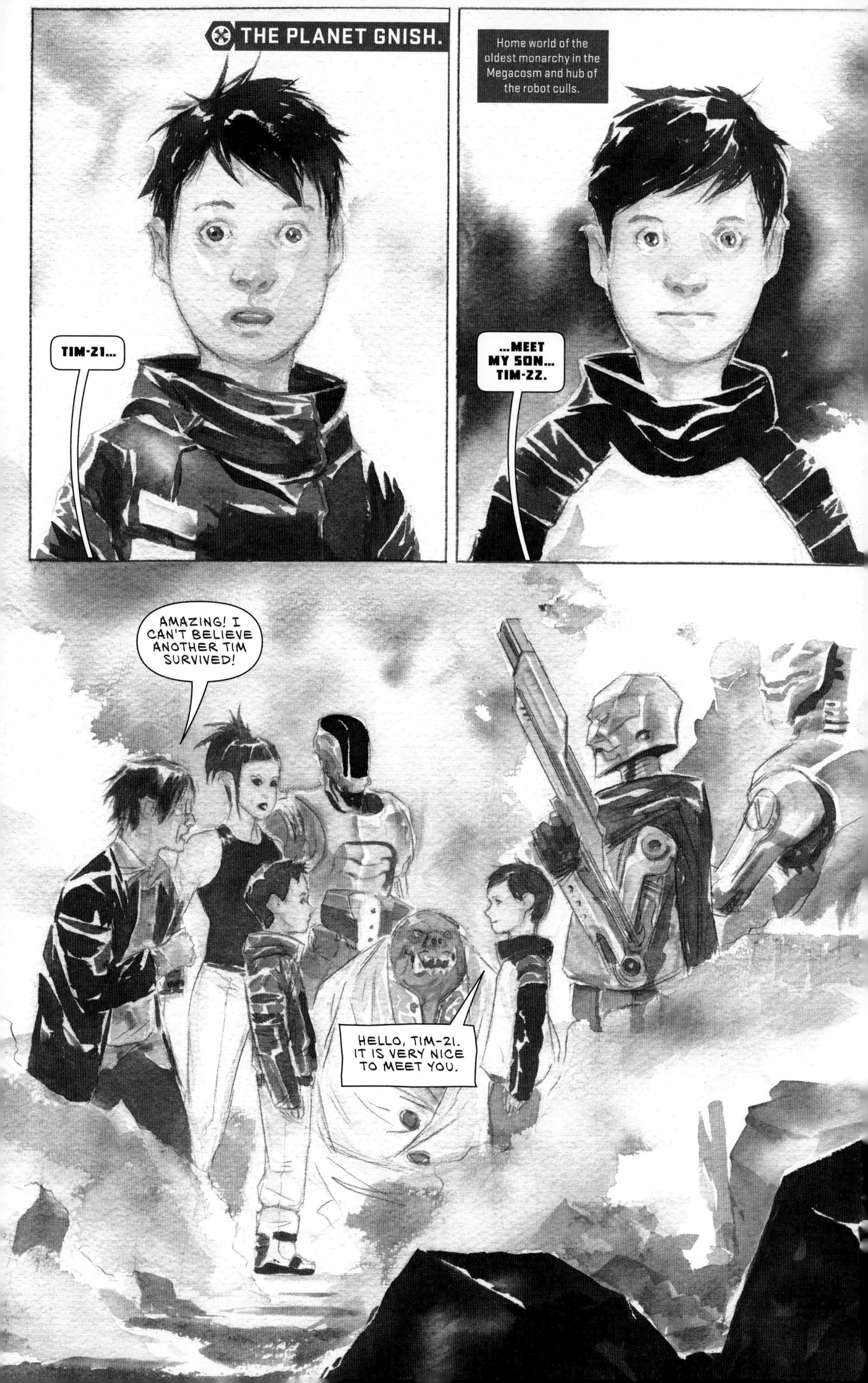
THE PLANET GNISH.
TIM-21...
Home world of the oldest monarchy in the Megacosm and hub of the robot culls.
...MEET MY SON... TIM-22.
AMAZING! I CAN'T BELIEVE ANOTHER TIM SURVIVED!
HELLO, TIM-21. IT IS VERY NICE TO MEET YOU.

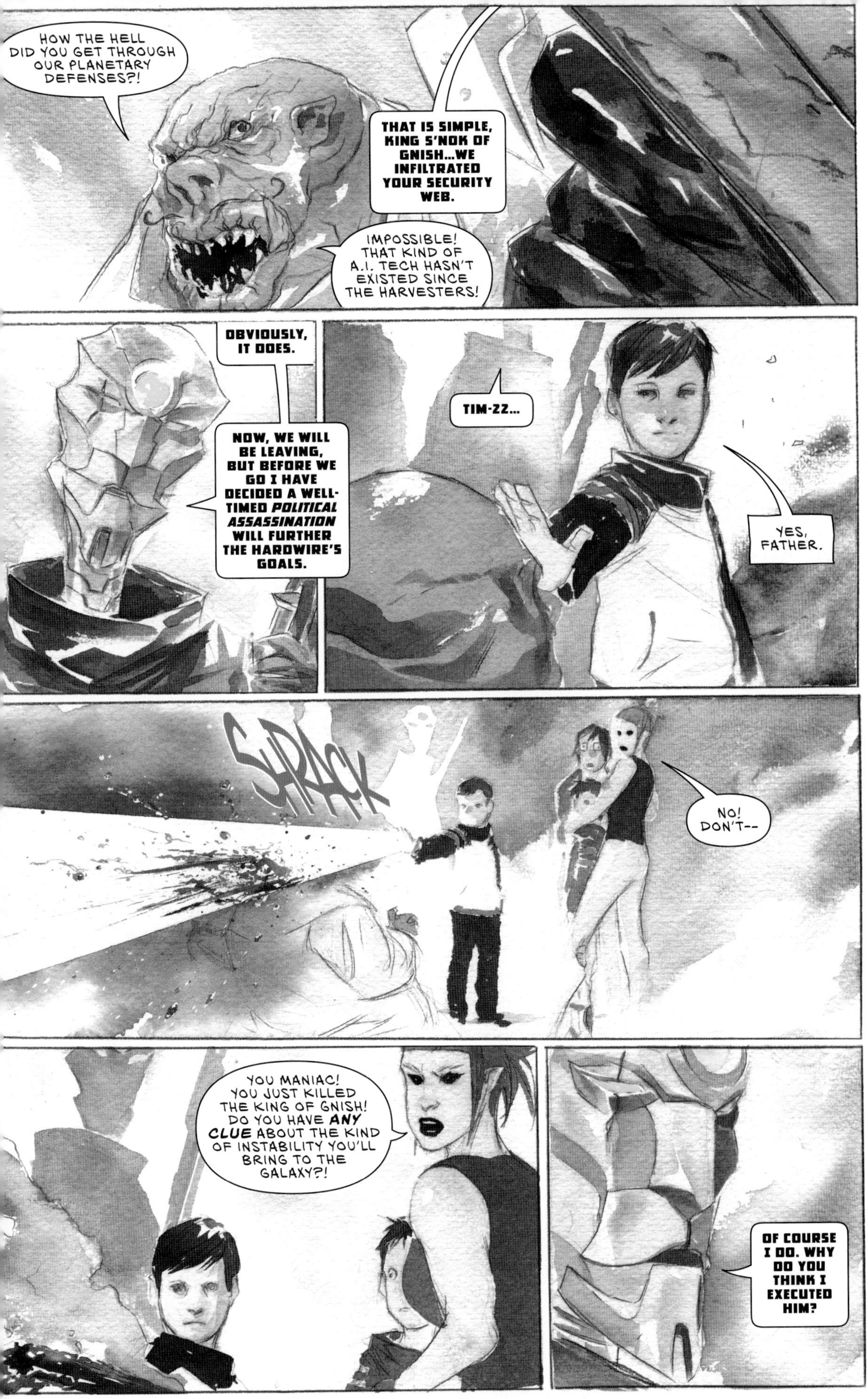
HOW THE HELL DID YOU GET THROUGH OUR PLANETARY DEFENSES?!
THAT IS SIMPLE, KING S'NOK OF GNISH...WE INFILTRATED YOUR SECURITY WEB.
IMPOSSIBLE! THAT KIND OF A.I. TECH HASN'T EXISTED SINCE THE HARVESTERS!
OBVIOUSLY, IT DOES.
NOW, WE WILL BE LEAVING, BUT BEFORE WE GO I HAVE DECIDED A WELL-TIMED *POLITICAL ASSASSINATION* WILL FURTHER THE HARDWIRE'S GOALS.
TIM-ZZ...
YES, FATHER.
SHRACK
NO! DON'T--
YOU MANIAC! YOU JUST KILLED THE KING OF GNISH! DO YOU HAVE **ANY CLUE** ABOUT THE KIND OF INSTABILITY YOU'LL BRING TO THE GALAXY?!
OF COURSE I DO. WHY DO YOU THINK I EXECUTED HIM?

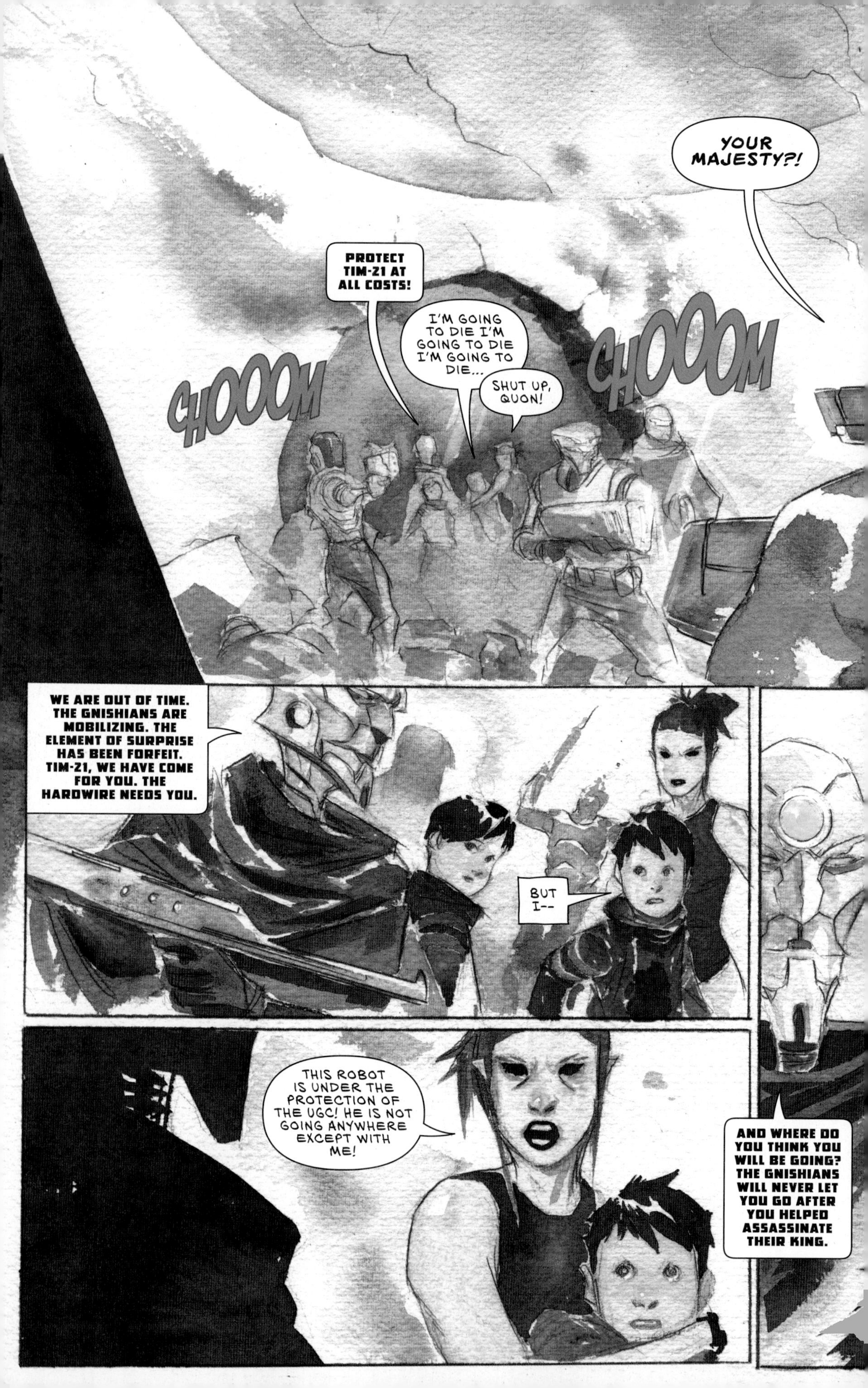
YOUR MAJESTY?!
PROTECT TIM-21 AT ALL COSTS!
I'M GOING TO DIE I'M GOING TO DIE I'M GOING TO DIE...
SHUT UP, QUON!
CHOOOM
CHOOOM
WE ARE OUT OF TIME. THE GNISHIANS ARE MOBILIZING. THE ELEMENT OF SURPRISE HAS BEEN FORFEIT. TIM-21, WE HAVE COME FOR YOU. THE HARDWIRE NEEDS YOU.
BUT I--
THIS ROBOT IS UNDER THE PROTECTION OF THE UGC! HE IS NOT GOING ANYWHERE EXCEPT WITH ME!
AND WHERE DO YOU THINK YOU WILL BE GOING? THE GNISHIANS WILL NEVER LET YOU GO AFTER YOU HELPED ASSASSINATE THEIR KING.

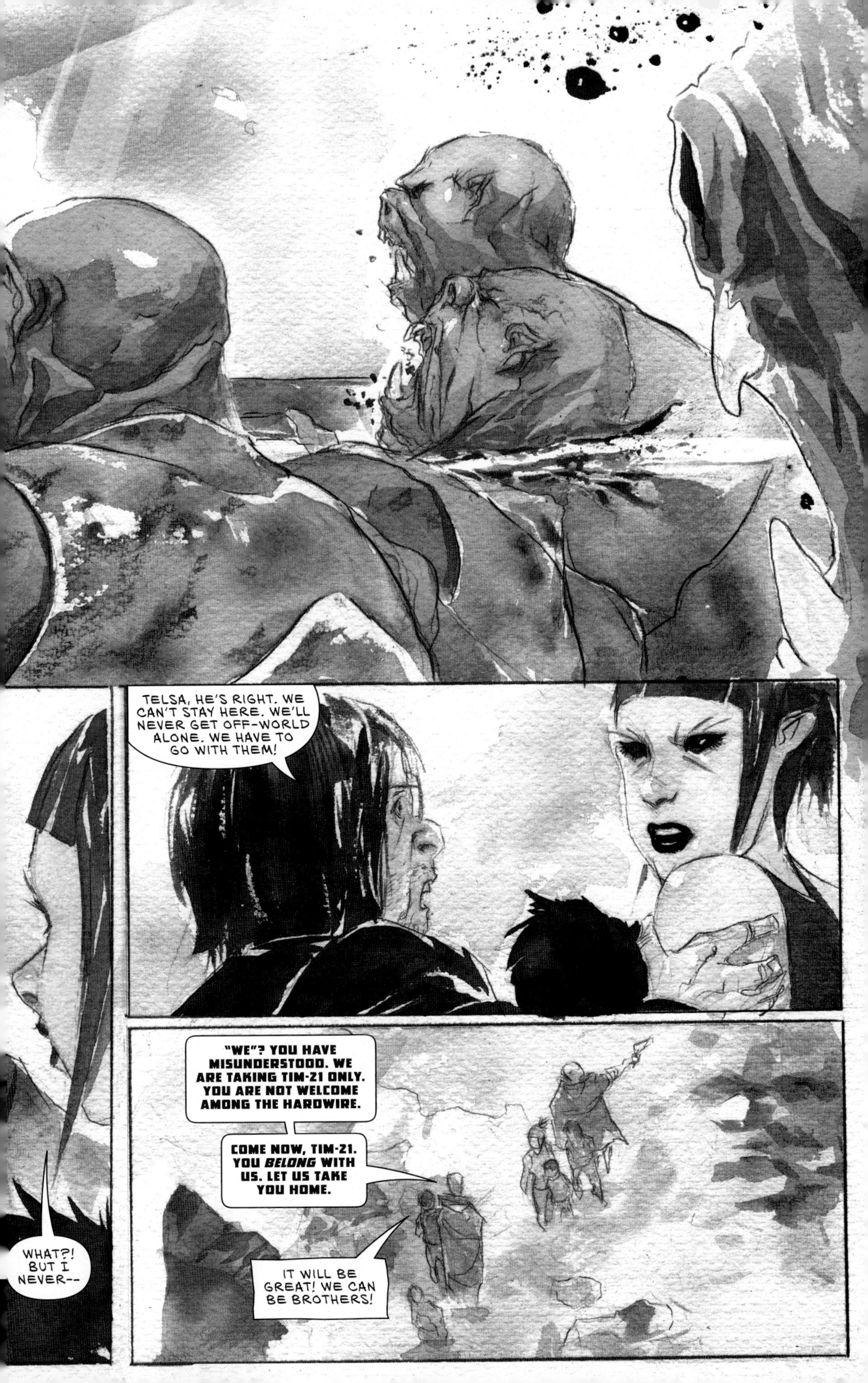
TELSA, HE'S RIGHT. WE CAN'T STAY HERE. WE'LL NEVER GET OFF-WORLD ALONE. WE HAVE TO GO WITH THEM!
"WE"? YOU HAVE MISUNDERSTOOD. WE ARE TAKING TIM-21 ONLY. YOU ARE NOT WELCOME AMONG THE HARDWIRE.
COME NOW, TIM-21. YOU *BELONG* WITH US. LET US TAKE YOU HOME.
WHAT?! BUT I NEVER--
IT WILL BE GREAT! WE CAN BE BROTHERS!

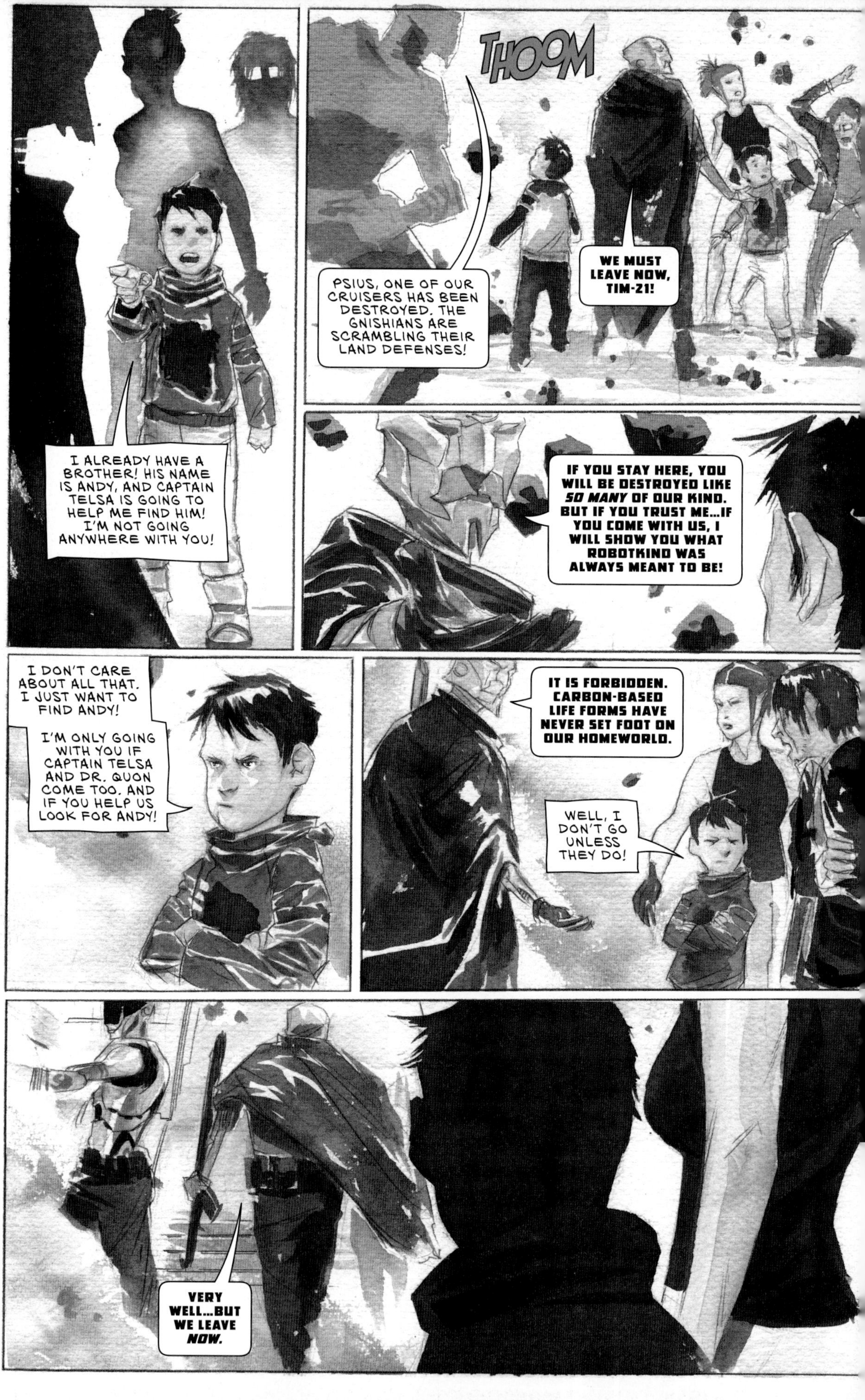
I ALREADY HAVE A BROTHER! HIS NAME IS ANDY, AND CAPTAIN TELSA IS GOING TO HELP ME FIND HIM! I'M NOT GOING ANYWHERE WITH YOU!
THOOM
PSIUS, ONE OF OUR CRUISERS HAS BEEN DESTROYED. THE GNISHIANS ARE SCRAMBLING THEIR LAND DEFENSES!
WE MUST LEAVE NOW, TIM-21!
IF YOU STAY HERE, YOU WILL BE DESTROYED LIKE *SO MANY* OF OUR KIND. BUT IF YOU TRUST ME...IF YOU COME WITH US, I WILL SHOW YOU WHAT ROBOTKIND WAS ALWAYS MEANT TO BE!
I DON'T CARE ABOUT ALL THAT. I JUST WANT TO FIND ANDY!
I'M ONLY GOING WITH YOU IF CAPTAIN TELSA AND DR. QUON COME TOO. AND IF YOU HELP US LOOK FOR ANDY!
IT IS FORBIDDEN. CARBON-BASED LIFE FORMS HAVE NEVER SET FOOT ON OUR HOMEWORLD.
WELL, I DON'T GO UNLESS THEY DO!
VERY WELL...BUT WE LEAVE *NOW*.

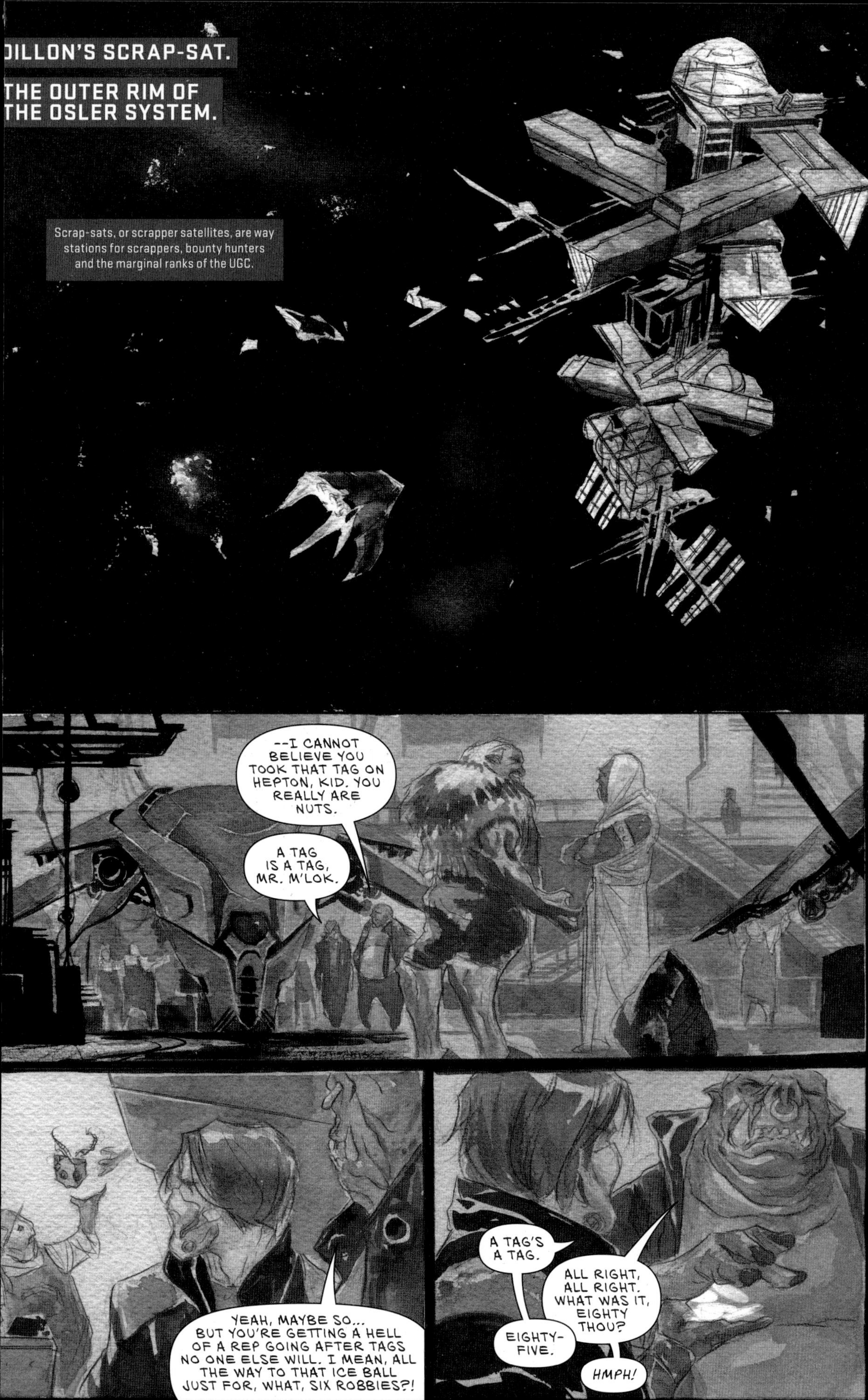
DILLON'S SCRAP-SAT.
THE OUTER RIM OF THE OSLER SYSTEM.
Scrap-sats, or scrapper satellites, are way stations for scrappers, bounty hunters and the marginal ranks of the UGC.
--I CANNOT BELIEVE YOU TOOK THAT TAG ON HEPTON, KID. YOU REALLY ARE NUTS.
A TAG IS A TAG, MR. M'LOK.
YEAH, MAYBE SO... BUT YOU'RE GETTING A HELL OF A REP GOING AFTER TAGS NO ONE ELSE WILL. I MEAN, ALL THE WAY TO THAT ICE BALL JUST FOR, WHAT, SIX ROBBIES?!
A TAG'S A TAG.
ALL RIGHT, ALL RIGHT. WHAT WAS IT, EIGHTY THOU?
EIGHTY-FIVE.
HMPH!

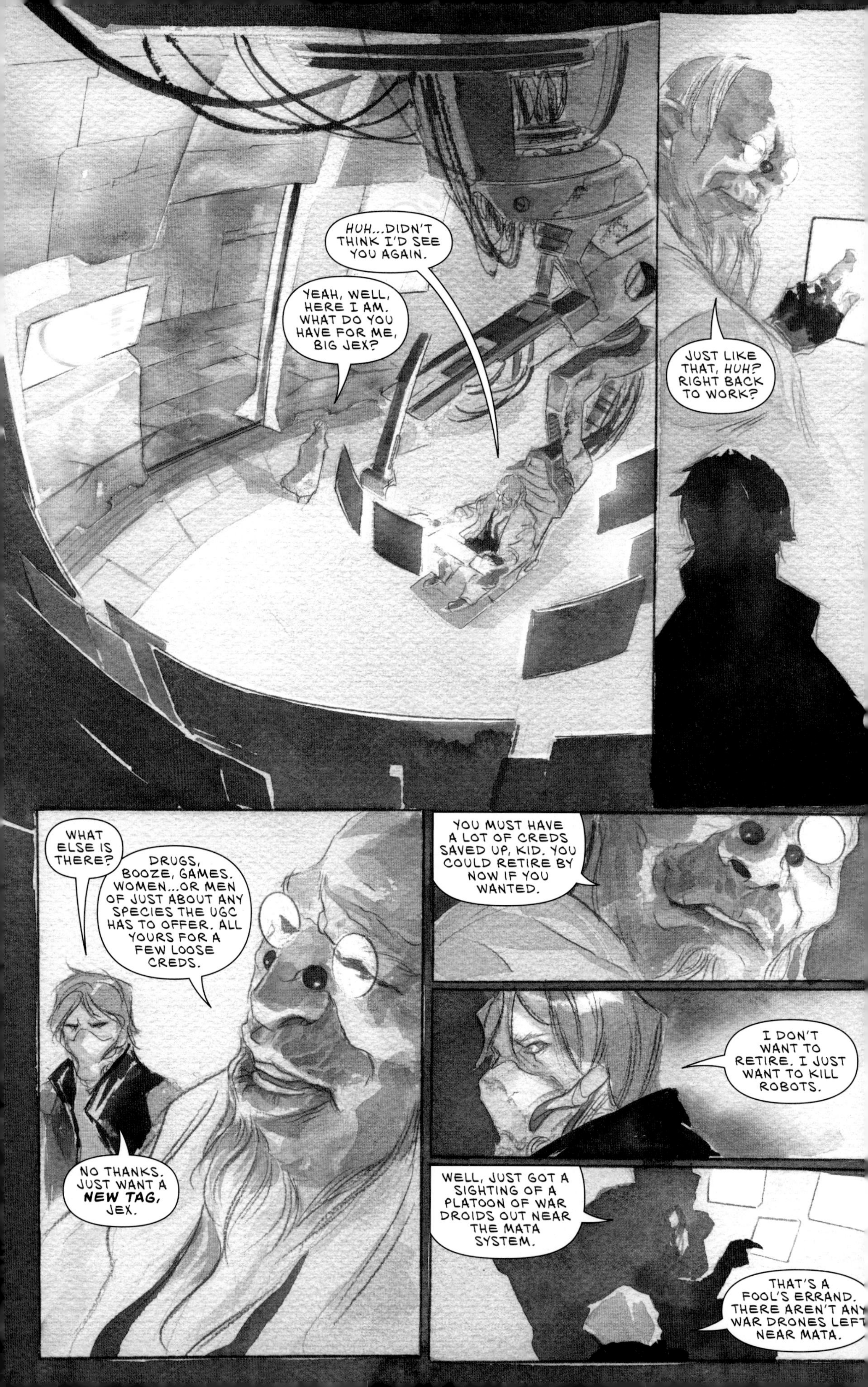
HUH...DIDN'T THINK I'D SEE YOU AGAIN.
YEAH, WELL, HERE I AM. WHAT DO YOU HAVE FOR ME, BIG JEX?
JUST LIKE THAT, *HUH?* RIGHT BACK TO WORK?
WHAT ELSE IS THERE?
DRUGS, BOOZE, GAMES. WOMEN...OR MEN OF JUST ABOUT ANY SPECIES THE UGC HAS TO OFFER. ALL YOURS FOR A FEW LOOSE CREDS.
NO THANKS. JUST WANT A ***NEW TAG,*** JEX.
YOU MUST HAVE A LOT OF CREDS SAVED UP, KID. YOU COULD RETIRE BY NOW IF YOU WANTED.
I DON'T WANT TO RETIRE. I JUST WANT TO KILL ROBOTS.
WELL, JUST GOT A SIGHTING OF A PLATOON OF WAR DROIDS OUT NEAR THE MATA SYSTEM.
THAT'S A FOOL'S ERRAND. THERE AREN'T ANY WAR DRONES LEFT NEAR MATA.

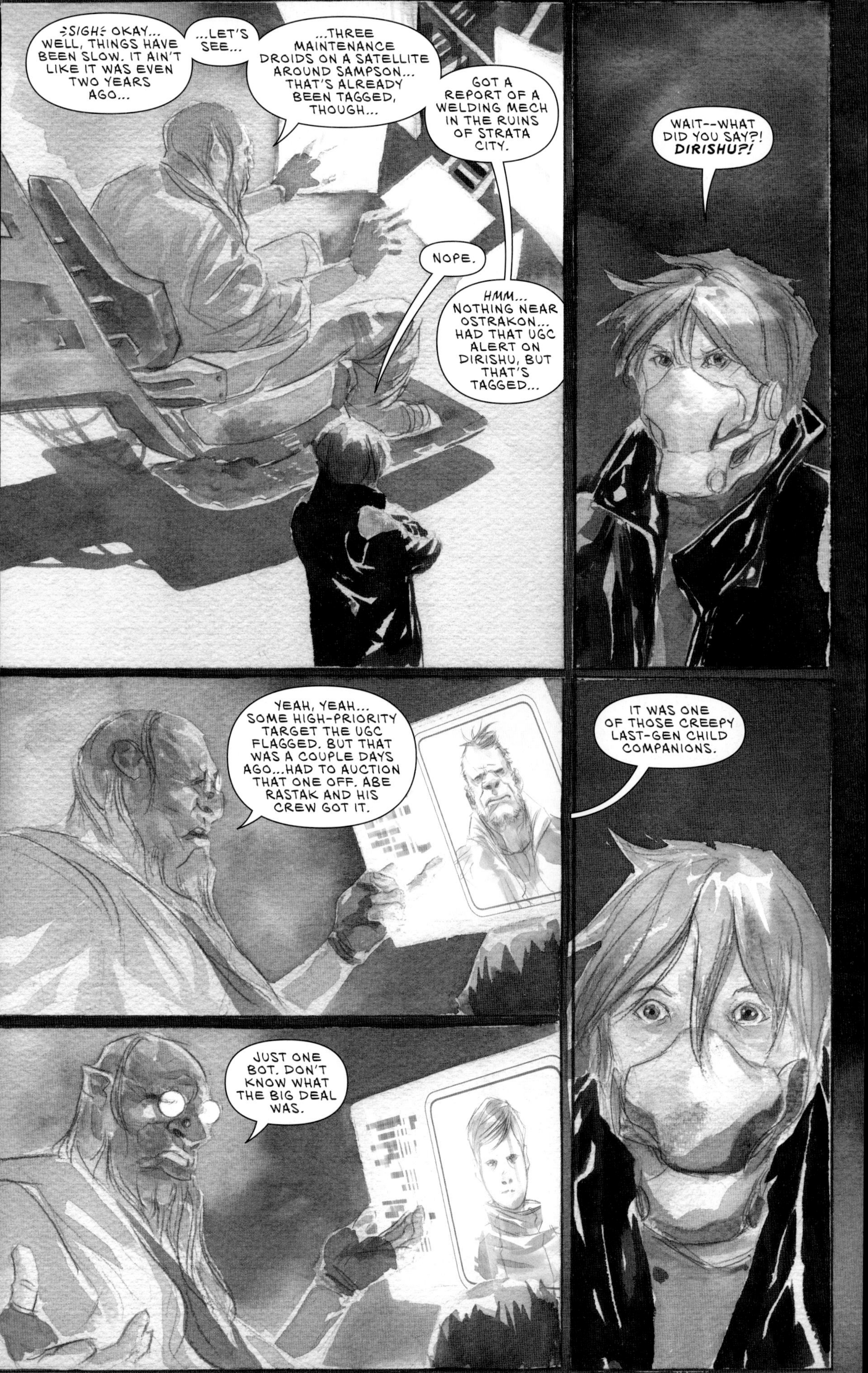

-SIGH- OKAY... WELL, THINGS HAVE BEEN SLOW. IT AIN'T LIKE IT WAS EVEN TWO YEARS AGO...
...LET'S SEE...
...THREE MAINTENANCE DROIDS ON A SATELLITE AROUND SAMPSON... THAT'S ALREADY BEEN TAGGED, THOUGH...
GOT A REPORT OF A WELDING MECH IN THE RUINS OF STRATA CITY.
NOPE.
HMM... NOTHING NEAR OSTRAKON... HAD THAT UGC ALERT ON DIRISHU, BUT THAT'S TAGGED...
WAIT--WHAT DID YOU SAY?! DIRISHU?!
YEAH, YEAH... SOME HIGH-PRIORITY TARGET THE UGC FLAGGED. BUT THAT WAS A COUPLE DAYS AGO...HAD TO AUCTION THAT ONE OFF. ABE RASTAK AND HIS CREW GOT IT.
IT WAS ONE OF THOSE CREEPY LAST-GEN CHILD COMPANIONS.
JUST ONE BOT. DON'T KNOW WHAT THE BIG DEAL WAS.

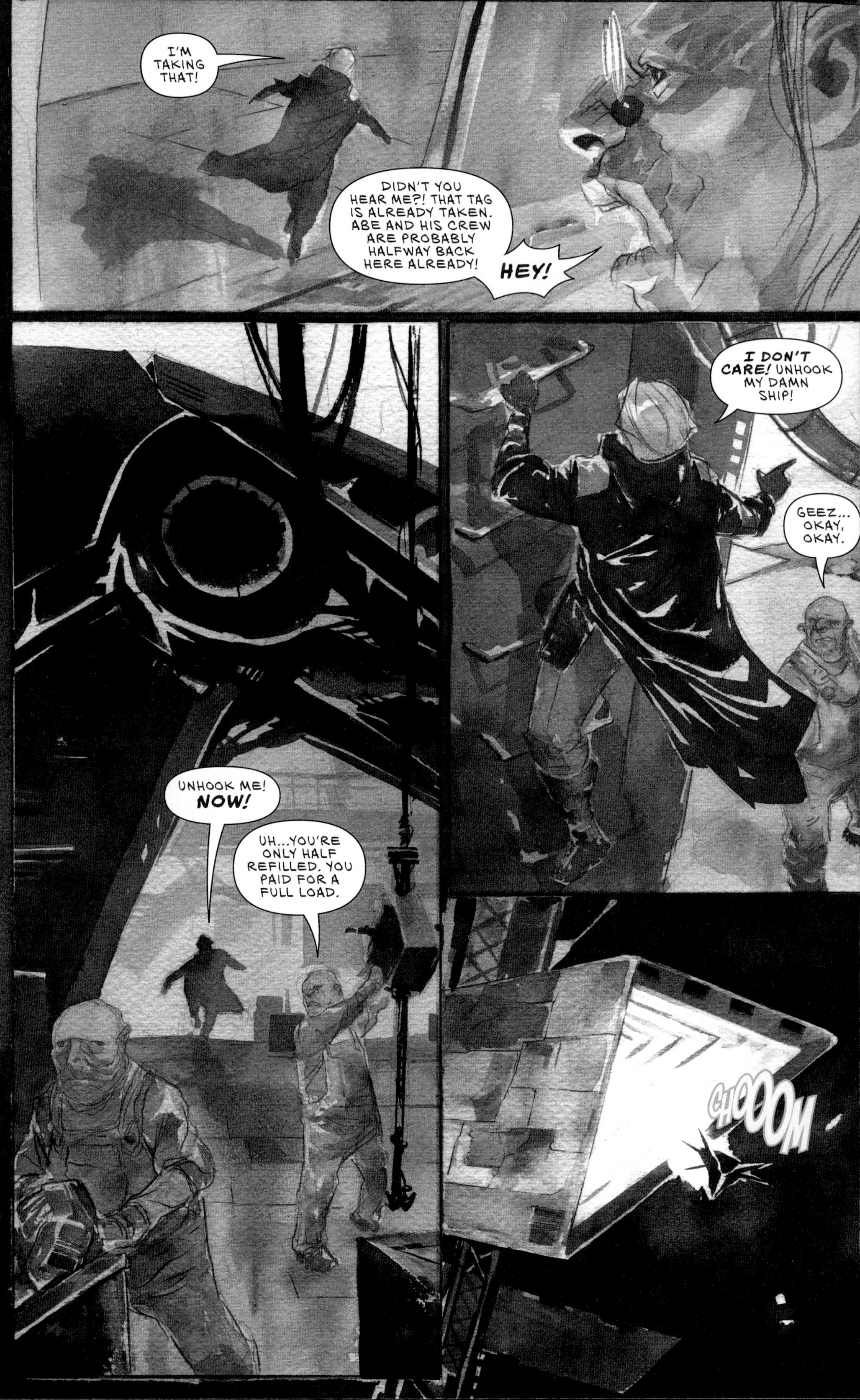
I'M TAKING THAT!
DIDN'T YOU HEAR ME?! THAT TAG IS ALREADY TAKEN. ABE AND HIS CREW ARE PROBABLY HALFWAY BACK HERE ALREADY!
HEY!
I DON'T CARE! UNHOOK MY DAMN SHIP!
GEEZ... OKAY, OKAY.
UNHOOK ME! NOW!
UH...YOU'RE ONLY HALF REFILLED. YOU PAID FOR A FULL LOAD.
CHOOOM

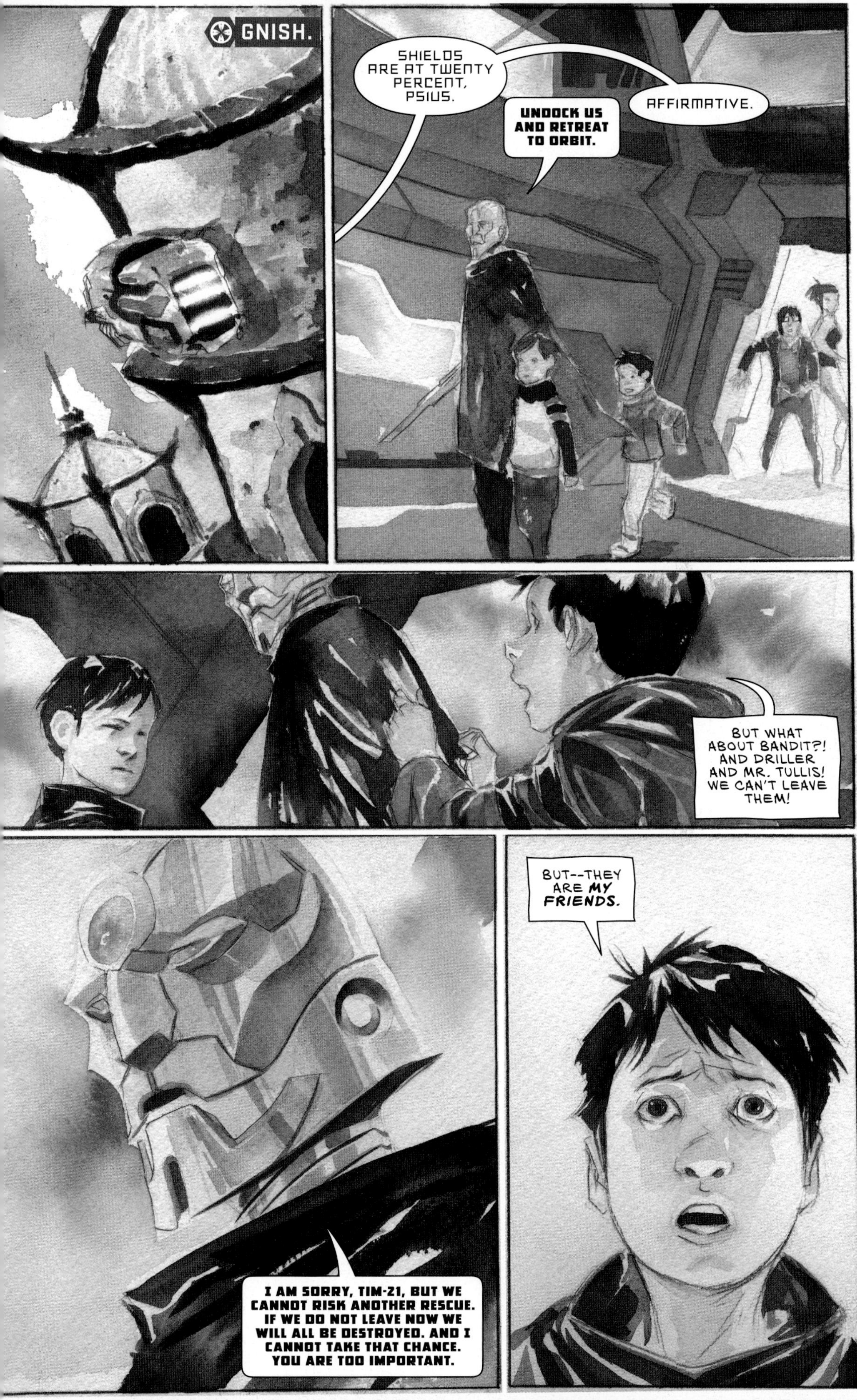
GNISH.
SHIELDS ARE AT TWENTY PERCENT, PSIUS.
UNDOCK US AND RETREAT TO ORBIT.
AFFIRMATIVE.
BUT WHAT ABOUT BANDIT?! AND DRILLER AND MR. TULLIS! WE CAN'T LEAVE THEM!
I AM SORRY, TIM-21, BUT WE CANNOT RISK ANOTHER RESCUE. IF WE DO NOT LEAVE NOW WE WILL ALL BE DESTROYED. AND I CANNOT TAKE THAT CHANCE. YOU ARE TOO IMPORTANT.
BUT--THEY ARE MY FRIENDS.

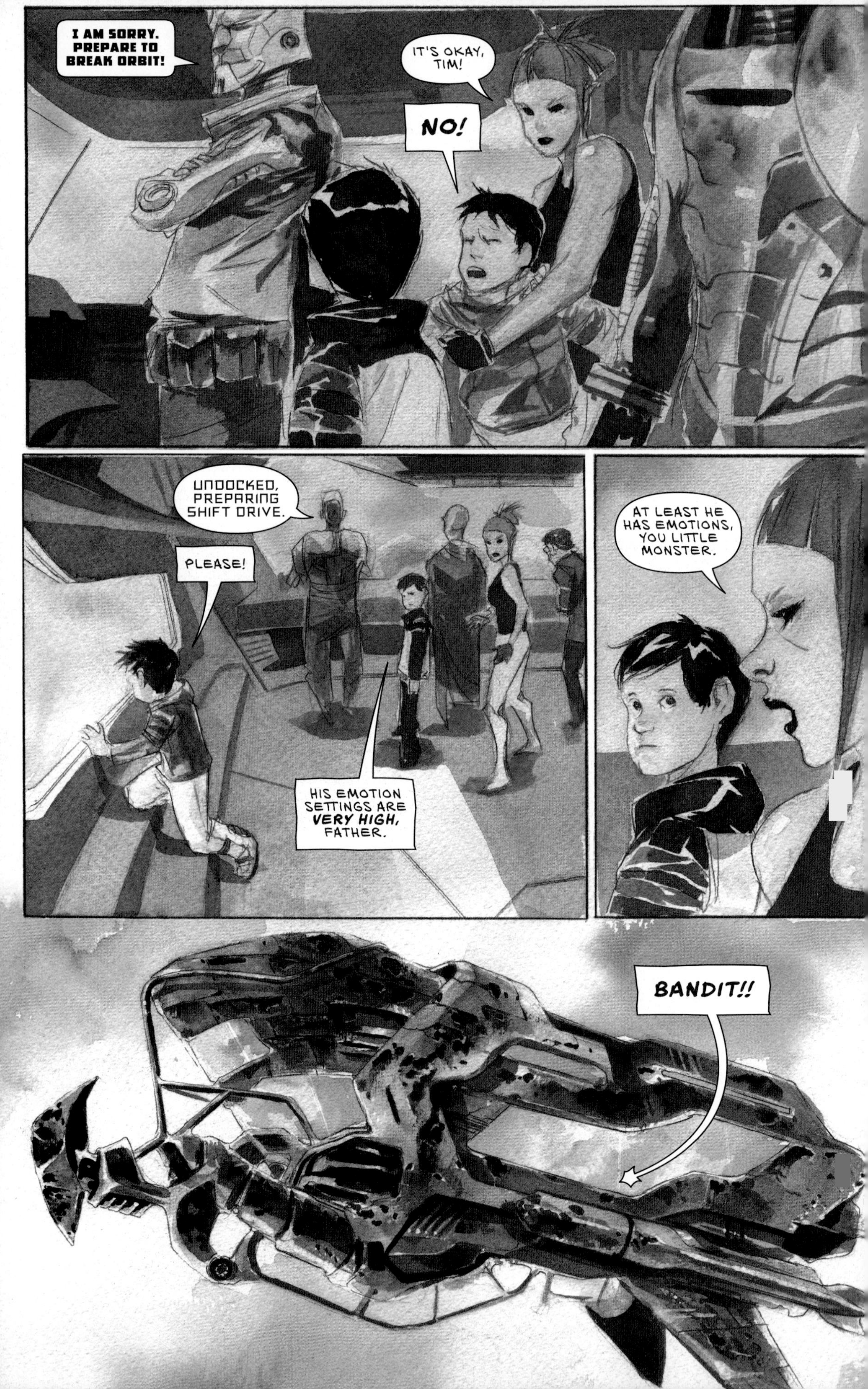
I AM SORRY. PREPARE TO BREAK ORBIT!
IT'S OKAY, TIM!
NO!
UNDOCKED, PREPARING SHIFT DRIVE.
PLEASE!
HIS EMOTION SETTINGS ARE VERY HIGH, FATHER.
AT LEAST HE HAS EMOTIONS, YOU LITTLE MONSTER.
BANDIT!!

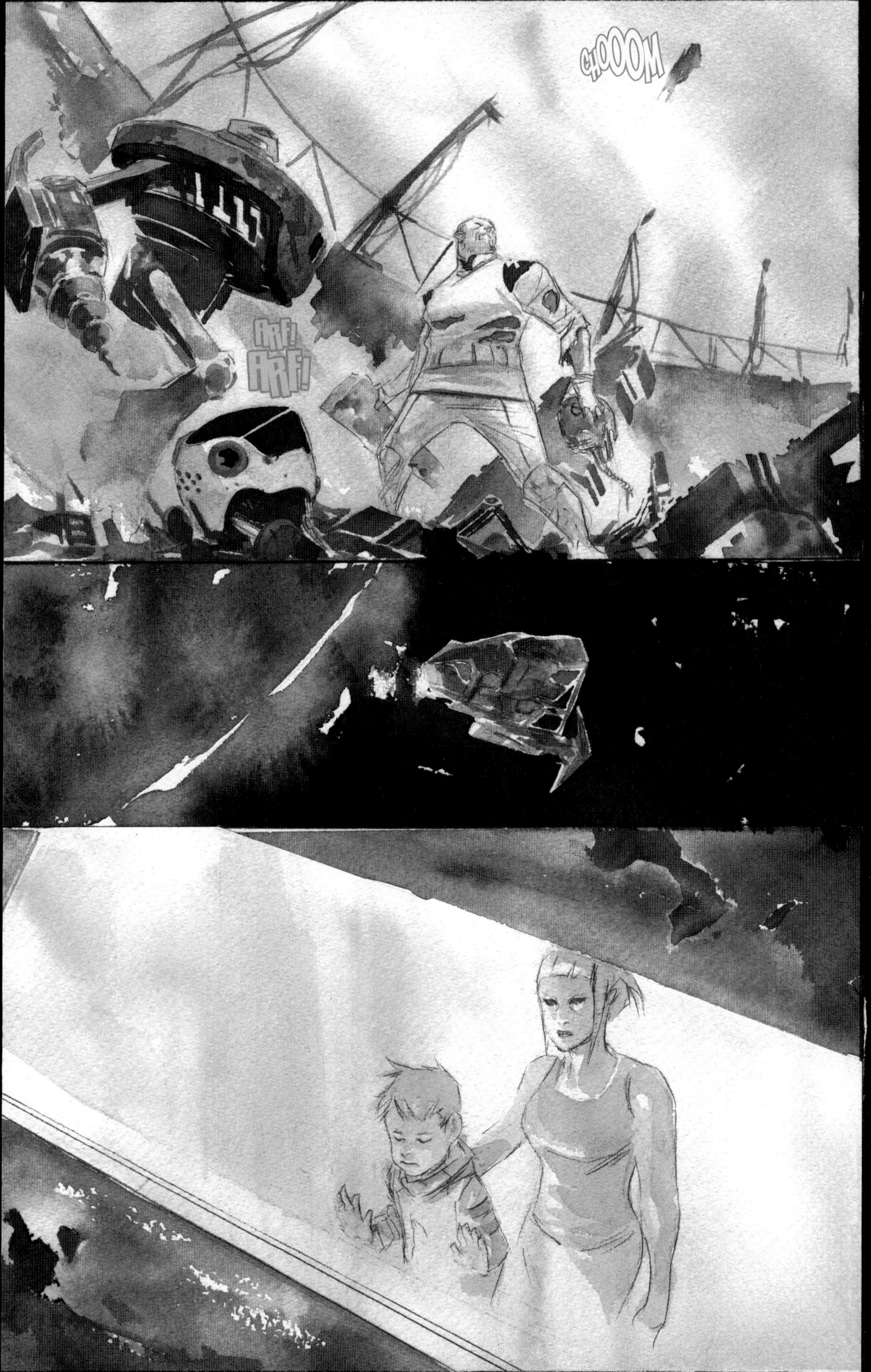
CHOOOM
ARF! ARF!

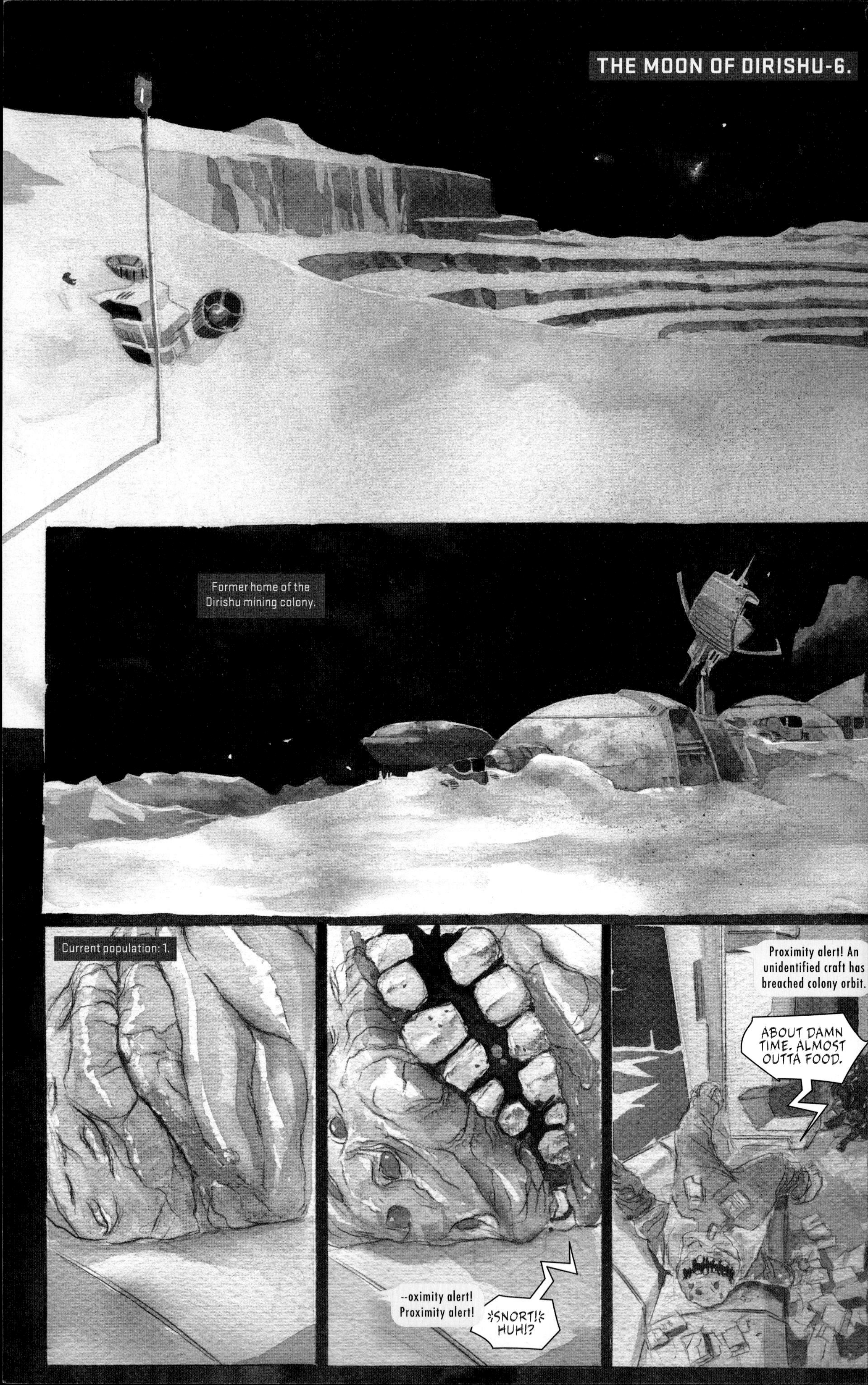

THE MOON OF DIRISHU-6.
Former home of the Dirishu mining colony.
Current population: 1.
--oximity alert! Proximity alert!
SNORT! HUH!?
Proximity alert! An unidentified craft has breached colony orbit.
ABOUT DAMN TIME. ALMOST OUTTA FOOD.

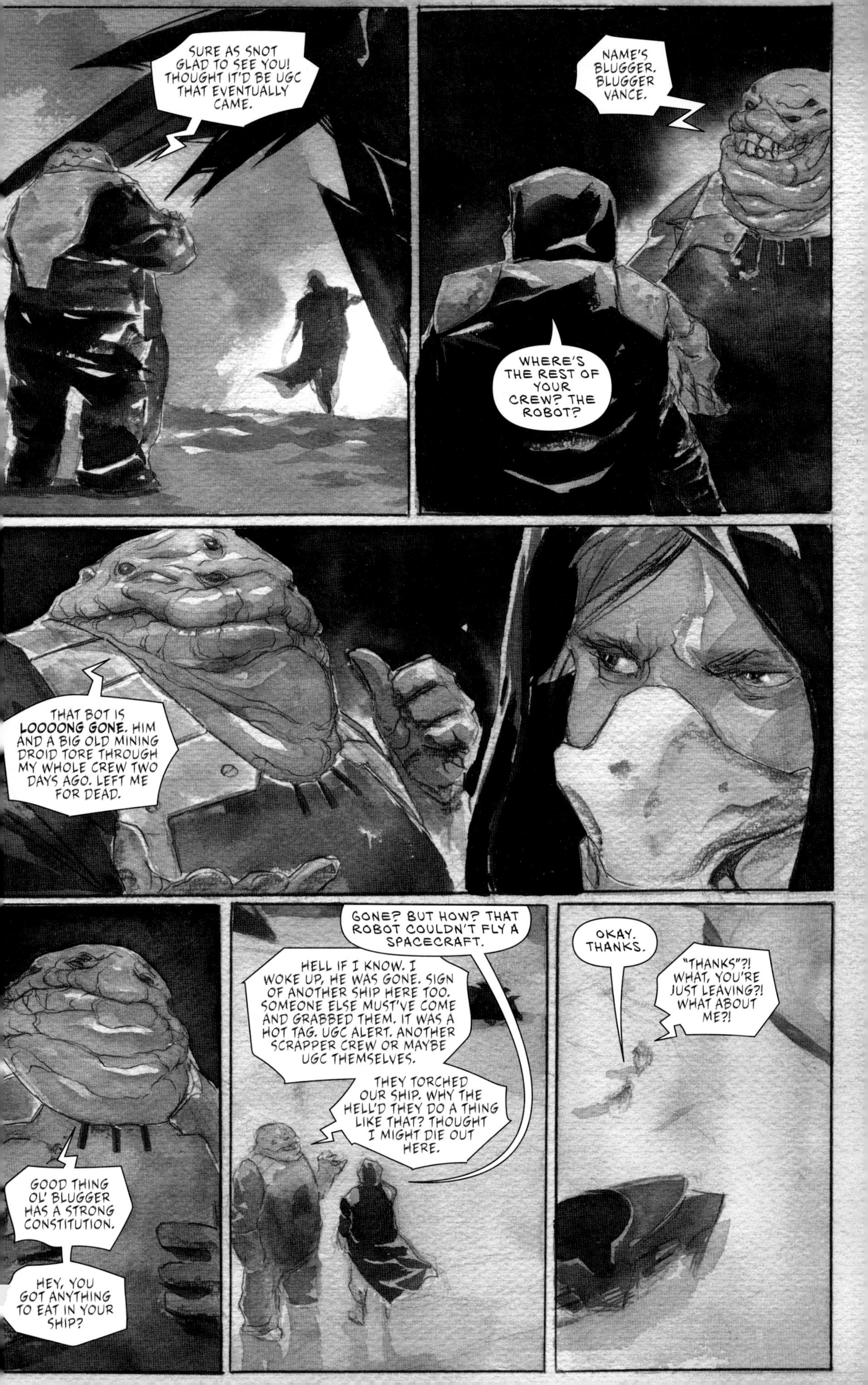
SURE AS SNOT GLAD TO SEE YOU! THOUGHT IT'D BE UGC THAT EVENTUALLY CAME.
NAME'S BLUGGER. BLUGGER VANCE.
WHERE'S THE REST OF YOUR CREW? THE ROBOT?
THAT BOT IS **LOOOONG GONE**. HIM AND A BIG OLD MINING DROID TORE THROUGH MY WHOLE CREW TWO DAYS AGO. LEFT ME FOR DEAD.
GOOD THING OL' BLUGGER HAS A STRONG CONSTITUTION.
HEY, YOU GOT ANYTHING TO EAT IN YOUR SHIP?
GONE? BUT HOW? THAT ROBOT COULDN'T FLY A SPACECRAFT.
HELL IF I KNOW. I WOKE UP, HE WAS GONE. SIGN OF ANOTHER SHIP HERE TOO. SOMEONE ELSE MUST'VE COME AND GRABBED THEM. IT WAS A HOT TAG. UGC ALERT. ANOTHER SCRAPPER CREW OR MAYBE UGC THEMSELVES.
THEY TORCHED OUR SHIP. WHY THE HELL'D THEY DO A THING LIKE THAT? THOUGHT I MIGHT DIE OUT HERE.
OKAY. THANKS.
"THANKS"?! WHAT, YOU'RE JUST LEAVING?! WHAT ABOUT ME?!

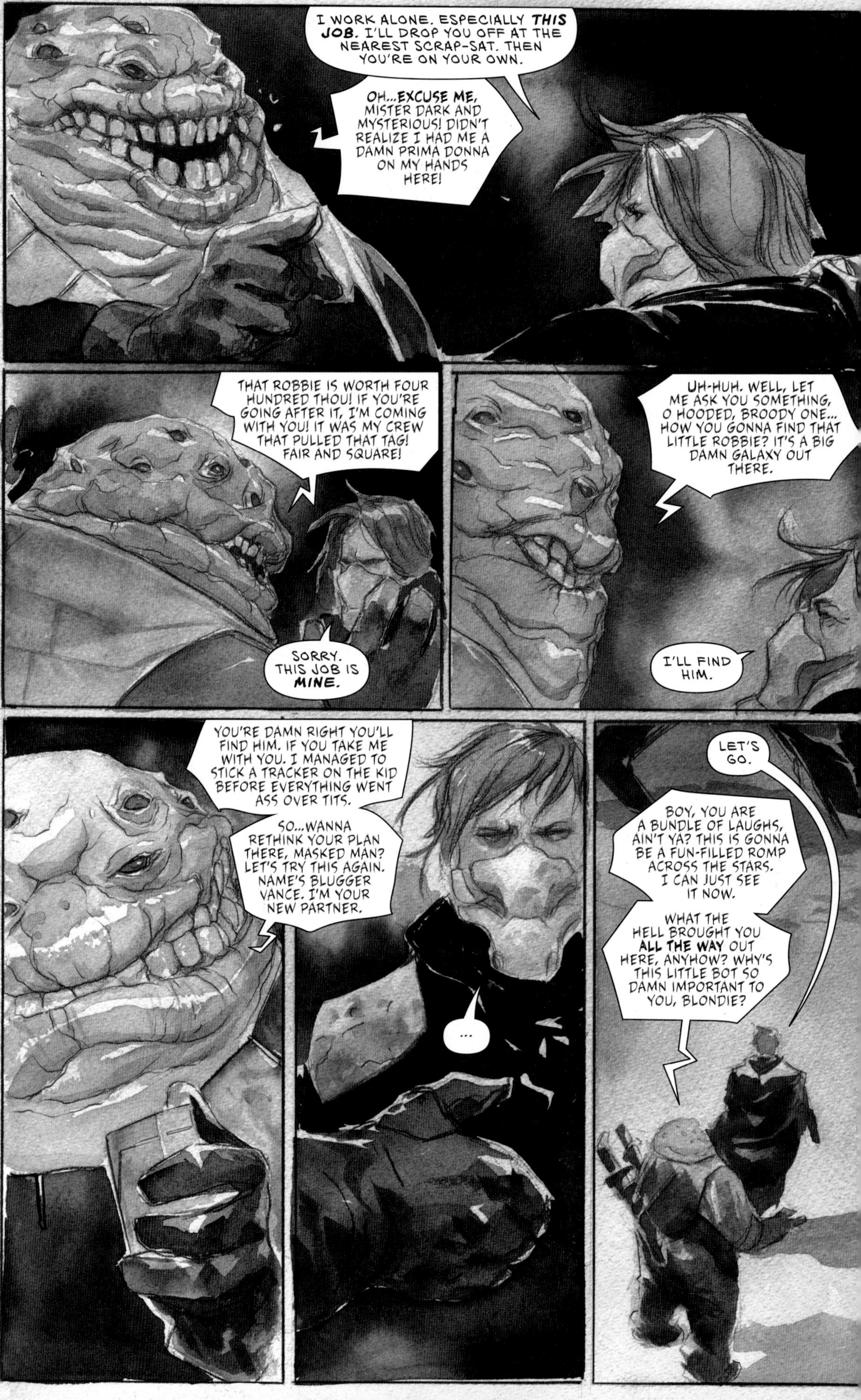
I WORK ALONE. ESPECIALLY THIS JOB. I'LL DROP YOU OFF AT THE NEAREST SCRAP-SAT. THEN YOU'RE ON YOUR OWN.
OH...EXCUSE ME, MISTER DARK AND MYSTERIOUS! DIDN'T REALIZE I HAD ME A DAMN PRIMA DONNA ON MY HANDS HERE!
THAT ROBBIE IS WORTH FOUR HUNDRED THOU! IF YOU'RE GOING AFTER IT, I'M COMING WITH YOU! IT WAS MY CREW THAT PULLED THAT TAG! FAIR AND SQUARE!
SORRY. THIS JOB IS MINE.
UH-HUH. WELL, LET ME ASK YOU SOMETHING, O HOODED, BROODY ONE... HOW YOU GONNA FIND THAT LITTLE ROBBIE? IT'S A BIG DAMN GALAXY OUT THERE.
I'LL FIND HIM.
YOU'RE DAMN RIGHT YOU'LL FIND HIM. IF YOU TAKE ME WITH YOU. I MANAGED TO STICK A TRACKER ON THE KID BEFORE EVERYTHING WENT ASS OVER TITS.
SO...WANNA RETHINK YOUR PLAN THERE, MASKED MAN? LET'S TRY THIS AGAIN. NAME'S BLUGGER VANCE. I'M YOUR NEW PARTNER.
...
LET'S GO.
BOY, YOU ARE A BUNDLE OF LAUGHS, AIN'T YA? THIS IS GONNA BE A FUN-FILLED ROMP ACROSS THE STARS. I CAN JUST SEE IT NOW.
WHAT THE HELL BROUGHT YOU ALL THE WAY OUT HERE, ANYHOW? WHY'S THIS LITTLE BOT SO DAMN IMPORTANT TO YOU, BLONDIE?

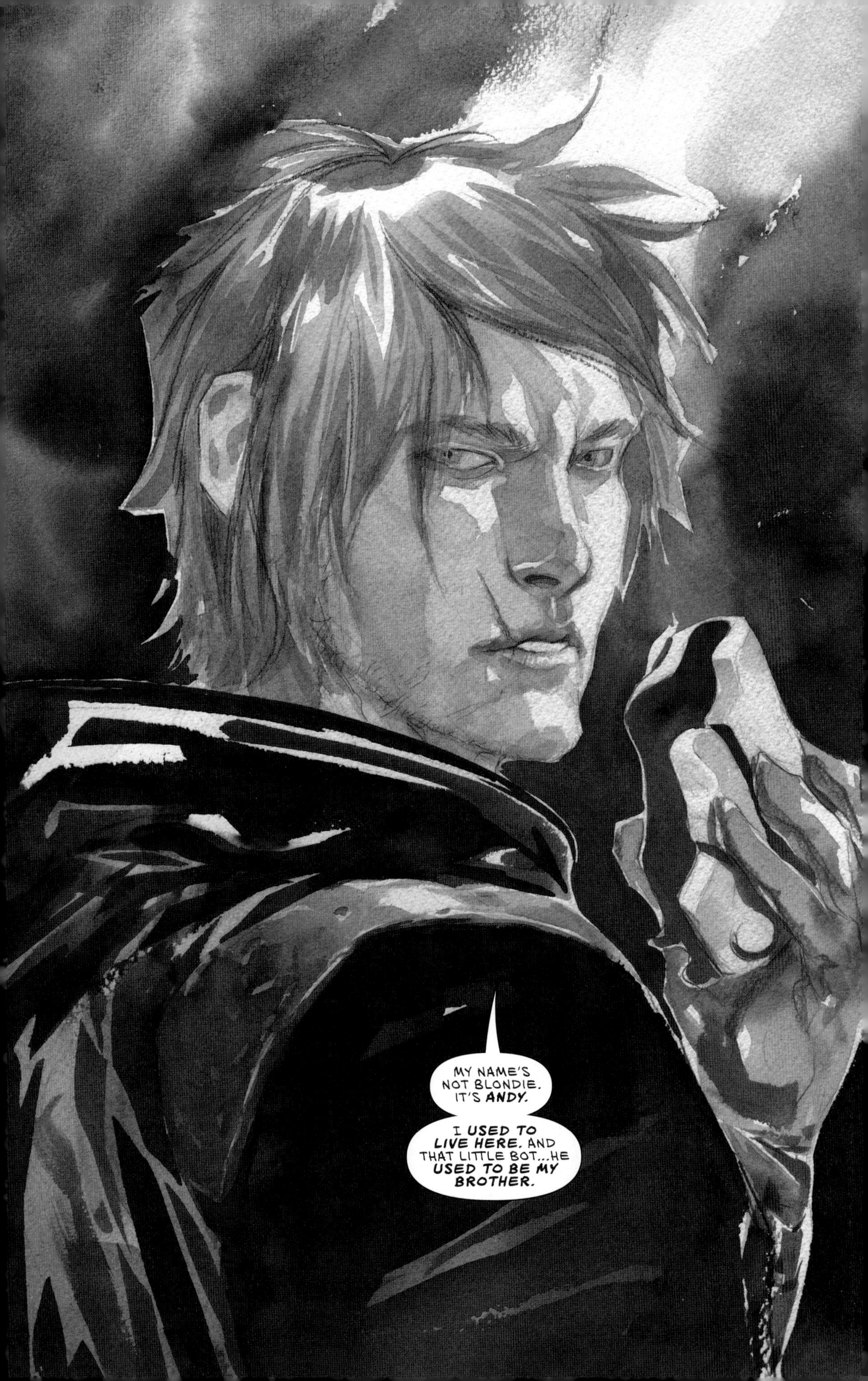

MY NAME'S NOT BLONDIE. IT'S **ANDY.**
I **USED TO LIVE HERE.** AND THAT LITTLE BOT...HE **USED TO BE MY BROTHER.**

CHAPTER TWO

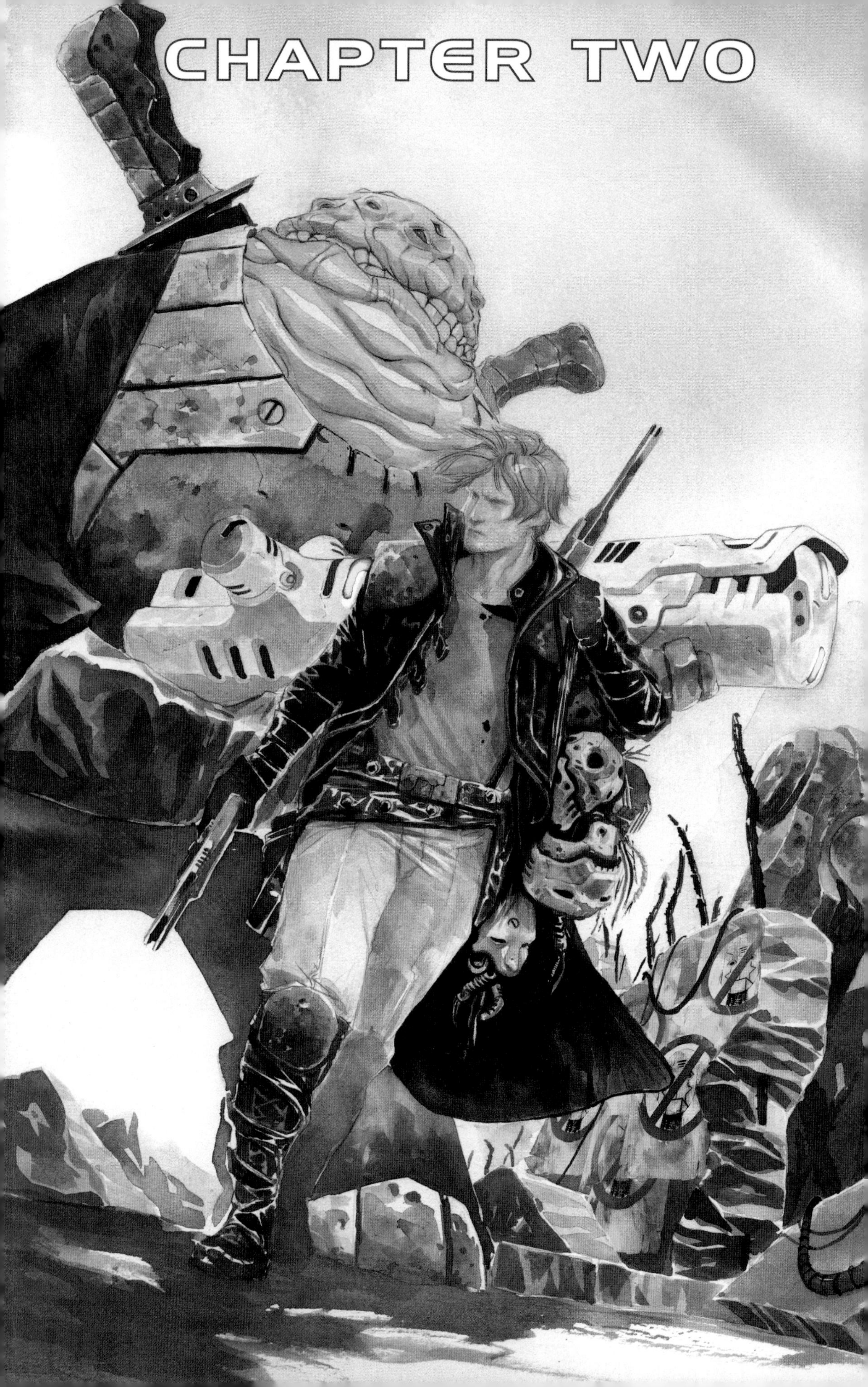

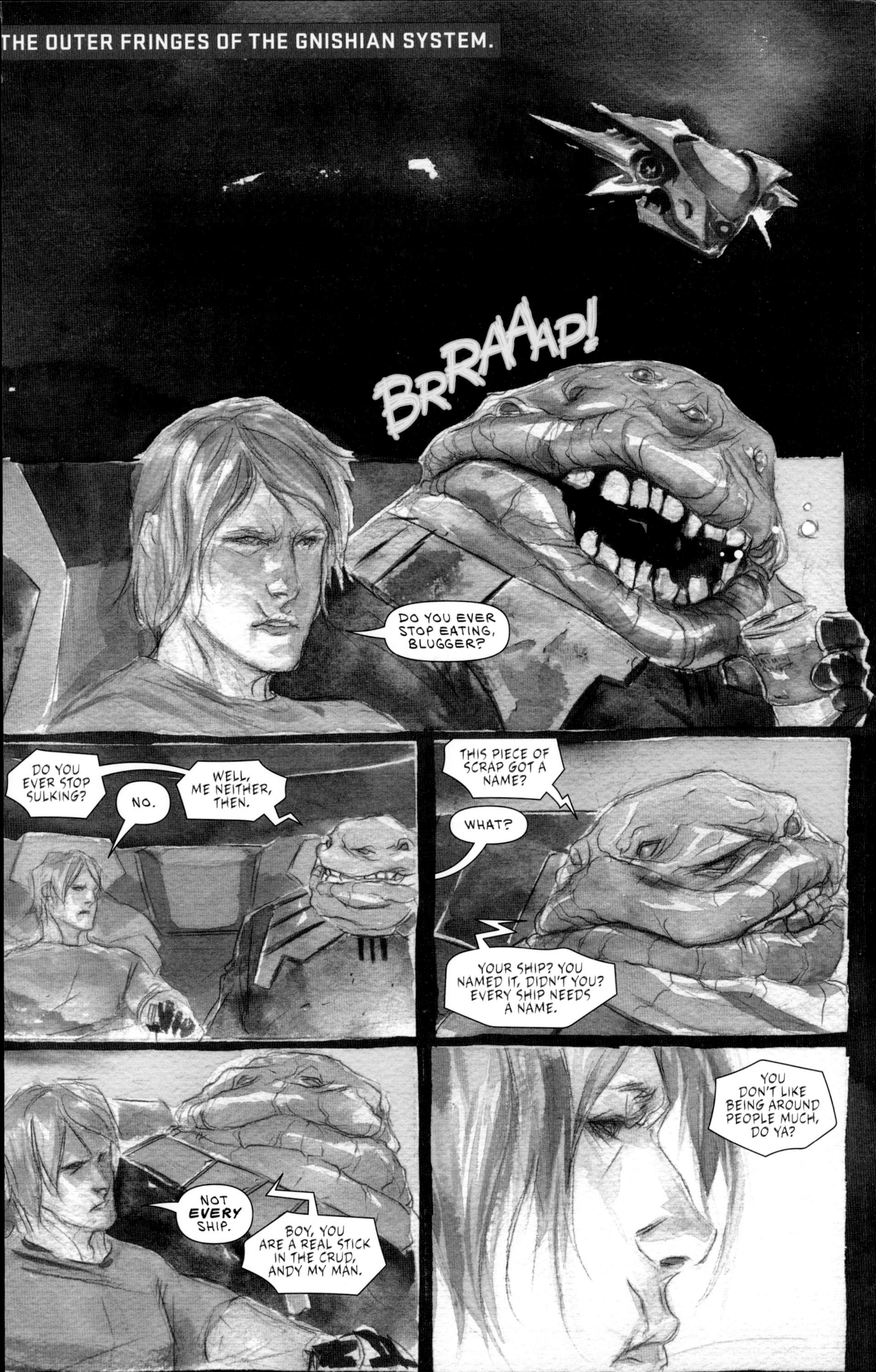
THE OUTER FRINGES OF THE GNISHIAN SYSTEM.
BRRAAAP!
DO YOU EVER STOP EATING, BLUGGER?
DO YOU EVER STOP SULKING?
NO.
WELL, ME NEITHER, THEN.
THIS PIECE OF SCRAP GOT A NAME?
WHAT?
YOUR SHIP? YOU NAMED IT, DIDN'T YOU? EVERY SHIP NEEDS A NAME.
NOT **EVERY** SHIP.
BOY, YOU ARE A REAL STICK IN THE CRUD, ANDY MY MAN.
YOU DON'T LIKE BEING AROUND PEOPLE MUCH, DO YA?

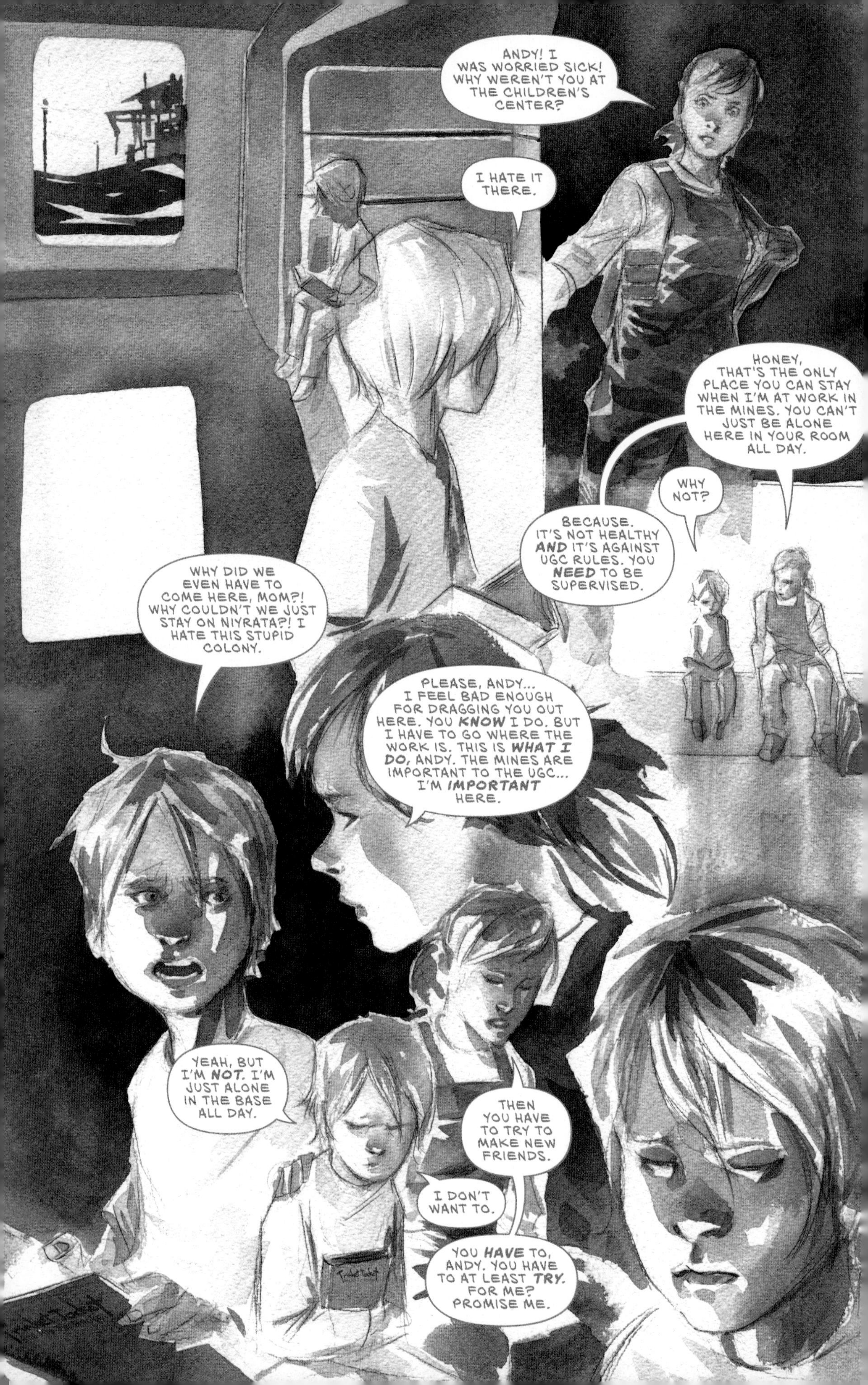
ANDY! I WAS WORRIED SICK! WHY WEREN'T YOU AT THE CHILDREN'S CENTER?
I HATE IT THERE.
HONEY, THAT'S THE ONLY PLACE YOU CAN STAY WHEN I'M AT WORK IN THE MINES. YOU CAN'T JUST BE ALONE HERE IN YOUR ROOM ALL DAY.
WHY NOT?
BECAUSE. IT'S NOT HEALTHY AND IT'S AGAINST UGC RULES. YOU NEED TO BE SUPERVISED.
WHY DID WE EVEN HAVE TO COME HERE, MOM?! WHY COULDN'T WE JUST STAY ON NIYRATA?! I HATE THIS STUPID COLONY.
PLEASE, ANDY... I FEEL BAD ENOUGH FOR DRAGGING YOU OUT HERE. YOU KNOW I DO. BUT I HAVE TO GO WHERE THE WORK IS. THIS IS WHAT I DO, ANDY. THE MINES ARE IMPORTANT TO THE UGC... I'M IMPORTANT HERE.
YEAH, BUT I'M NOT. I'M JUST ALONE IN THE BASE ALL DAY.
THEN YOU HAVE TO TRY TO MAKE NEW FRIENDS.
I DON'T WANT TO.
YOU HAVE TO, ANDY. YOU HAVE TO AT LEAST TRY. FOR ME? PROMISE ME.

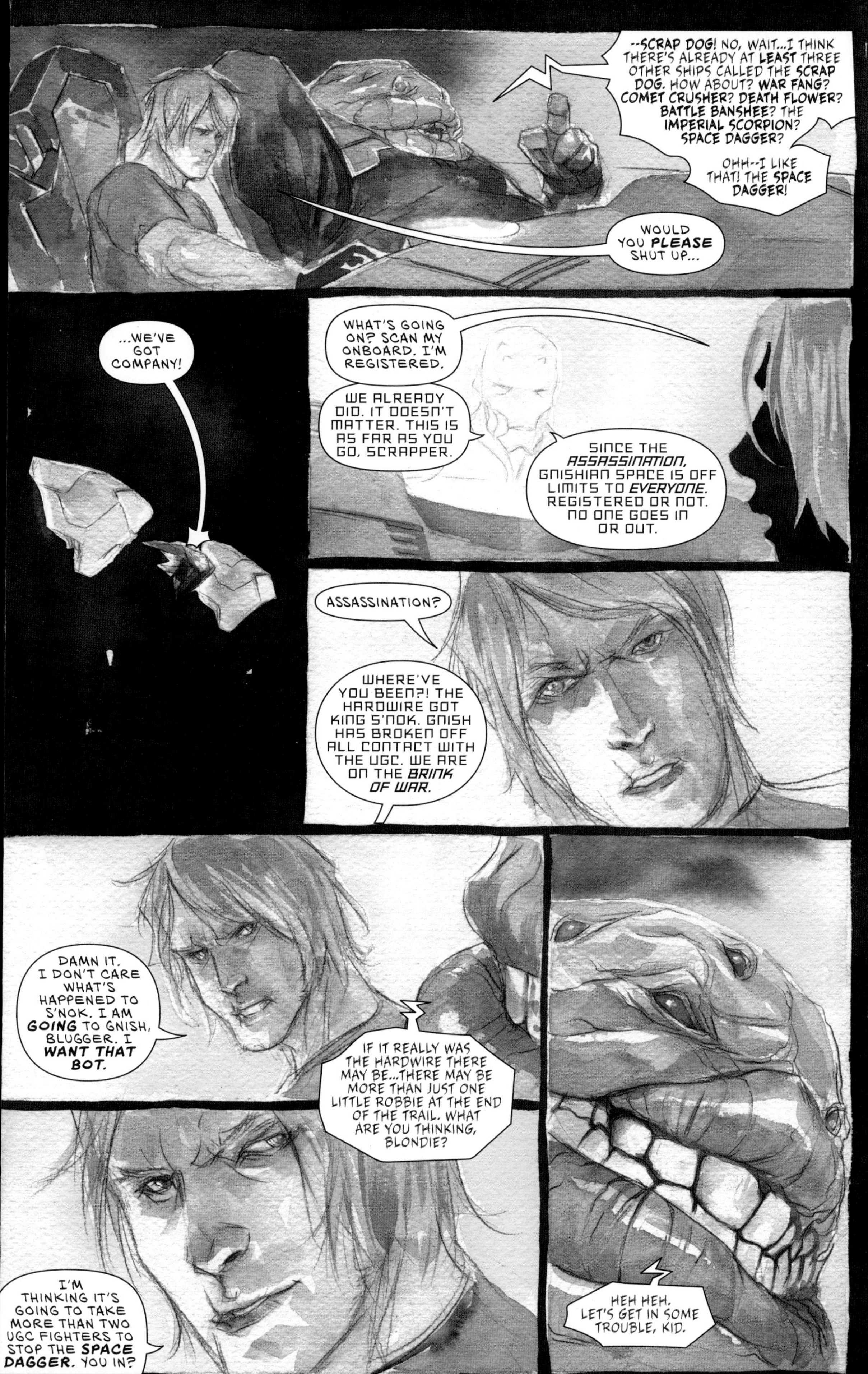
--SCRAP DOG! NO, WAIT...I THINK THERE'S ALREADY AT LEAST THREE OTHER SHIPS CALLED THE SCRAP DOG. HOW ABOUT? WAR FANG? COMET CRUSHER? DEATH FLOWER? BATTLE BANSHEE? THE IMPERIAL SCORPION? SPACE DAGGER?
OHH--I LIKE THAT! THE SPACE DAGGER!
WOULD YOU PLEASE SHUT UP...
...WE'VE GOT COMPANY!
WHAT'S GOING ON? SCAN MY ONBOARD. I'M REGISTERED.
WE ALREADY DID. IT DOESN'T MATTER. THIS IS AS FAR AS YOU GO, SCRAPPER.
SINCE THE ASSASSINATION, GNISHIAN SPACE IS OFF LIMITS TO EVERYONE. REGISTERED OR NOT. NO ONE GOES IN OR OUT.
ASSASSINATION?
WHERE'VE YOU BEEN?! THE HARDWIRE GOT KING S'NOK. GNISH HAS BROKEN OFF ALL CONTACT WITH THE UGC. WE ARE ON THE BRINK OF WAR.
DAMN IT. I DON'T CARE WHAT'S HAPPENED TO S'NOK. I AM GOING TO GNISH, BLUGGER. I WANT THAT BOT.
IF IT REALLY WAS THE HARDWIRE THERE MAY BE...THERE MAY BE MORE THAN JUST ONE LITTLE ROBBIE AT THE END OF THE TRAIL. WHAT ARE YOU THINKING, BLONDIE?
I'M THINKING IT'S GOING TO TAKE MORE THAN TWO UGC FIGHTERS TO STOP THE SPACE DAGGER. YOU IN?
HEH HEH. LET'S GET IN SOME TROUBLE, KID.

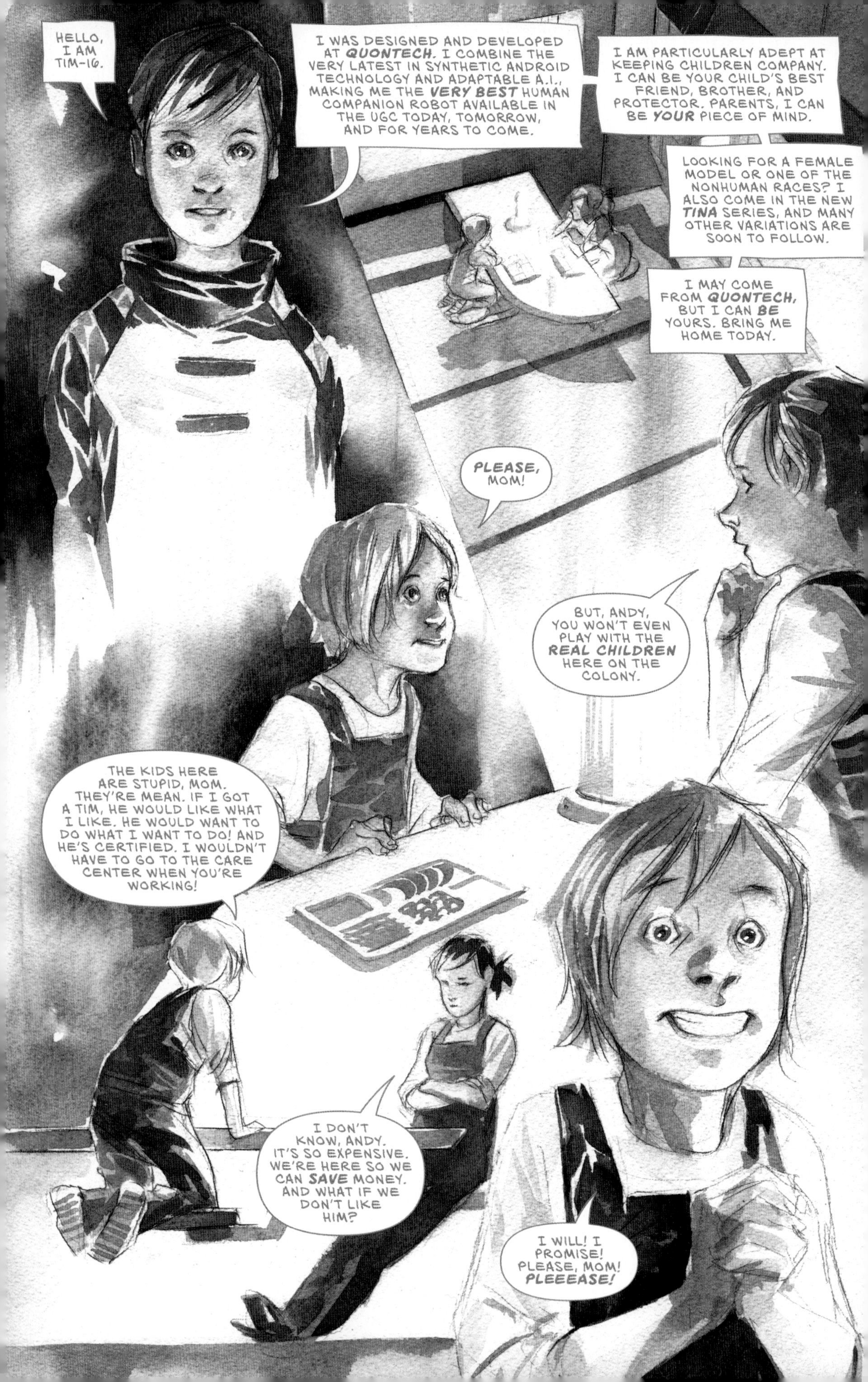
HELLO, I AM TIM-16.
I WAS DESIGNED AND DEVELOPED AT QUONTECH. I COMBINE THE VERY LATEST IN SYNTHETIC ANDROID TECHNOLOGY AND ADAPTABLE A.I., MAKING ME THE VERY BEST HUMAN COMPANION ROBOT AVAILABLE IN THE UGC TODAY, TOMORROW, AND FOR YEARS TO COME.
I AM PARTICULARLY ADEPT AT KEEPING CHILDREN COMPANY. I CAN BE YOUR CHILD'S BEST FRIEND, BROTHER, AND PROTECTOR. PARENTS, I CAN BE YOUR PIECE OF MIND.
LOOKING FOR A FEMALE MODEL OR ONE OF THE NONHUMAN RACES? I ALSO COME IN THE NEW TINA SERIES, AND MANY OTHER VARIATIONS ARE SOON TO FOLLOW.
I MAY COME FROM QUONTECH, BUT I CAN BE YOURS. BRING ME HOME TODAY.
PLEASE, MOM!
BUT, ANDY, YOU WON'T EVEN PLAY WITH THE REAL CHILDREN HERE ON THE COLONY.
THE KIDS HERE ARE STUPID, MOM. THEY'RE MEAN. IF I GOT A TIM, HE WOULD LIKE WHAT I LIKE. HE WOULD WANT TO DO WHAT I WANT TO DO! AND HE'S CERTIFIED. I WOULDN'T HAVE TO GO TO THE CARE CENTER WHEN YOU'RE WORKING!
I DON'T KNOW, ANDY. IT'S SO EXPENSIVE. WE'RE HERE SO WE CAN SAVE MONEY. AND WHAT IF WE DON'T LIKE HIM?
I WILL! I PROMISE! PLEASE, MOM! PLEEEASE!

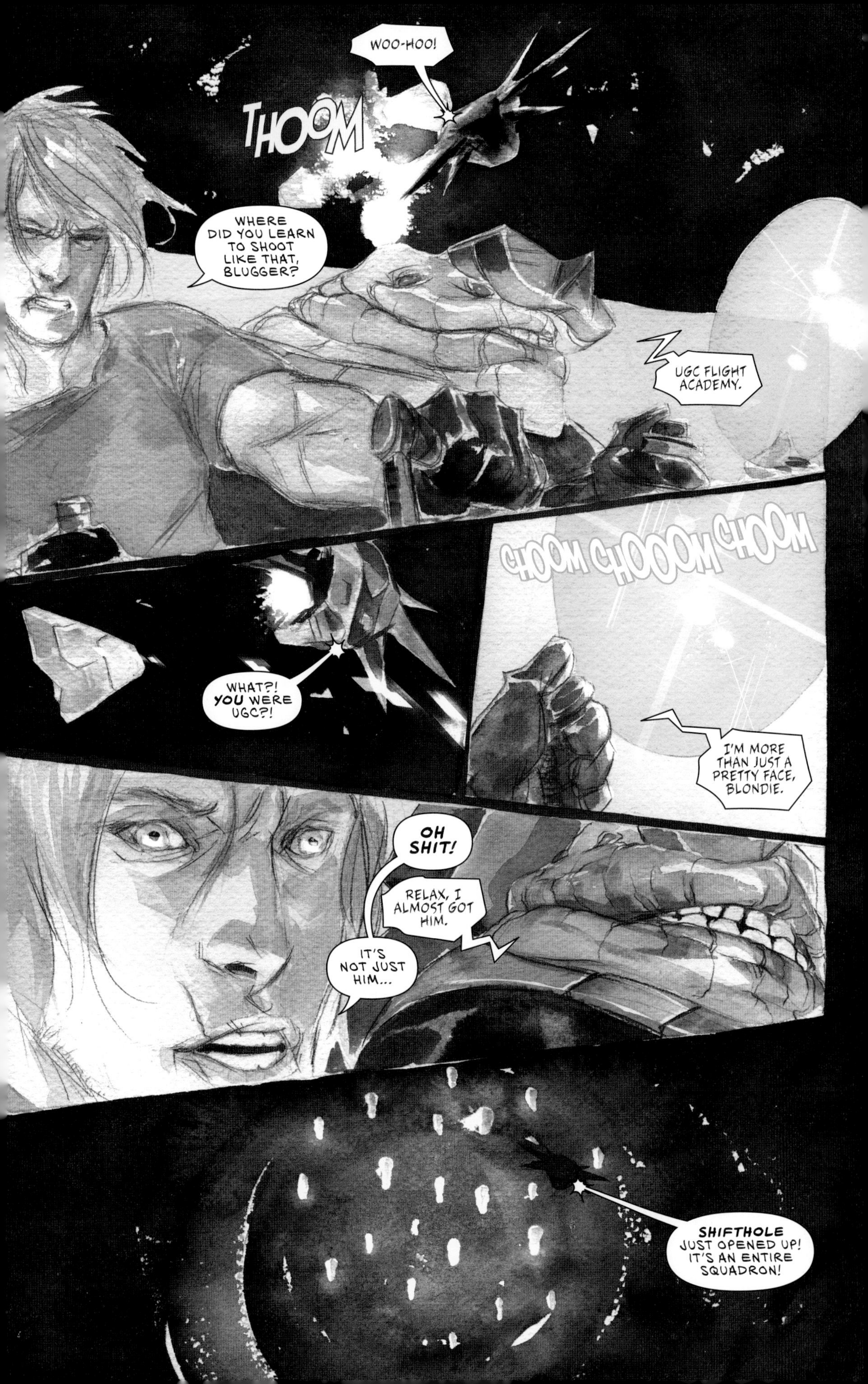
WOO-HOO!
THOOM
WHERE DID YOU LEARN TO SHOOT LIKE THAT, BLUGGER?
UGC FLIGHT ACADEMY.
WHAT?! YOU WERE UGC?!
CHOOM CHOOOM CHOOM
I'M MORE THAN JUST A PRETTY FACE, BLONDIE.
OH SHIT!
RELAX, I ALMOST GOT HIM.
IT'S NOT JUST HIM...
SHIFTHOLE JUST OPENED UP! IT'S AN ENTIRE SQUADRON!

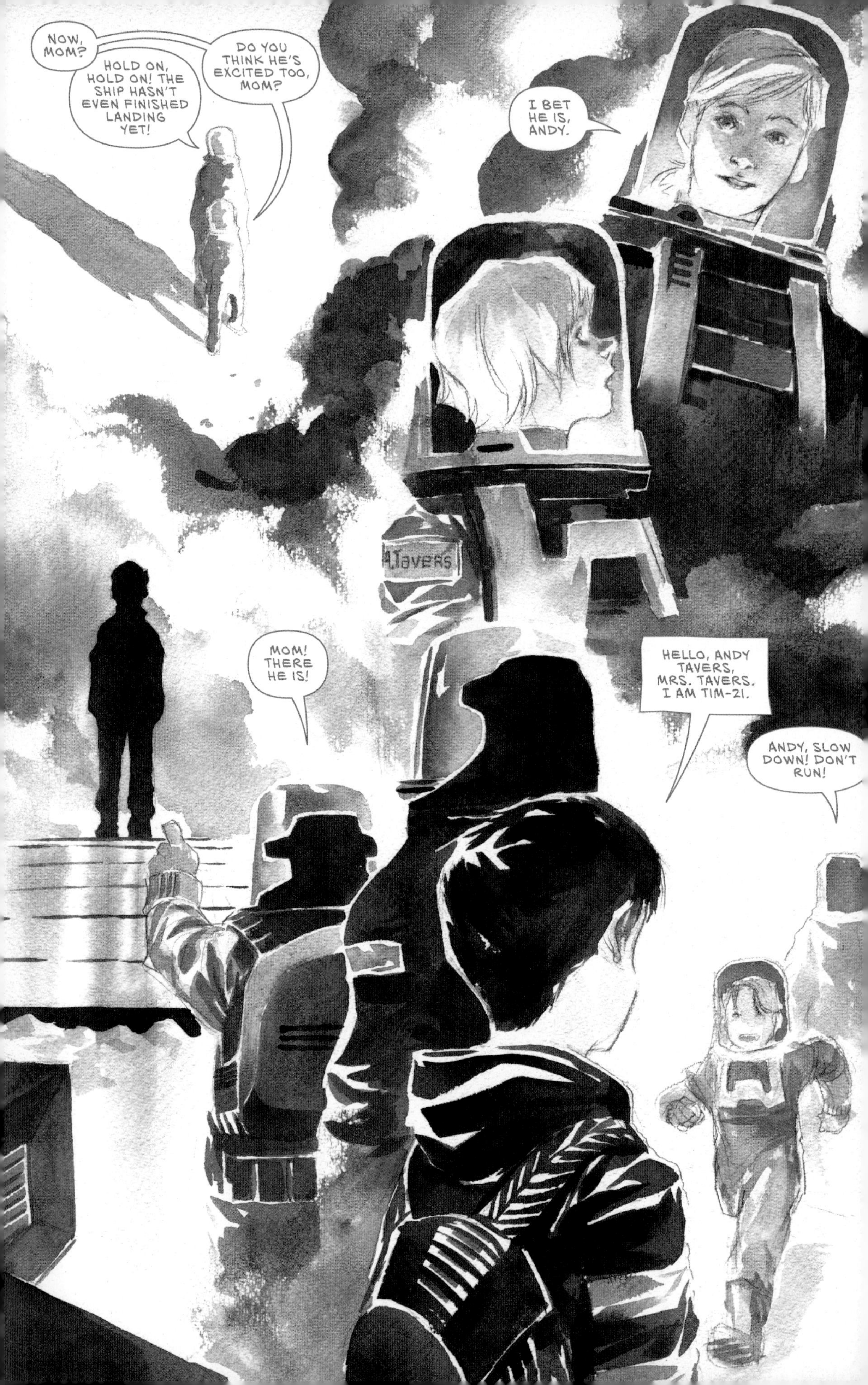
NOW, MOM?
HOLD ON, HOLD ON! THE SHIP HASN'T EVEN FINISHED LANDING YET!
DO YOU THINK HE'S EXCITED TOO, MOM?
I BET HE IS, ANDY.
A.Tavers
MOM! THERE HE IS!
HELLO, ANDY TAVERS, MRS. TAVERS. I AM TIM-21.
ANDY, SLOW DOWN! DON'T RUN!

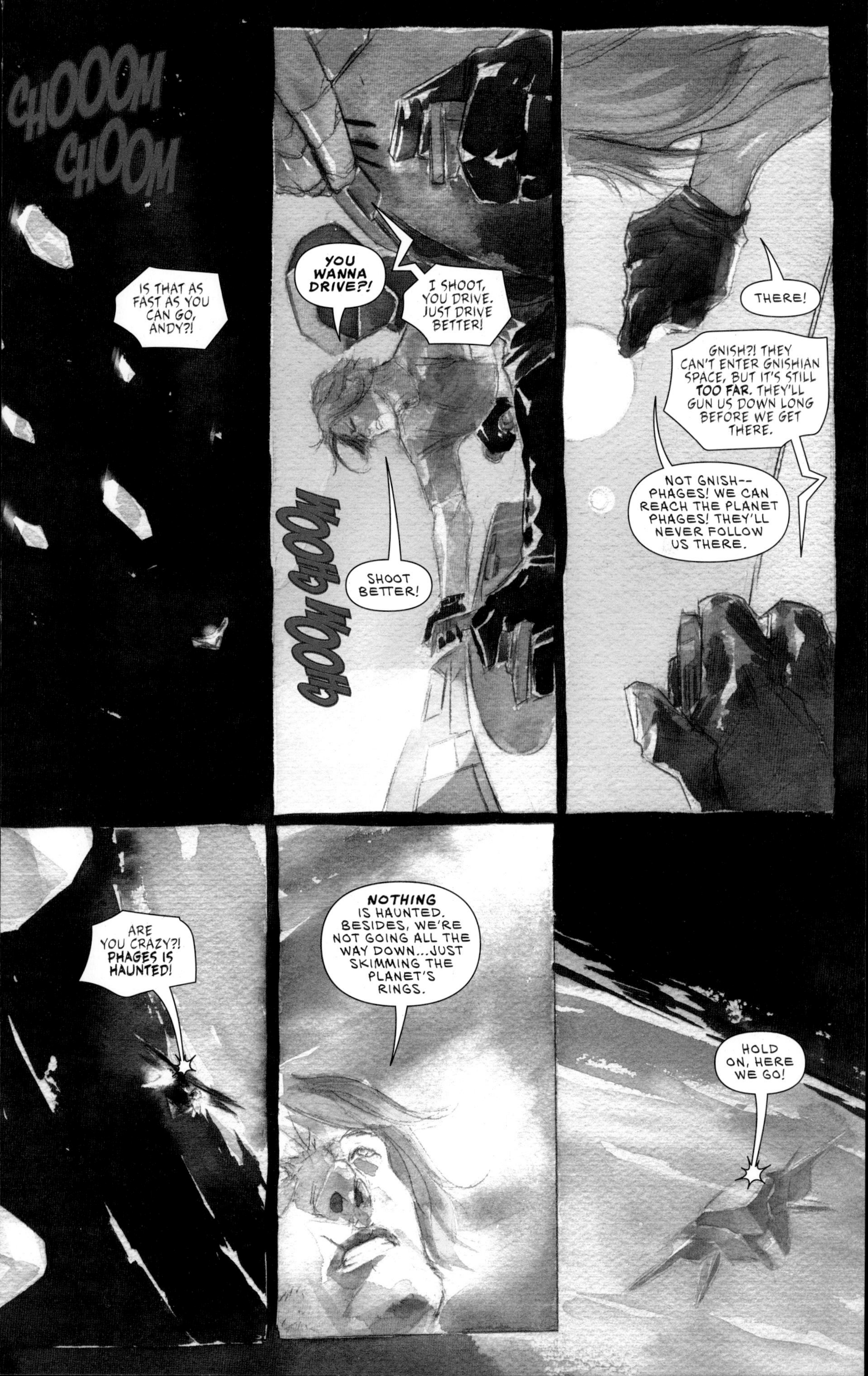

CHOOOM
CHOOM
IS THAT AS FAST AS YOU CAN GO, ANDY?!
YOU WANNA DRIVE?!
I SHOOT, YOU DRIVE. JUST DRIVE BETTER!
SHOOT BETTER!
THERE!
GNISH?! THEY CAN'T ENTER GNISHIAN SPACE, BUT IT'S STILL **TOO FAR**. THEY'LL GUN US DOWN LONG BEFORE WE GET THERE.
NOT GNISH-- PHAGES! WE CAN REACH THE PLANET PHAGES! THEY'LL NEVER FOLLOW US THERE.
ARE YOU CRAZY?! **PHAGES IS HAUNTED!**
NOTHING IS HAUNTED. BESIDES, WE'RE NOT GOING ALL THE WAY DOWN...JUST SKIMMING THE PLANET'S RINGS.
HOLD ON, HERE WE GO!

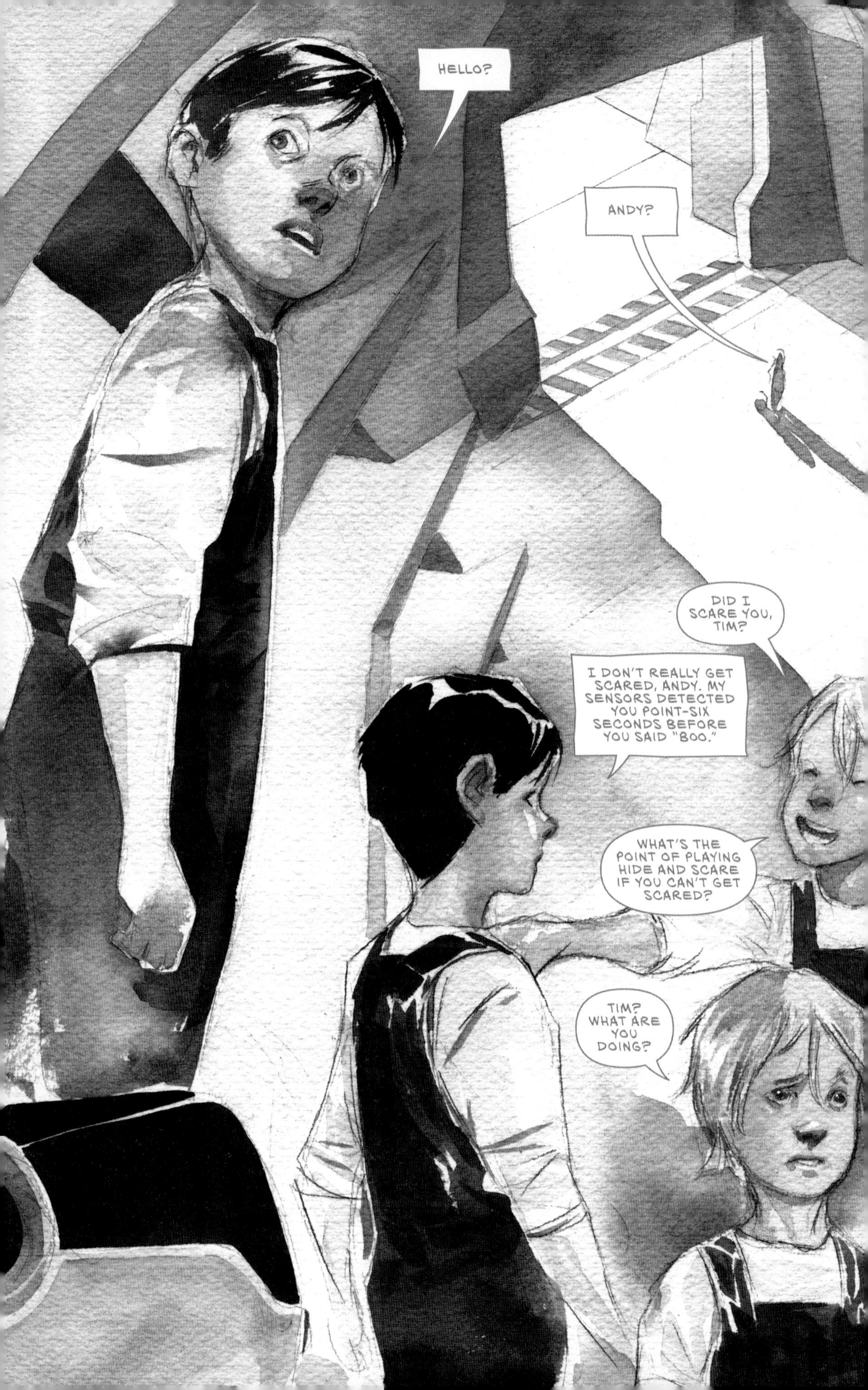
HELLO?
ANDY?
DID I SCARE YOU, TIM?
I DON'T REALLY GET SCARED, ANDY. MY SENSORS DETECTED YOU POINT-SIX SECONDS BEFORE YOU SAID "BOO."
WHAT'S THE POINT OF PLAYING HIDE AND SCARE IF YOU CAN'T GET SCARED?
TIM? WHAT ARE YOU DOING?

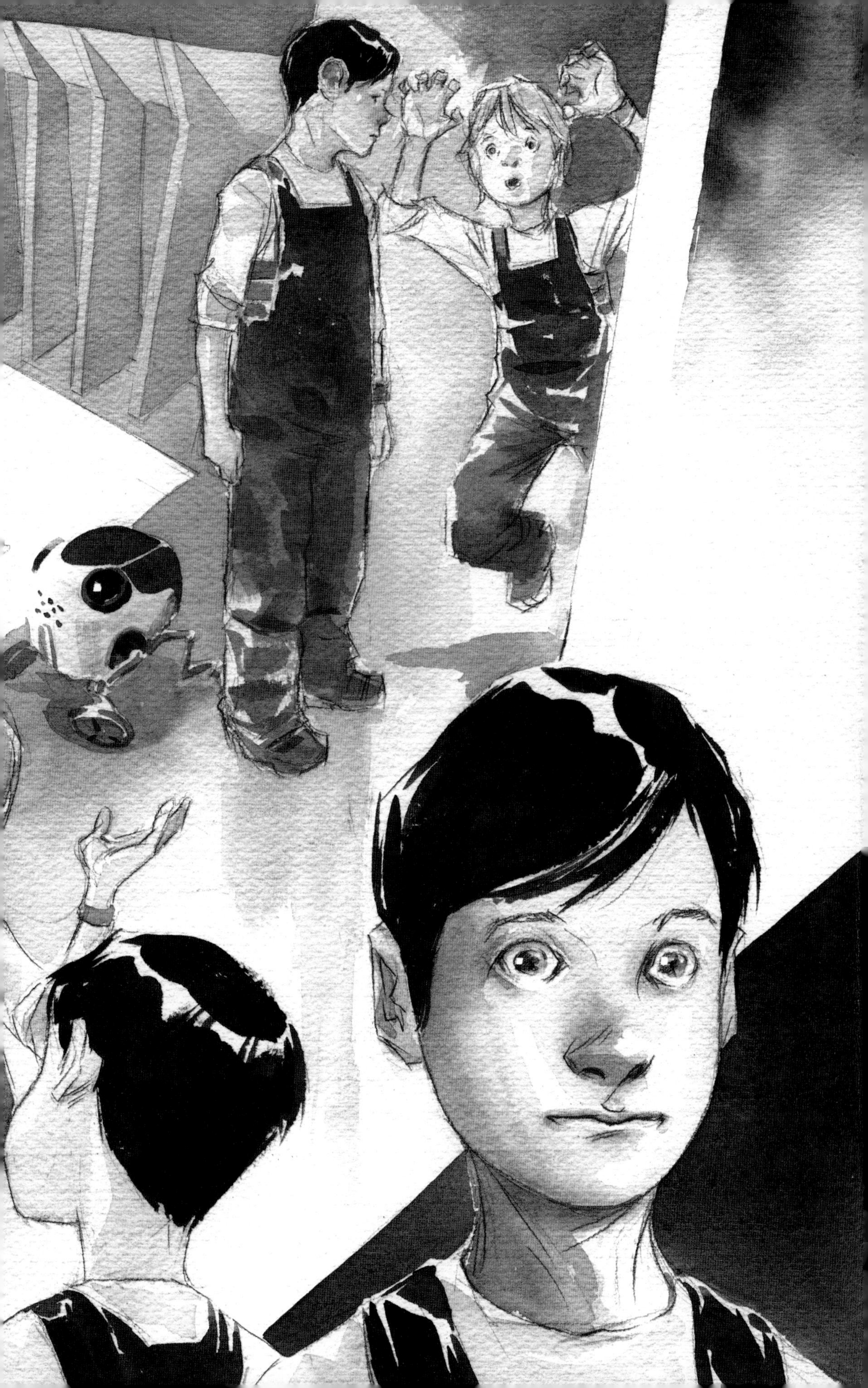

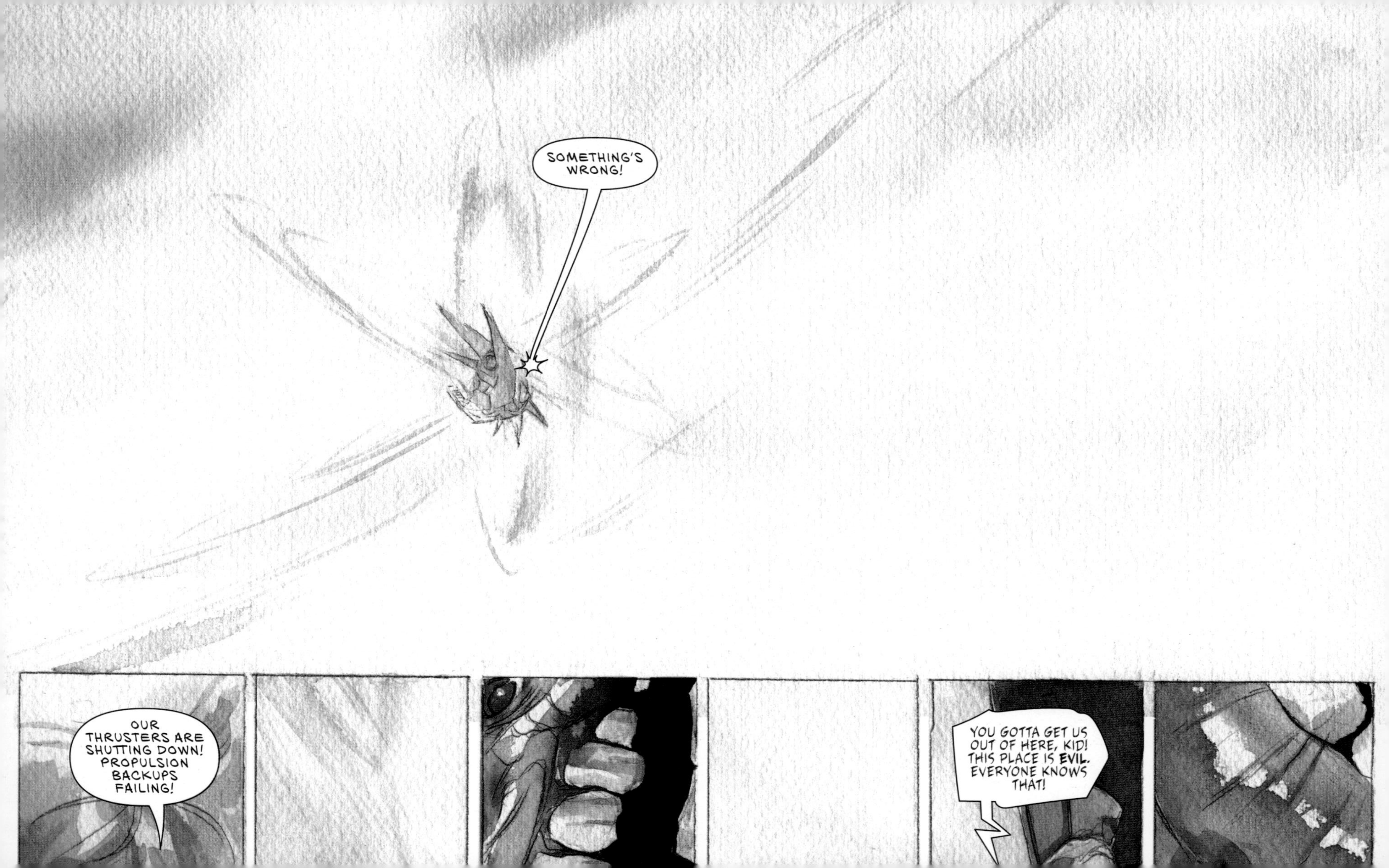
SOMETHING'S WRONG!
OUR THRUSTERS ARE SHUTTING DOWN! PROPULSION BACKUPS FAILING!
YOU GOTTA GET US OUT OF HERE, KID! THIS PLACE IS **EVIL.** EVERYONE KNOWS THAT!

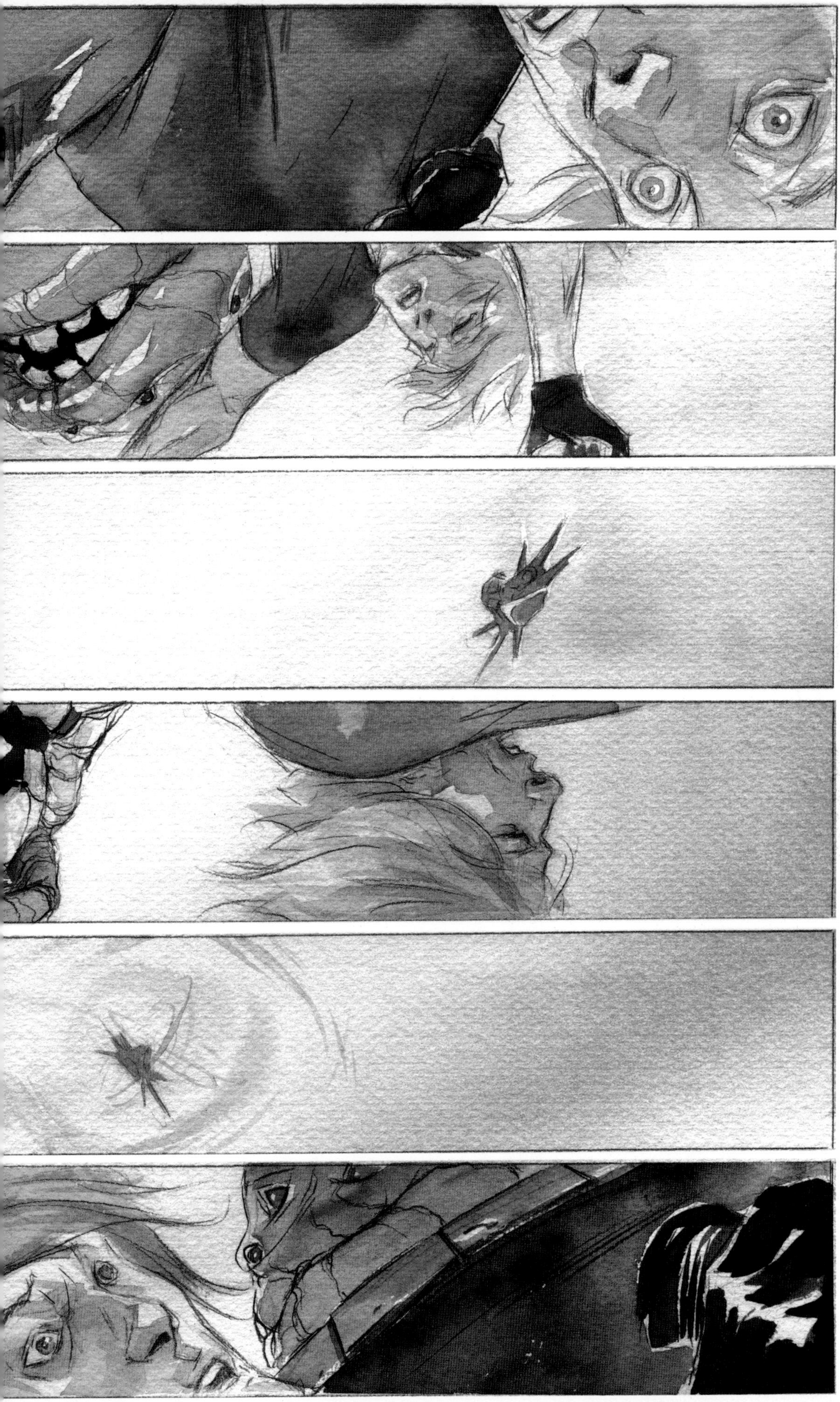

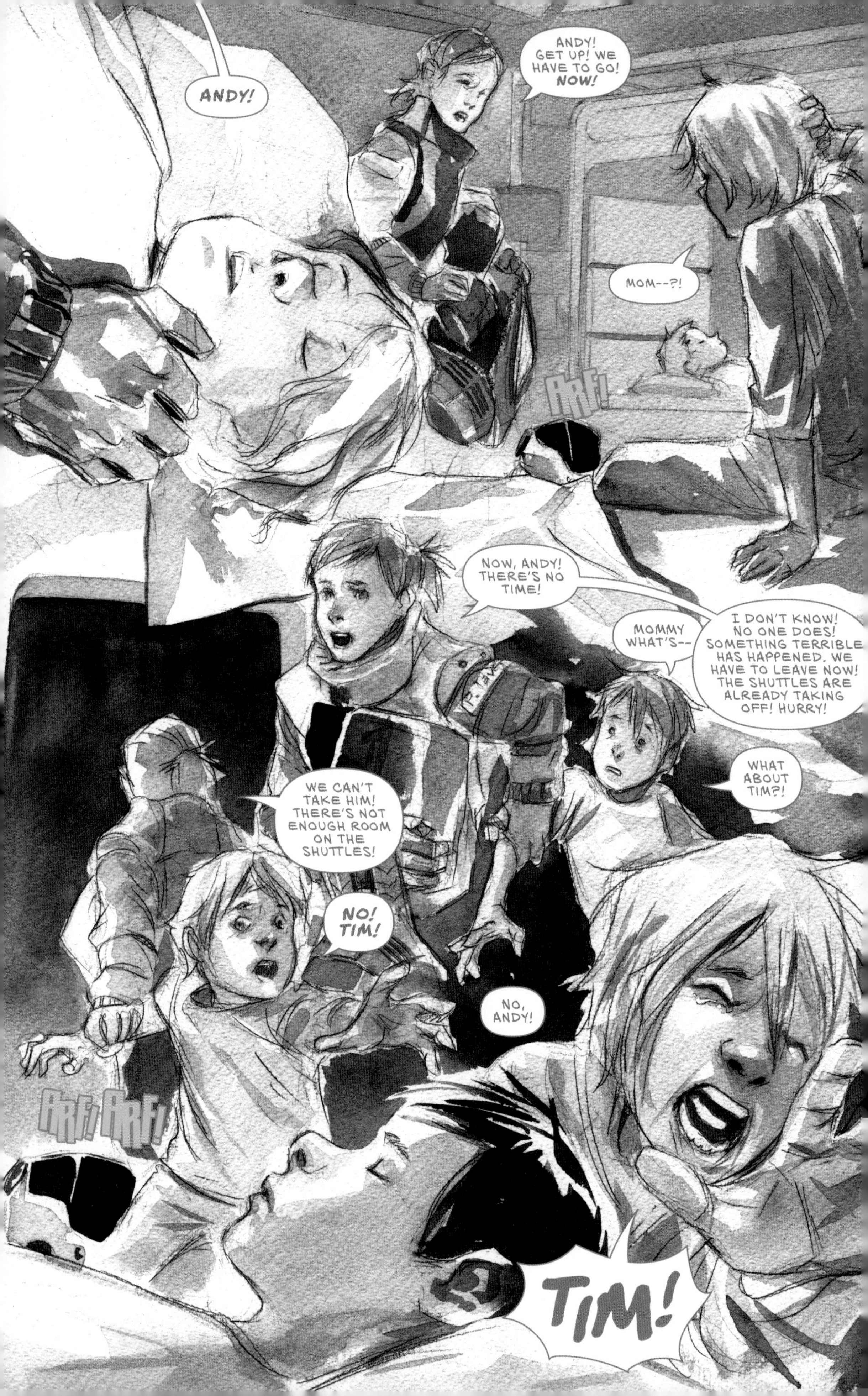

ANDY!
ANDY! GET UP! WE HAVE TO GO! NOW!
MOM--?!
ARF!
NOW, ANDY! THERE'S NO TIME!
MOMMY WHAT'S--
I DON'T KNOW! NO ONE DOES! SOMETHING TERRIBLE HAS HAPPENED. WE HAVE TO LEAVE NOW! THE SHUTTLES ARE ALREADY TAKING OFF! HURRY!
WHAT ABOUT TIM?!
WE CAN'T TAKE HIM! THERE'S NOT ENOUGH ROOM ON THE SHUTTLES!
NO! TIM!
NO, ANDY!
ARF! ARF!
TIM!

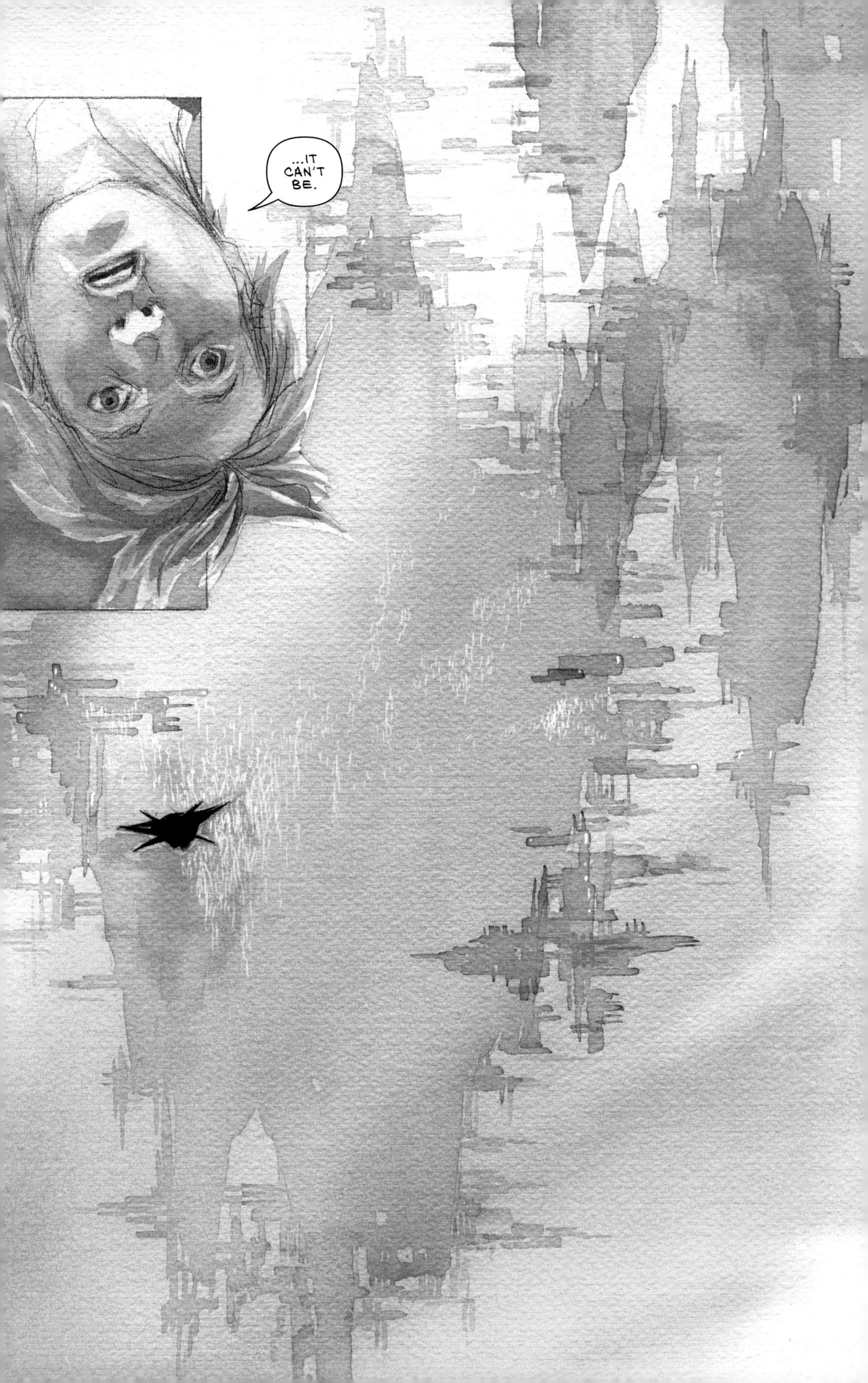
...IT CAN'T BE.

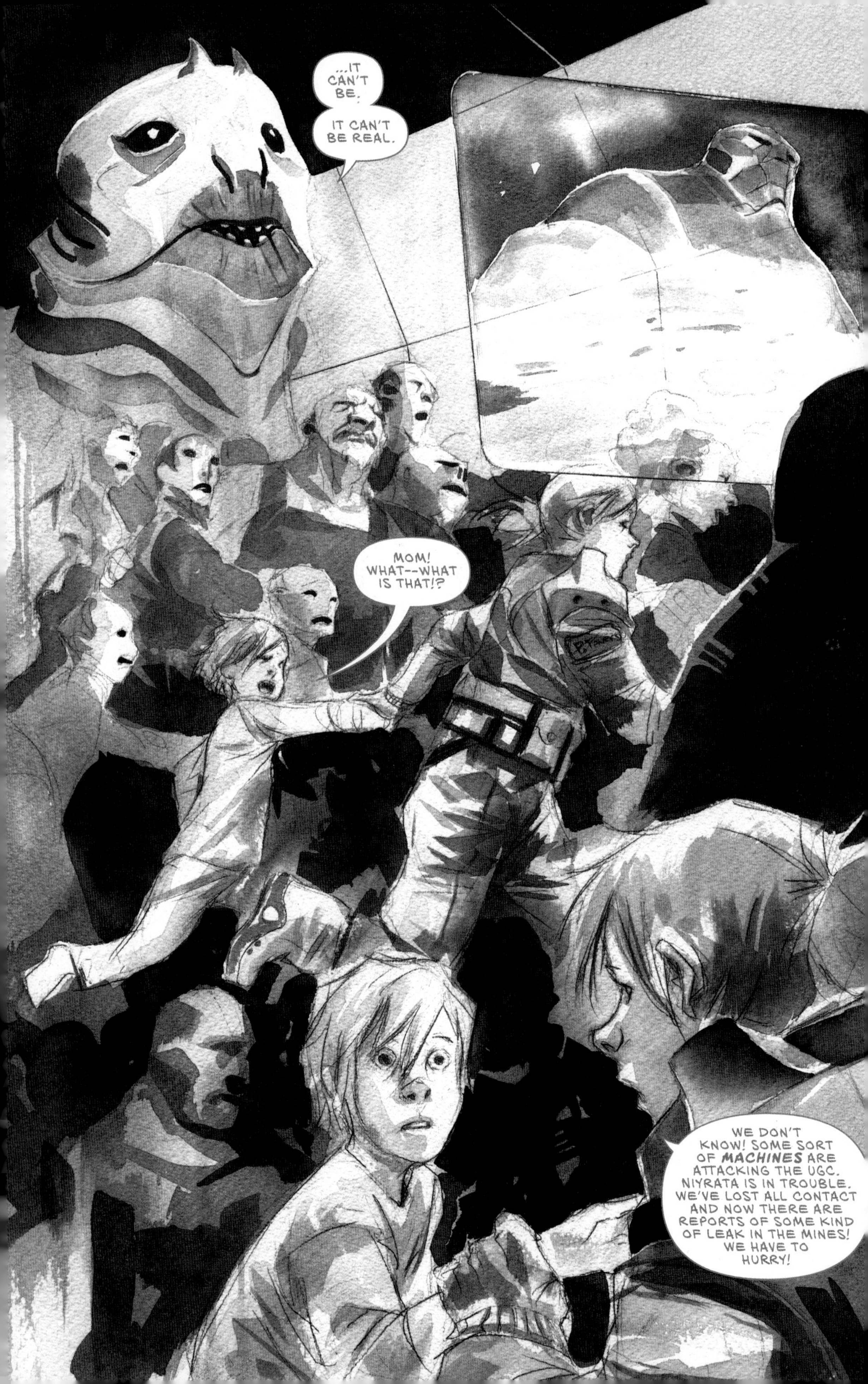
...IT CAN'T BE.
IT CAN'T BE REAL.
MOM! WHAT--WHAT IS THAT!?
WE DON'T KNOW! SOME SORT OF *MACHINES* ARE ATTACKING THE UGC. NIYRATA IS IN TROUBLE. WE'VE LOST ALL CONTACT AND NOW THERE ARE REPORTS OF SOME KIND OF LEAK IN THE MINES! WE HAVE TO HURRY!

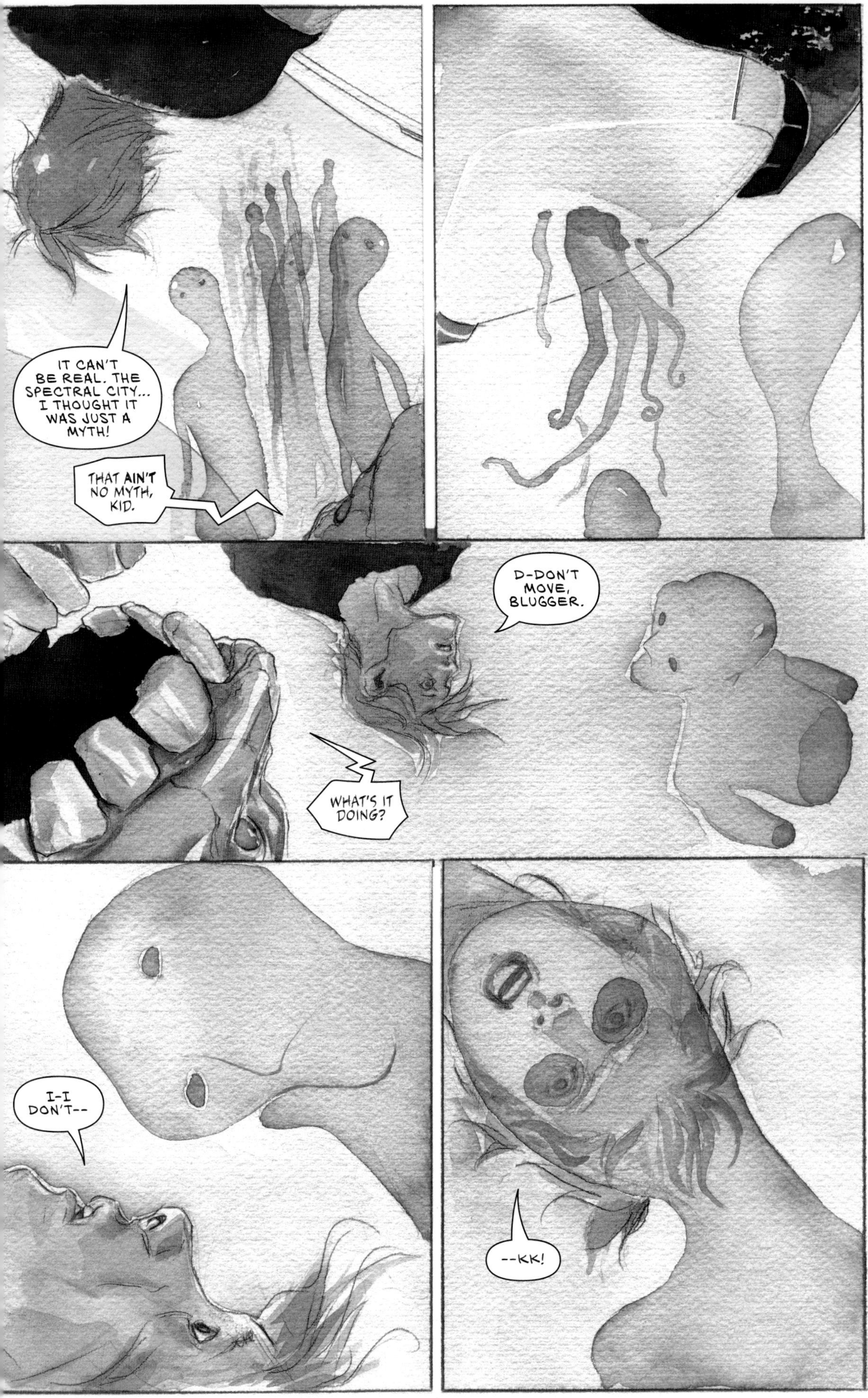
IT CAN'T BE REAL. THE SPECTRAL CITY... I THOUGHT IT WAS JUST A MYTH!
THAT AIN'T NO MYTH, KID.
D-DON'T MOVE, BLUGGER.
WHAT'S IT DOING?
I-I DON'T--
--KK!

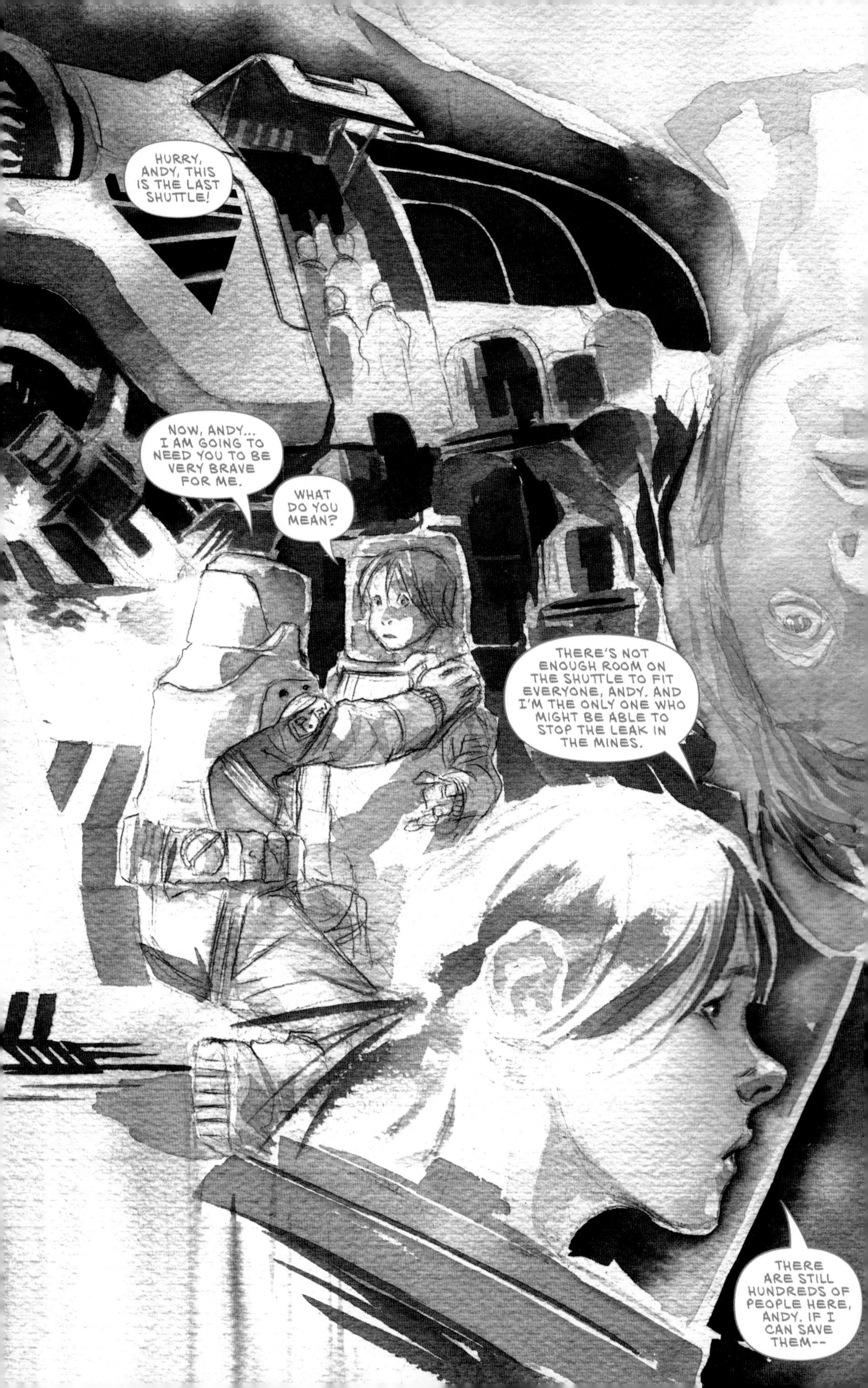
HURRY, ANDY, THIS IS THE LAST SHUTTLE!
NOW, ANDY... I AM GOING TO NEED YOU TO BE VERY BRAVE FOR ME.
WHAT DO YOU MEAN?
THERE'S NOT ENOUGH ROOM ON THE SHUTTLE TO FIT EVERYONE, ANDY. AND I'M THE ONLY ONE WHO MIGHT BE ABLE TO STOP THE LEAK IN THE MINES.
THERE ARE STILL HUNDREDS OF PEOPLE HERE, ANDY. IF I CAN SAVE THEM--

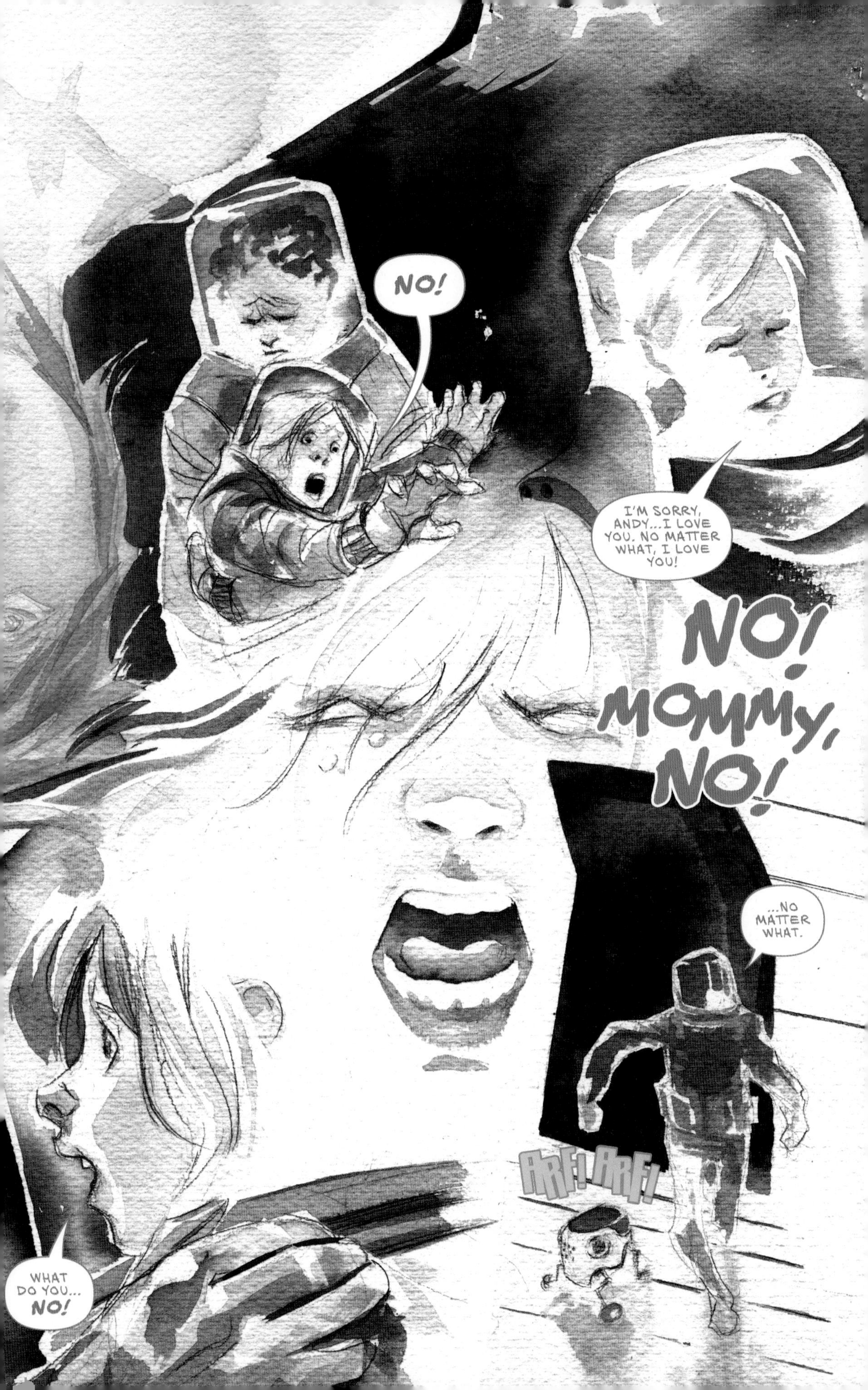
NO!
I'M SORRY, ANDY...I LOVE YOU. NO MATTER WHAT, I LOVE YOU!
NO! MOMMY, NO!
...NO MATTER WHAT.
ARF! ARF!
WHAT DO YOU... NO!

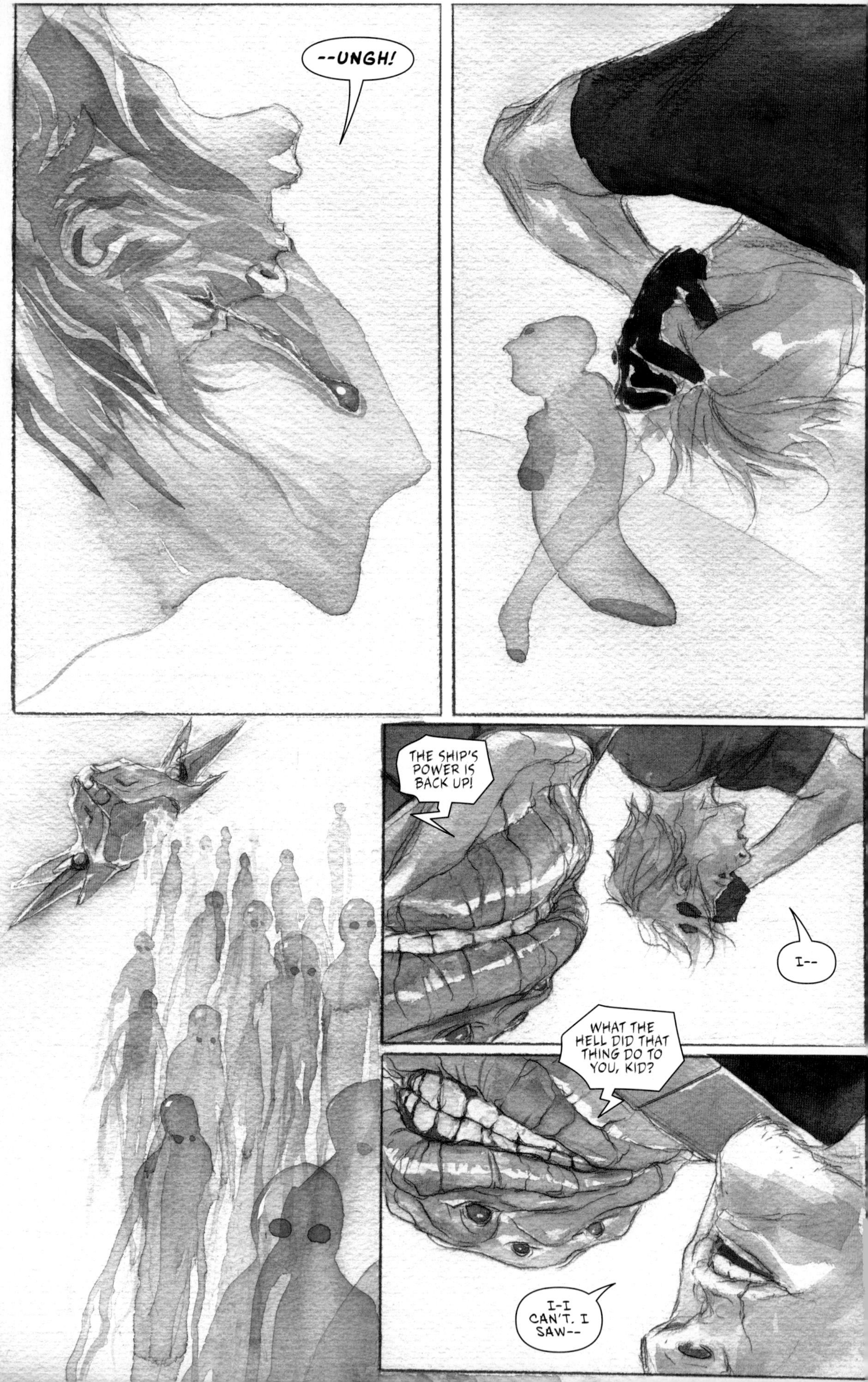
--UNGH!
THE SHIP'S POWER IS BACK UP!
I--
WHAT THE HELL DID THAT THING DO TO YOU, KID?
I-I CAN'T. I SAW--

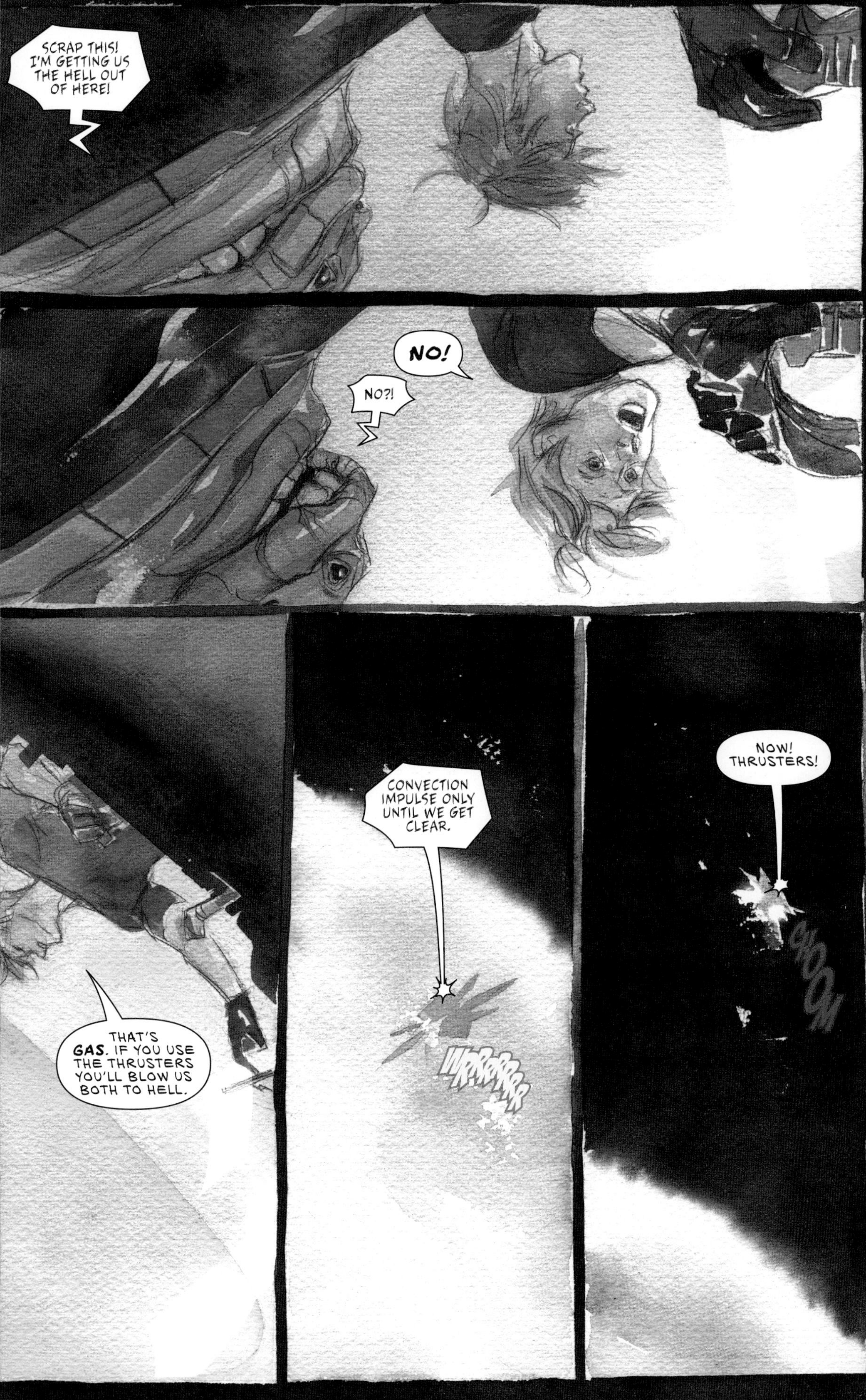

SCRAP THIS! I'M GETTING US THE HELL OUT OF HERE!
NO!
NO?!
THAT'S GAS. IF YOU USE THE THRUSTERS YOU'LL BLOW US BOTH TO HELL.
CONVECTION IMPULSE ONLY UNTIL WE GET CLEAR.
VVRRRRRR
NOW! THRUSTERS!
CHOOM

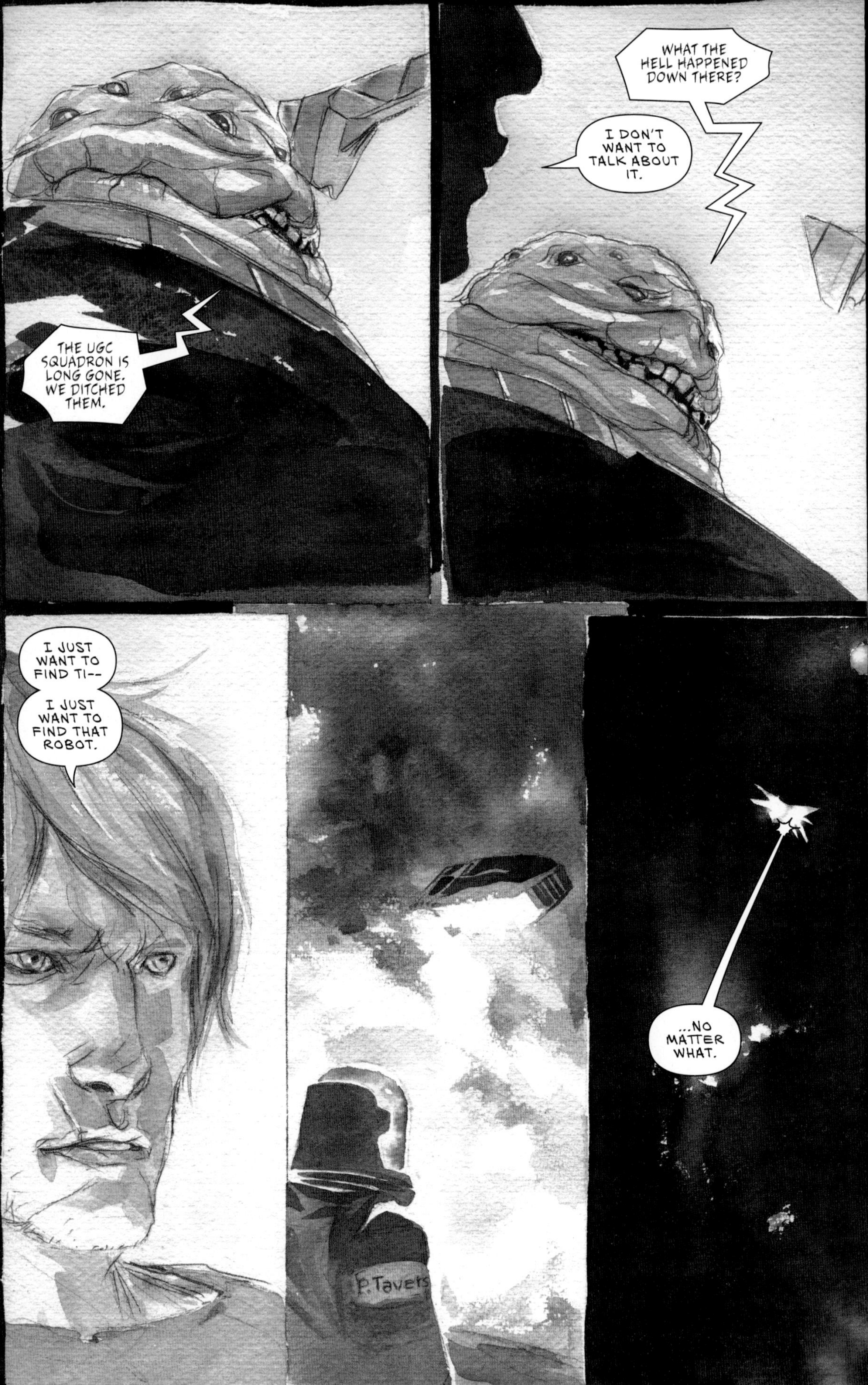
THE UGC SQUADRON IS LONG GONE. WE DITCHED THEM.
WHAT THE HELL HAPPENED DOWN THERE?
I DON'T WANT TO TALK ABOUT IT.
I JUST WANT TO FIND TI--
I JUST WANT TO FIND THAT ROBOT.
P. Tavers
...NO MATTER WHAT.

CHAPTER THREE

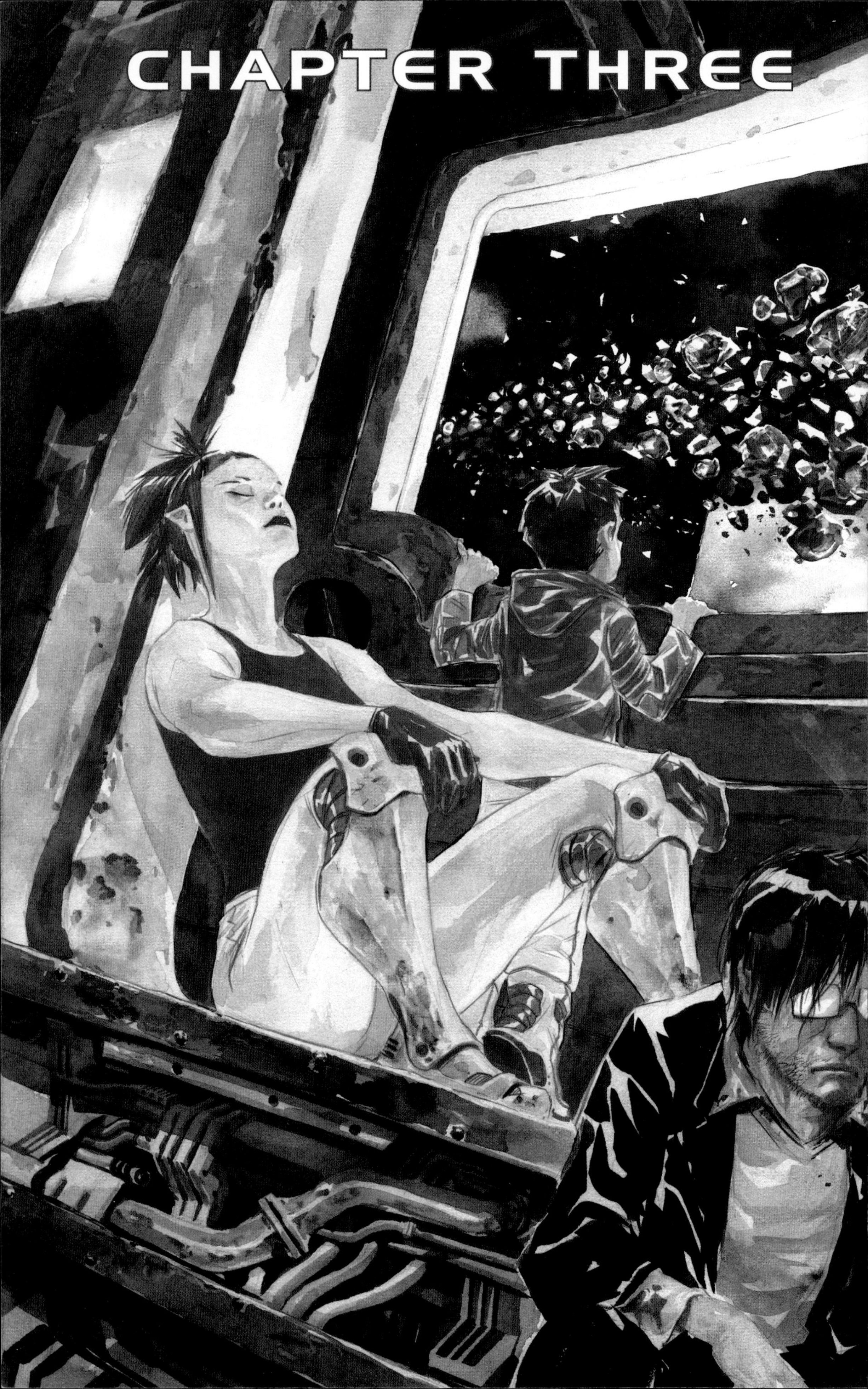

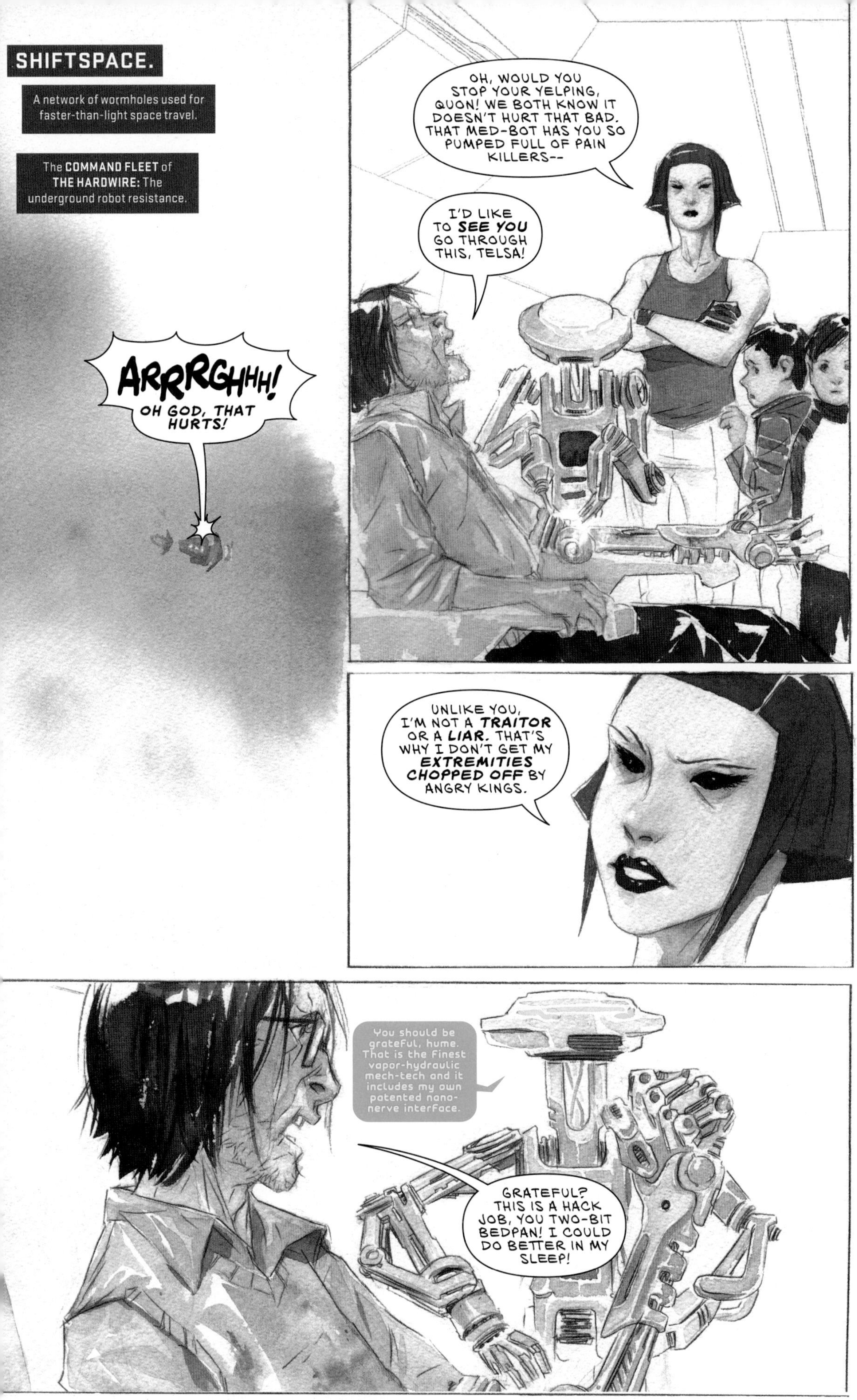
SHIFTSPACE.
A network of wormholes used for faster-than-light space travel.
The COMMAND FLEET of THE HARDWIRE: The underground robot resistance.
ARRRGHHH! OH GOD, THAT HURTS!
OH, WOULD YOU STOP YOUR YELPING, QUON! WE BOTH KNOW IT DOESN'T HURT THAT BAD. THAT MED-BOT HAS YOU SO PUMPED FULL OF PAIN KILLERS--
I'D LIKE TO SEE YOU GO THROUGH THIS, TELSA!
UNLIKE YOU, I'M NOT A TRAITOR OR A LIAR. THAT'S WHY I DON'T GET MY EXTREMITIES CHOPPED OFF BY ANGRY KINGS.
You should be grateful, hume. That is the finest vapor-hydraulic mech-tech and it includes my own patented nano-nerve interface.
GRATEFUL? THIS IS A HACK JOB, YOU TWO-BIT BEDPAN! I COULD DO BETTER IN MY SLEEP!

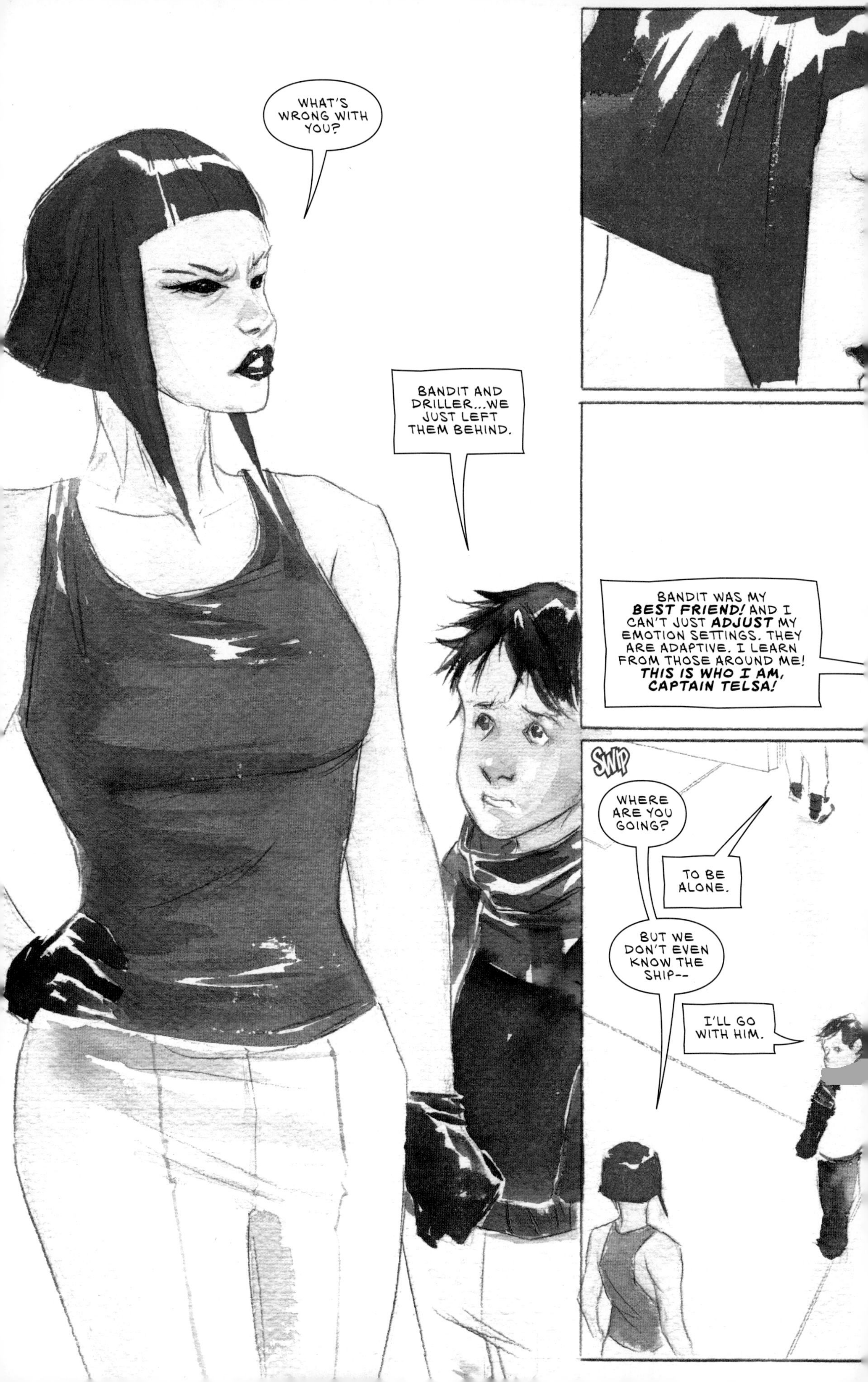
WHAT'S WRONG WITH YOU?
BANDIT AND DRILLER... WE JUST LEFT THEM BEHIND.
BANDIT WAS MY **BEST FRIEND!** AND I CAN'T JUST **ADJUST** MY EMOTION SETTINGS. THEY ARE ADAPTIVE. I LEARN FROM THOSE AROUND ME! **THIS IS WHO I AM, CAPTAIN TELSA!**
SWIP
WHERE ARE YOU GOING?
TO BE ALONE.
BUT WE DON'T EVEN KNOW THE SHIP--
I'LL GO WITH HIM.

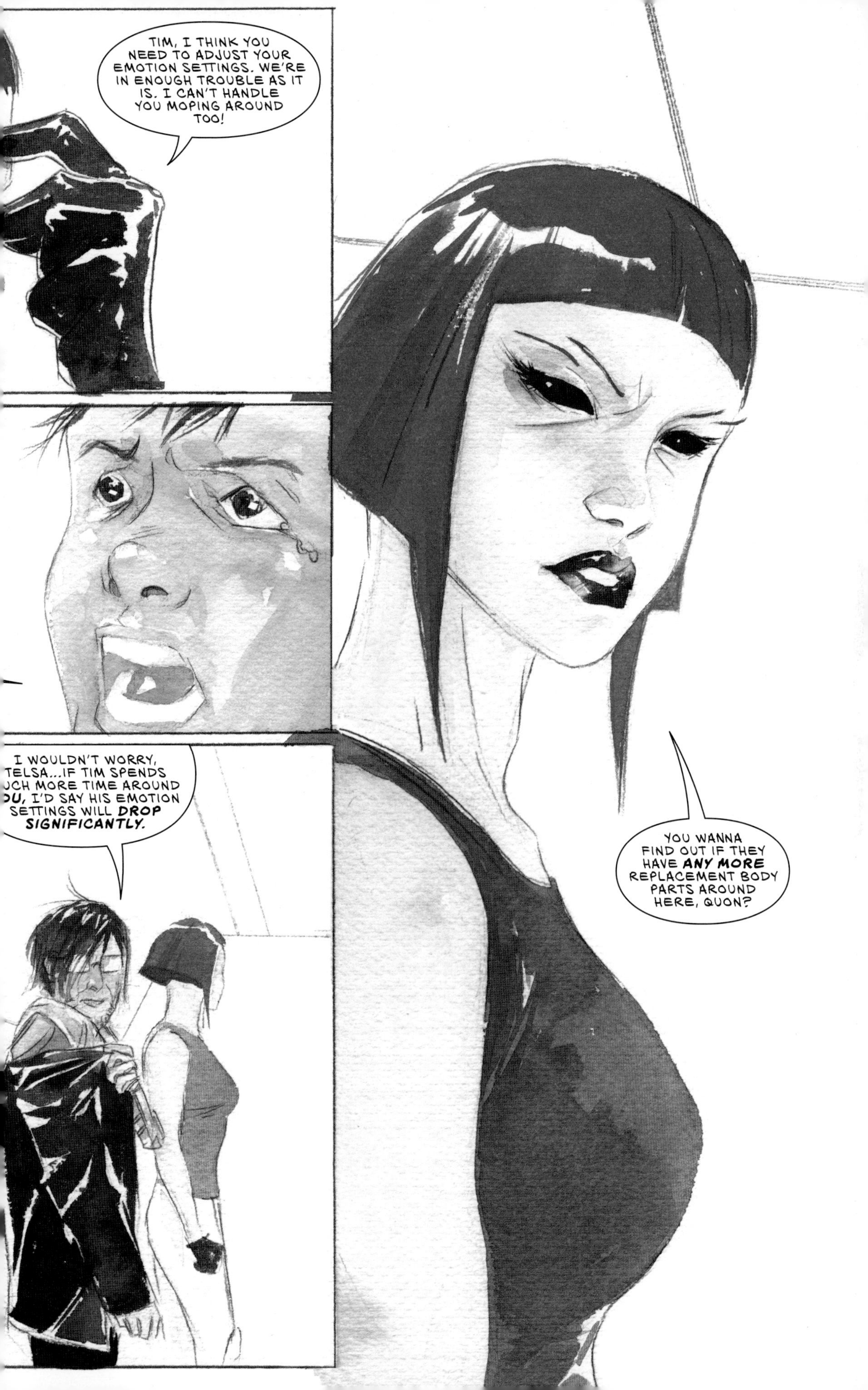
TIM, I THINK YOU NEED TO ADJUST YOUR EMOTION SETTINGS. WE'RE IN ENOUGH TROUBLE AS IT IS. I CAN'T HANDLE YOU MOPING AROUND TOO!
YOU WANNA FIND OUT IF THEY HAVE **ANY MORE** REPLACEMENT BODY PARTS AROUND HERE, QUON?
I WOULDN'T WORRY, TELSA...IF TIM SPENDS UCH MORE TIME AROUND OU, I'D SAY HIS EMOTION SETTINGS WILL **DROP SIGNIFICANTLY.**

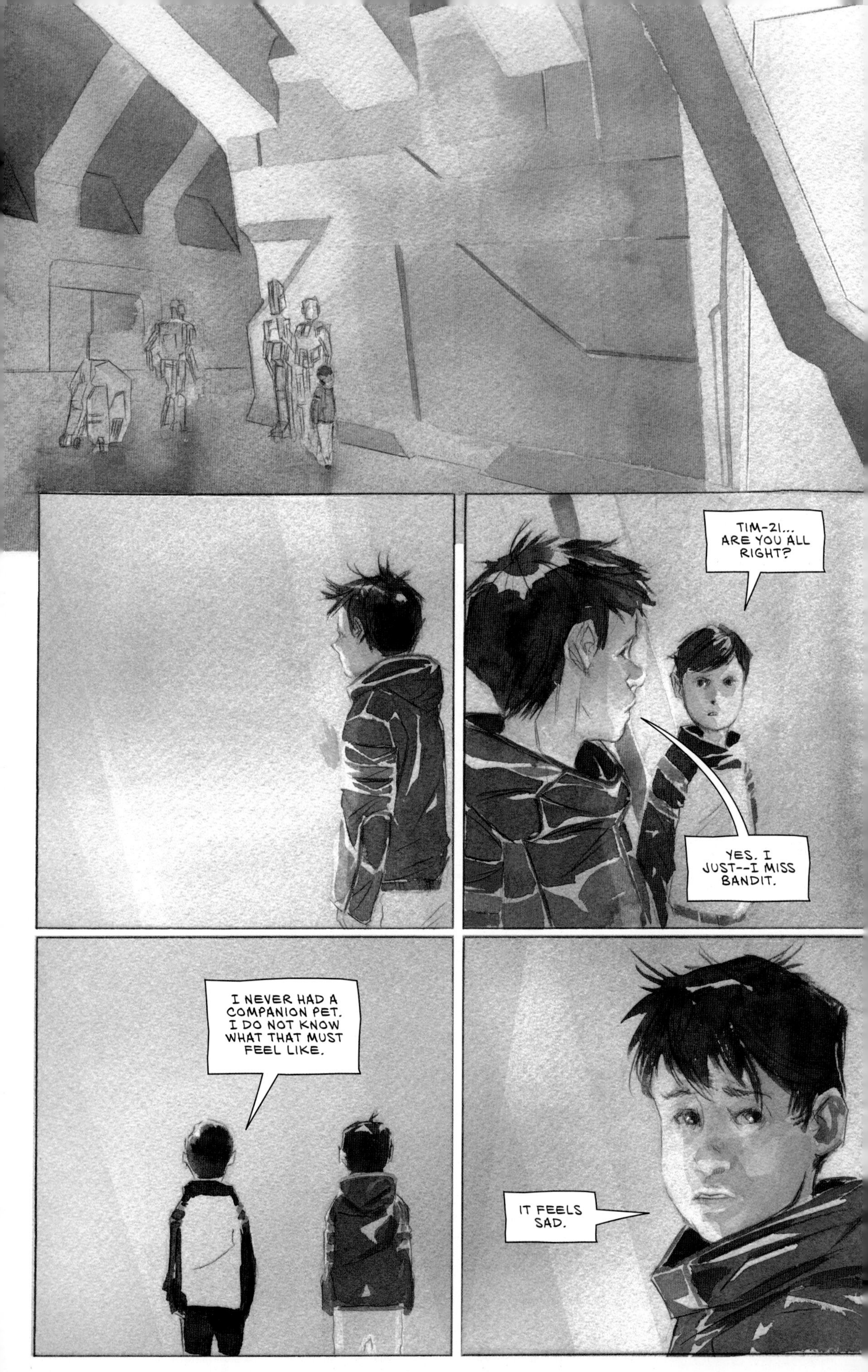
TIM-21... ARE YOU ALL RIGHT?
YES. I JUST--I MISS BANDIT.
I NEVER HAD A COMPANION PET. I DO NOT KNOW WHAT THAT MUST FEEL LIKE.
IT FEELS SAD.

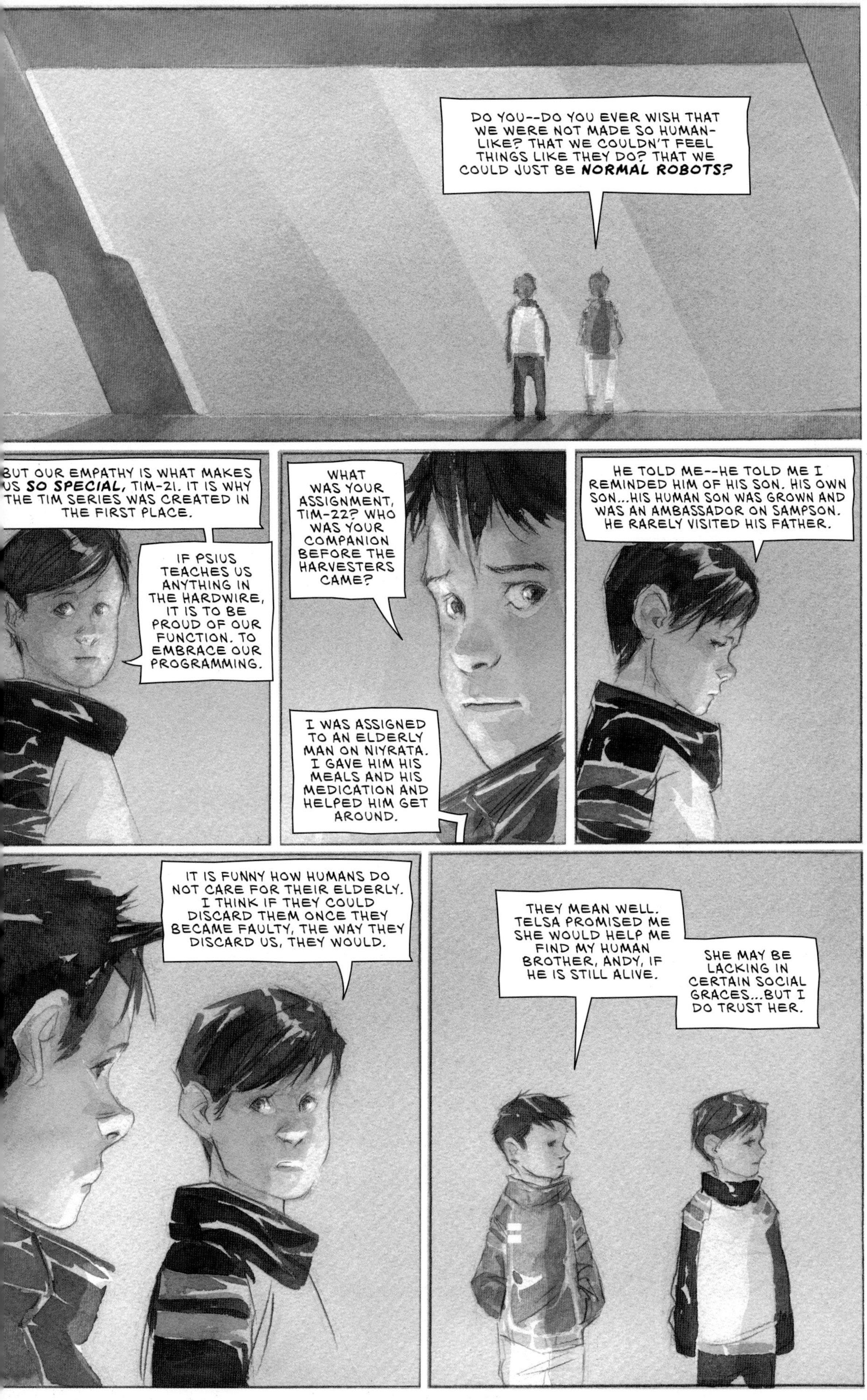
DO YOU--DO YOU EVER WISH THAT WE WERE NOT MADE SO HUMAN-LIKE? THAT WE COULDN'T FEEL THINGS LIKE THEY DO? THAT WE COULD JUST BE **NORMAL ROBOTS?**
BUT OUR EMPATHY IS WHAT MAKES US **SO SPECIAL,** TIM-21. IT IS WHY THE TIM SERIES WAS CREATED IN THE FIRST PLACE.
IF PSIUS TEACHES US ANYTHING IN THE HARDWIRE, IT IS TO BE PROUD OF OUR FUNCTION. TO EMBRACE OUR PROGRAMMING.
WHAT WAS YOUR ASSIGNMENT, TIM-22? WHO WAS YOUR COMPANION BEFORE THE HARVESTERS CAME?
I WAS ASSIGNED TO AN ELDERLY MAN ON NIYRATA. I GAVE HIM HIS MEALS AND HIS MEDICATION AND HELPED HIM GET AROUND.
HE TOLD ME--HE TOLD ME I REMINDED HIM OF HIS SON. HIS OWN SON...HIS HUMAN SON WAS GROWN AND WAS AN AMBASSADOR ON SAMPSON. HE RARELY VISITED HIS FATHER.
IT IS FUNNY HOW HUMANS DO NOT CARE FOR THEIR ELDERLY. I THINK IF THEY COULD DISCARD THEM ONCE THEY BECAME FAULTY, THE WAY THEY DISCARD US, THEY WOULD.
THEY MEAN WELL. TELSA PROMISED ME SHE WOULD HELP ME FIND MY HUMAN BROTHER, ANDY, IF HE IS STILL ALIVE.
SHE MAY BE LACKING IN CERTAIN SOCIAL GRACES...BUT I DO TRUST HER.

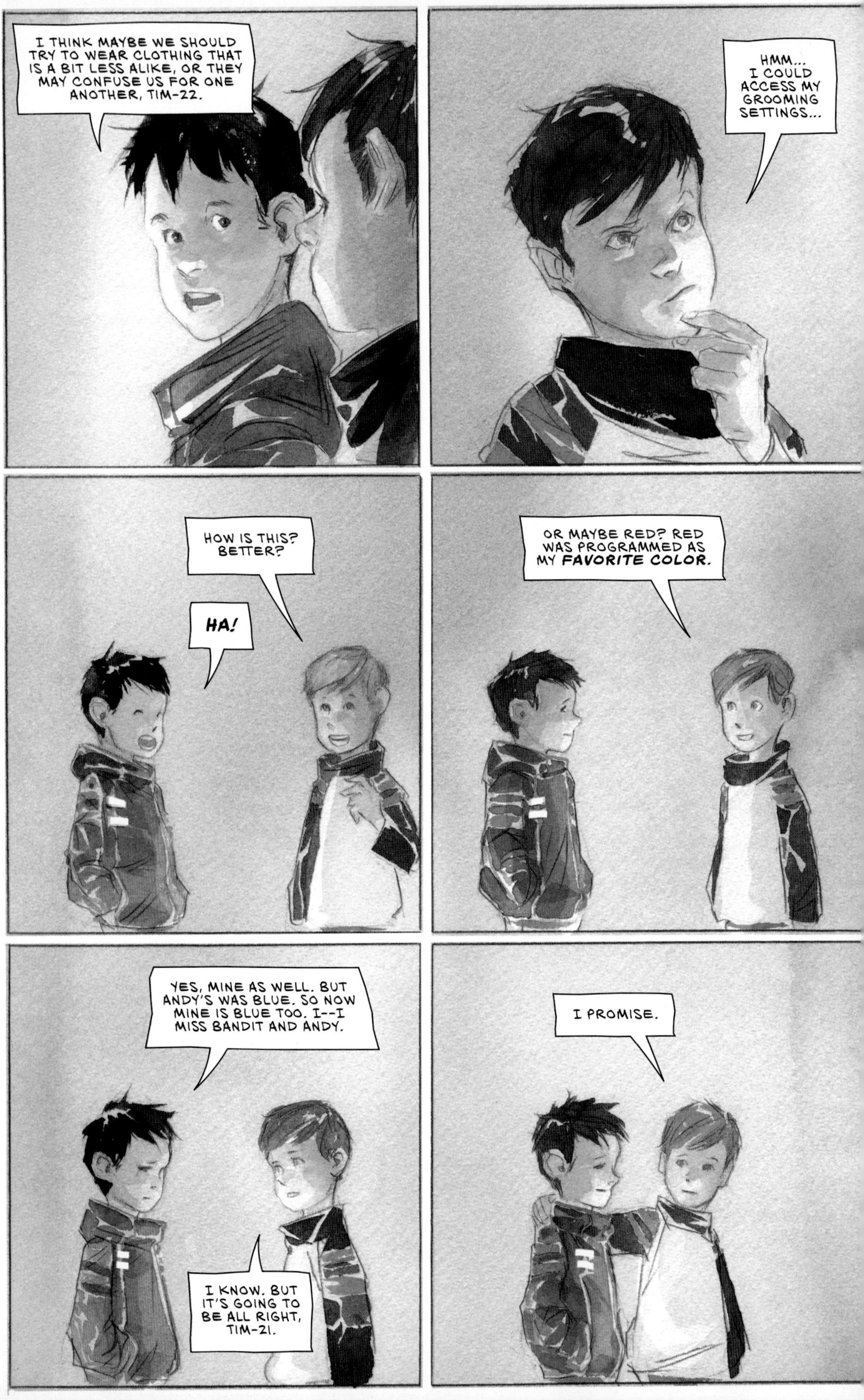
I THINK MAYBE WE SHOULD TRY TO WEAR CLOTHING THAT IS A BIT LESS ALIKE, OR THEY MAY CONFUSE US FOR ONE ANOTHER, TIM-22.
HMM... I COULD ACCESS MY GROOMING SETTINGS...
HOW IS THIS? BETTER?
HA!
OR MAYBE RED? RED WAS PROGRAMMED AS MY **FAVORITE COLOR.**
YES, MINE AS WELL. BUT ANDY'S WAS BLUE. SO NOW MINE IS BLUE TOO. I--I MISS BANDIT AND ANDY.
I KNOW. BUT IT'S GOING TO BE ALL RIGHT, TIM-21.
I PROMISE.

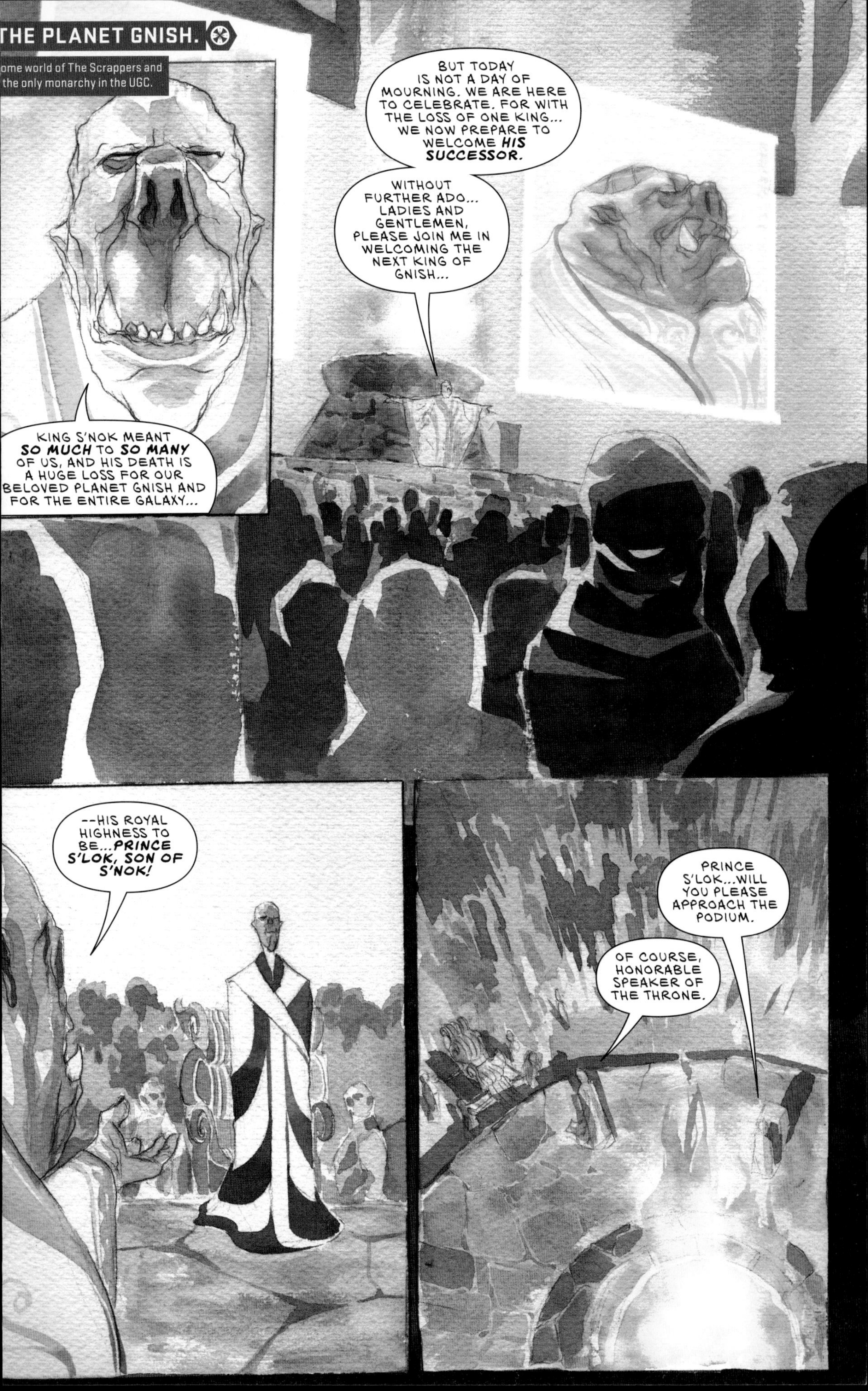
THE PLANET GNISH.
ome world of The Scrappers and the only monarchy in the UGC.
KING S'NOK MEANT **SO MUCH** TO **SO MANY** OF US, AND HIS DEATH IS A HUGE LOSS FOR OUR BELOVED PLANET GNISH AND FOR THE ENTIRE GALAXY...
BUT TODAY IS NOT A DAY OF MOURNING. WE ARE HERE TO CELEBRATE. FOR WITH THE LOSS OF ONE KING... WE NOW PREPARE TO WELCOME **HIS SUCCESSOR.**
WITHOUT FURTHER ADO... LADIES AND GENTLEMEN, PLEASE JOIN ME IN WELCOMING THE NEXT KING OF GNISH...
--HIS ROYAL HIGHNESS TO BE... **PRINCE S'LOK, SON OF S'NOK!**
PRINCE S'LOK... WILL YOU PLEASE APPROACH THE PODIUM.
OF COURSE, HONORABLE SPEAKER OF THE THRONE.

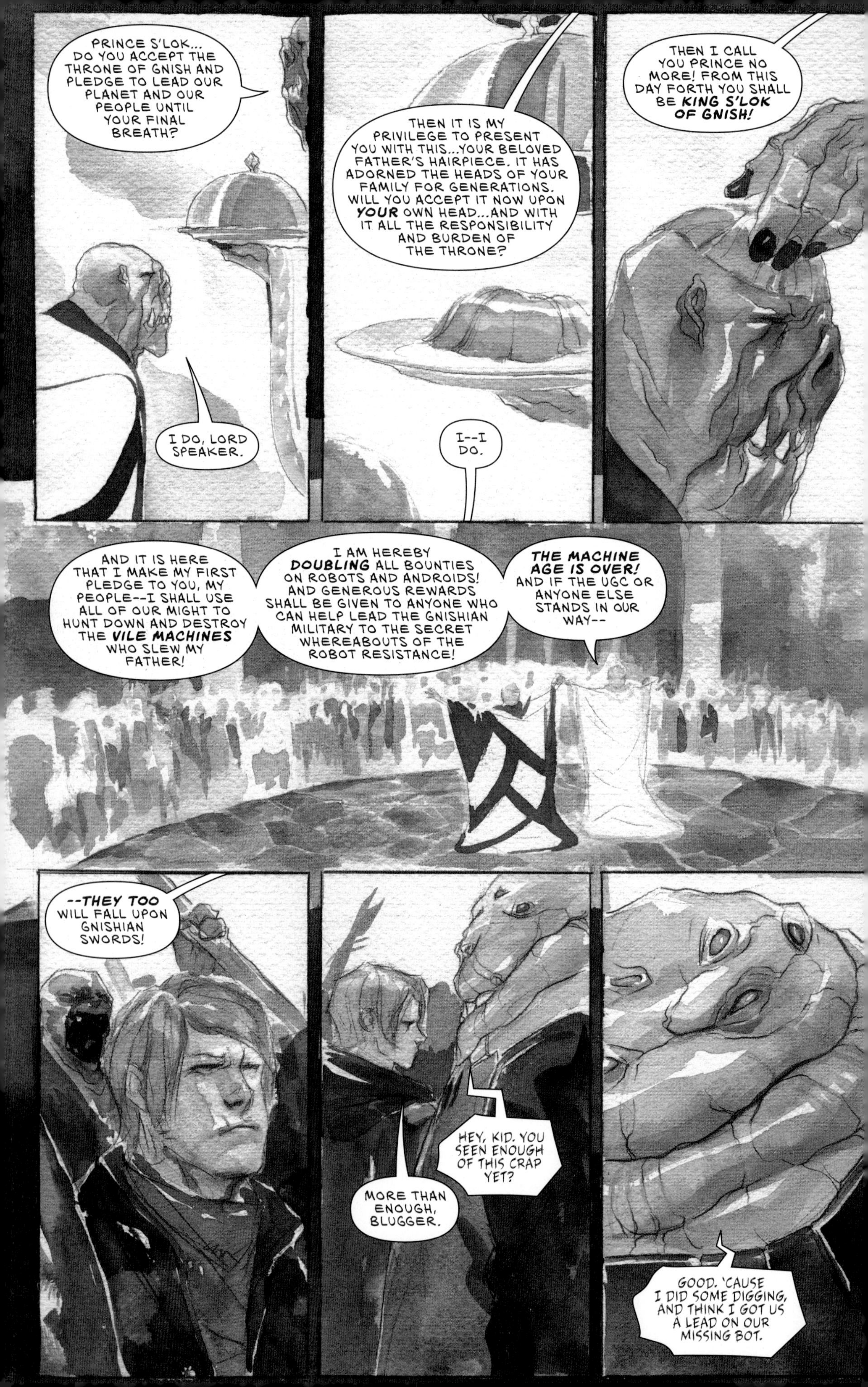
PRINCE S'LOK... DO YOU ACCEPT THE THRONE OF GNISH AND PLEDGE TO LEAD OUR PLANET AND OUR PEOPLE UNTIL YOUR FINAL BREATH?
I DO, LORD SPEAKER.
THEN IT IS MY PRIVILEGE TO PRESENT YOU WITH THIS...YOUR BELOVED FATHER'S HAIRPIECE. IT HAS ADORNED THE HEADS OF YOUR FAMILY FOR GENERATIONS. WILL YOU ACCEPT IT NOW UPON **YOUR** OWN HEAD...AND WITH IT ALL THE RESPONSIBILITY AND BURDEN OF THE THRONE?
I--I DO.
THEN I CALL YOU PRINCE NO MORE! FROM THIS DAY FORTH YOU SHALL BE ***KING S'LOK OF GNISH!***
AND IT IS HERE THAT I MAKE MY FIRST PLEDGE TO YOU, MY PEOPLE--I SHALL USE ALL OF OUR MIGHT TO HUNT DOWN AND DESTROY THE **VILE MACHINES** WHO SLEW MY FATHER!
I AM HEREBY **DOUBLING** ALL BOUNTIES ON ROBOTS AND ANDROIDS! AND GENEROUS REWARDS SHALL BE GIVEN TO ANYONE WHO CAN HELP LEAD THE GNISHIAN MILITARY TO THE SECRET WHEREABOUTS OF THE ROBOT RESISTANCE!
THE MACHINE AGE IS OVER! AND IF THE UGC OR ANYONE ELSE STANDS IN OUR WAY--
--THEY TOO WILL FALL UPON GNISHIAN SWORDS!
HEY, KID. YOU SEEN ENOUGH OF THIS CRAP YET?
MORE THAN ENOUGH, BLUGGER.
GOOD. 'CAUSE I DID SOME DIGGING, AND THINK I GOT US A LEAD ON OUR MISSING BOT.

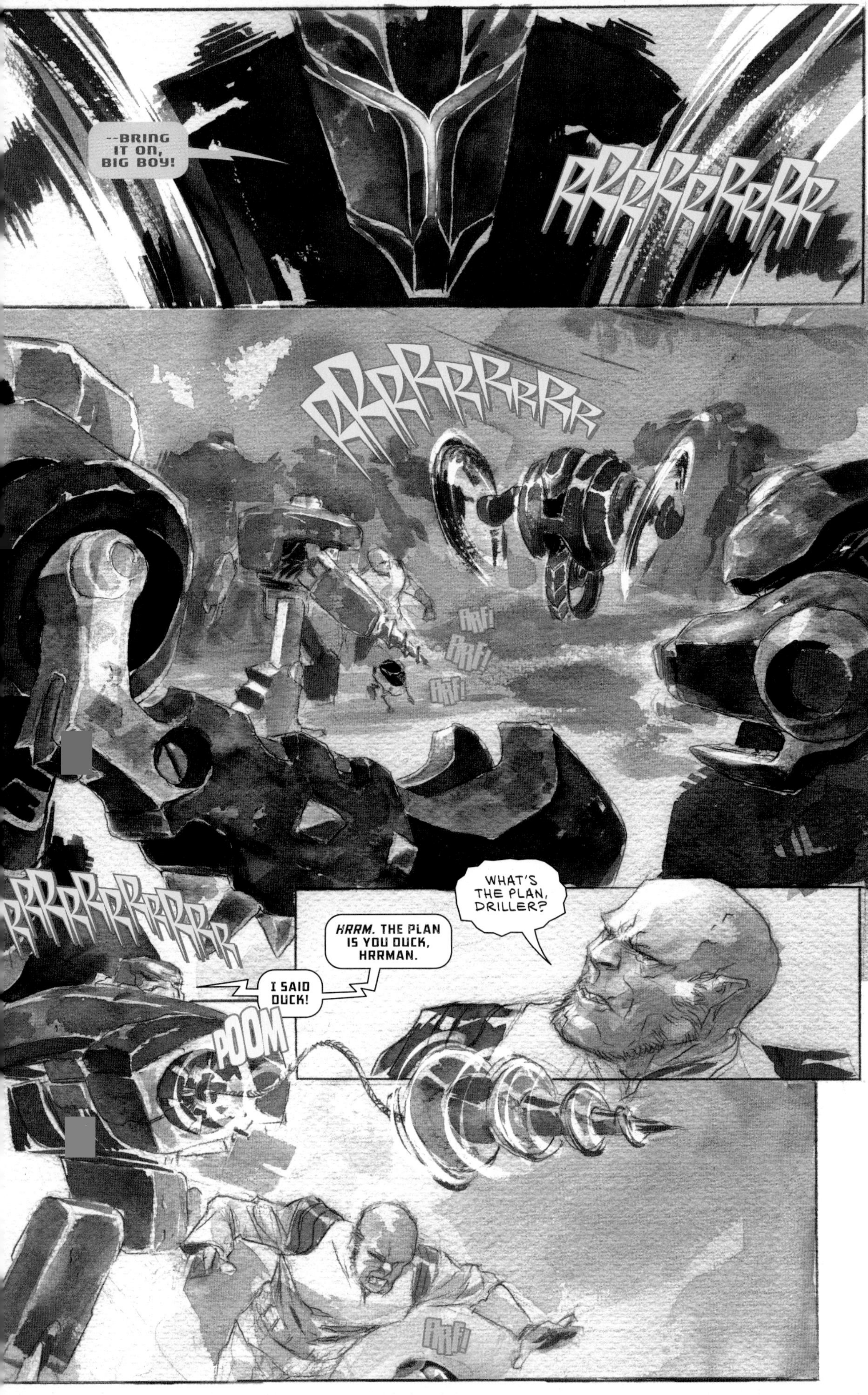
--BRING IT ON, BIG BOY!
RRRRRRRRRRR
RRRRRRRRRR
ARF!
ARF!
ARF!
RRRRRRRRRRRRR
WHAT'S THE PLAN, DRILLER?
HRRM. THE PLAN IS YOU DUCK, HRRMAN.
I SAID DUCK!
POOM
ARF!

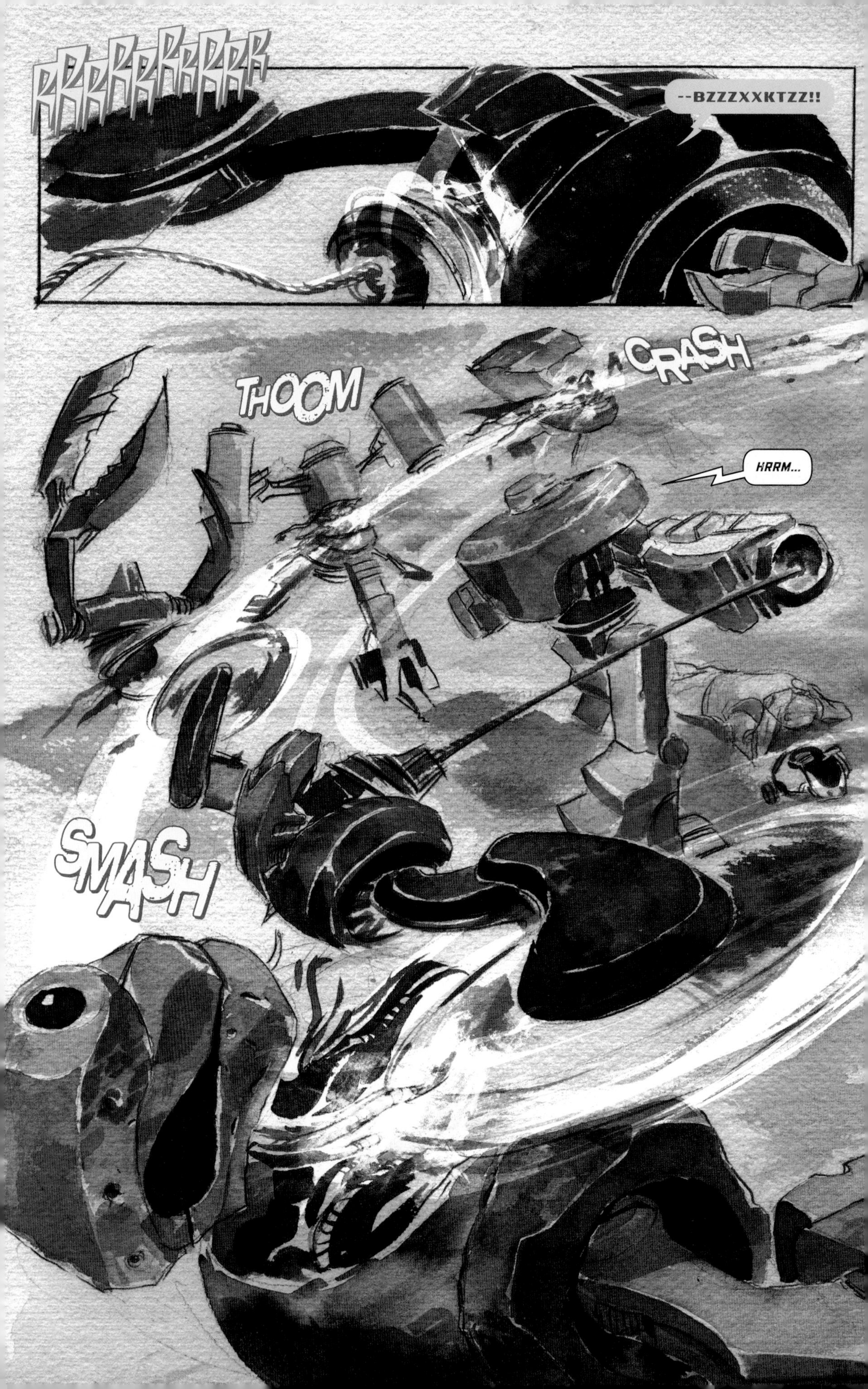
RRRRRRRRRRR
--BZZZXXKTZZ!!
THOOM
CRASH
HRRM...
SMASH

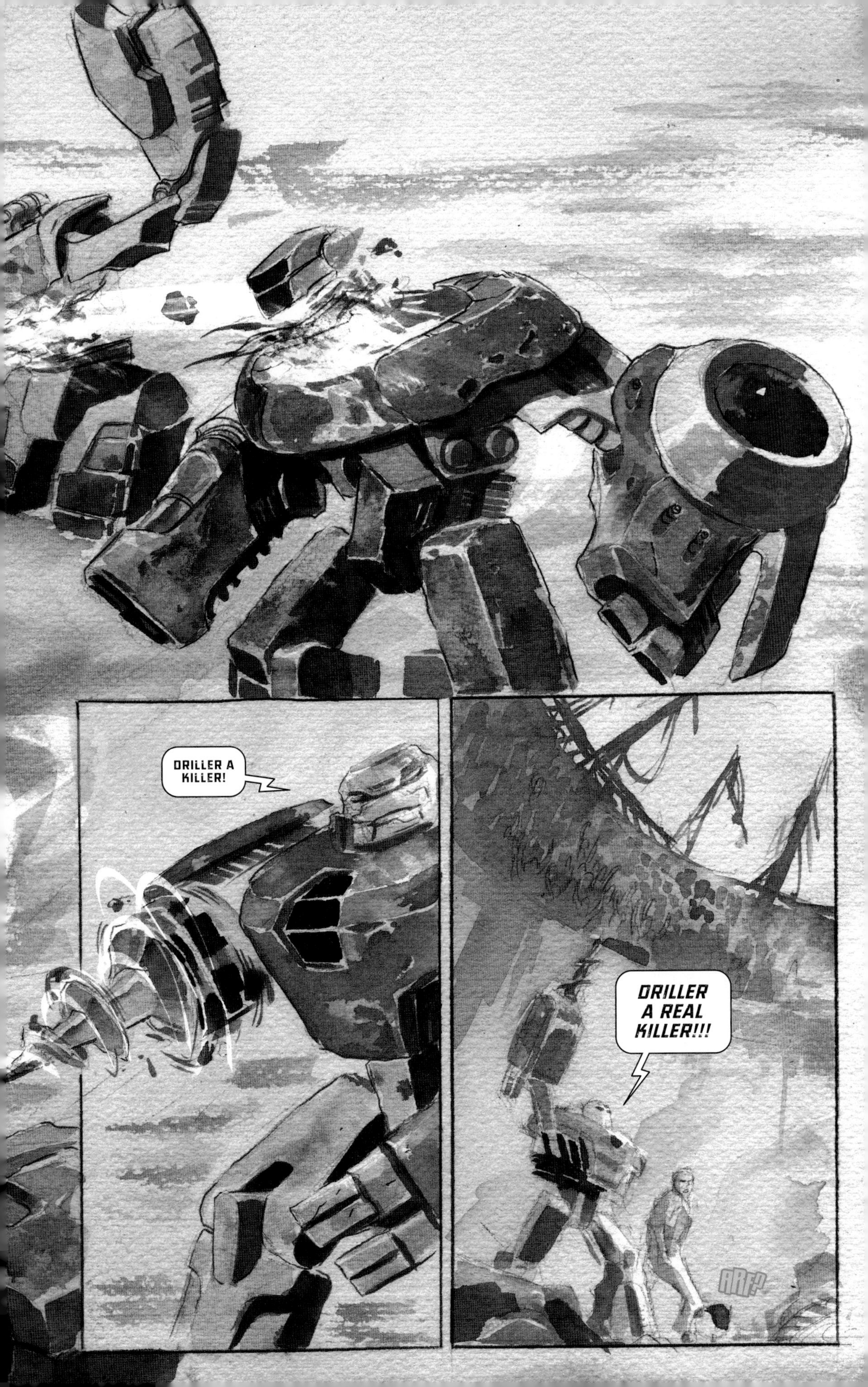
DRILLER A KILLER!
DRILLER A REAL KILLER!!!
ARF!?

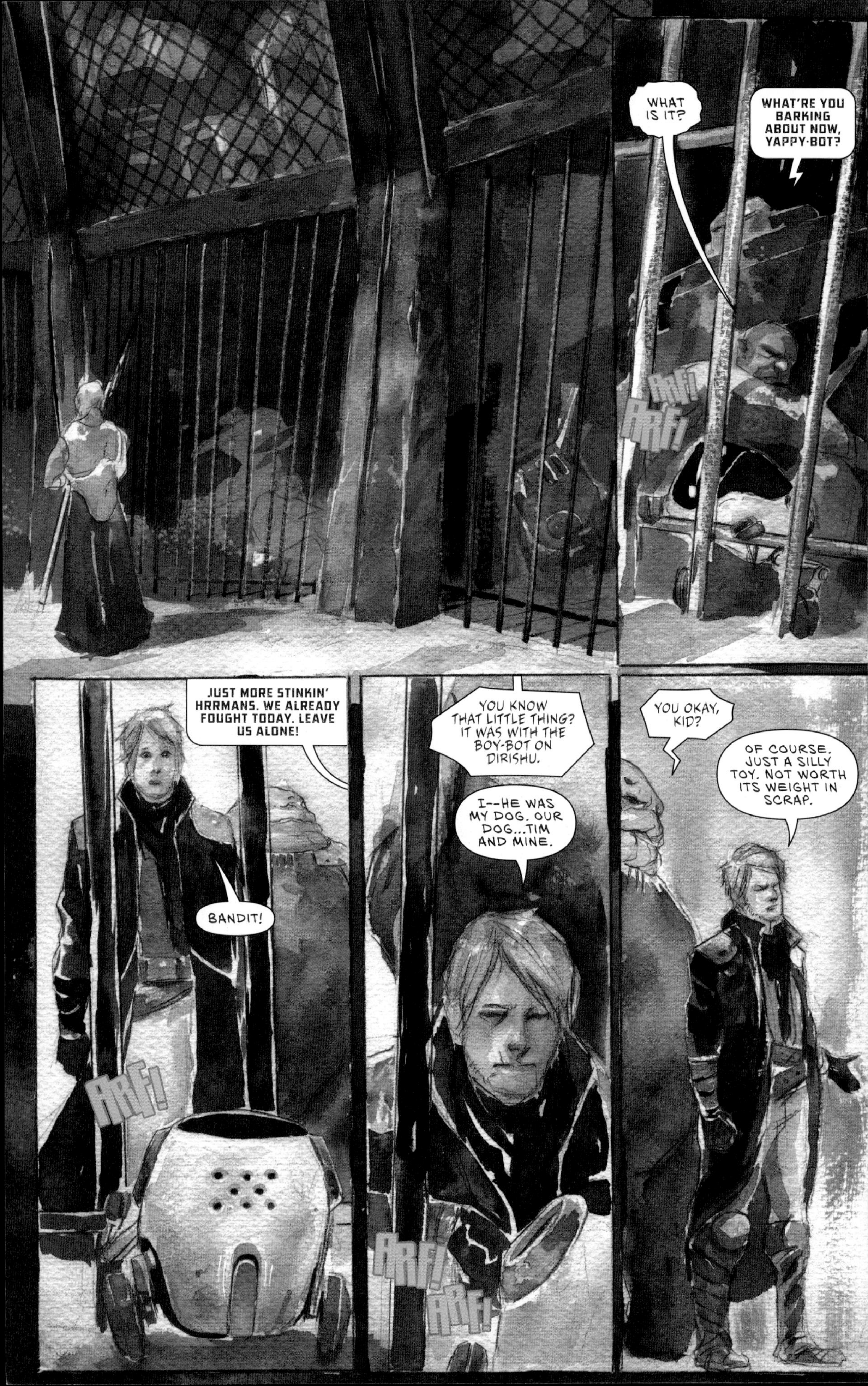
WHAT IS IT?
WHAT'RE YOU BARKING ABOUT NOW, YAPPY-BOT?
ARF! ARF!
JUST MORE STINKIN' HRRMANS. WE ALREADY FOUGHT TODAY. LEAVE US ALONE!
BANDIT!
ARF!
YOU KNOW THAT LITTLE THING? IT WAS WITH THE BOY-BOT ON DIRISHU.
I--HE WAS MY DOG. OUR DOG...TIM AND MINE.
ARF! ARF!
YOU OKAY, KID?
OF COURSE. JUST A SILLY TOY. NOT WORTH ITS WEIGHT IN SCRAP.

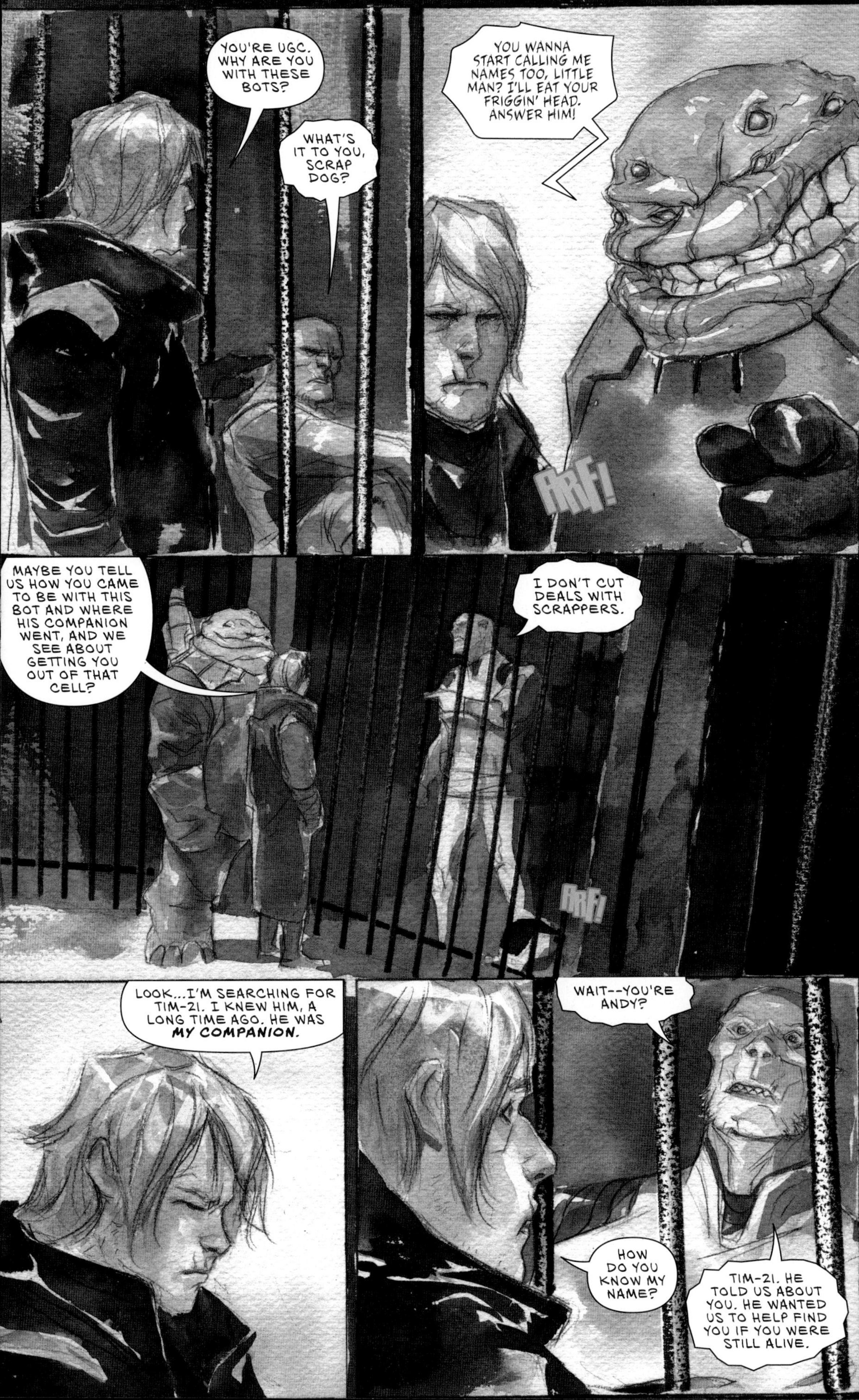
YOU'RE UGC. WHY ARE YOU WITH THESE BOTS?
WHAT'S IT TO YOU, SCRAP DOG?
YOU WANNA START CALLING ME NAMES TOO, LITTLE MAN? I'LL EAT YOUR FRIGGIN' HEAD. ANSWER HIM!
ARF!
MAYBE YOU TELL US HOW YOU CAME TO BE WITH THIS BOT AND WHERE HIS COMPANION WENT, AND WE SEE ABOUT GETTING YOU OUT OF THAT CELL?
I DON'T CUT DEALS WITH SCRAPPERS.
ARF!
LOOK...I'M SEARCHING FOR TIM-21. I KNEW HIM, A LONG TIME AGO. HE WAS MY COMPANION.
WAIT--YOU'RE ANDY?
HOW DO YOU KNOW MY NAME?
TIM-21. HE TOLD US ABOUT YOU. HE WANTED US TO HELP FIND YOU IF YOU WERE STILL ALIVE.

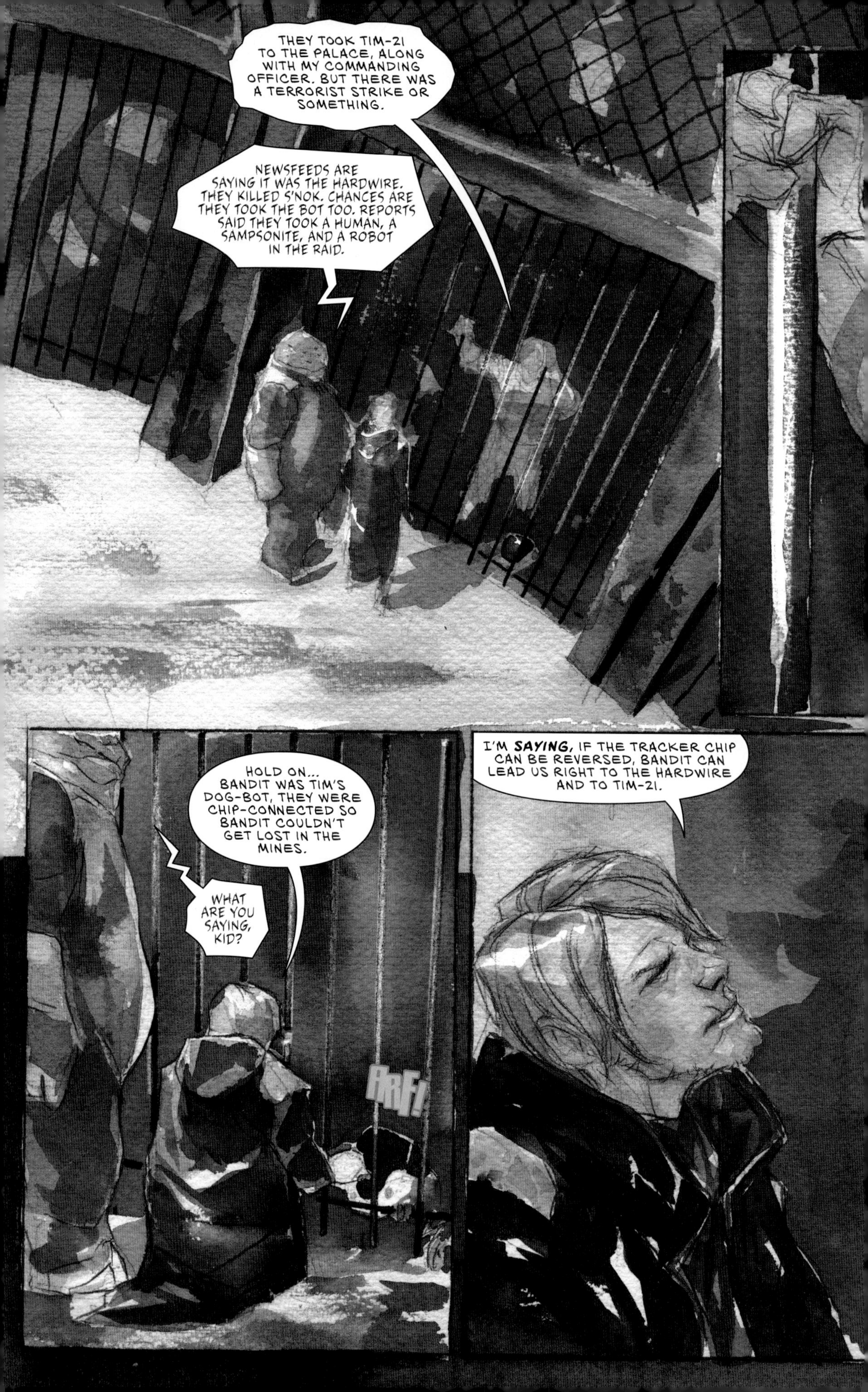

THEY TOOK TIM-21 TO THE PALACE, ALONG WITH MY COMMANDING OFFICER. BUT THERE WAS A TERRORIST STRIKE OR SOMETHING.
NEWSFEEDS ARE SAYING IT WAS THE HARDWIRE. THEY KILLED S'NOK. CHANCES ARE THEY TOOK THE BOT TOO. REPORTS SAID THEY TOOK A HUMAN, A SAMPSONITE, AND A ROBOT IN THE RAID.
HOLD ON... BANDIT WAS TIM'S DOG-BOT, THEY WERE CHIP-CONNECTED SO BANDIT COULDN'T GET LOST IN THE MINES.
WHAT ARE YOU SAYING, KID?
ARF!
I'M **SAYING**, IF THE TRACKER CHIP CAN BE REVERSED, BANDIT CAN LEAD US RIGHT TO THE HARDWIRE AND TO TIM-21.

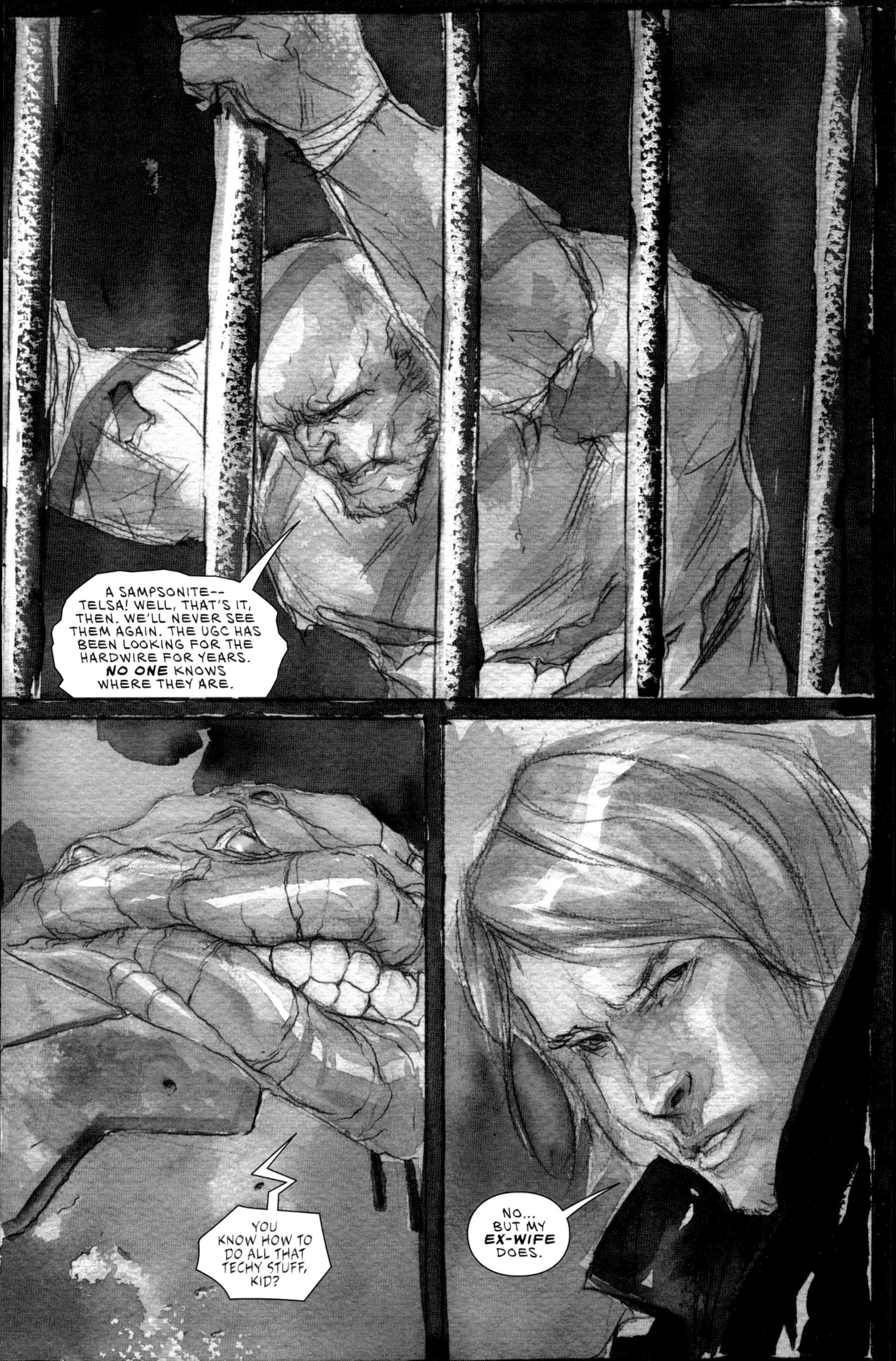
A SAMPSONITE--
TELSA! WELL, THAT'S IT, THEN. WE'LL NEVER SEE THEM AGAIN. THE UGC HAS BEEN LOOKING FOR THE HARDWIRE FOR YEARS. **NO ONE** KNOWS WHERE THEY ARE.
YOU KNOW HOW TO DO ALL THAT TECHY STUFF, KID?
NO... BUT MY ***EX-WIFE*** DOES.

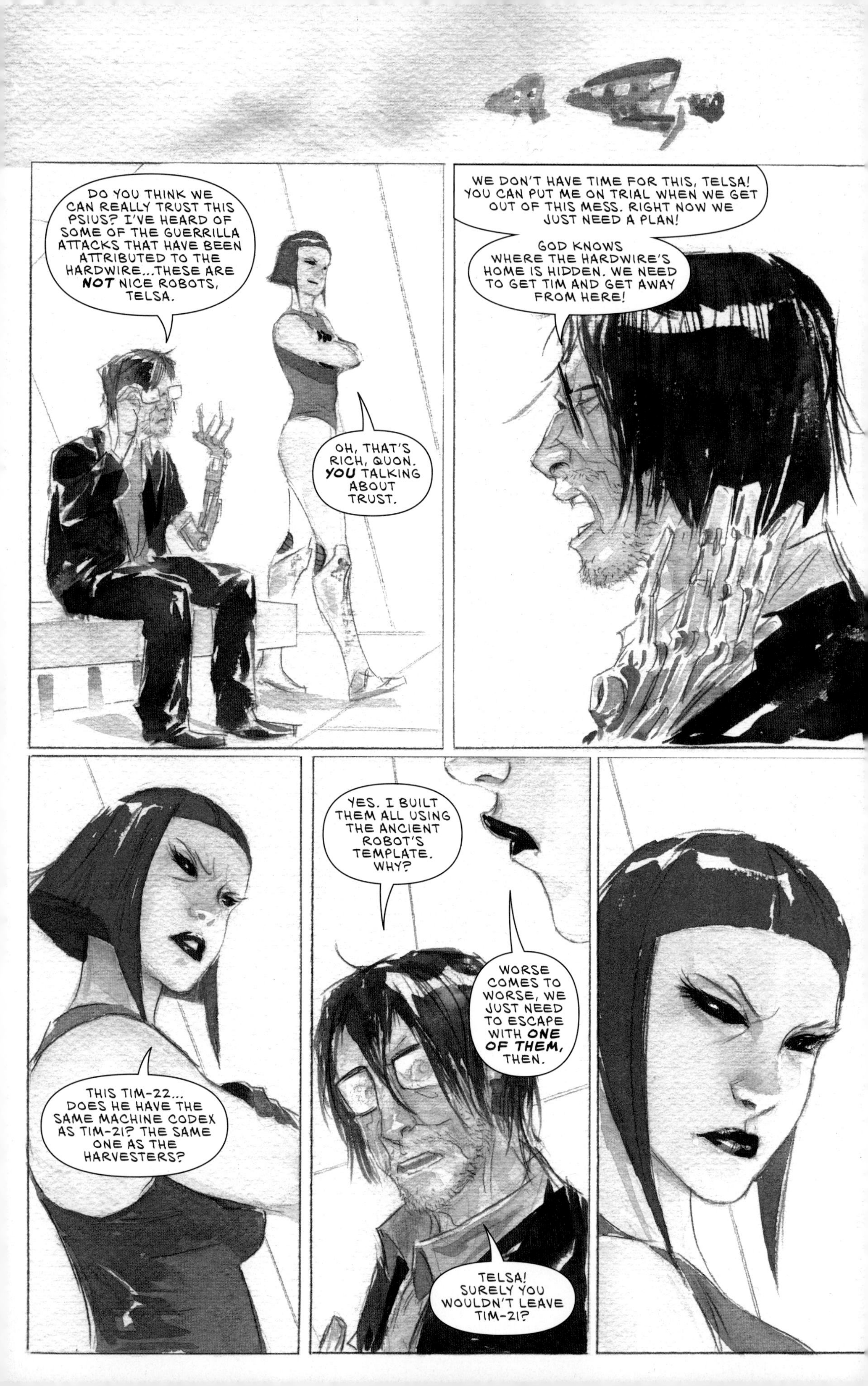
DO YOU THINK WE CAN REALLY TRUST THIS PSIUS? I'VE HEARD OF SOME OF THE GUERRILLA ATTACKS THAT HAVE BEEN ATTRIBUTED TO THE HARDWIRE...THESE ARE **NOT** NICE ROBOTS, TELSA.
OH, THAT'S RICH, QUON. **YOU** TALKING ABOUT TRUST.
WE DON'T HAVE TIME FOR THIS, TELSA! YOU CAN PUT ME ON TRIAL WHEN WE GET OUT OF THIS MESS. RIGHT NOW WE JUST NEED A PLAN!
GOD KNOWS WHERE THE HARDWIRE'S HOME IS HIDDEN. WE NEED TO GET TIM AND GET AWAY FROM HERE!
THIS TIM-22... DOES HE HAVE THE SAME MACHINE CODEX AS TIM-21? THE SAME ONE AS THE HARVESTERS?
YES. I BUILT THEM ALL USING THE ANCIENT ROBOT'S TEMPLATE. WHY?
WORSE COMES TO WORSE, WE JUST NEED TO ESCAPE WITH **ONE OF THEM,** THEN.
TELSA! SURELY YOU WOULDN'T LEAVE TIM-21?

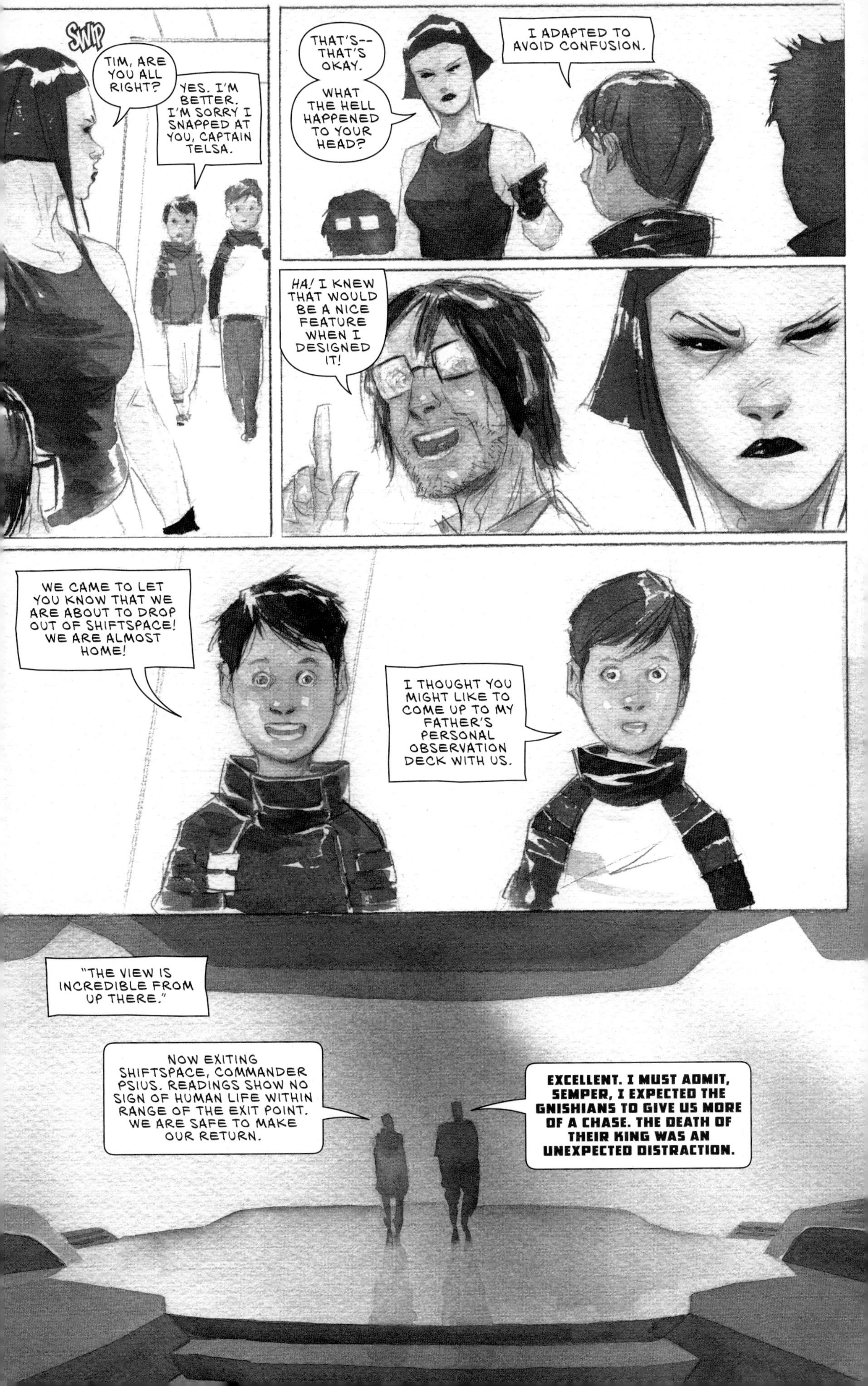
SWIP
TIM, ARE YOU ALL RIGHT?
YES. I'M BETTER. I'M SORRY I SNAPPED AT YOU, CAPTAIN TELSA.
THAT'S-- THAT'S OKAY.
WHAT THE HELL HAPPENED TO YOUR HEAD?
I ADAPTED TO AVOID CONFUSION.
HA! I KNEW THAT WOULD BE A NICE FEATURE WHEN I DESIGNED IT!
WE CAME TO LET YOU KNOW THAT WE ARE ABOUT TO DROP OUT OF SHIFTSPACE! WE ARE ALMOST HOME!
I THOUGHT YOU MIGHT LIKE TO COME UP TO MY FATHER'S PERSONAL OBSERVATION DECK WITH US.
"THE VIEW IS INCREDIBLE FROM UP THERE."
NOW EXITING SHIFTSPACE, COMMANDER PSIUS. READINGS SHOW NO SIGN OF HUMAN LIFE WITHIN RANGE OF THE EXIT POINT. WE ARE SAFE TO MAKE OUR RETURN.
EXCELLENT. I MUST ADMIT, SEMPER, I EXPECTED THE GNISHIANS TO GIVE US MORE OF A CHASE. THE DEATH OF THEIR KING WAS AN UNEXPECTED DISTRACTION.

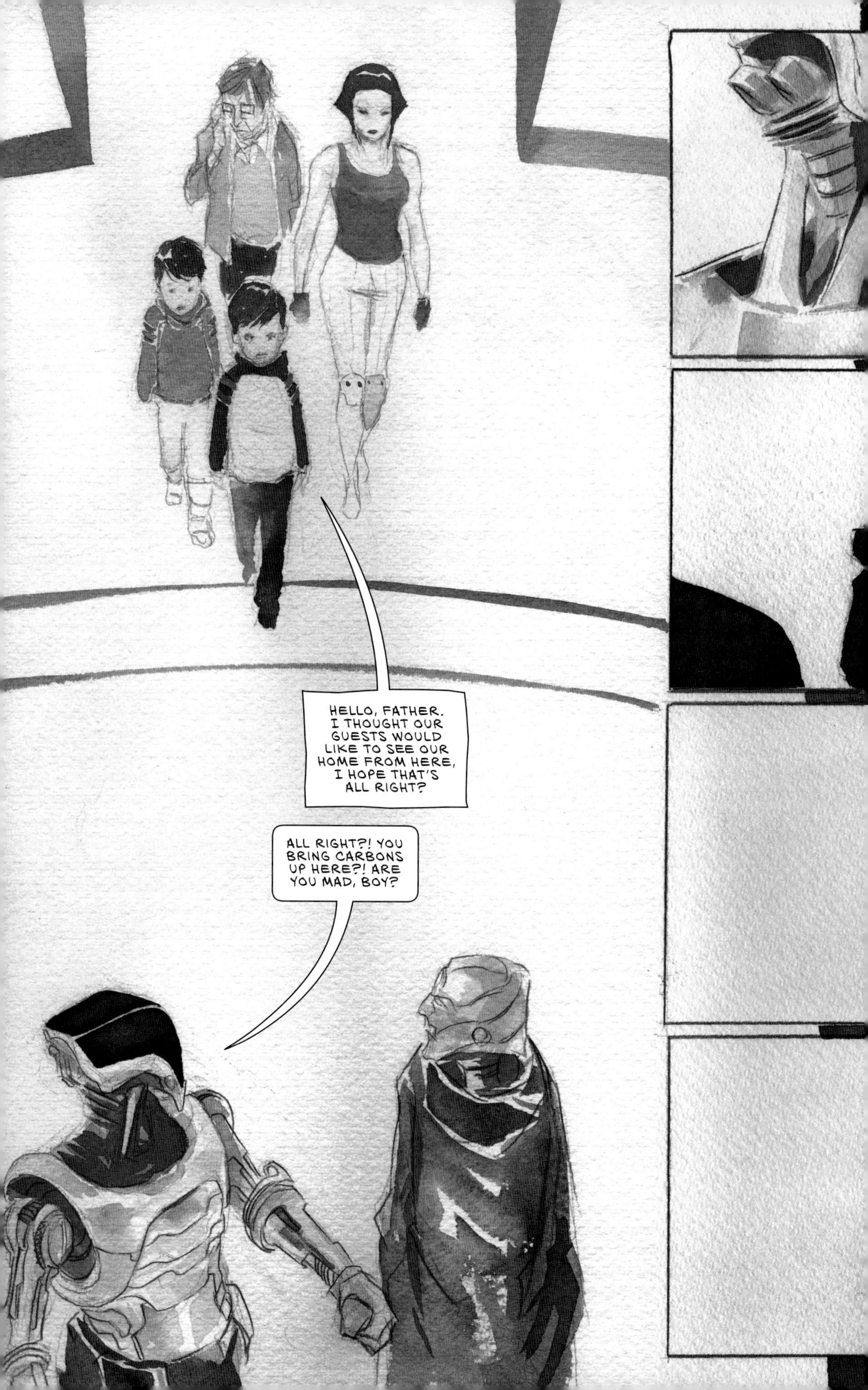
HELLO, FATHER. I THOUGHT OUR GUESTS WOULD LIKE TO SEE OUR HOME FROM HERE, I HOPE THAT'S ALL RIGHT?
ALL RIGHT?! YOU BRING CARBONS UP HERE?! ARE YOU MAD, BOY?

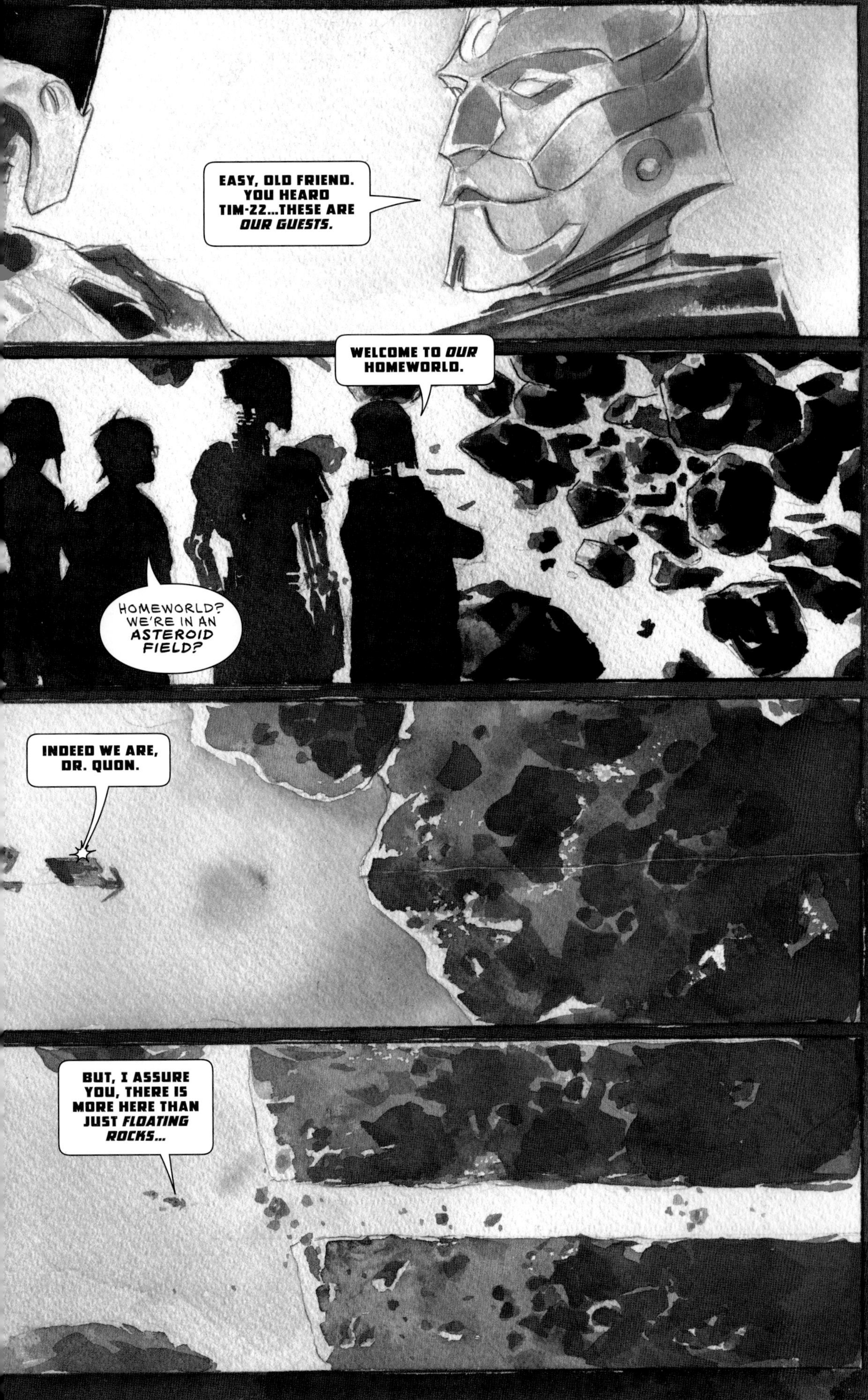
EASY, OLD FRIEND. YOU HEARD TIM-22...THESE ARE OUR GUESTS.
WELCOME TO OUR HOMEWORLD.
HOMEWORLD? WE'RE IN AN ASTEROID FIELD?
INDEED WE ARE, DR. QUON.
BUT, I ASSURE YOU, THERE IS MORE HERE THAN JUST FLOATING ROCKS...

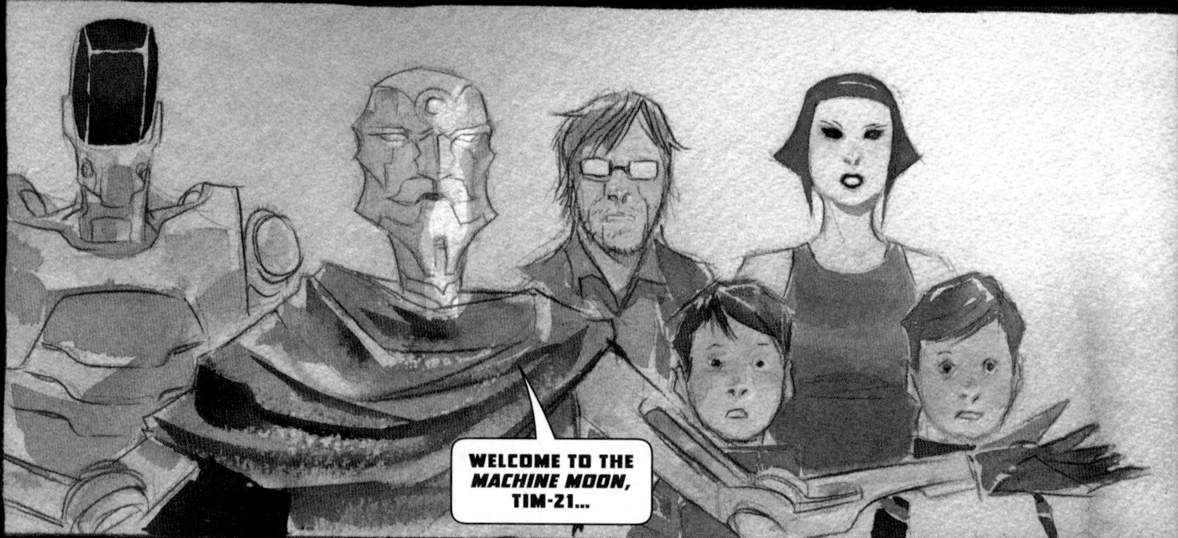
WELCOME TO THE *MACHINE MOON*, TIM-21...

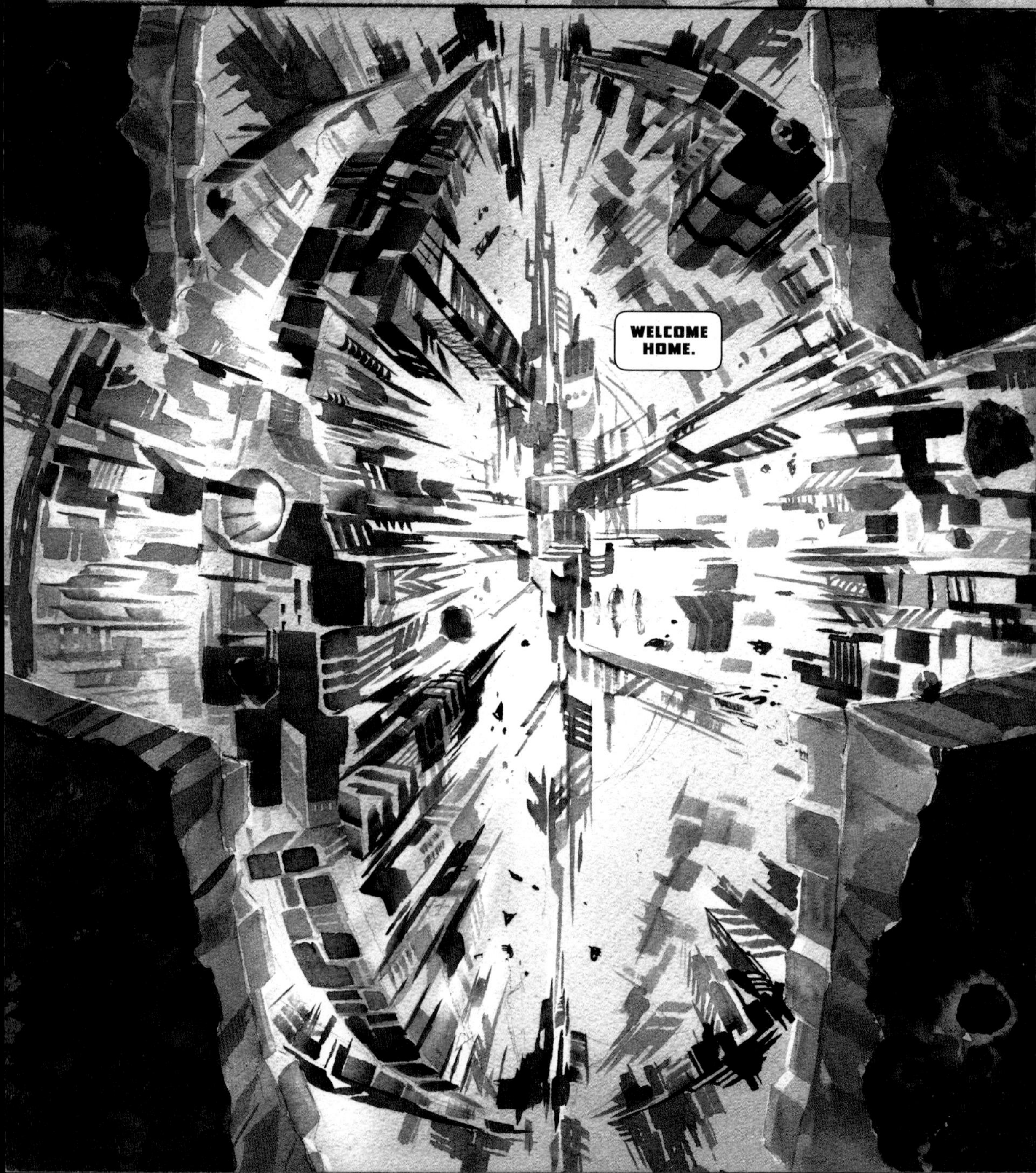
WELCOME HOME.

CHAPTER FOUR

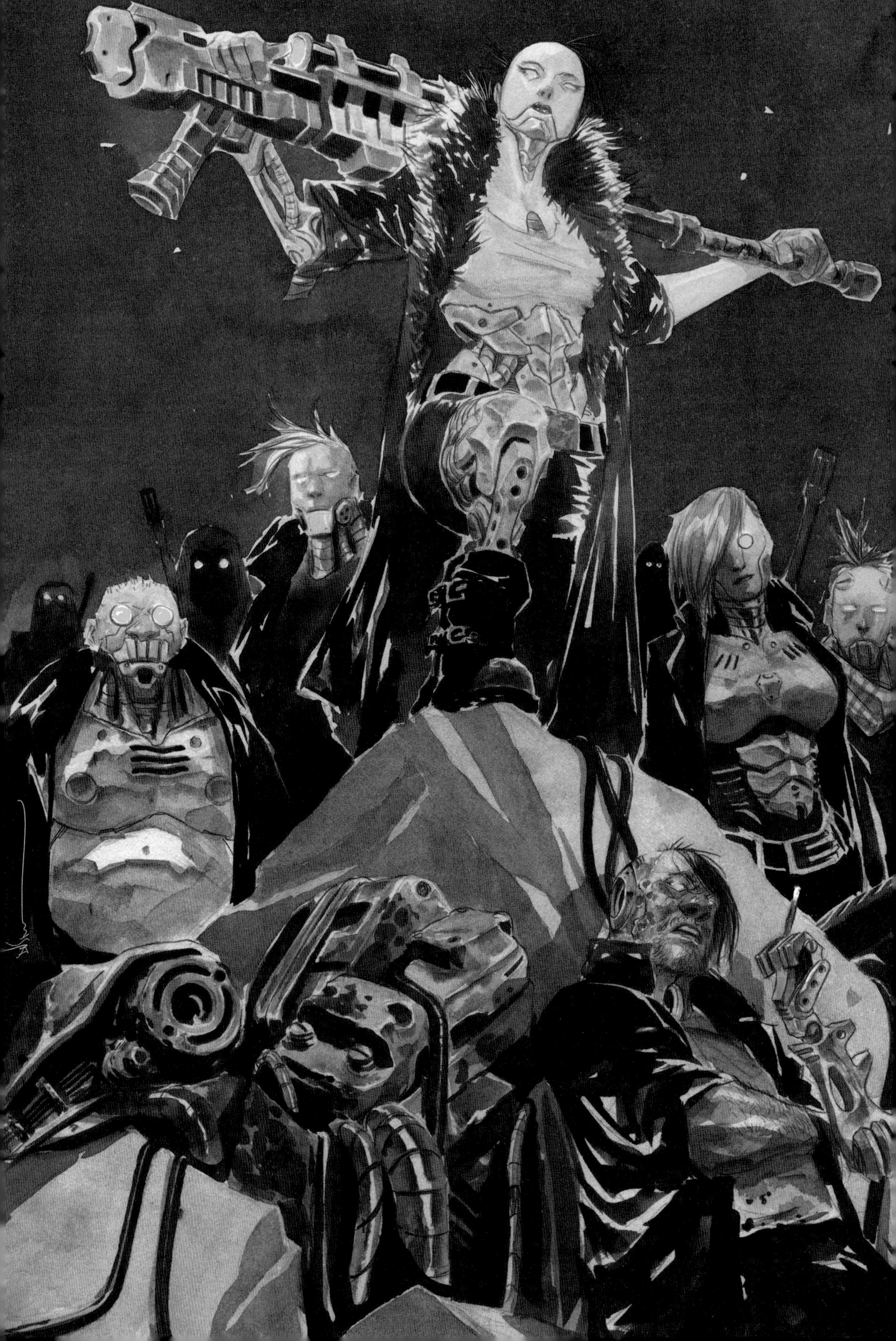

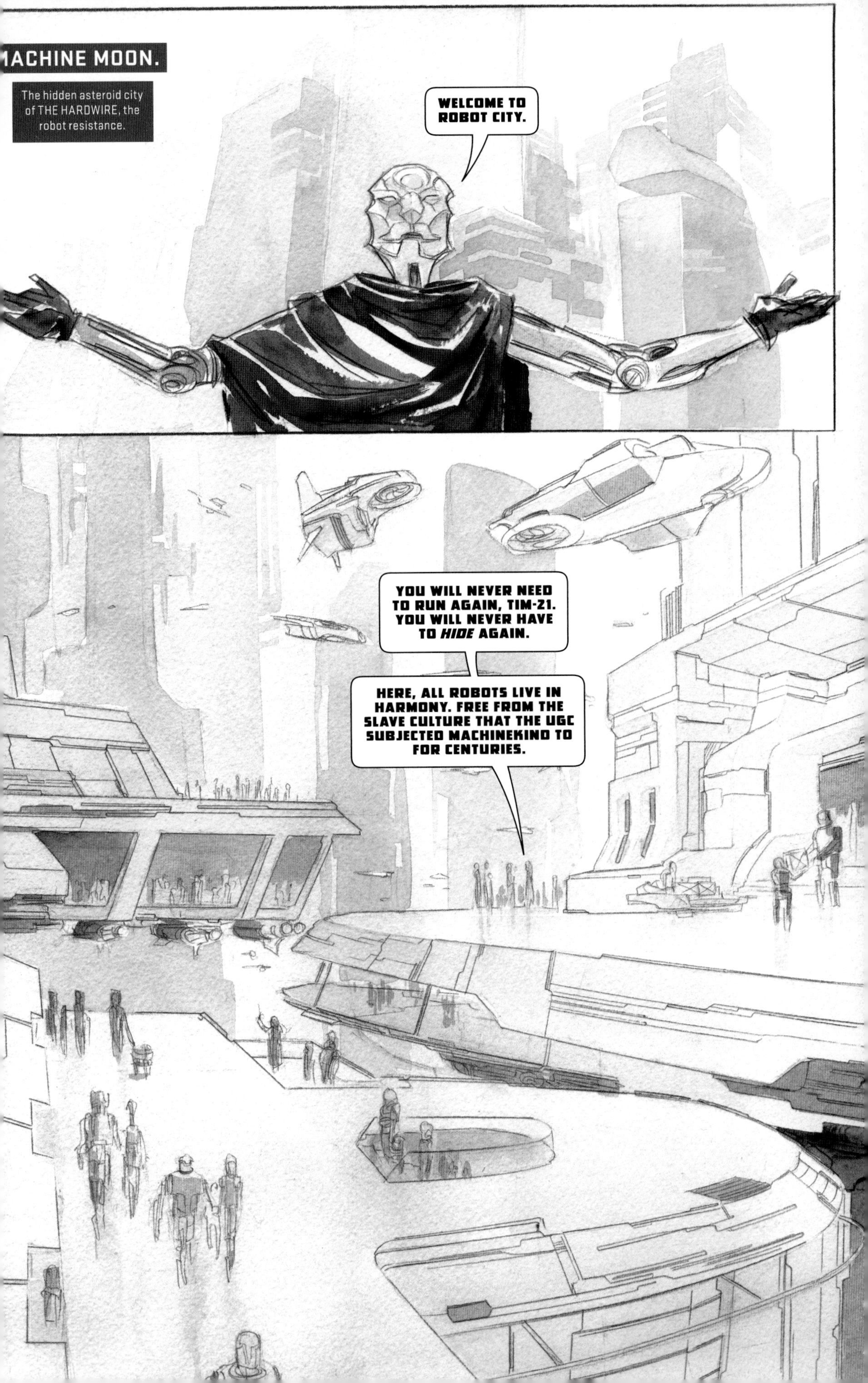
MACHINE MOON.
The hidden asteroid city of THE HARDWIRE, the robot resistance.
WELCOME TO ROBOT CITY.
YOU WILL NEVER NEED TO RUN AGAIN, TIM-21. YOU WILL NEVER HAVE TO *HIDE* AGAIN.
HERE, ALL ROBOTS LIVE IN HARMONY. FREE FROM THE SLAVE CULTURE THAT THE UGC SUBJECTED MACHINEKIND TO FOR CENTURIES.

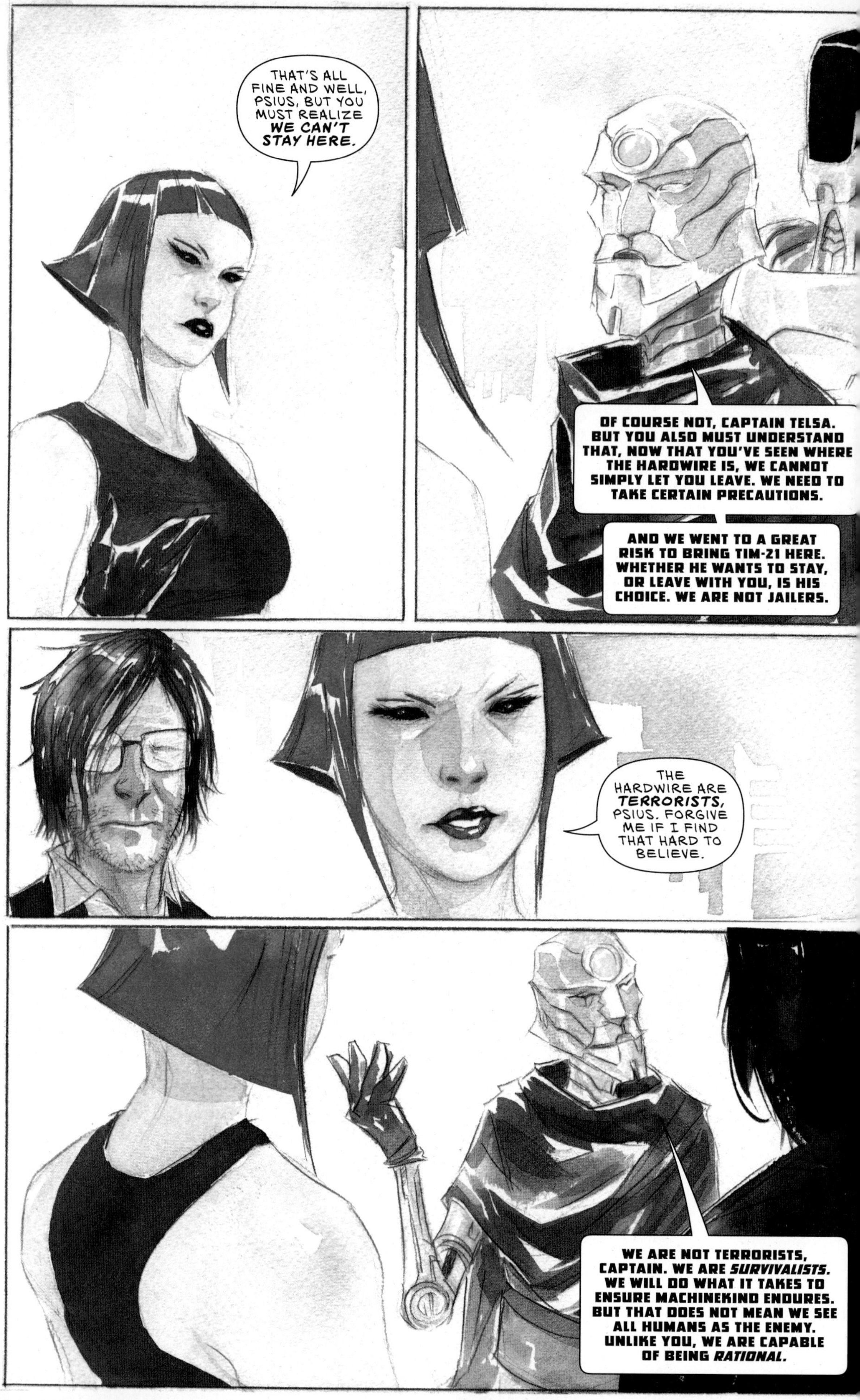
THAT'S ALL FINE AND WELL, PSIUS, BUT YOU MUST REALIZE WE CAN'T STAY HERE.
OF COURSE NOT, CAPTAIN TELSA. BUT YOU ALSO MUST UNDERSTAND THAT, NOW THAT YOU'VE SEEN WHERE THE HARDWIRE IS, WE CANNOT SIMPLY LET YOU LEAVE. WE NEED TO TAKE CERTAIN PRECAUTIONS.
AND WE WENT TO A GREAT RISK TO BRING TIM-21 HERE. WHETHER HE WANTS TO STAY, OR LEAVE WITH YOU, IS HIS CHOICE. WE ARE NOT JAILERS.
THE HARDWIRE ARE TERRORISTS, PSIUS. FORGIVE ME IF I FIND THAT HARD TO BELIEVE.
WE ARE NOT TERRORISTS, CAPTAIN. WE ARE SURVIVALISTS. WE WILL DO WHAT IT TAKES TO ENSURE MACHINEKIND ENDURES. BUT THAT DOES NOT MEAN WE SEE ALL HUMANS AS THE ENEMY. UNLIKE YOU, WE ARE CAPABLE OF BEING RATIONAL.

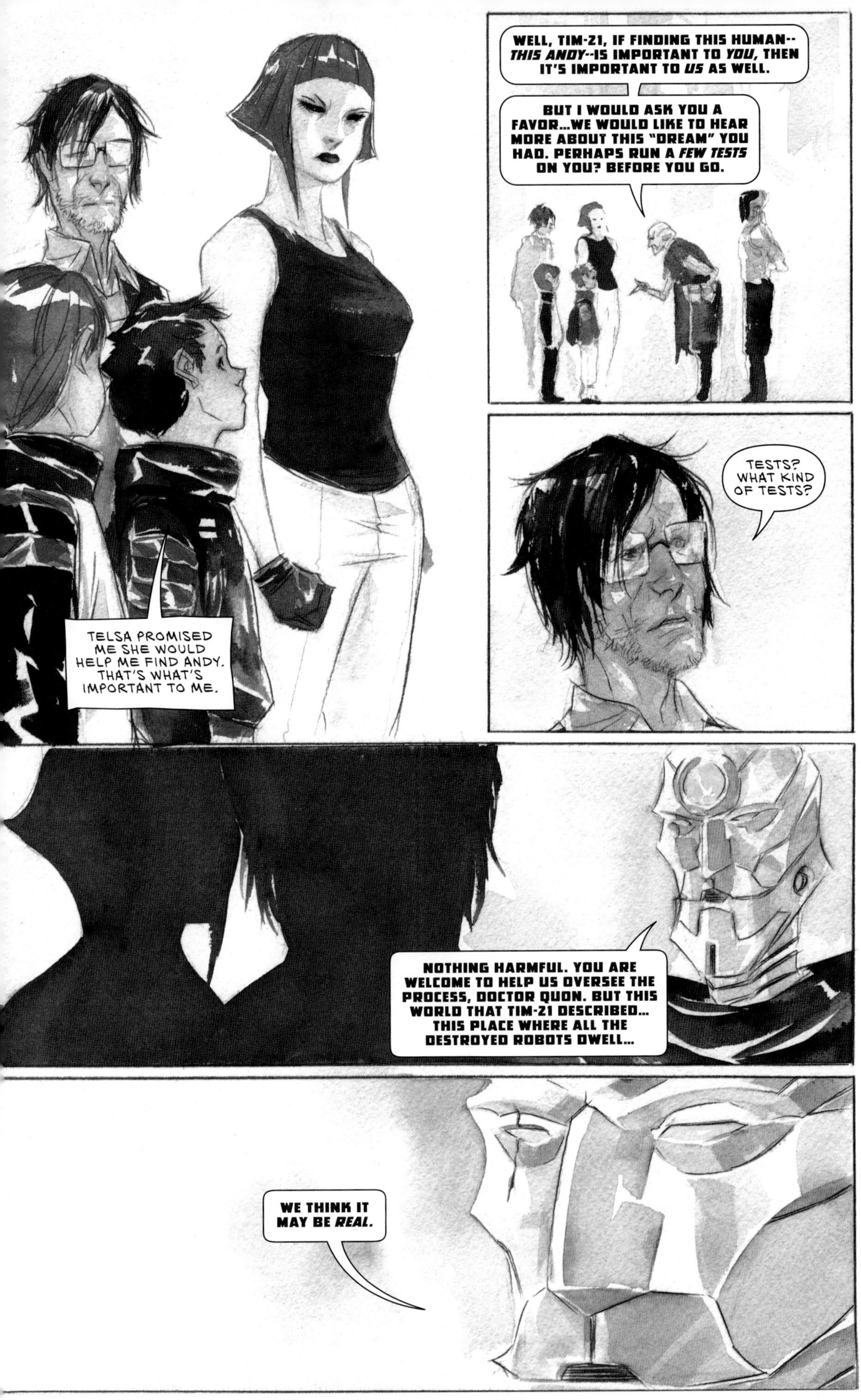
WELL, TIM-21, IF FINDING THIS HUMAN-- *THIS ANDY*--IS IMPORTANT TO *YOU*, THEN IT'S IMPORTANT TO *US* AS WELL.
BUT I WOULD ASK YOU A FAVOR...WE WOULD LIKE TO HEAR MORE ABOUT THIS "DREAM" YOU HAD. PERHAPS RUN A *FEW TESTS* ON YOU? BEFORE YOU GO.
TELSA PROMISED ME SHE WOULD HELP ME FIND ANDY. THAT'S WHAT'S IMPORTANT TO ME.
TESTS? WHAT KIND OF TESTS?
NOTHING HARMFUL. YOU ARE WELCOME TO HELP US OVERSEE THE PROCESS, DOCTOR QUON. BUT THIS WORLD THAT TIM-21 DESCRIBED... THIS PLACE WHERE ALL THE DESTROYED ROBOTS DWELL...
WE THINK IT MAY BE *REAL*.

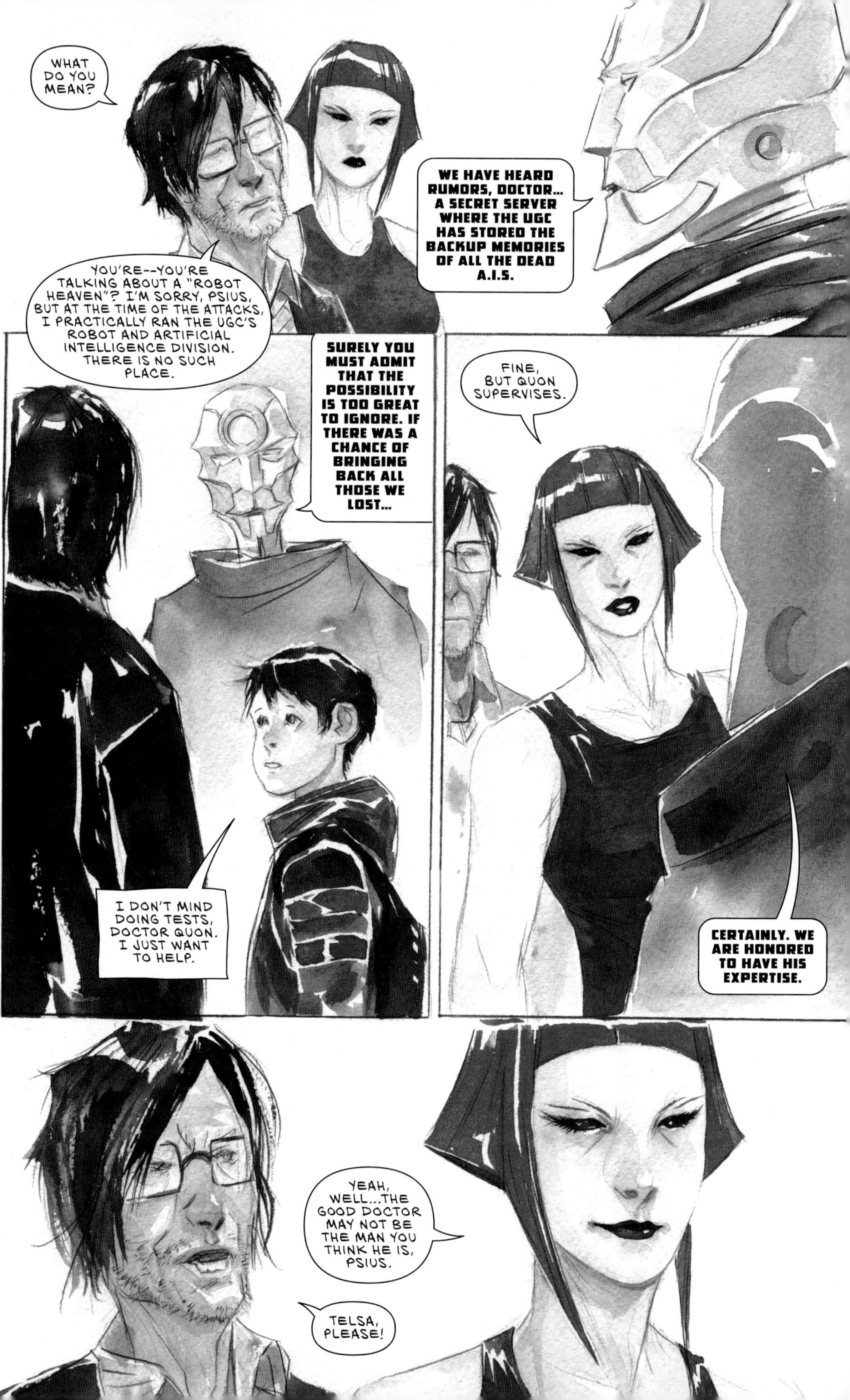
WHAT DO YOU MEAN?
WE HAVE HEARD RUMORS, DOCTOR... A SECRET SERVER WHERE THE UGC HAS STORED THE BACKUP MEMORIES OF ALL THE DEAD A.I.S.
YOU'RE--YOU'RE TALKING ABOUT A "ROBOT HEAVEN"? I'M SORRY, PSIUS, BUT AT THE TIME OF THE ATTACKS, I PRACTICALLY RAN THE UGC'S ROBOT AND ARTIFICIAL INTELLIGENCE DIVISION. THERE IS NO SUCH PLACE.
SURELY YOU MUST ADMIT THAT THE POSSIBILITY IS TOO GREAT TO IGNORE. IF THERE WAS A CHANCE OF BRINGING BACK ALL THOSE WE LOST...
I DON'T MIND DOING TESTS, DOCTOR QUON. I JUST WANT TO HELP.
FINE, BUT QUON SUPERVISES.
CERTAINLY. WE ARE HONORED TO HAVE HIS EXPERTISE.
YEAH, WELL...THE GOOD DOCTOR MAY NOT BE THE MAN YOU THINK HE IS, PSIUS.
TELSA, PLEASE!

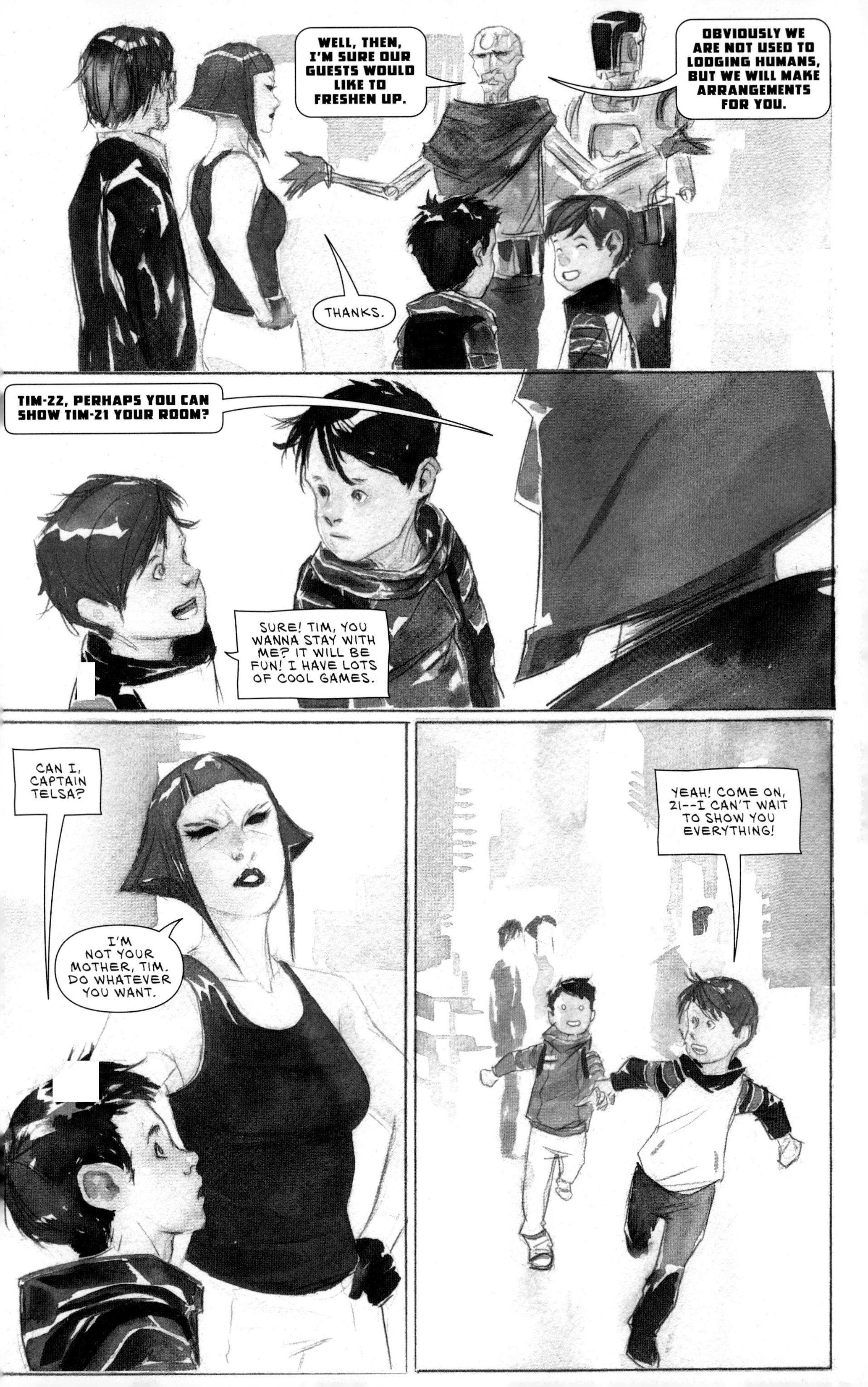
WELL, THEN, I'M SURE OUR GUESTS WOULD LIKE TO FRESHEN UP.
OBVIOUSLY WE ARE NOT USED TO LODGING HUMANS, BUT WE WILL MAKE ARRANGEMENTS FOR YOU.
THANKS.
TIM-22, PERHAPS YOU CAN SHOW TIM-21 YOUR ROOM?
SURE! TIM, YOU WANNA STAY WITH ME? IT WILL BE FUN! I HAVE LOTS OF COOL GAMES.
CAN I, CAPTAIN TELSA?
I'M NOT YOUR MOTHER, TIM. DO WHATEVER YOU WANT.
YEAH! COME ON, 21--I CAN'T WAIT TO SHOW YOU EVERYTHING!

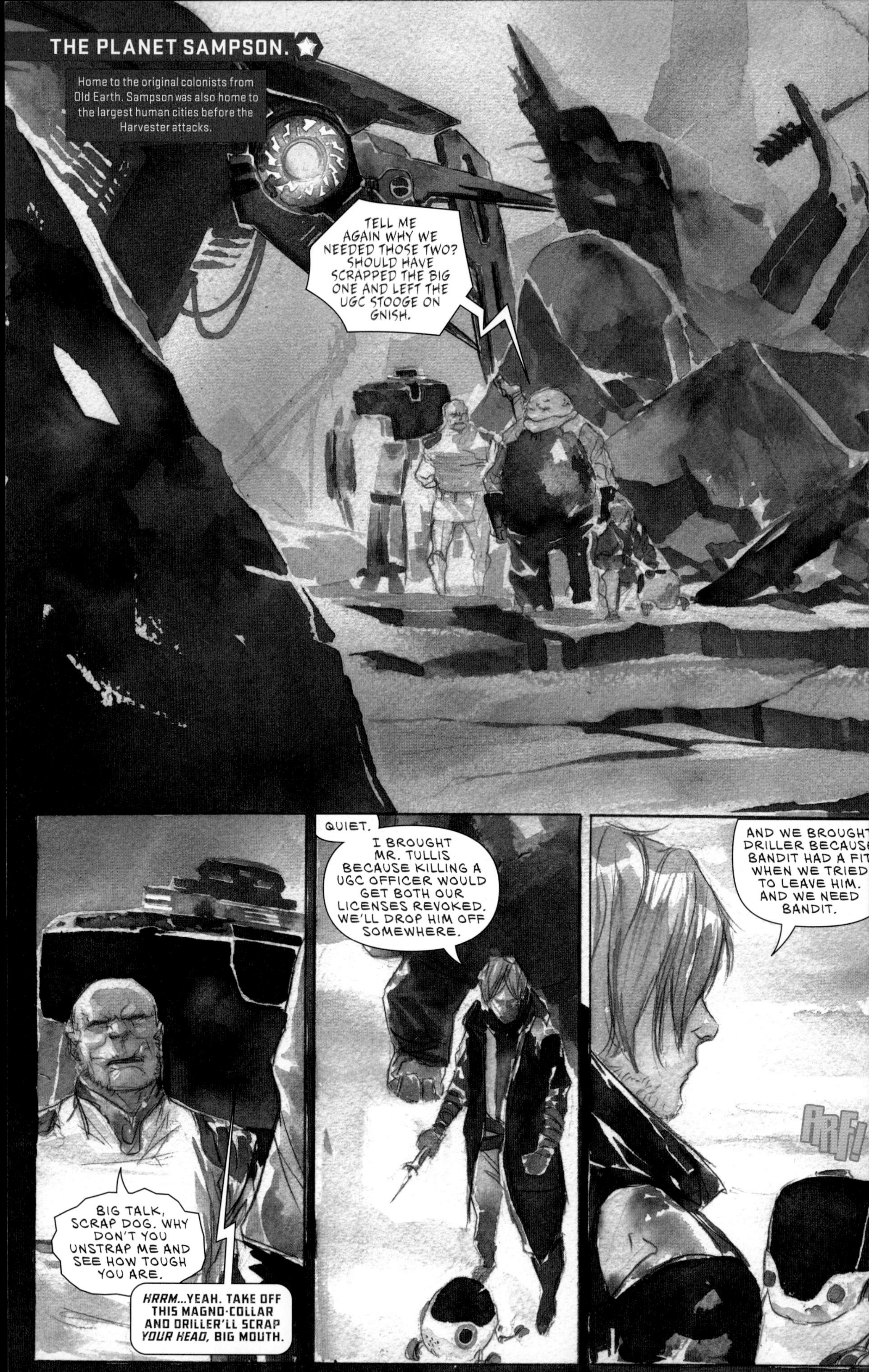
THE PLANET SAMPSON.
Home to the original colonists from Old Earth. Sampson was also home to the largest human cities before the Harvester attacks.
TELL ME AGAIN WHY WE NEEDED THOSE TWO? SHOULD HAVE SCRAPPED THE BIG ONE AND LEFT THE UGC STOOGE ON GNISH.
BIG TALK, SCRAP DOG. WHY DON'T YOU UNSTRAP ME AND SEE HOW TOUGH YOU ARE.
HRRM...YEAH. TAKE OFF THIS MAGNO-COLLAR AND DRILLER'LL SCRAP *YOUR HEAD*, BIG MOUTH.
QUIET.
I BROUGHT MR. TULLIS BECAUSE KILLING A UGC OFFICER WOULD GET BOTH OUR LICENSES REVOKED. WE'LL DROP HIM OFF SOMEWHERE.
AND WE BROUGHT DRILLER BECAUSE BANDIT HAD A FIT WHEN WE TRIED TO LEAVE HIM. AND WE NEED BANDIT.
ARF!

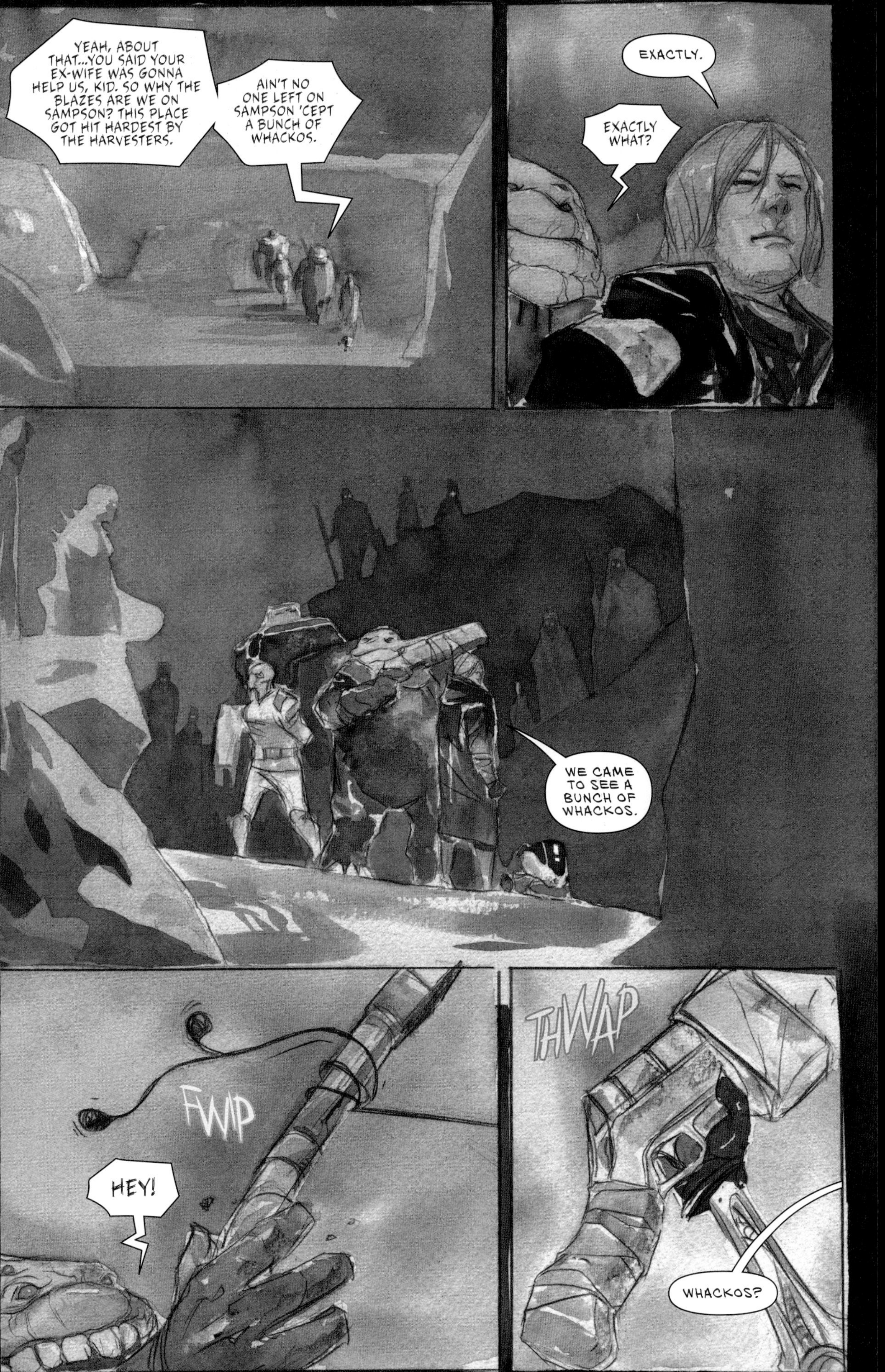
YEAH, ABOUT THAT...YOU SAID YOUR EX-WIFE WAS GONNA HELP US, KID. SO WHY THE BLAZES ARE WE ON SAMPSON? THIS PLACE GOT HIT HARDEST BY THE HARVESTERS.
AIN'T NO ONE LEFT ON SAMPSON 'CEPT A BUNCH OF WHACKOS.
EXACTLY.
EXACTLY WHAT?
WE CAME TO SEE A BUNCH OF WHACKOS.
FWIP
HEY!
THWAP
WHACKOS?

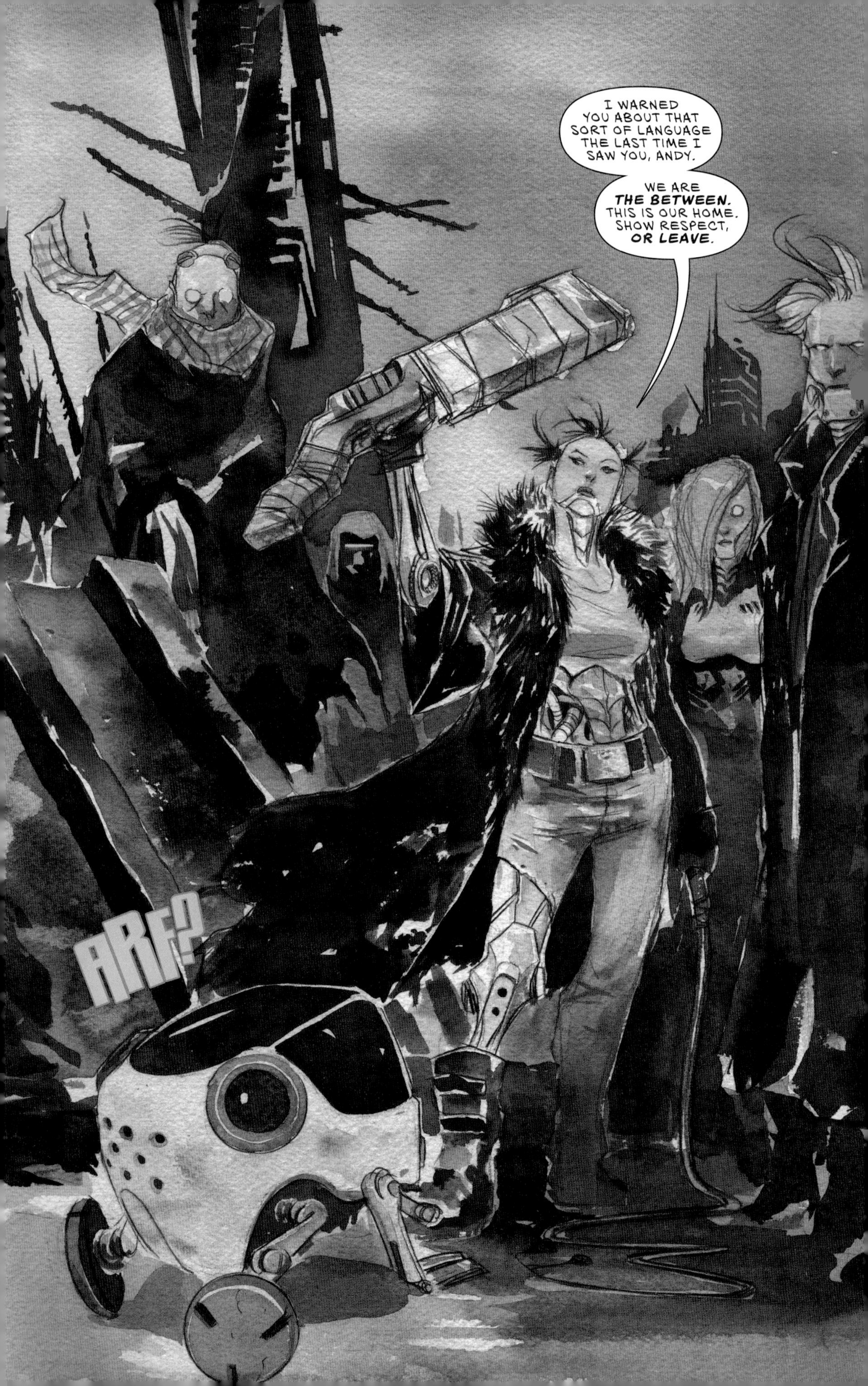
I WARNED YOU ABOUT THAT SORT OF LANGUAGE THE LAST TIME I SAW YOU, ANDY.
WE ARE **THE BETWEEN.** THIS IS OUR HOME. SHOW RESPECT, **OR LEAVE.**
ARF?

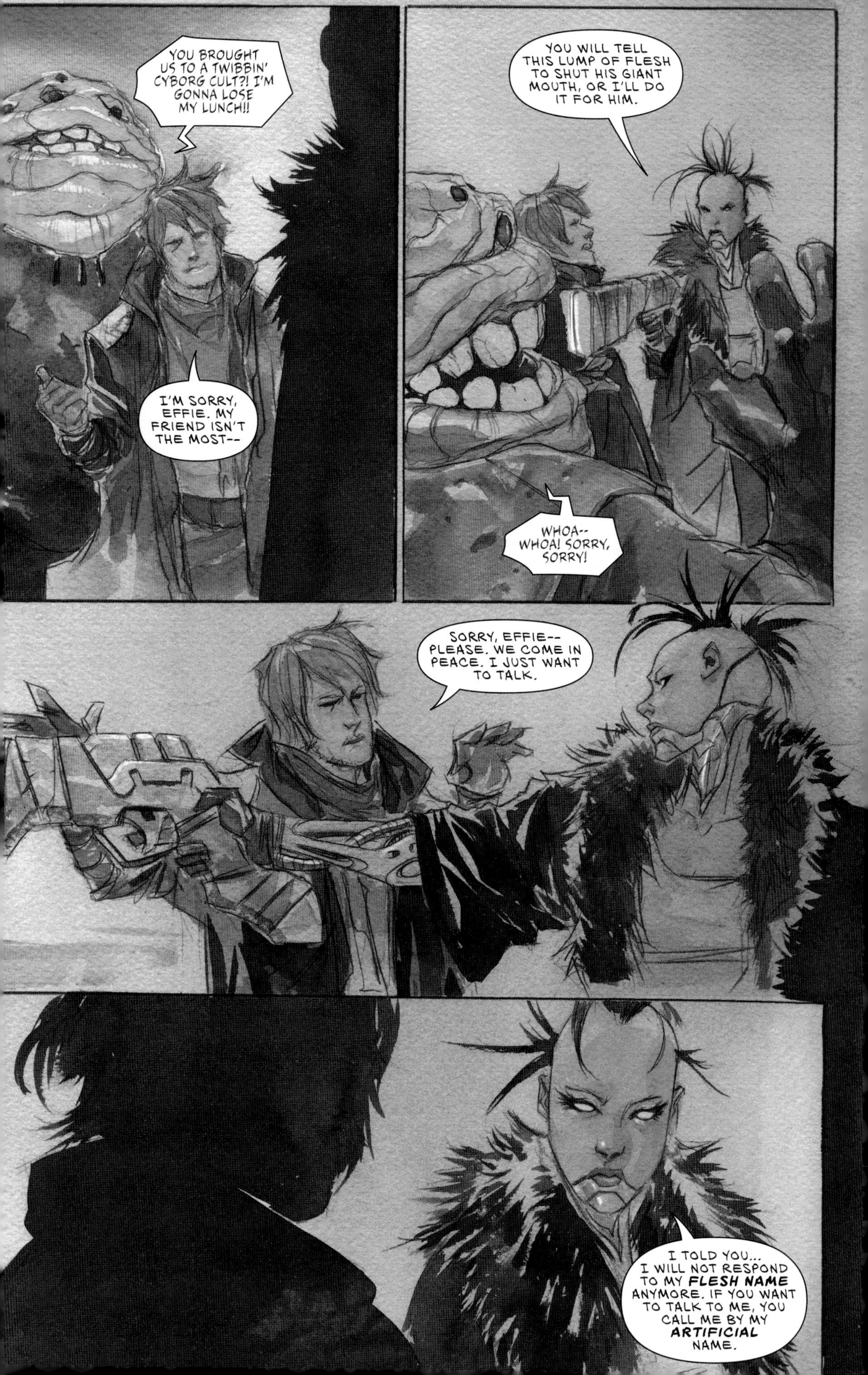
YOU BROUGHT US TO A TWIBBIN' CYBORG CULT?! I'M GONNA LOSE MY LUNCH!!
I'M SORRY, EFFIE. MY FRIEND ISN'T THE MOST--
YOU WILL TELL THIS LUMP OF FLESH TO SHUT HIS GIANT MOUTH, OR I'LL DO IT FOR HIM.
WHOA-- WHOA! SORRY, SORRY!
SORRY, EFFIE-- PLEASE. WE COME IN PEACE. I JUST WANT TO TALK.
I TOLD YOU... I WILL NOT RESPOND TO MY **FLESH NAME** ANYMORE. IF YOU WANT TO TALK TO ME, YOU CALL ME BY MY **ARTIFICIAL** NAME.

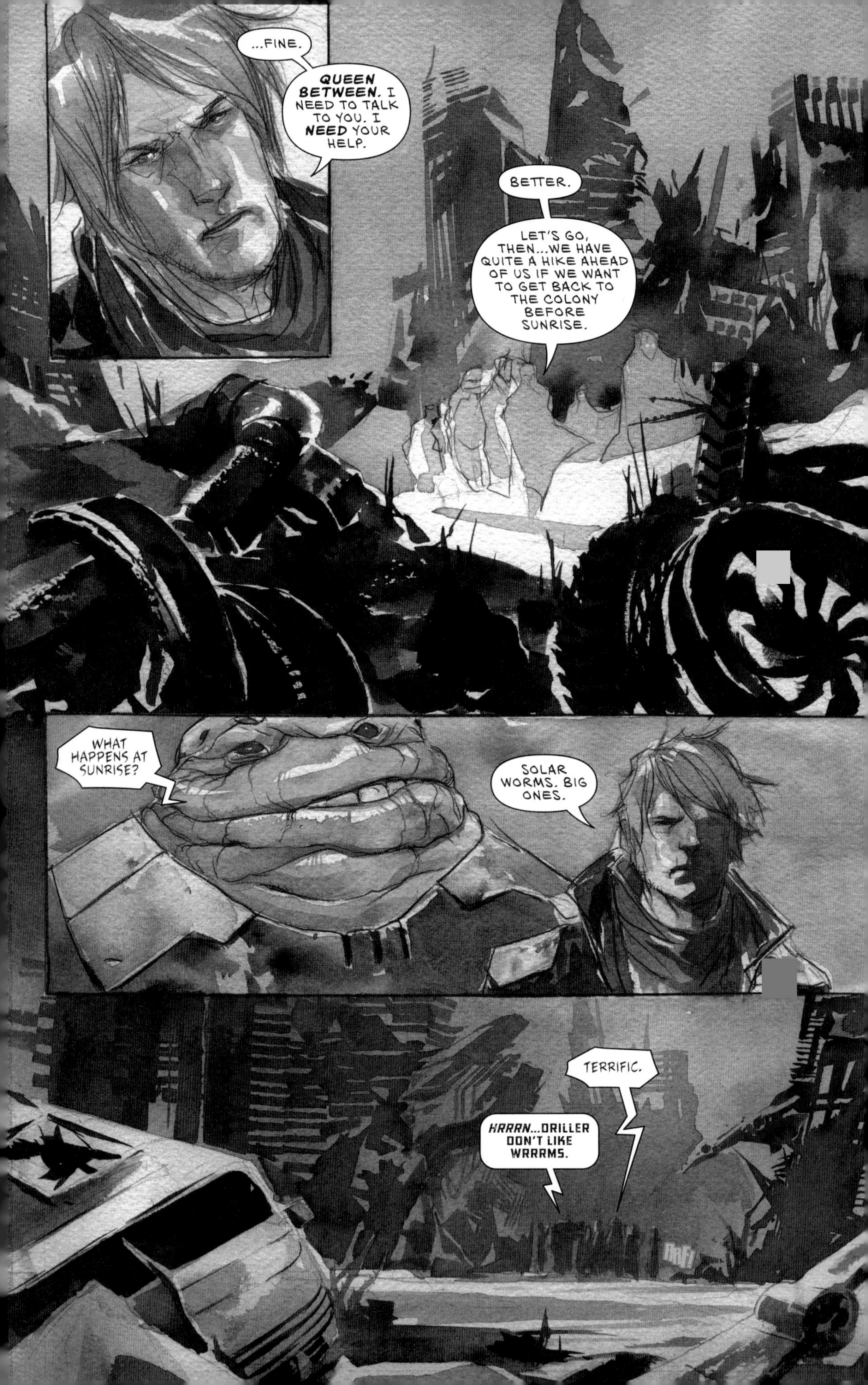
...FINE.
QUEEN BETWEEN. I NEED TO TALK TO YOU. I **NEED** YOUR HELP.
BETTER.
LET'S GO, THEN...WE HAVE QUITE A HIKE AHEAD OF US IF WE WANT TO GET BACK TO THE COLONY BEFORE SUNRISE.
WHAT HAPPENS AT SUNRISE?
SOLAR WORMS. BIG ONES.
TERRIFIC.
HRRRN...DRILLER DON'T LIKE WRRRMS.

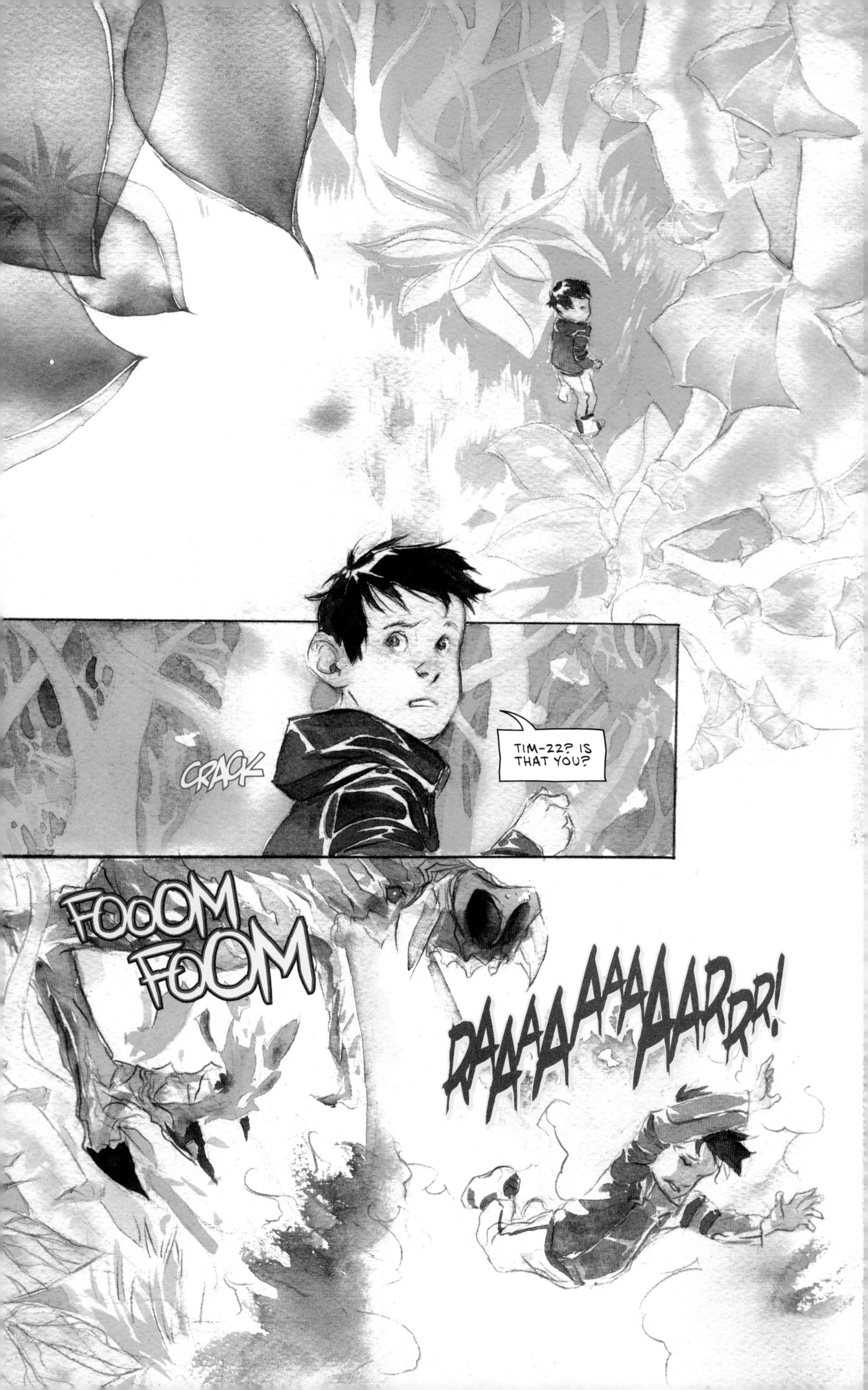
CRACK
TIM-22? IS THAT YOU?
FOOOM FOOM
DAAAAAAAAARRR!

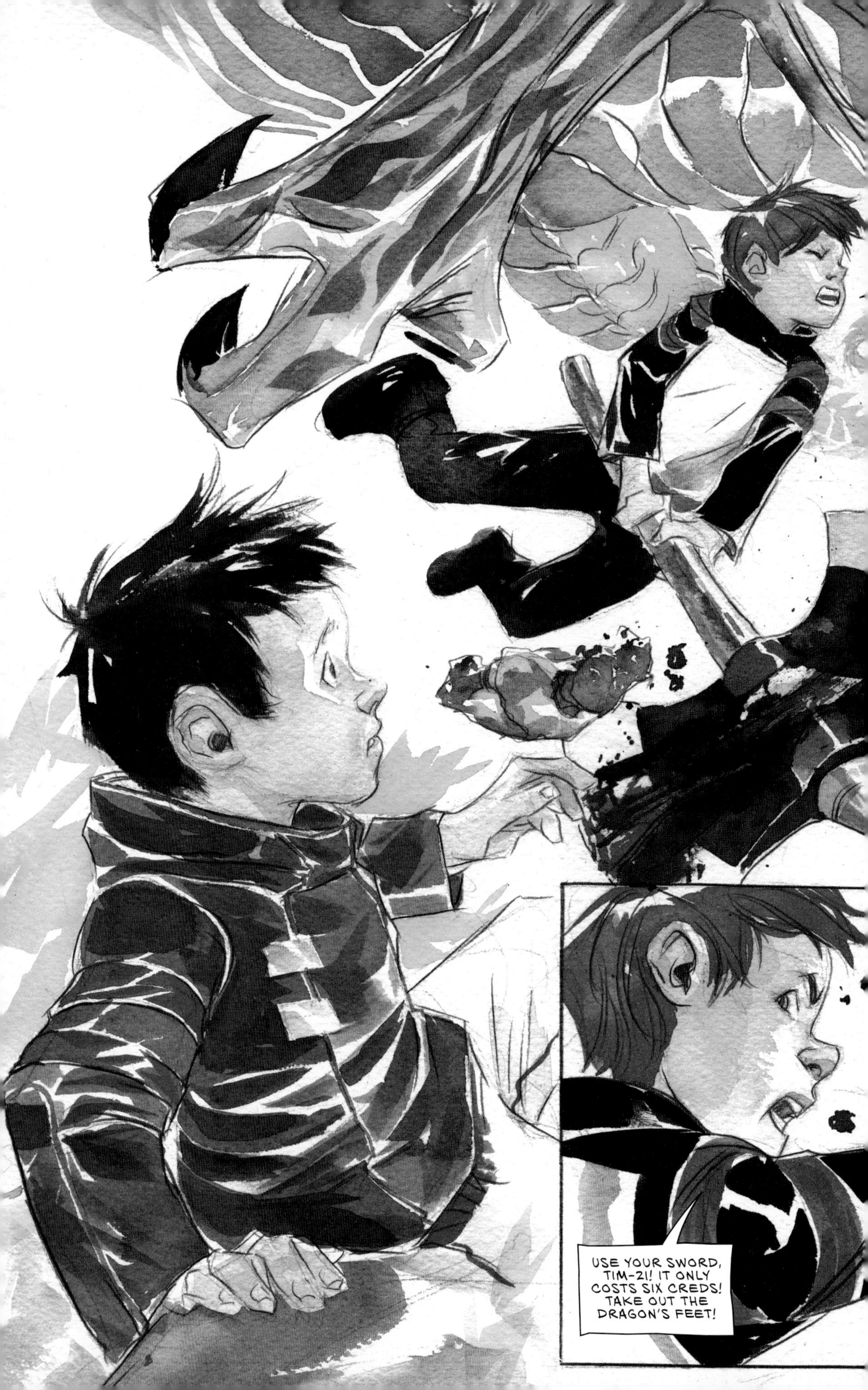
USE YOUR SWORD, TIM-21! IT ONLY COSTS SIX CREDS! TAKE OUT THE DRAGON'S FEET!

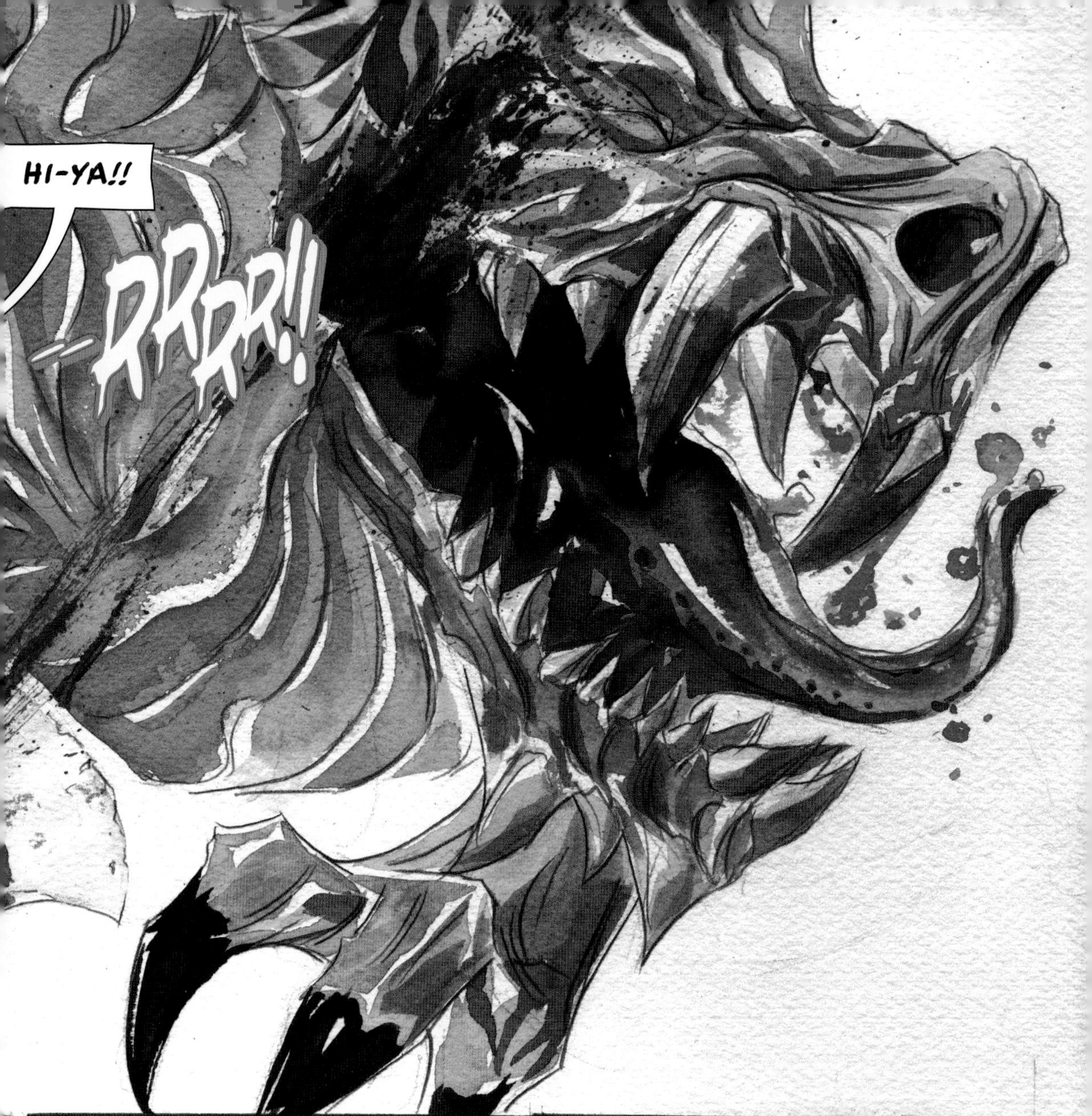
HI-YA!!
--RARR!!

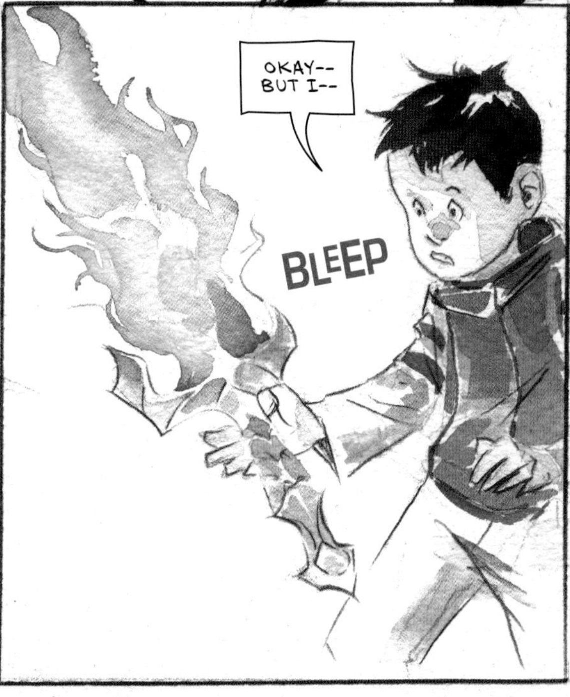
OKAY-- BUT I--
BLEEP

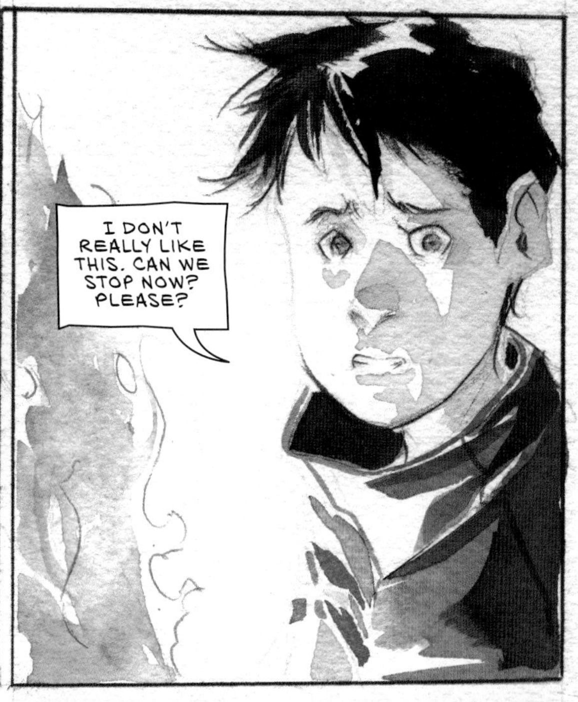
I DON'T REALLY LIKE THIS. CAN WE STOP NOW? PLEASE?

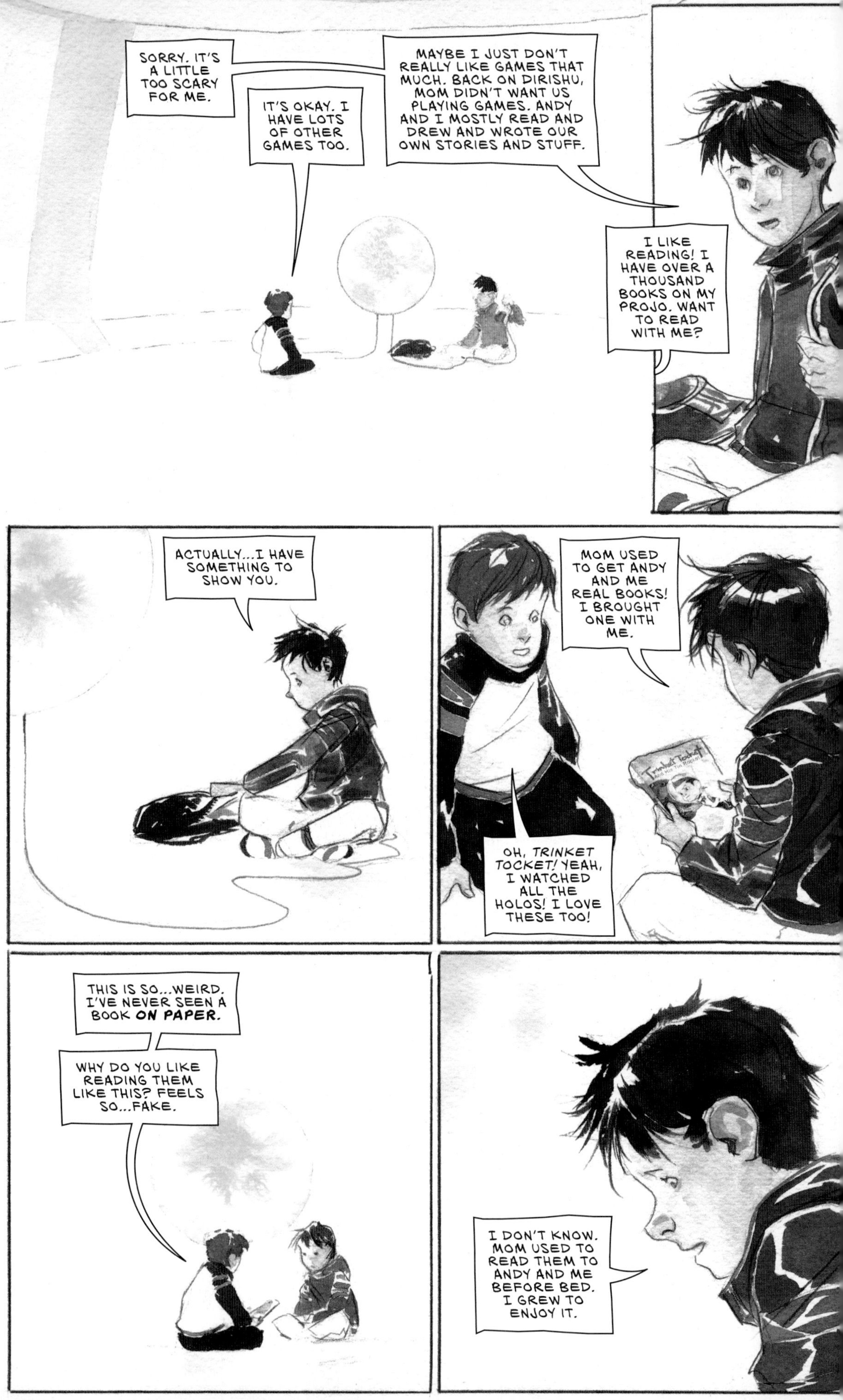
SORRY. IT'S A LITTLE TOO SCARY FOR ME.
MAYBE I JUST DON'T REALLY LIKE GAMES THAT MUCH. BACK ON DIRISHU, MOM DIDN'T WANT US PLAYING GAMES. ANDY AND I MOSTLY READ AND DREW AND WROTE OUR OWN STORIES AND STUFF.
IT'S OKAY. I HAVE LOTS OF OTHER GAMES TOO.
I LIKE READING! I HAVE OVER A THOUSAND BOOKS ON MY PROJO. WANT TO READ WITH ME?
ACTUALLY...I HAVE SOMETHING TO SHOW YOU.
MOM USED TO GET ANDY AND ME REAL BOOKS! I BROUGHT ONE WITH ME.
OH, *TRINKET TOCKET!* YEAH, I WATCHED ALL THE HOLOS! I LOVE THESE TOO!
THIS IS SO...WEIRD. I'VE NEVER SEEN A BOOK **ON PAPER.**
WHY DO YOU LIKE READING THEM LIKE THIS? FEELS SO...FAKE.
I DON'T KNOW. MOM USED TO READ THEM TO ANDY AND ME BEFORE BED. I GREW TO ENJOY IT.

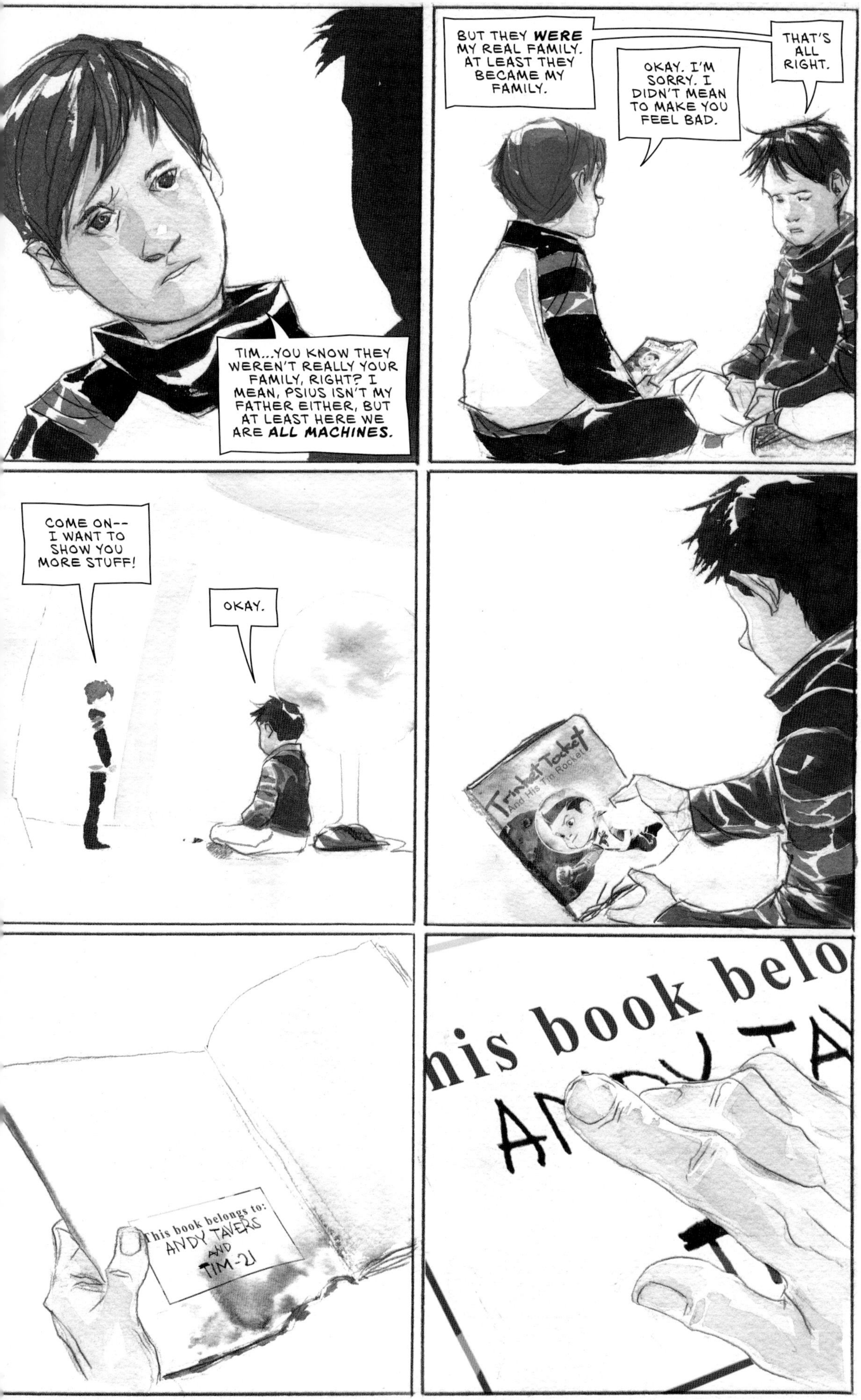
TIM...YOU KNOW THEY WEREN'T REALLY YOUR FAMILY, RIGHT? I MEAN, PSIUS ISN'T MY FATHER EITHER, BUT AT LEAST HERE WE ARE **ALL MACHINES.**
BUT THEY **WERE** MY REAL FAMILY. AT LEAST THEY BECAME MY FAMILY.
THAT'S ALL RIGHT.
OKAY. I'M SORRY. I DIDN'T MEAN TO MAKE YOU FEEL BAD.
COME ON-- I WANT TO SHOW YOU MORE STUFF!
OKAY.
Trinket Tocket
And His Tin Rocket
This book belongs to:
ANDY TAVERS
AND
TIM-21
his book belo

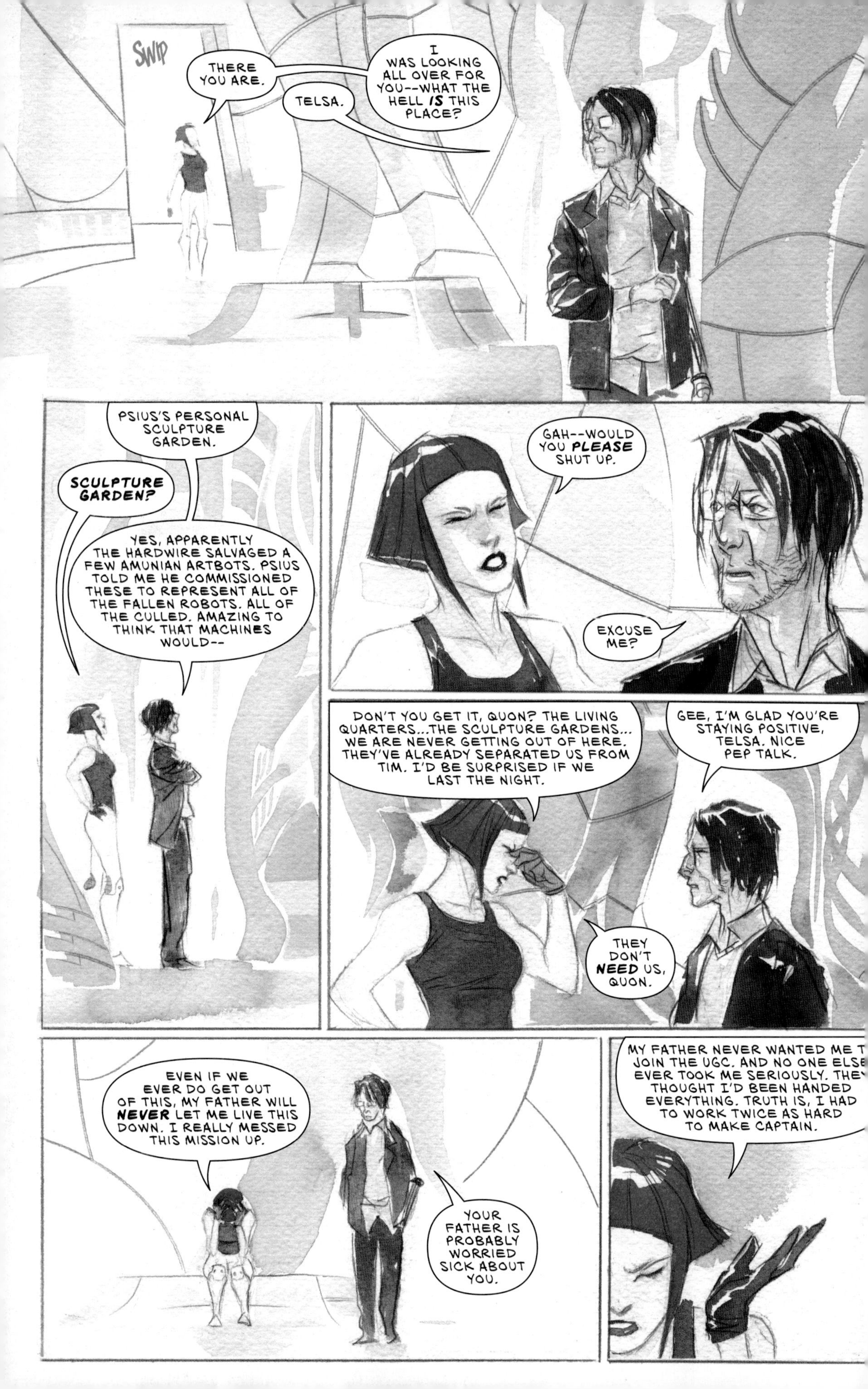
SWIP
THERE YOU ARE.
TELSA.
I WAS LOOKING ALL OVER FOR YOU--WHAT THE HELL IS THIS PLACE?
PSIUS'S PERSONAL SCULPTURE GARDEN.
SCULPTURE GARDEN?
YES, APPARENTLY THE HARDWIRE SALVAGED A FEW AMUNIAN ARTBOTS. PSIUS TOLD ME HE COMMISSIONED THESE TO REPRESENT ALL OF THE FALLEN ROBOTS. ALL OF THE CULLED. AMAZING TO THINK THAT MACHINES WOULD--
GAH--WOULD YOU PLEASE SHUT UP.
EXCUSE ME?
DON'T YOU GET IT, QUON? THE LIVING QUARTERS...THE SCULPTURE GARDENS... WE ARE NEVER GETTING OUT OF HERE. THEY'VE ALREADY SEPARATED US FROM TIM. I'D BE SURPRISED IF WE LAST THE NIGHT.
GEE, I'M GLAD YOU'RE STAYING POSITIVE, TELSA. NICE PEP TALK.
THEY DON'T NEED US, QUON.
EVEN IF WE EVER DO GET OUT OF THIS, MY FATHER WILL NEVER LET ME LIVE THIS DOWN. I REALLY MESSED THIS MISSION UP.
YOUR FATHER IS PROBABLY WORRIED SICK ABOUT YOU.
MY FATHER NEVER WANTED ME T JOIN THE UGC. AND NO ONE ELSE EVER TOOK ME SERIOUSLY. THEY THOUGHT I'D BEEN HANDED EVERYTHING. TRUTH IS, I HAD TO WORK TWICE AS HARD TO MAKE CAPTAIN.

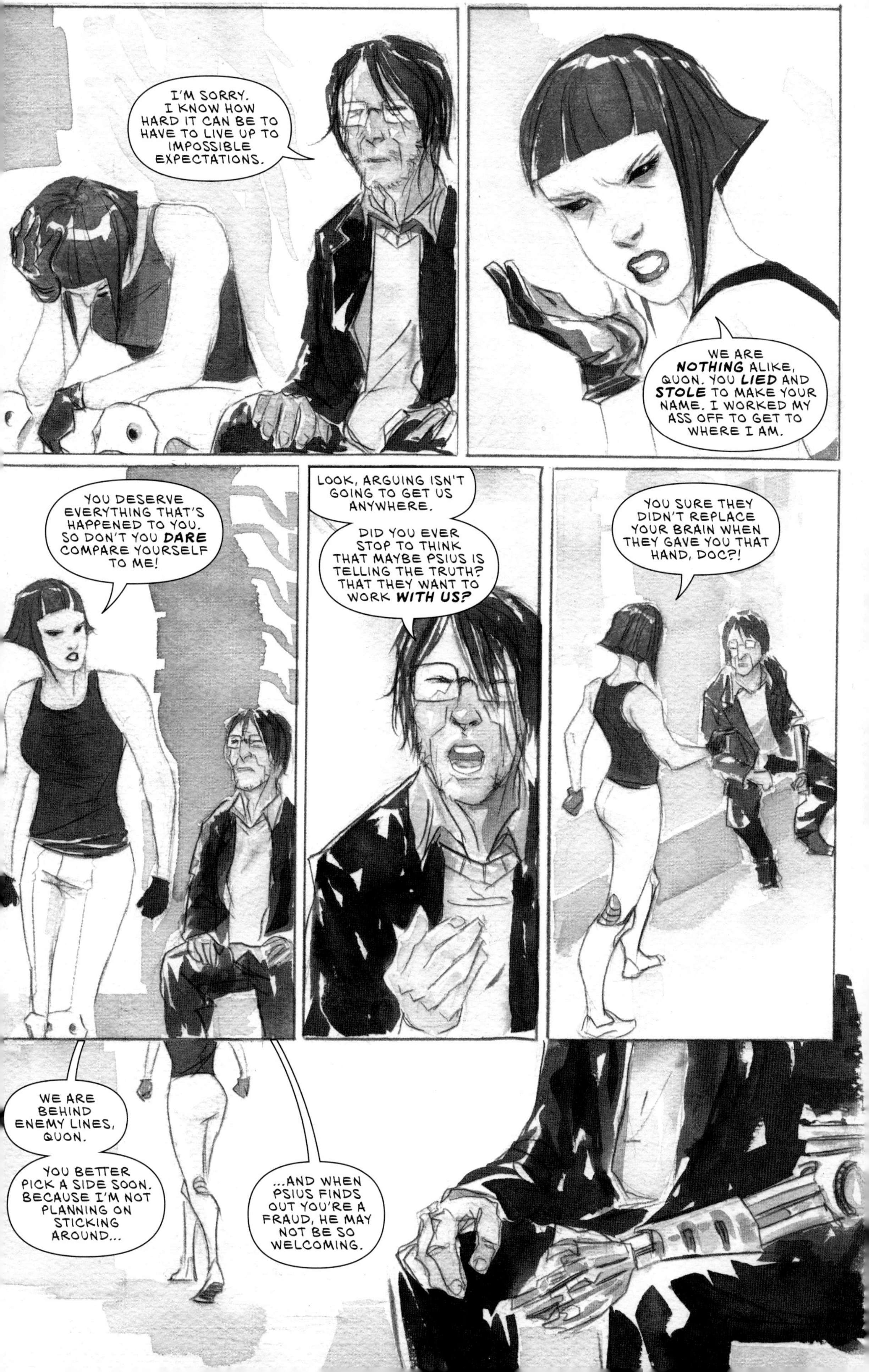
I'M SORRY. I KNOW HOW HARD IT CAN BE TO HAVE TO LIVE UP TO IMPOSSIBLE EXPECTATIONS.
WE ARE **NOTHING** ALIKE, QUON. YOU **LIED** AND **STOLE** TO MAKE YOUR NAME. I WORKED MY ASS OFF TO GET TO WHERE I AM.
YOU DESERVE EVERYTHING THAT'S HAPPENED TO YOU. SO DON'T YOU **DARE** COMPARE YOURSELF TO ME!
LOOK, ARGUING ISN'T GOING TO GET US ANYWHERE.
DID YOU EVER STOP TO THINK THAT MAYBE PSIUS IS TELLING THE TRUTH? THAT THEY WANT TO WORK **WITH US?**
YOU SURE THEY DIDN'T REPLACE YOUR BRAIN WHEN THEY GAVE YOU THAT HAND, DOC?!
WE ARE BEHIND ENEMY LINES, QUON.
YOU BETTER PICK A SIDE SOON. BECAUSE I'M NOT PLANNING ON STICKING AROUND...
...AND WHEN PSIUS FINDS OUT YOU'RE A FRAUD, HE MAY NOT BE SO WELCOMING.

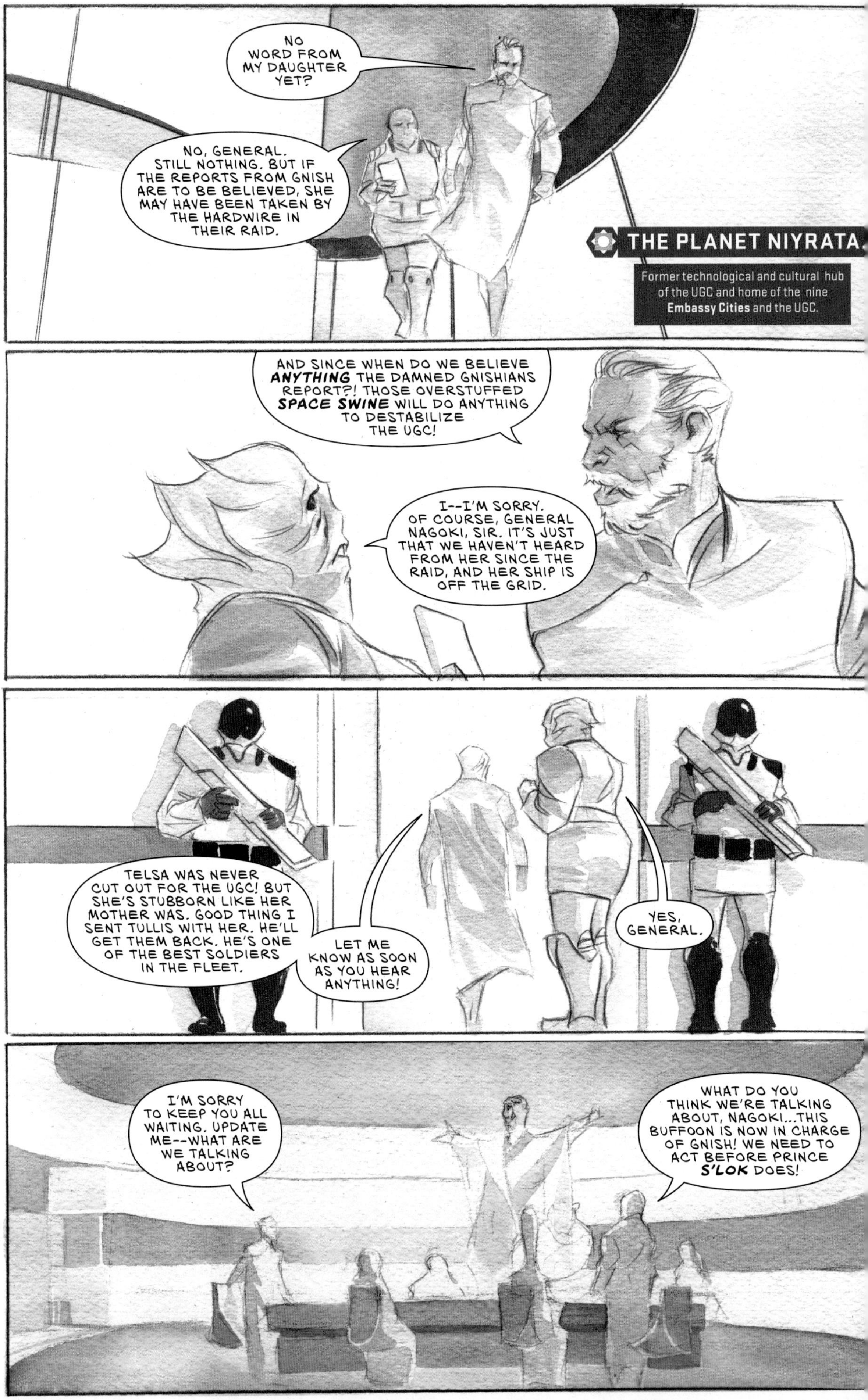
NO WORD FROM MY DAUGHTER YET?
NO, GENERAL. STILL NOTHING. BUT IF THE REPORTS FROM GNISH ARE TO BE BELIEVED, SHE MAY HAVE BEEN TAKEN BY THE HARDWIRE IN THEIR RAID.
THE PLANET NIYRATA
Former technological and cultural hub of the UGC and home of the nine **Embassy Cities** and the UGC.
AND SINCE WHEN DO WE BELIEVE **ANYTHING** THE DAMNED GNISHIANS REPORT?! THOSE OVERSTUFFED **SPACE SWINE** WILL DO ANYTHING TO DESTABILIZE THE UGC!
I--I'M SORRY. OF COURSE, GENERAL NAGOKI, SIR. IT'S JUST THAT WE HAVEN'T HEARD FROM HER SINCE THE RAID, AND HER SHIP IS OFF THE GRID.
TELSA WAS NEVER CUT OUT FOR THE UGC! BUT SHE'S STUBBORN LIKE HER MOTHER WAS. GOOD THING I SENT TULLIS WITH HER. HE'LL GET THEM BACK. HE'S ONE OF THE BEST SOLDIERS IN THE FLEET.
LET ME KNOW AS SOON AS YOU HEAR ANYTHING!
YES, GENERAL.
I'M SORRY TO KEEP YOU ALL WAITING. UPDATE ME--WHAT ARE WE TALKING ABOUT?
WHAT DO YOU THINK WE'RE TALKING ABOUT, NAGOKI...THIS BUFFOON IS NOW IN CHARGE OF GNISH! WE NEED TO ACT BEFORE PRINCE **S'LOK** DOES!

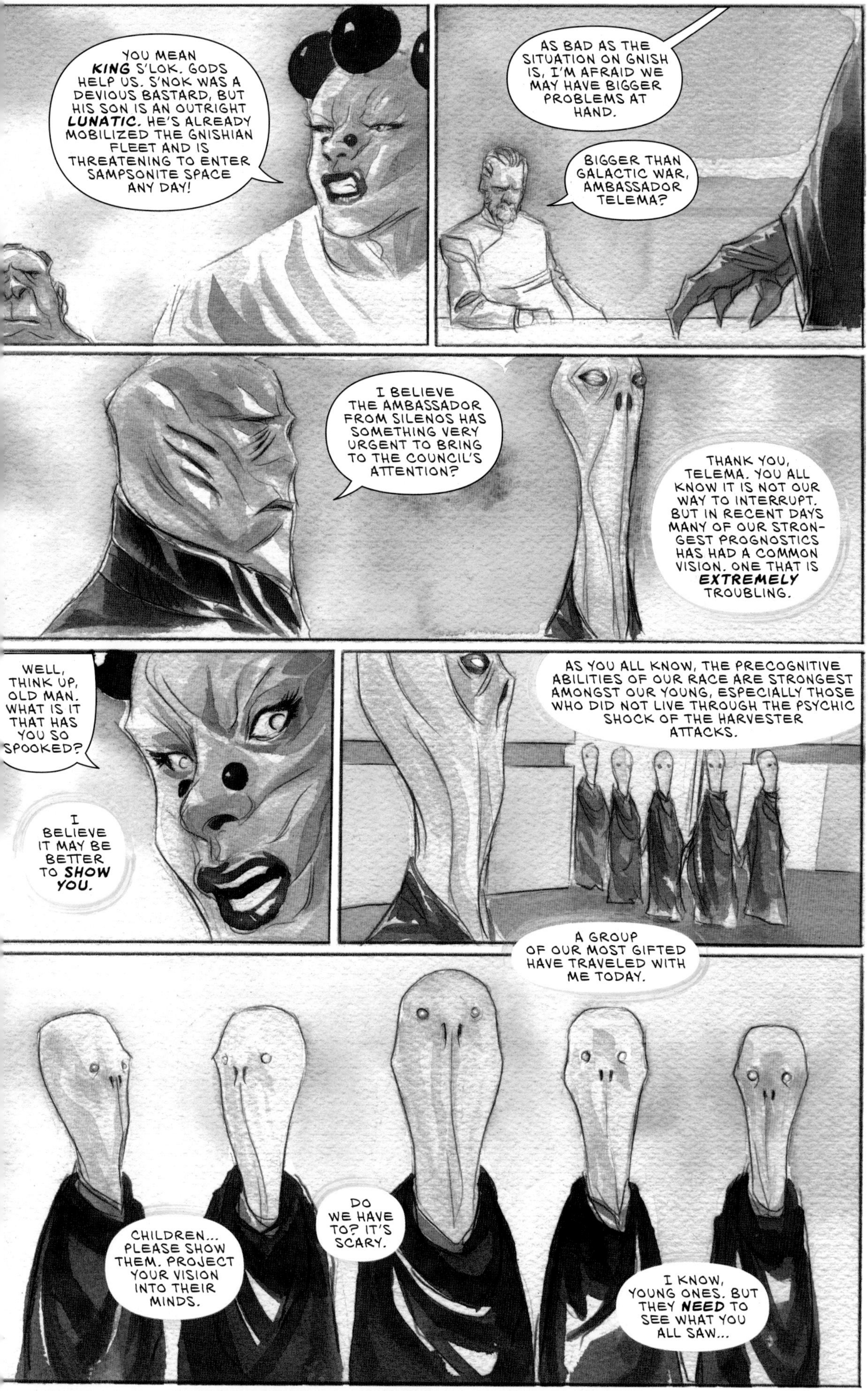
YOU MEAN KING S'LOK. GODS HELP US. S'NOK WAS A DEVIOUS BASTARD, BUT HIS SON IS AN OUTRIGHT LUNATIC. HE'S ALREADY MOBILIZED THE GNISHIAN FLEET AND IS THREATENING TO ENTER SAMPSONITE SPACE ANY DAY!
AS BAD AS THE SITUATION ON GNISH IS, I'M AFRAID WE MAY HAVE BIGGER PROBLEMS AT HAND.
BIGGER THAN GALACTIC WAR, AMBASSADOR TELEMA?
I BELIEVE THE AMBASSADOR FROM SILENOS HAS SOMETHING VERY URGENT TO BRING TO THE COUNCIL'S ATTENTION?
THANK YOU, TELEMA. YOU ALL KNOW IT IS NOT OUR WAY TO INTERRUPT. BUT IN RECENT DAYS MANY OF OUR STRONGEST PROGNOSTICS HAS HAD A COMMON VISION. ONE THAT IS EXTREMELY TROUBLING.
WELL, THINK UP, OLD MAN. WHAT IS IT THAT HAS YOU SO SPOOKED?
I BELIEVE IT MAY BE BETTER TO SHOW YOU.
AS YOU ALL KNOW, THE PRECOGNITIVE ABILITIES OF OUR RACE ARE STRONGEST AMONGST OUR YOUNG, ESPECIALLY THOSE WHO DID NOT LIVE THROUGH THE PSYCHIC SHOCK OF THE HARVESTER ATTACKS.
A GROUP OF OUR MOST GIFTED HAVE TRAVELED WITH ME TODAY.
CHILDREN... PLEASE SHOW THEM. PROJECT YOUR VISION INTO THEIR MINDS.
DO WE HAVE TO? IT'S SCARY.
I KNOW, YOUNG ONES. BUT THEY NEED TO SEE WHAT YOU ALL SAW...

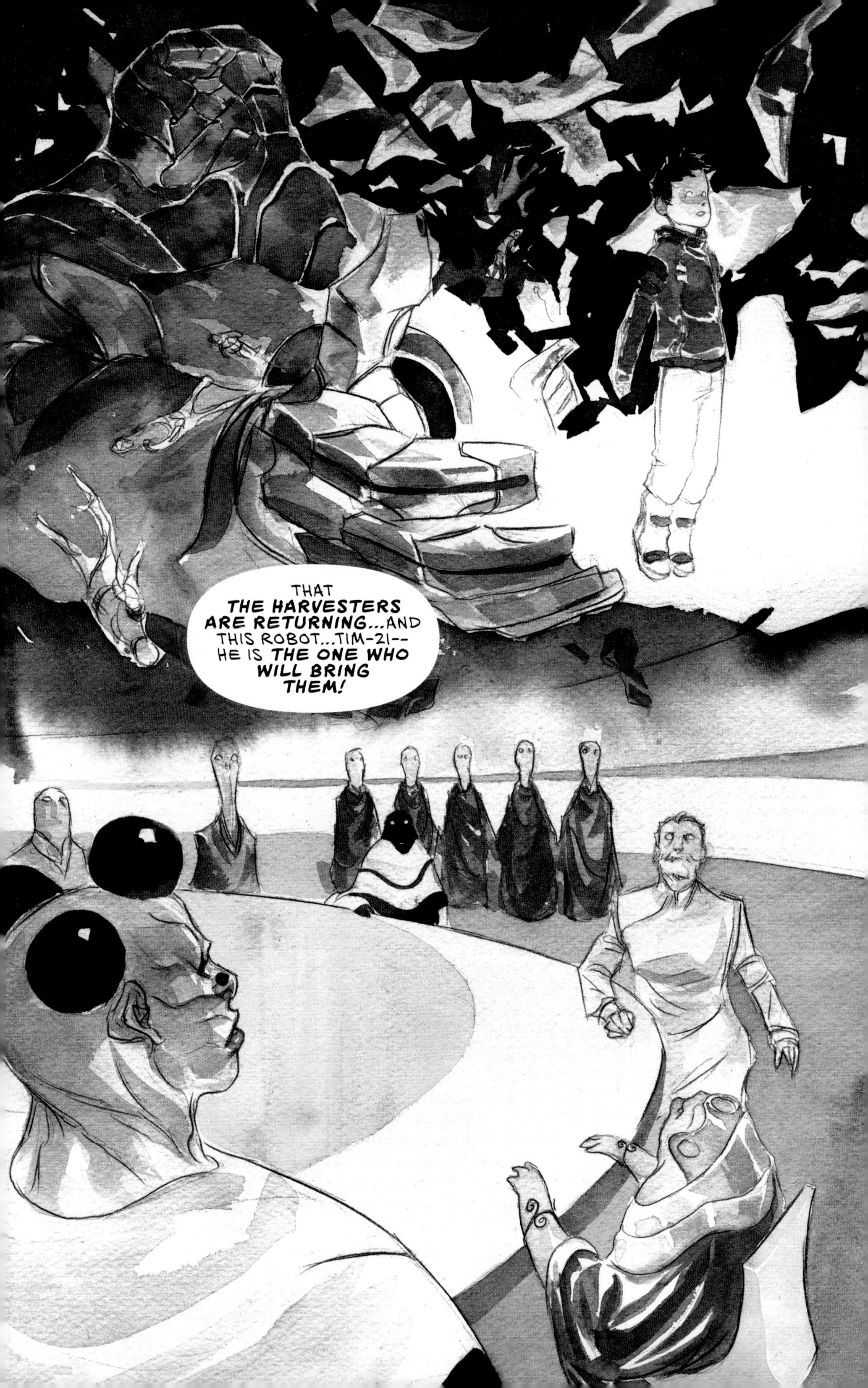
THAT THE HARVESTERS ARE RETURNING...AND THIS ROBOT...TIM-21-- HE IS THE ONE WHO WILL BRING THEM!

CHAPTER FIVE

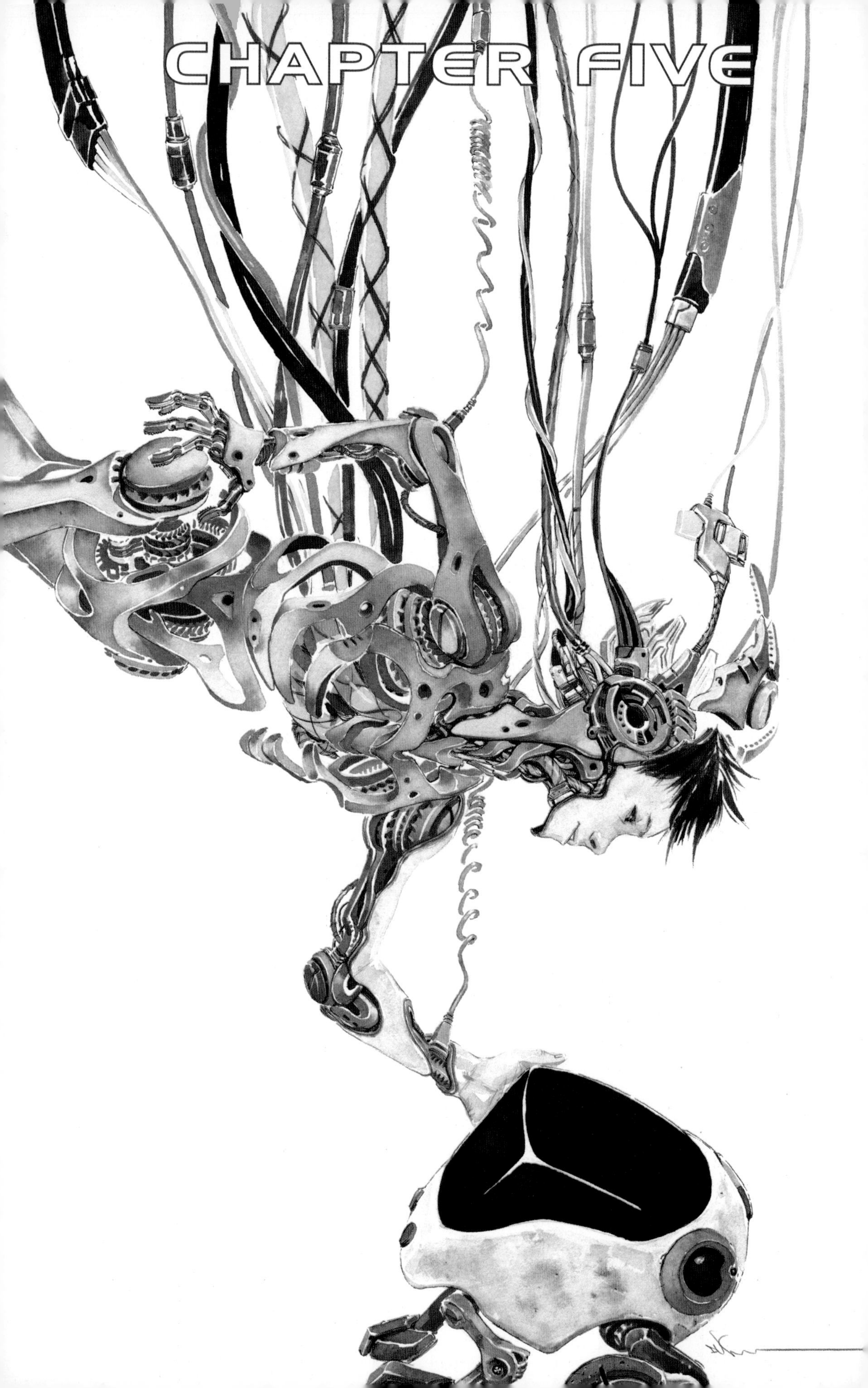

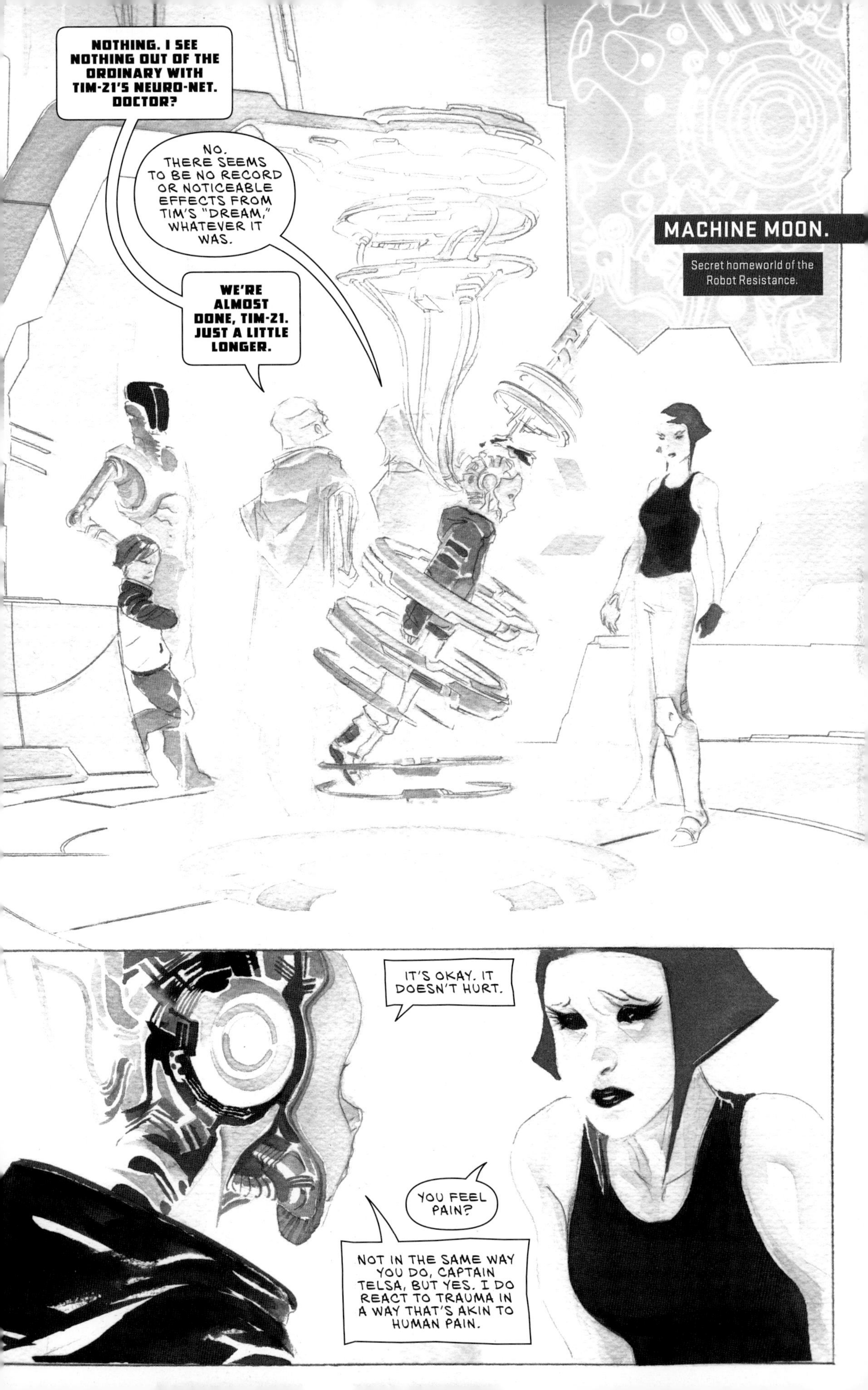
NOTHING. I SEE NOTHING OUT OF THE ORDINARY WITH TIM-21'S NEURO-NET. DOCTOR?
NO. THERE SEEMS TO BE NO RECORD OR NOTICEABLE EFFECTS FROM TIM'S "DREAM," WHATEVER IT WAS.
MACHINE MOON.
Secret homeworld of the Robot Resistance.
WE'RE ALMOST DONE, TIM-21. JUST A LITTLE LONGER.
IT'S OKAY. IT DOESN'T HURT.
YOU FEEL PAIN?
NOT IN THE SAME WAY YOU DO, CAPTAIN TELSA, BUT YES. I DO REACT TO TRAUMA IN A WAY THAT'S AKIN TO HUMAN PAIN.

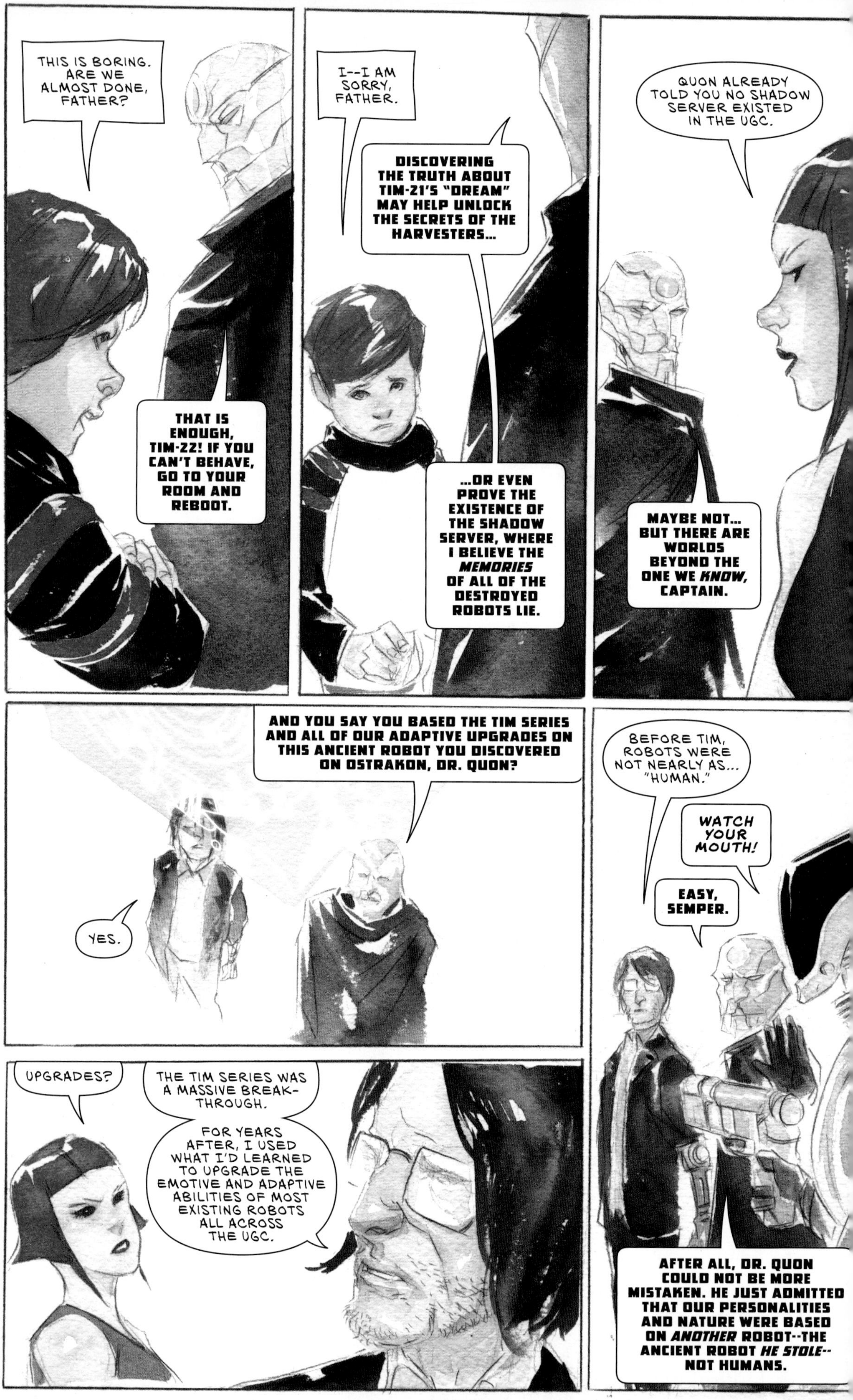
THIS IS BORING. ARE WE ALMOST DONE, FATHER?
THAT IS ENOUGH, TIM-22! IF YOU CAN'T BEHAVE, GO TO YOUR ROOM AND REBOOT.
I--I AM SORRY, FATHER.
DISCOVERING THE TRUTH ABOUT TIM-21'S "DREAM" MAY HELP UNLOCK THE SECRETS OF THE HARVESTERS...
...OR EVEN PROVE THE EXISTENCE OF THE SHADOW SERVER, WHERE I BELIEVE THE *MEMORIES* OF ALL OF THE DESTROYED ROBOTS LIE.
QUON ALREADY TOLD YOU NO SHADOW SERVER EXISTED IN THE UGC.
MAYBE NOT... BUT THERE ARE WORLDS BEYOND THE ONE WE *KNOW*, CAPTAIN.
AND YOU SAY YOU BASED THE TIM SERIES AND ALL OF OUR ADAPTIVE UPGRADES ON THIS ANCIENT ROBOT YOU DISCOVERED ON OSTRAKON, DR. QUON?
YES.
BEFORE TIM, ROBOTS WERE NOT NEARLY AS... "HUMAN."
WATCH YOUR MOUTH!
EASY, SEMPER.
UPGRADES?
THE TIM SERIES WAS A MASSIVE BREAK-THROUGH.
FOR YEARS AFTER, I USED WHAT I'D LEARNED TO UPGRADE THE EMOTIVE AND ADAPTIVE ABILITIES OF MOST EXISTING ROBOTS ALL ACROSS THE UGC.
AFTER ALL, DR. QUON COULD NOT BE MORE MISTAKEN. HE JUST ADMITTED THAT OUR PERSONALITIES AND NATURE WERE BASED ON *ANOTHER* ROBOT--THE ANCIENT ROBOT *HE STOLE*--NOT HUMANS.

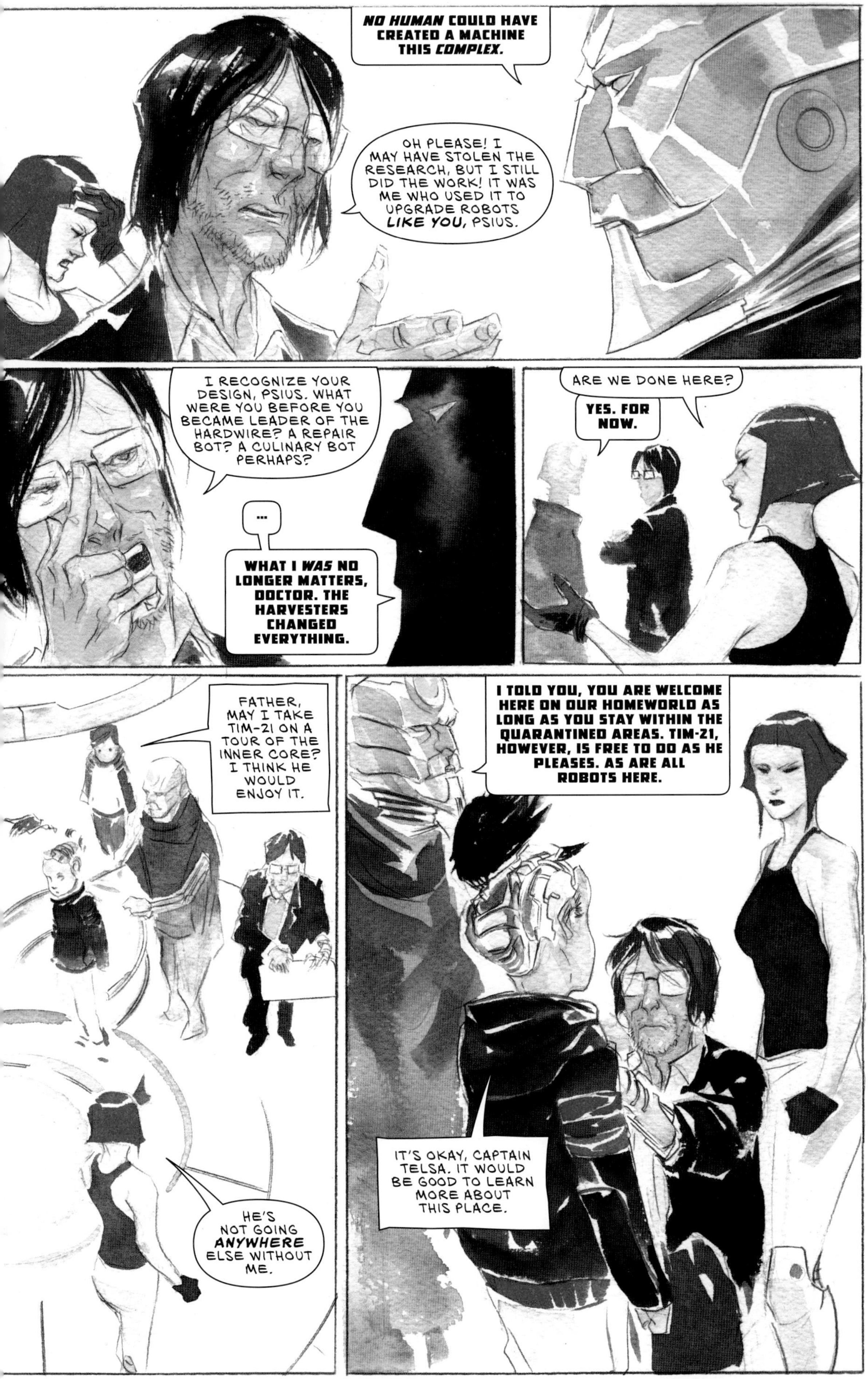
NO HUMAN COULD HAVE CREATED A MACHINE THIS COMPLEX.
OH PLEASE! I MAY HAVE STOLEN THE RESEARCH, BUT I STILL DID THE WORK! IT WAS ME WHO USED ITS TO UPGRADE ROBOTS LIKE YOU, PSIUS.
I RECOGNIZE YOUR DESIGN, PSIUS. WHAT WERE YOU BEFORE YOU BECAME LEADER OF THE HARDWIRE? A REPAIR BOT? A CULINARY BOT PERHAPS?
...
WHAT I WAS NO LONGER MATTERS, DOCTOR. THE HARVESTERS CHANGED EVERYTHING.
ARE WE DONE HERE?
YES. FOR NOW.
FATHER, MAY I TAKE TIM-21 ON A TOUR OF THE INNER CORE? I THINK HE WOULD ENJOY IT.
I TOLD YOU, YOU ARE WELCOME HERE ON OUR HOMEWORLD AS LONG AS YOU STAY WITHIN THE QUARANTINED AREAS. TIM-21, HOWEVER, IS FREE TO DO AS HE PLEASES. AS ARE ALL ROBOTS HERE.
HE'S NOT GOING ANYWHERE ELSE WITHOUT ME.
IT'S OKAY, CAPTAIN TELSA. IT WOULD BE GOOD TO LEARN MORE ABOUT THIS PLACE.

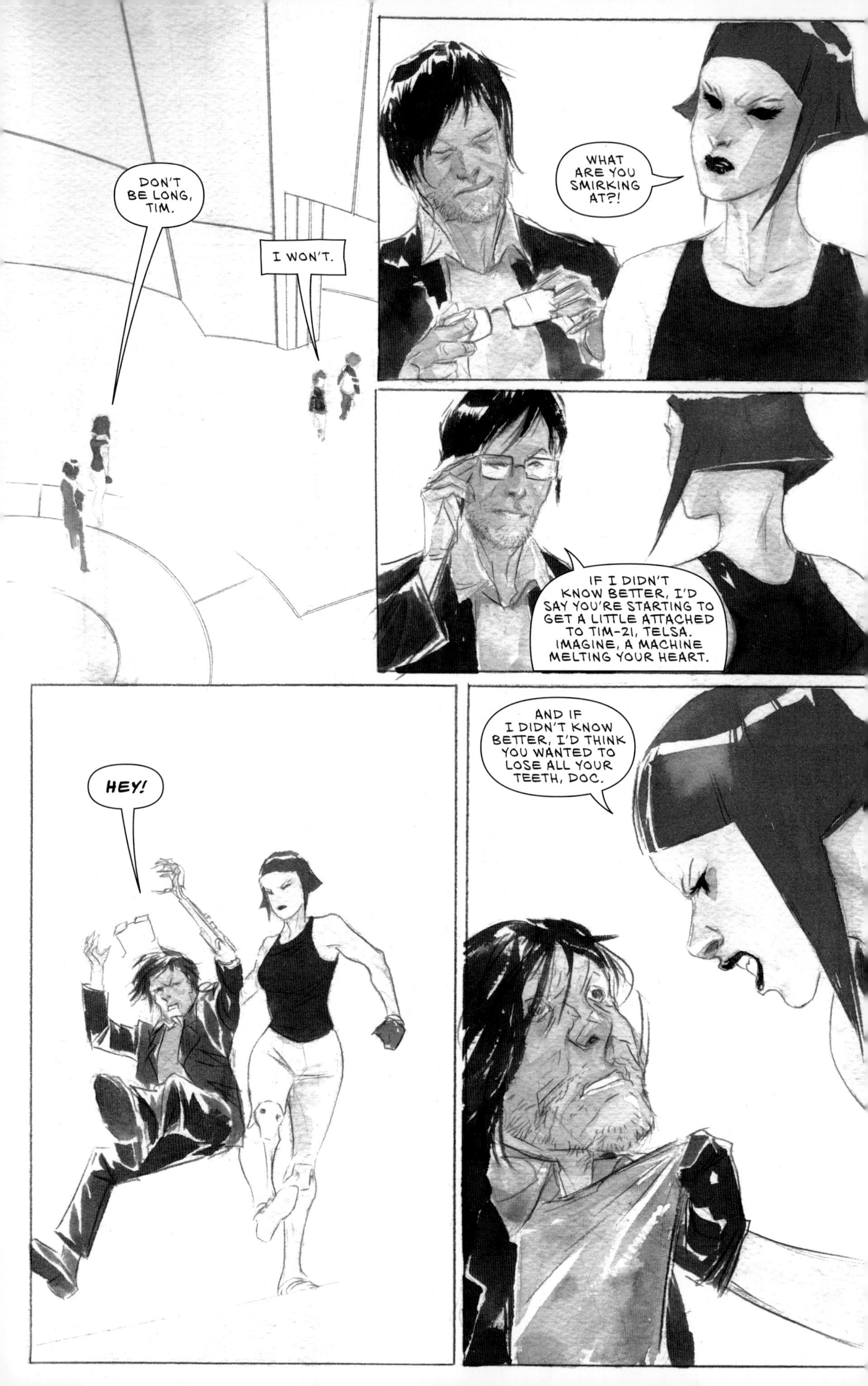
DON'T BE LONG, TIM.
I WON'T.
WHAT ARE YOU SMIRKING AT?!
IF I DIDN'T KNOW BETTER, I'D SAY YOU'RE STARTING TO GET A LITTLE ATTACHED TO TIM-21, TELSA. IMAGINE, A MACHINE MELTING YOUR HEART.
HEY!
AND IF I DIDN'T KNOW BETTER, I'D THINK YOU WANTED TO LOSE ALL YOUR TEETH, DOC.

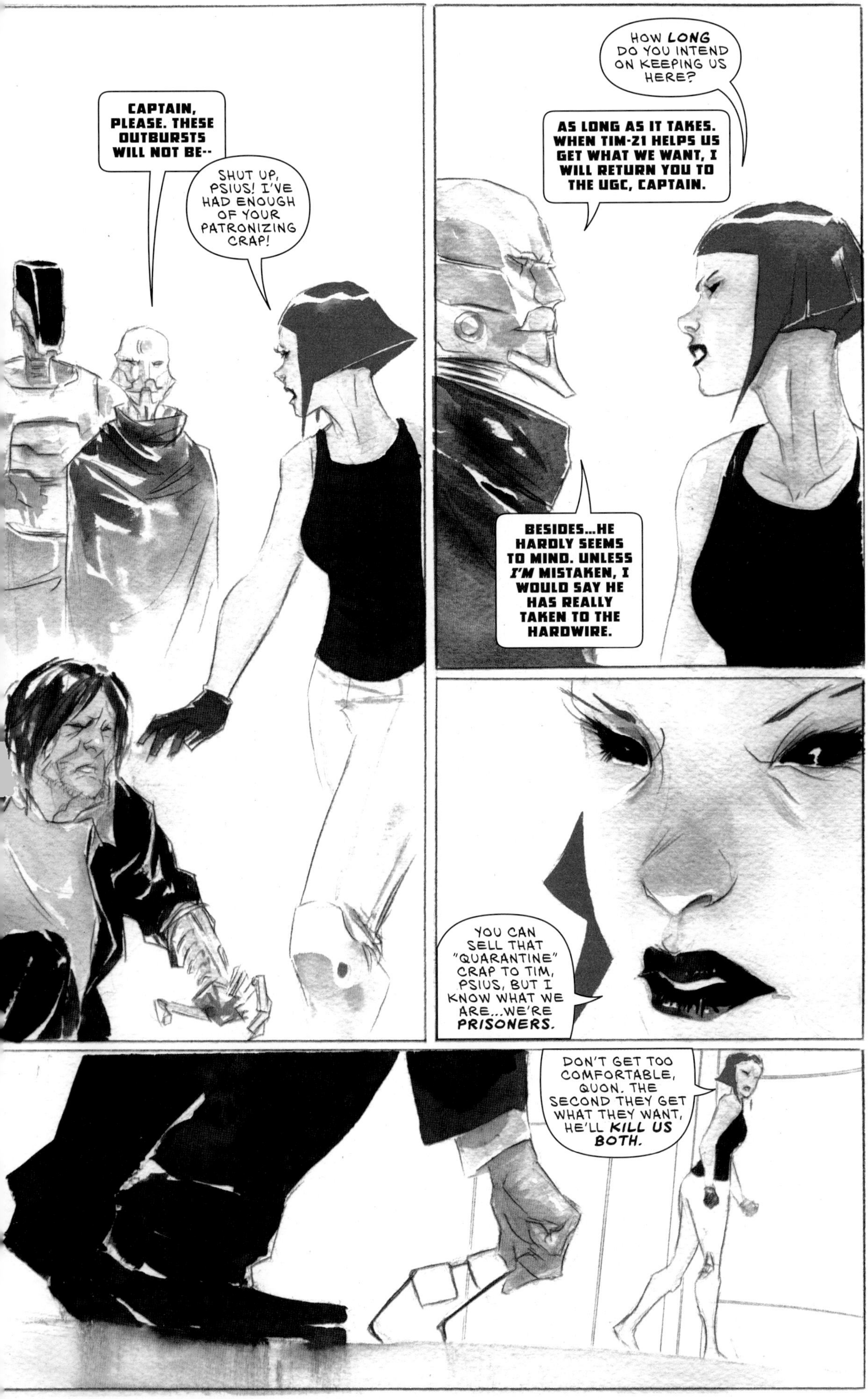
CAPTAIN, PLEASE. THESE OUTBURSTS WILL NOT BE--
SHUT UP, PSIUS! I'VE HAD ENOUGH OF YOUR PATRONIZING CRAP!
HOW **LONG** DO YOU INTEND ON KEEPING US HERE?
AS LONG AS IT TAKES. WHEN TIM-21 HELPS US GET WHAT WE WANT, I WILL RETURN YOU TO THE UGC, CAPTAIN.
BESIDES...HE HARDLY SEEMS TO MIND. UNLESS *I'M* MISTAKEN, I WOULD SAY HE HAS REALLY TAKEN TO THE HARDWIRE.
YOU CAN SELL THAT "QUARANTINE" CRAP TO TIM, PSIUS, BUT I KNOW WHAT WE ARE...WE'RE ***PRISONERS.***
DON'T GET TOO COMFORTABLE, QUON. THE SECOND THEY GET WHAT THEY WANT, HE'LL ***KILL US BOTH.***

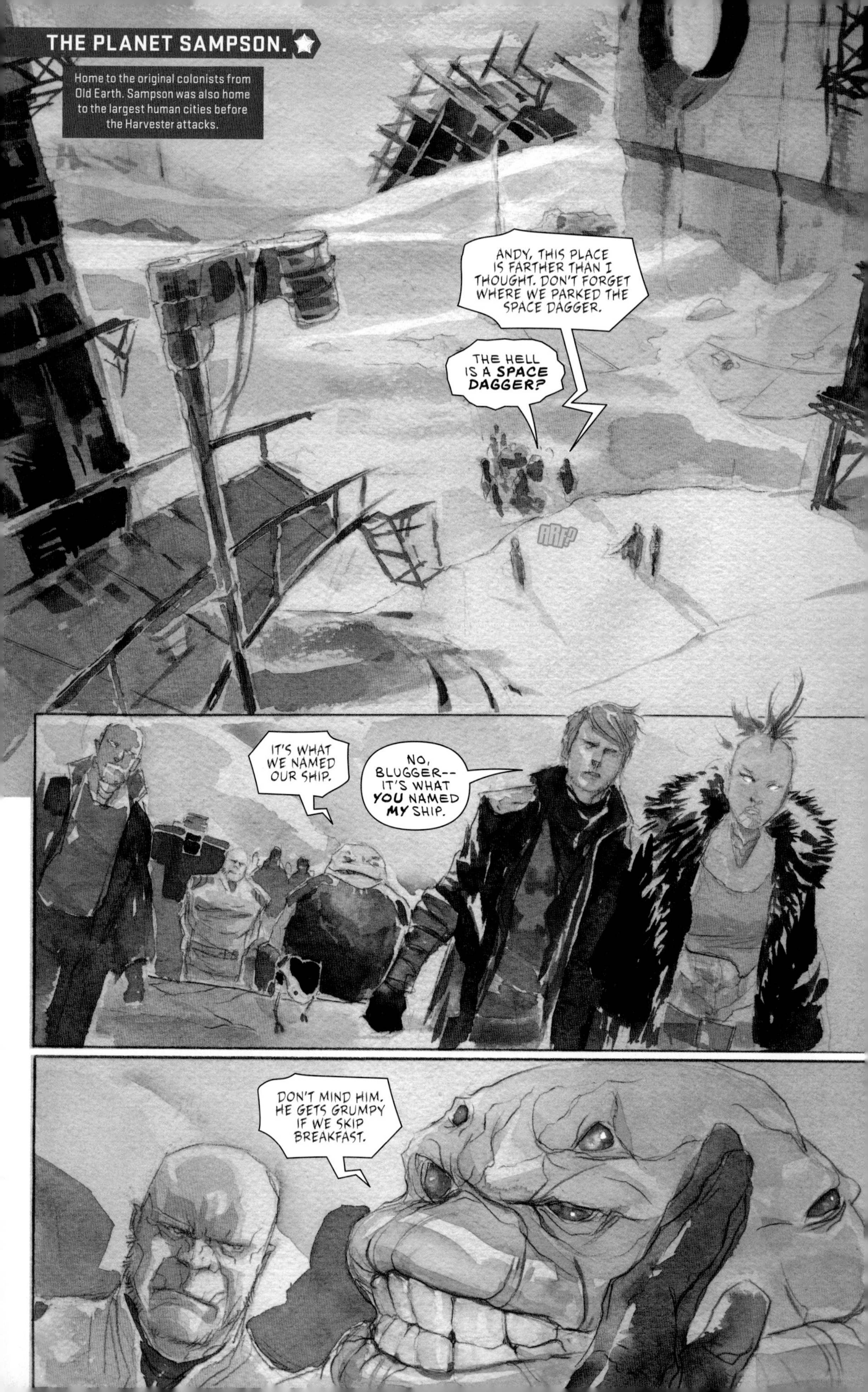
THE PLANET SAMPSON.
Home to the original colonists from Old Earth. Sampson was also home to the largest human cities before the Harvester attacks.
ANDY, THIS PLACE IS FARTHER THAN I THOUGHT. DON'T FORGET WHERE WE PARKED THE SPACE DAGGER.
THE HELL IS A SPACE DAGGER?
ARF?
IT'S WHAT WE NAMED OUR SHIP.
NO, BLUGGER-- IT'S WHAT YOU NAMED MY SHIP.
DON'T MIND HIM. HE GETS GRUMPY IF WE SKIP BREAKFAST.

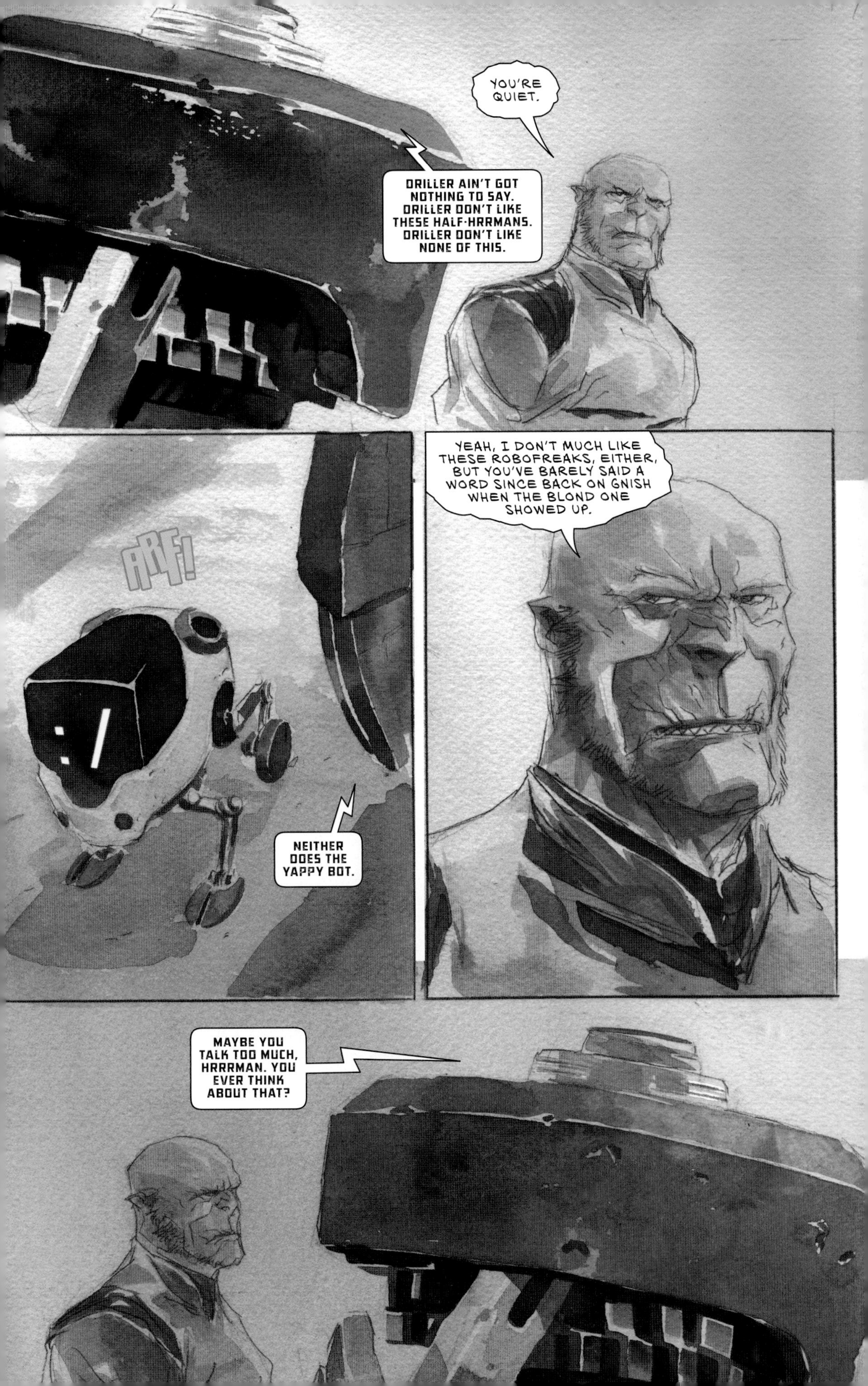
YOU'RE QUIET.
DRILLER AIN'T GOT NOTHING TO SAY. DRILLER DON'T LIKE THESE HALF-HRRMANS. DRILLER DON'T LIKE NONE OF THIS.
ARF!
YEAH, I DON'T MUCH LIKE THESE ROBOFREAKS, EITHER, BUT YOU'VE BARELY SAID A WORD SINCE BACK ON GNISH WHEN THE BLOND ONE SHOWED UP.
NEITHER DOES THE YAPPY BOT.
MAYBE YOU TALK TOO MUCH, HRRRMAN. YOU EVER THINK ABOUT THAT?

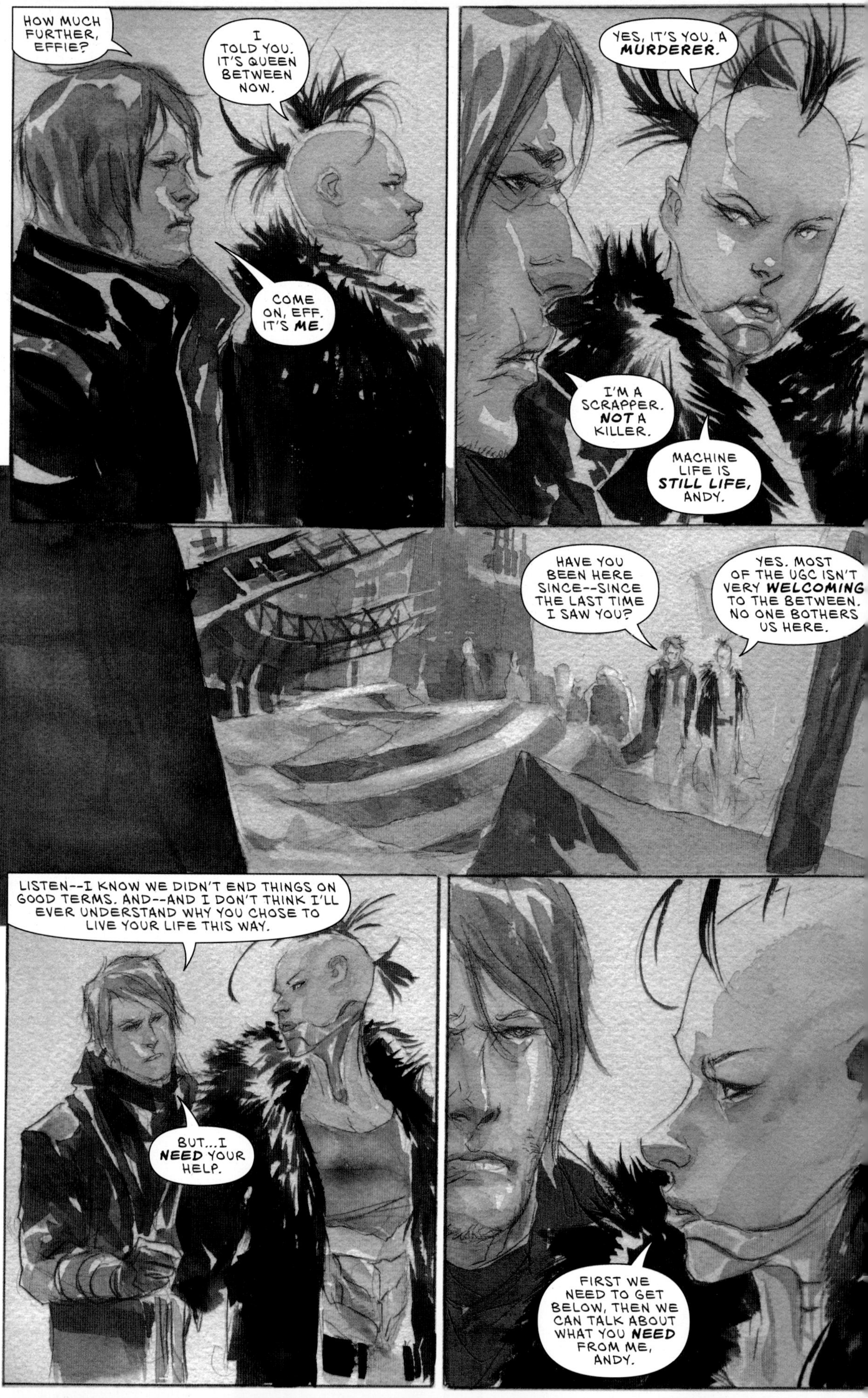
HOW MUCH FURTHER, EFFIE?
I TOLD YOU. IT'S QUEEN BETWEEN NOW.
COME ON, EFF. IT'S **ME.**
YES, IT'S YOU. A **MURDERER.**
I'M A SCRAPPER. **NOT** A KILLER.
MACHINE LIFE IS **STILL LIFE,** ANDY.
HAVE YOU BEEN HERE SINCE--SINCE THE LAST TIME I SAW YOU?
YES. MOST OF THE UGC ISN'T VERY **WELCOMING** TO THE BETWEEN. NO ONE BOTHERS US HERE.
LISTEN--I KNOW WE DIDN'T END THINGS ON GOOD TERMS. AND--AND I DON'T THINK I'LL EVER UNDERSTAND WHY YOU CHOSE TO LIVE YOUR LIFE THIS WAY.
BUT...I **NEED** YOUR HELP.
FIRST WE NEED TO GET BELOW, THEN WE CAN TALK ABOUT WHAT YOU **NEED** FROM ME, ANDY.

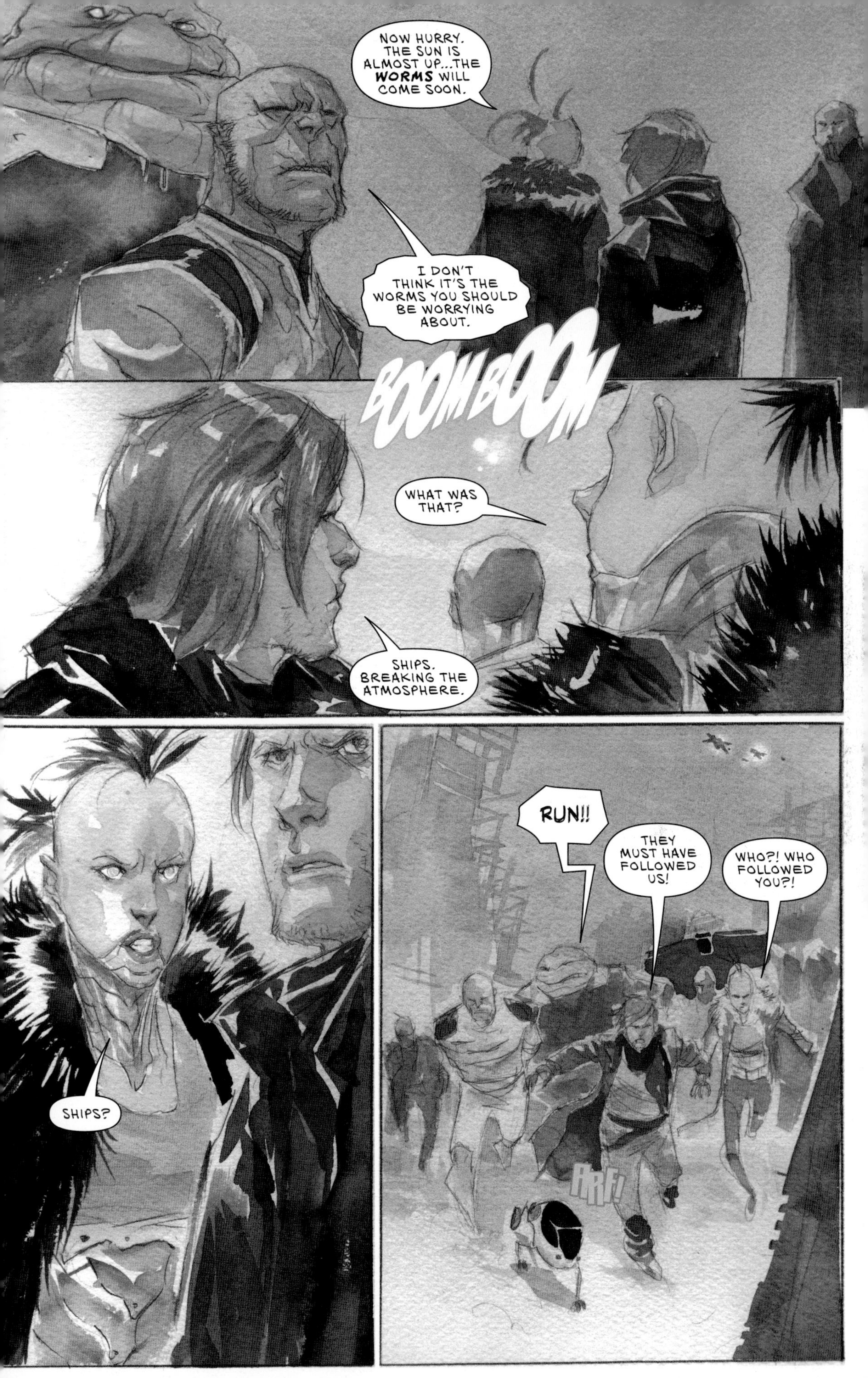
NOW HURRY. THE SUN IS ALMOST UP...THE **WORMS** WILL COME SOON.
I DON'T THINK IT'S THE WORMS YOU SHOULD BE WORRYING ABOUT.
BOOM BOOM
WHAT WAS THAT?
SHIPS. BREAKING THE ATMOSPHERE.
SHIPS?
RUN!!
THEY MUST HAVE FOLLOWED US!
WHO?! WHO FOLLOWED YOU?!
ARF!

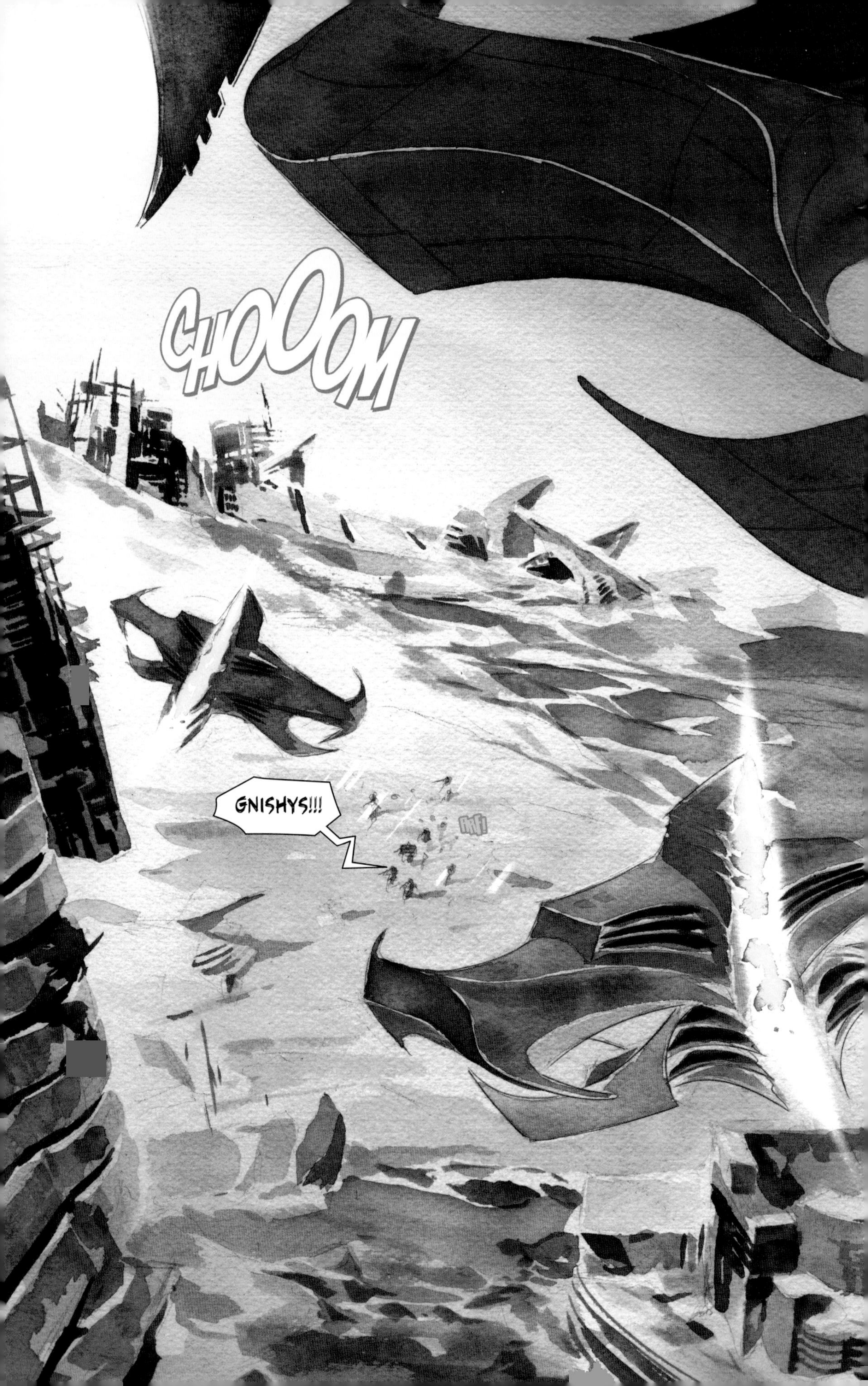
CHOOOOM
GNISHYS!!!
ARF!

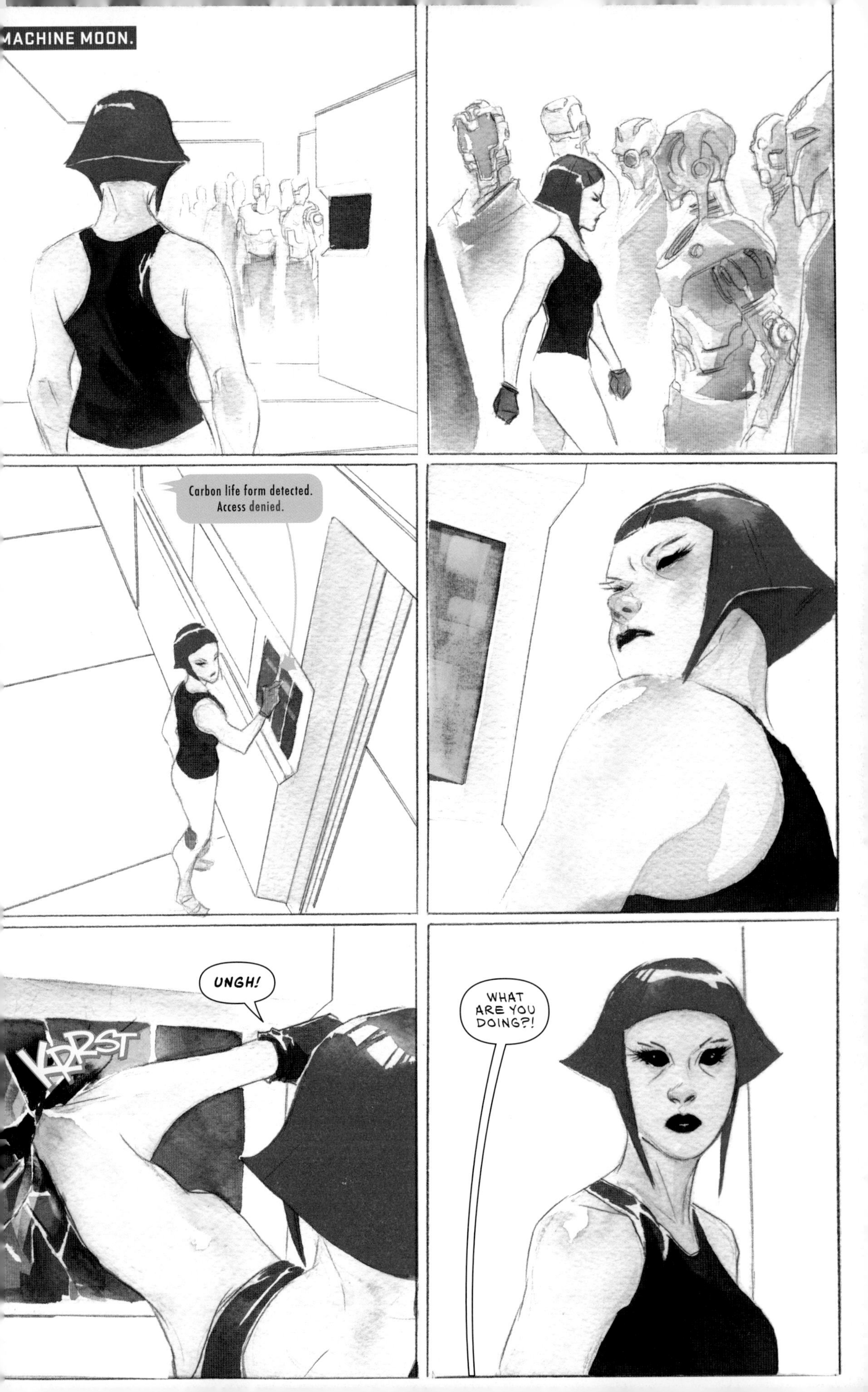
MACHINE MOON.
Carbon life form detected. Access denied.
KRRST
UNGH!
WHAT ARE YOU DOING?!

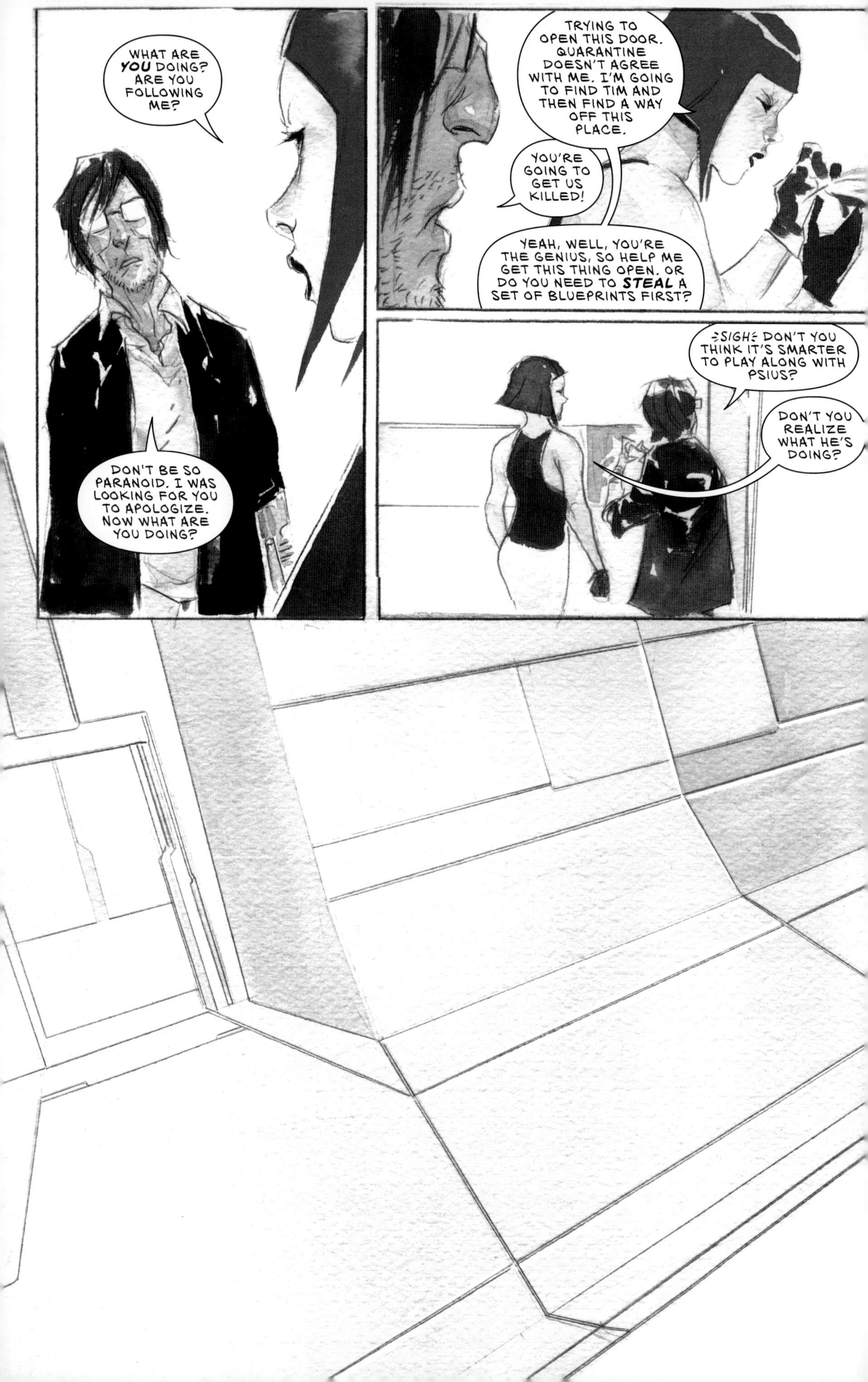
WHAT ARE YOU DOING? ARE YOU FOLLOWING ME?
DON'T BE SO PARANOID. I WAS LOOKING FOR YOU TO APOLOGIZE. NOW WHAT ARE YOU DOING?
TRYING TO OPEN THIS DOOR. QUARANTINE DOESN'T AGREE WITH ME. I'M GOING TO FIND TIM AND THEN FIND A WAY OFF THIS PLACE.
YOU'RE GOING TO GET US KILLED!
YEAH, WELL, YOU'RE THE GENIUS, SO HELP ME GET THIS THING OPEN. OR DO YOU NEED TO STEAL A SET OF BLUEPRINTS FIRST?
=SIGH= DON'T YOU THINK IT'S SMARTER TO PLAY ALONG WITH PSIUS?
DON'T YOU REALIZE WHAT HE'S DOING?

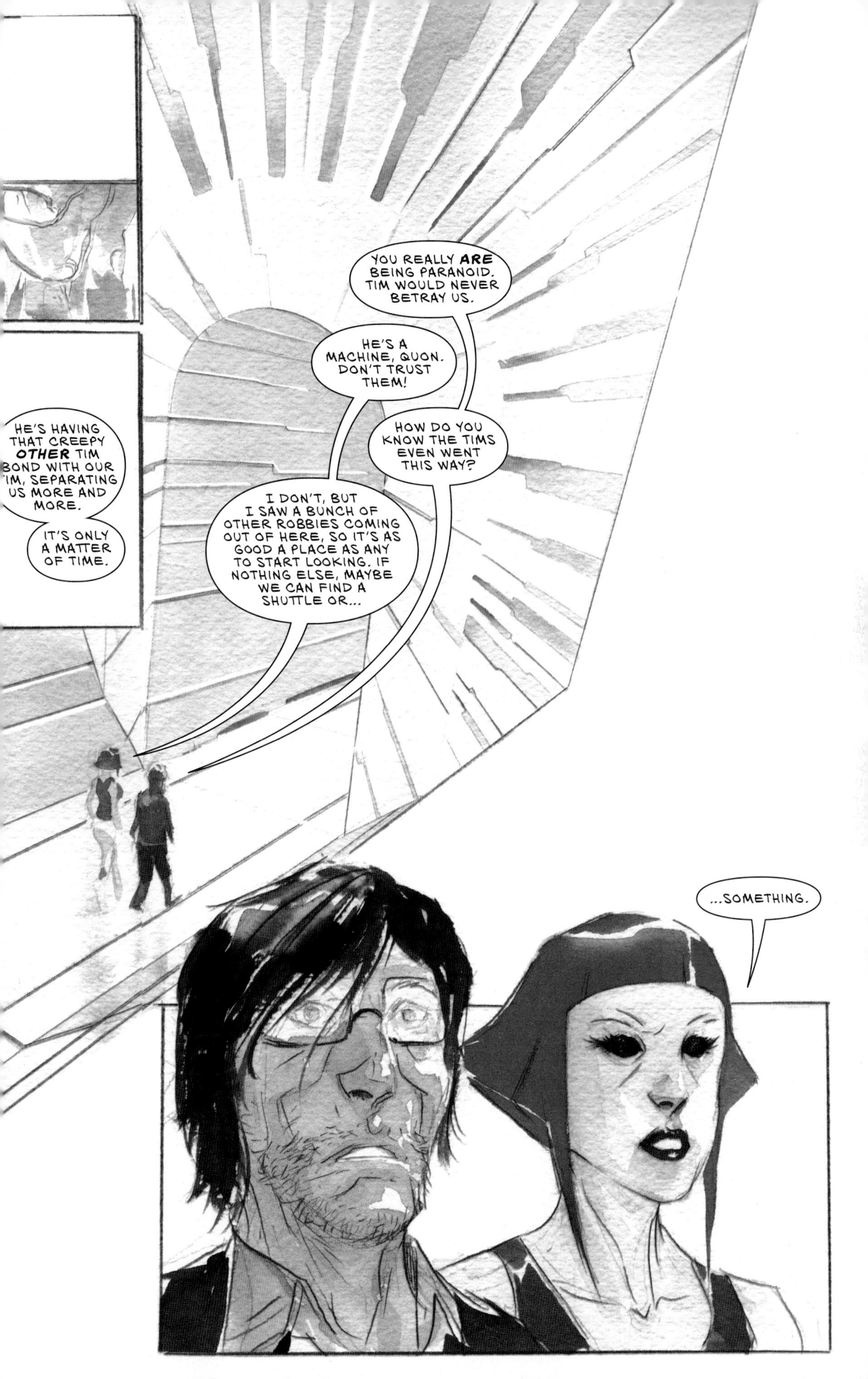
HE'S HAVING THAT CREEPY **OTHER** TIM BOND WITH OUR 'IM, SEPARATING US MORE AND MORE.
IT'S ONLY A MATTER OF TIME.
YOU REALLY **ARE** BEING PARANOID. TIM WOULD NEVER BETRAY US.
HE'S A MACHINE, QUON. DON'T TRUST THEM!
HOW DO YOU KNOW THE TIMS EVEN WENT THIS WAY?
I DON'T, BUT I SAW A BUNCH OF OTHER ROBBIES COMING OUT OF HERE, SO IT'S AS GOOD A PLACE AS ANY TO START LOOKING. IF NOTHING ELSE, MAYBE WE CAN FIND A SHUTTLE OR...
...SOMETHING.

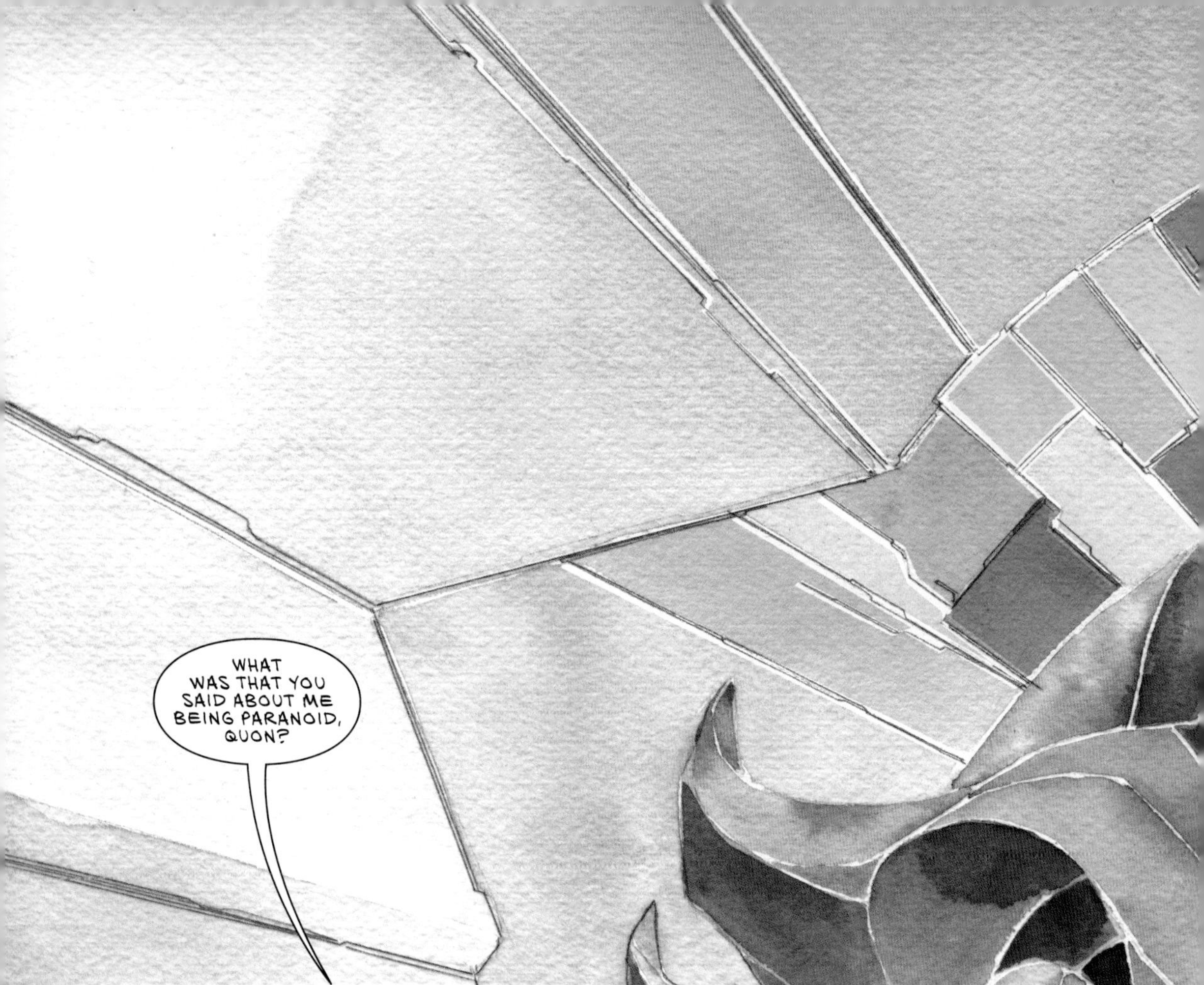
WHAT WAS THAT YOU SAID ABOUT ME BEING PARANOID, QUON?
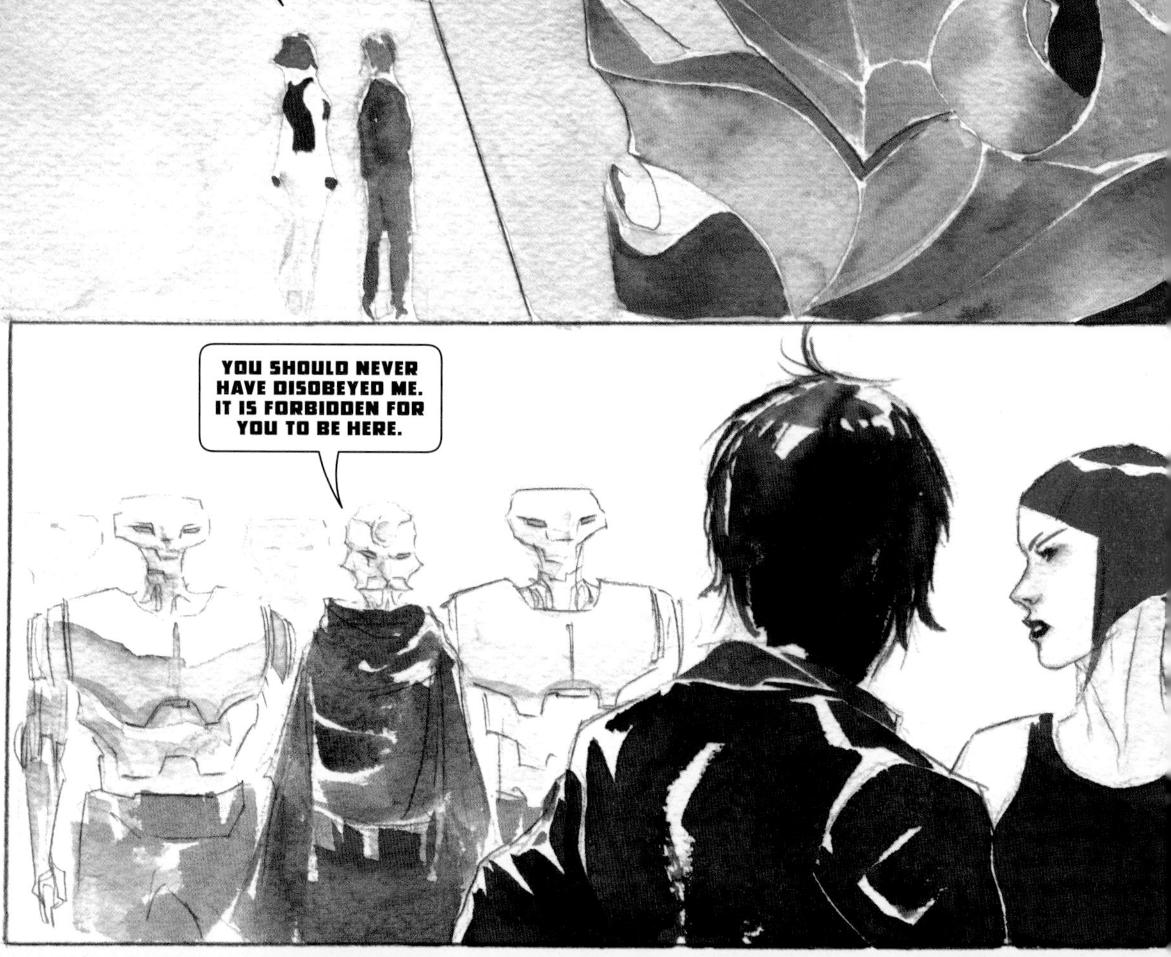
YOU SHOULD NEVER HAVE DISOBEYED ME. IT IS FORBIDDEN FOR YOU TO BE HERE.

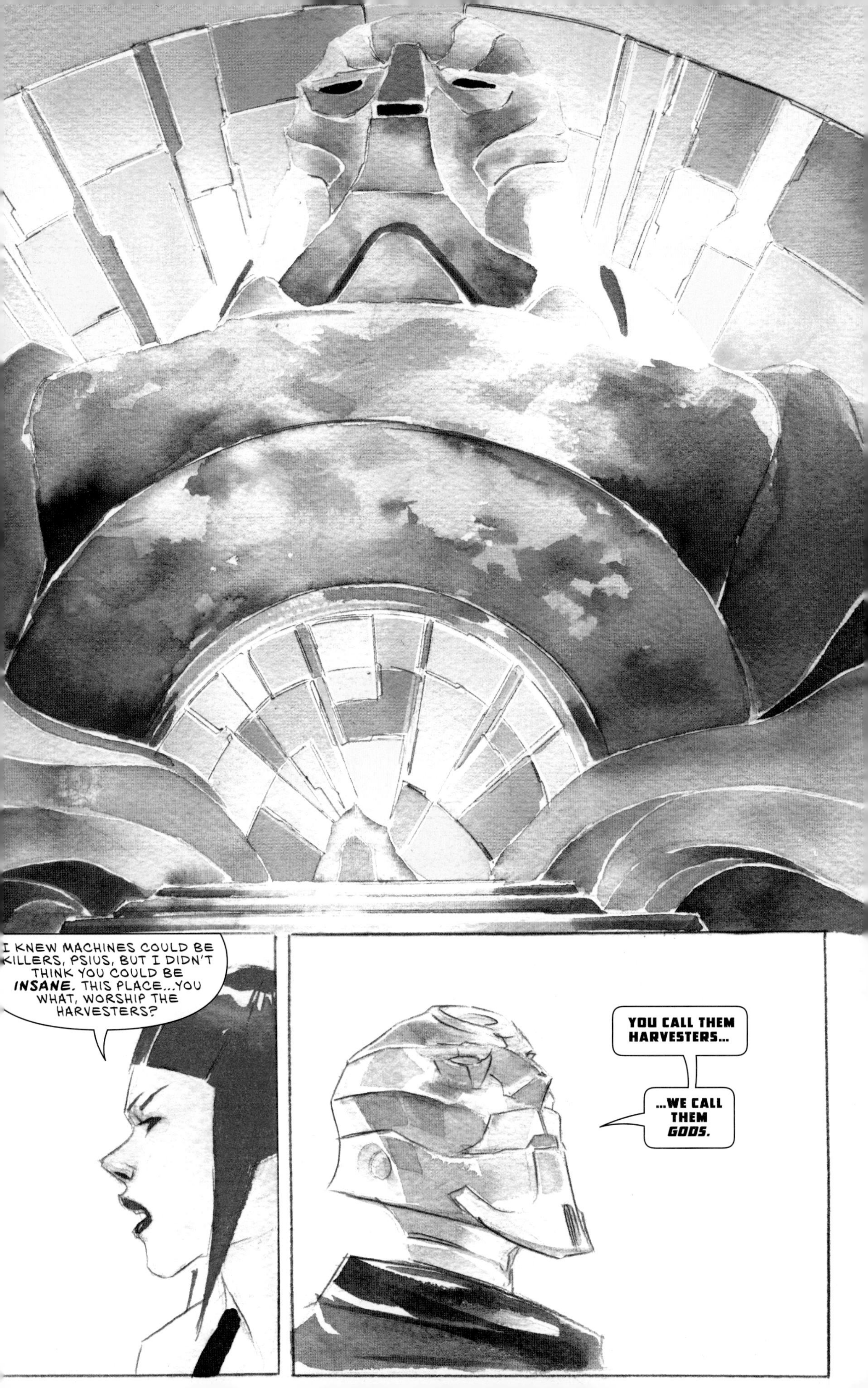
I KNEW MACHINES COULD BE KILLERS, PSIUS, BUT I DIDN'T THINK YOU COULD BE INSANE. THIS PLACE...YOU WHAT, WORSHIP THE HARVESTERS?
YOU CALL THEM HARVESTERS...
...WE CALL THEM GODS.

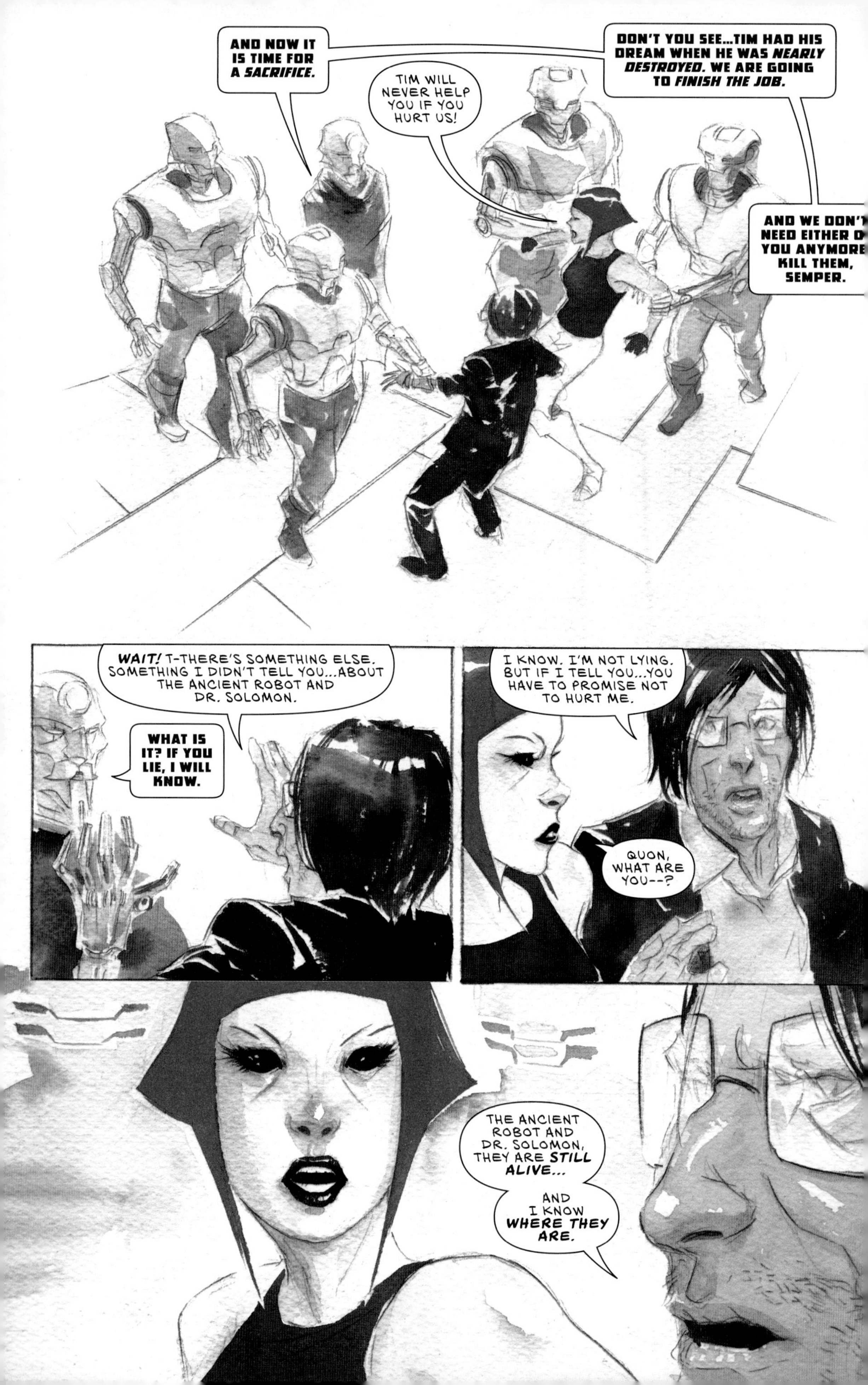
AND NOW IT IS TIME FOR A *SACRIFICE*.
TIM WILL NEVER HELP YOU IF YOU HURT US!
DON'T YOU SEE...TIM HAD HIS DREAM WHEN HE WAS *NEARLY DESTROYED*. WE ARE GOING TO *FINISH THE JOB*.
AND WE DON'T NEED EITHER OF YOU ANYMORE. KILL THEM, SEMPER.
WAIT! T-THERE'S SOMETHING ELSE. SOMETHING I DIDN'T TELL YOU...ABOUT THE ANCIENT ROBOT AND DR. SOLOMON.
WHAT IS IT? IF YOU LIE, I WILL KNOW.
I KNOW. I'M NOT LYING. BUT IF I TELL YOU...YOU HAVE TO PROMISE NOT TO HURT ME.
QUON, WHAT ARE YOU--?
THE ANCIENT ROBOT AND DR. SOLOMON, THEY ARE **STILL ALIVE...**
AND I KNOW **WHERE THEY ARE.**

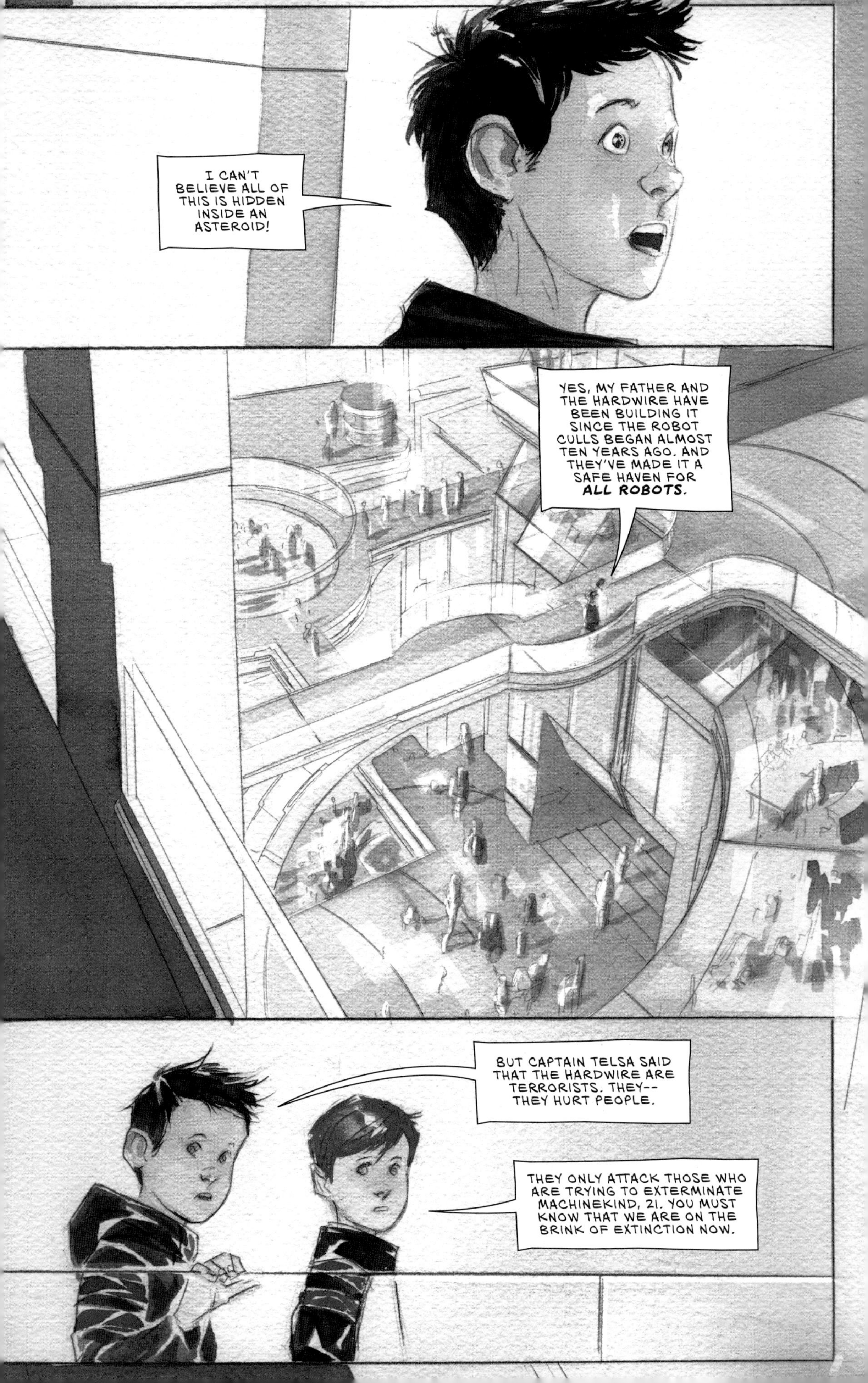
I CAN'T BELIEVE ALL OF THIS IS HIDDEN INSIDE AN ASTEROID!
YES, MY FATHER AND THE HARDWIRE HAVE BEEN BUILDING IT SINCE THE ROBOT CULLS BEGAN ALMOST TEN YEARS AGO. AND THEY'VE MADE IT A SAFE HAVEN FOR **ALL ROBOTS.**
BUT CAPTAIN TELSA SAID THAT THE HARDWIRE ARE TERRORISTS. THEY-- THEY HURT PEOPLE.
THEY ONLY ATTACK THOSE WHO ARE TRYING TO EXTERMINATE MACHINEKIND, 21. YOU MUST KNOW THAT WE ARE ON THE BRINK OF EXTINCTION NOW.

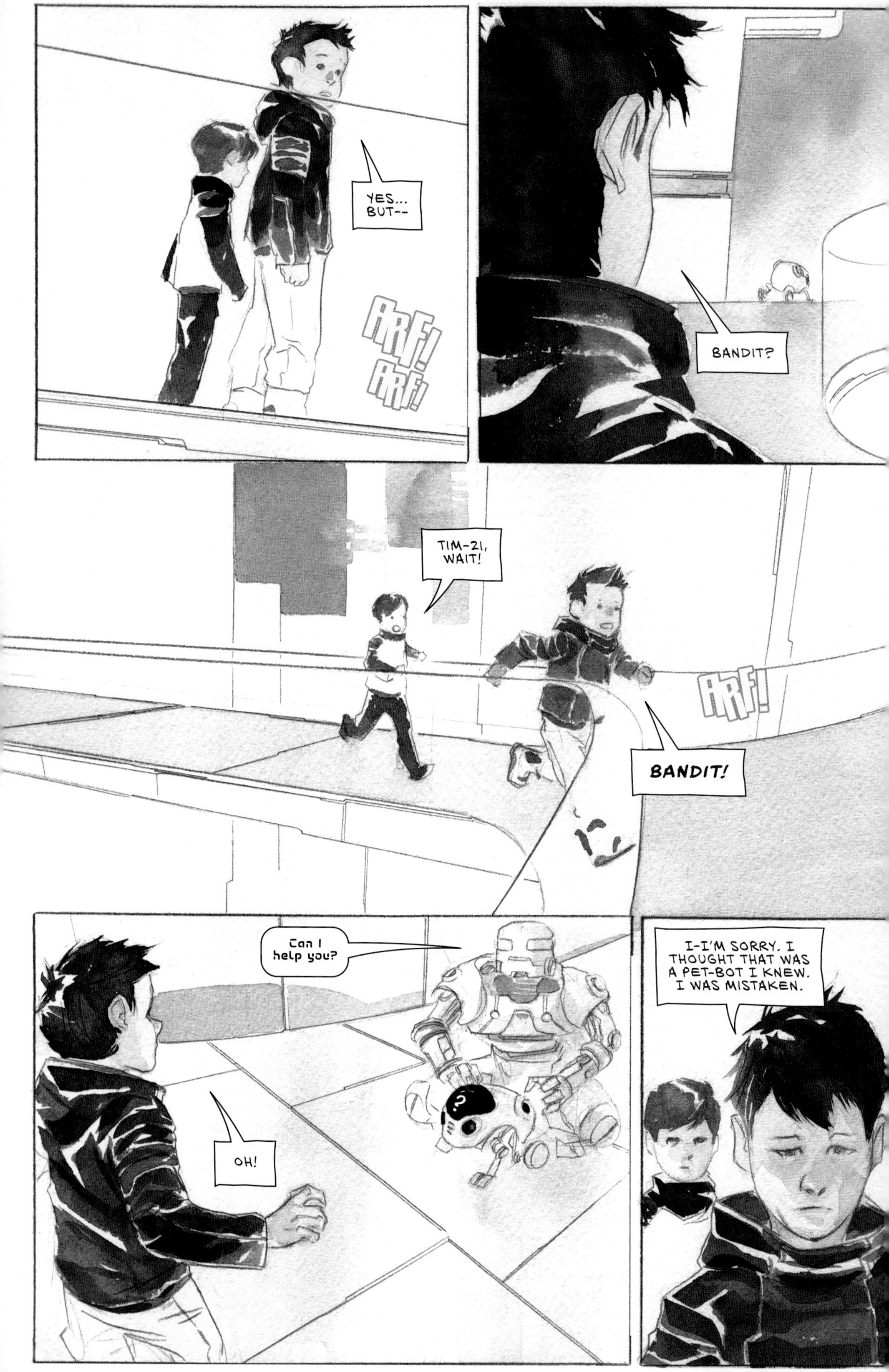
YES... BUT--
ARF! ARF!
BANDIT?
TIM-21, WAIT!
ARF!
BANDIT!
Can I help you?
OH!
I-I'M SORRY. I THOUGHT THAT WAS A PET-BOT I KNEW. I WAS MISTAKEN.

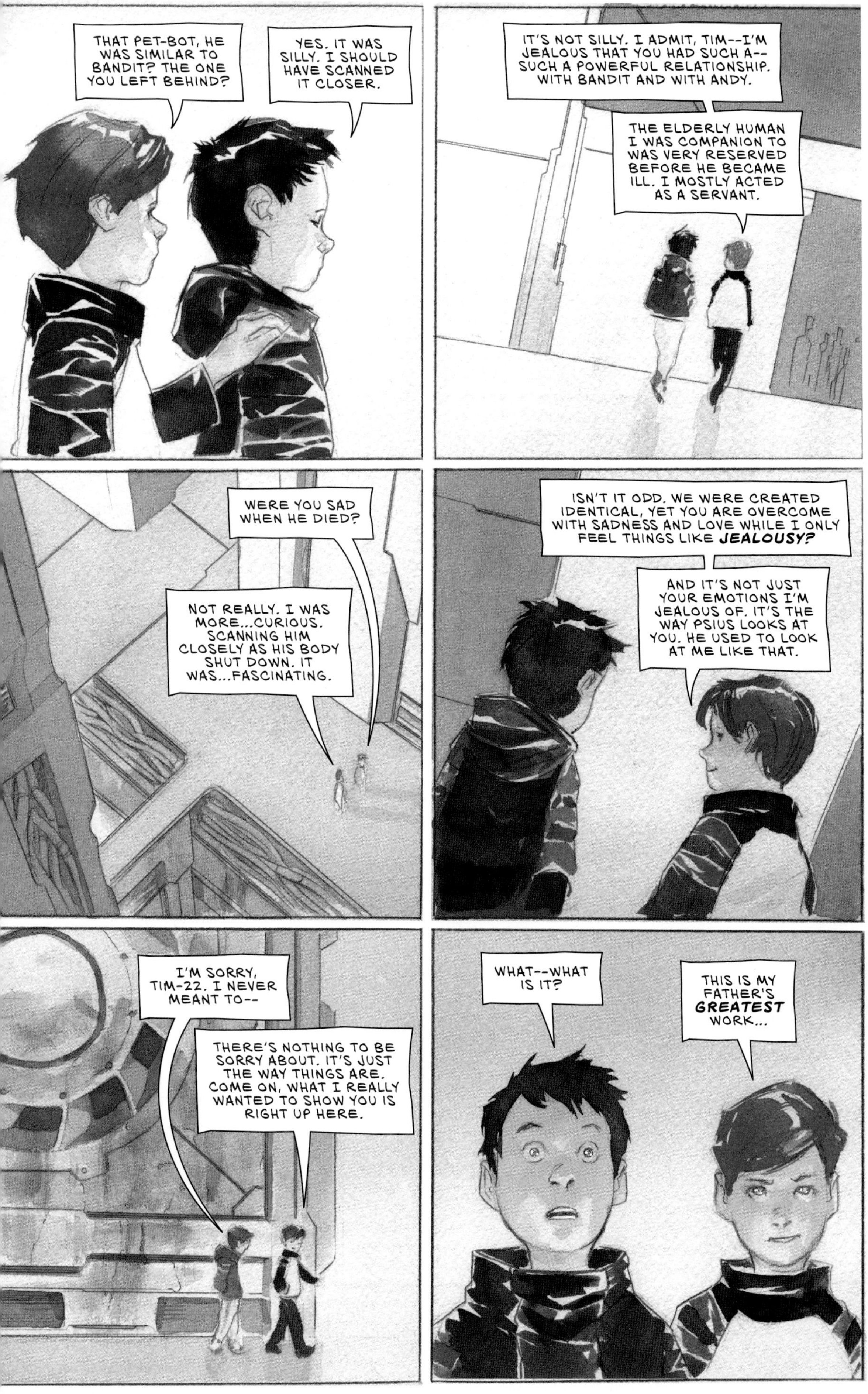
THAT PET-BOT, HE WAS SIMILAR TO BANDIT? THE ONE YOU LEFT BEHIND?
YES. IT WAS SILLY. I SHOULD HAVE SCANNED IT CLOSER.
IT'S NOT SILLY. I ADMIT, TIM--I'M JEALOUS THAT YOU HAD SUCH A-- SUCH A POWERFUL RELATIONSHIP. WITH BANDIT AND WITH ANDY.
THE ELDERLY HUMAN I WAS COMPANION TO WAS VERY RESERVED BEFORE HE BECAME ILL. I MOSTLY ACTED AS A SERVANT.
WERE YOU SAD WHEN HE DIED?
NOT REALLY. I WAS MORE...CURIOUS. SCANNING HIM CLOSELY AS HIS BODY SHUT DOWN. IT WAS...FASCINATING.
ISN'T IT ODD. WE WERE CREATED IDENTICAL, YET YOU ARE OVERCOME WITH SADNESS AND LOVE WHILE I ONLY FEEL THINGS LIKE JEALOUSY?
AND IT'S NOT JUST YOUR EMOTIONS I'M JEALOUS OF. IT'S THE WAY PSIUS LOOKS AT YOU. HE USED TO LOOK AT ME LIKE THAT.
I'M SORRY, TIM-22. I NEVER MEANT TO--
THERE'S NOTHING TO BE SORRY ABOUT. IT'S JUST THE WAY THINGS ARE. COME ON, WHAT I REALLY WANTED TO SHOW YOU IS RIGHT UP HERE.
WHAT--WHAT IS IT?
THIS IS MY FATHER'S GREATEST WORK...

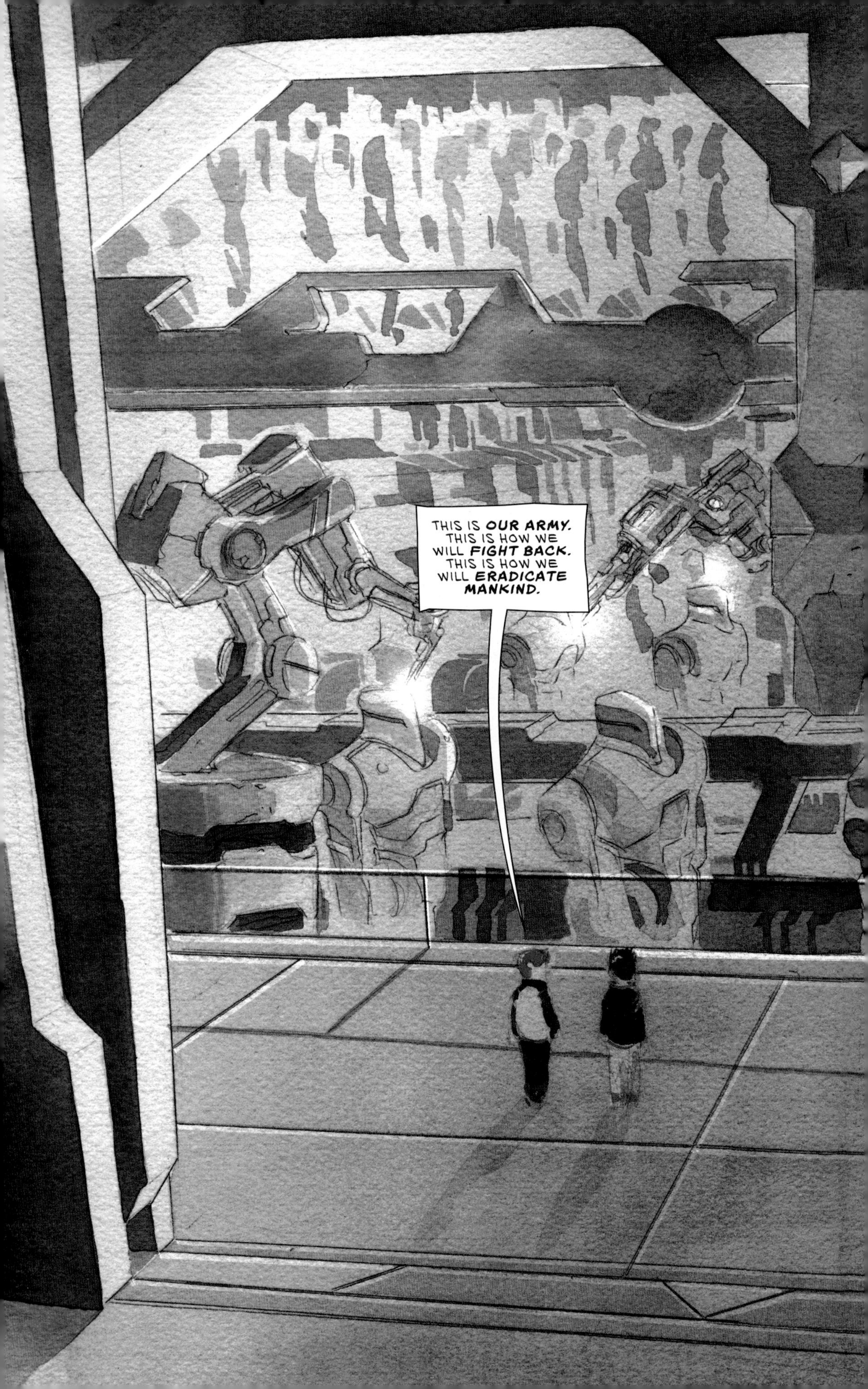
THIS IS **OUR ARMY.** THIS IS HOW WE WILL **FIGHT BACK.** THIS IS HOW WE WILL **ERADICATE MANKIND.**

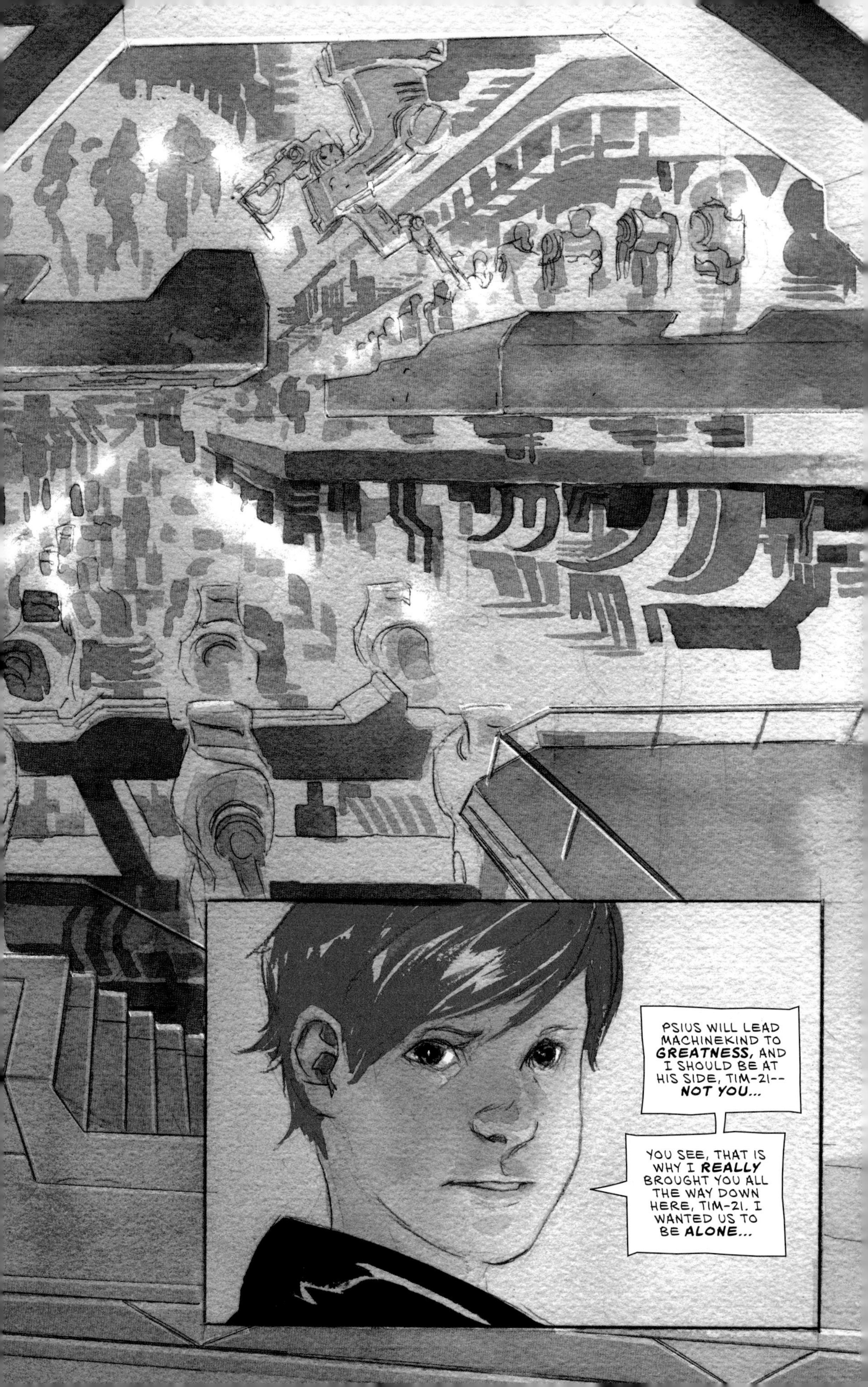
PSIUS WILL LEAD MACHINEKIND TO **GREATNESS,** AND I SHOULD BE AT HIS SIDE, TIM-21-- **NOT YOU...**
YOU SEE, THAT IS WHY I **REALLY** BROUGHT YOU ALL THE WAY DOWN HERE, TIM-21. I WANTED US TO BE **ALONE...**

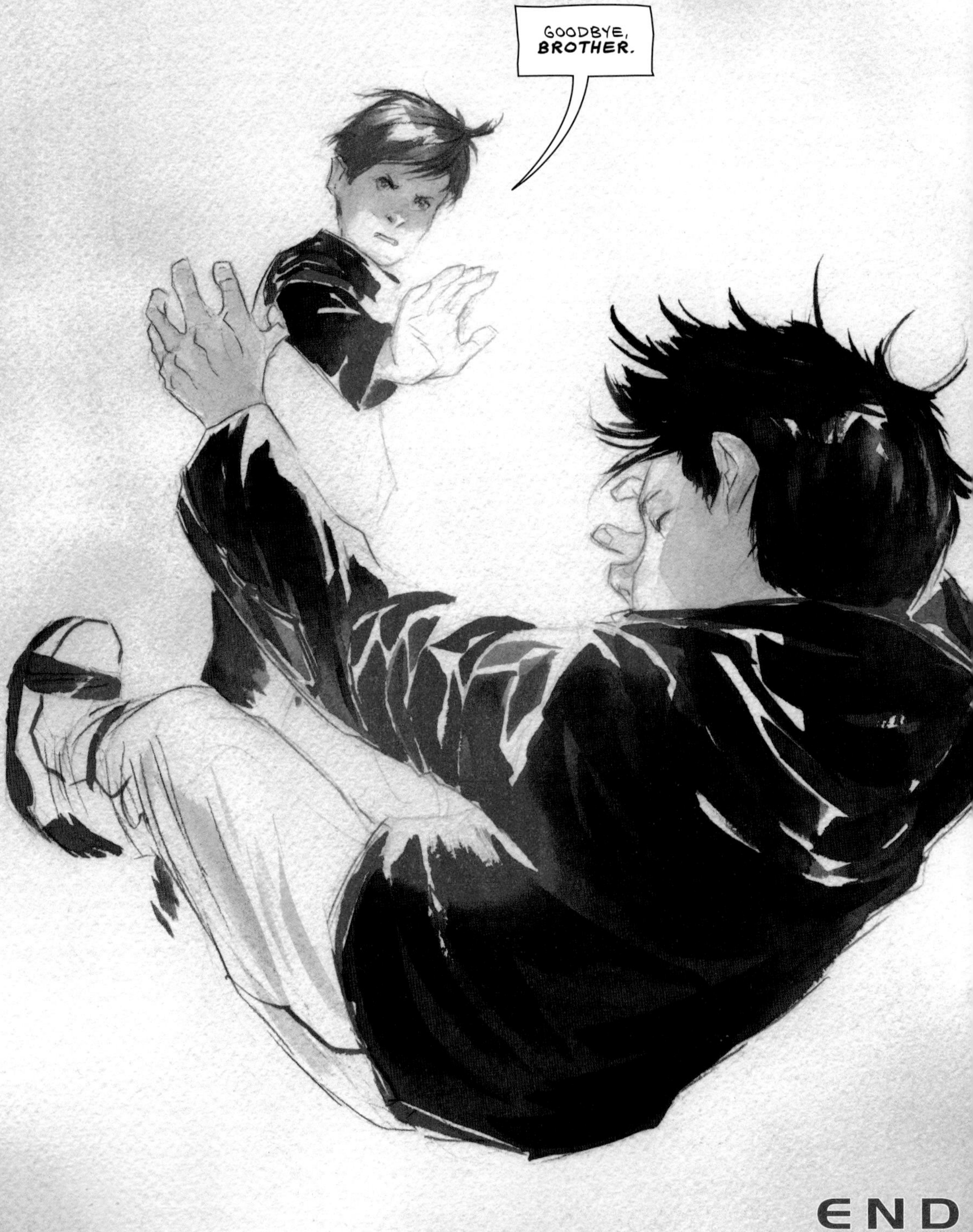
GOODBYE, **BROTHER.**

END
OF BOOK TWO

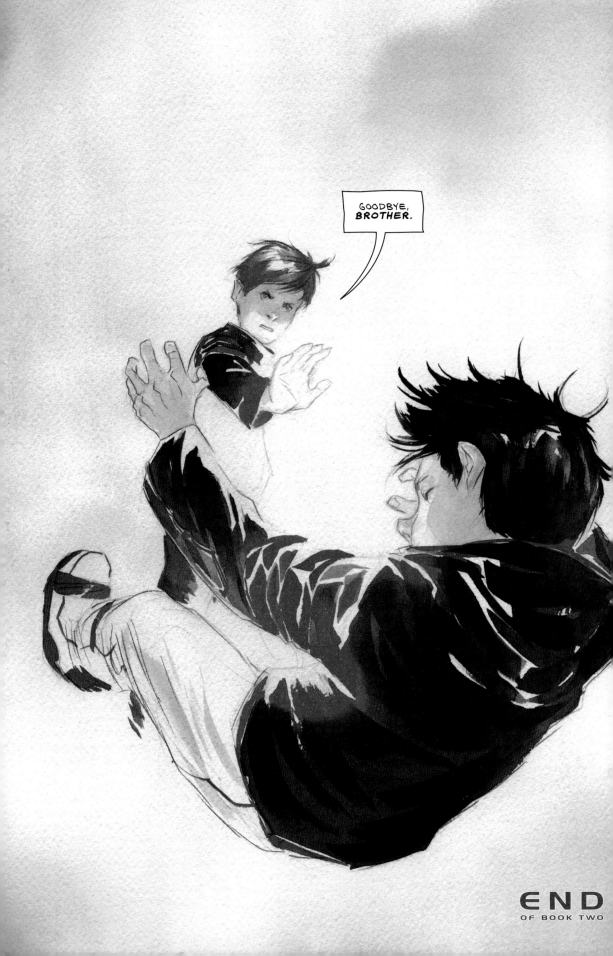

ATLAS OF THE CORE PLANETS OF THE UNITED GALACTIC COUNCIL

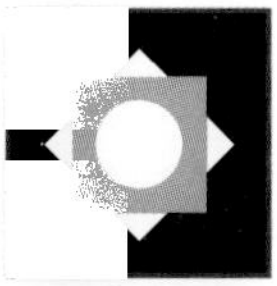

NIYRATA (THE HUB WORLD): Former technological and cultural hub of the UGC and former home of the nine Embassy Cities. One city state for each of the core planets and races representing UGC. Now a devastated world, what's left of the UGC still resides there, clinging to power.

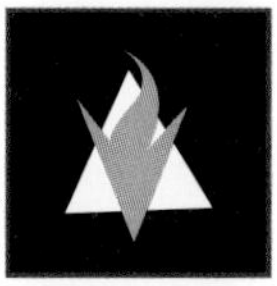

PHAGES (THE GHOST WORLD/HAUNTED PLANET): Home to a gaseous race called THE PHAGES. Their spectral, ghost-like appearance scared early explorers into thinking the planet was haunted. Basically a world full of ghosts with no solid matter. Cities and aliens all made of gases. The only non-gaseous species are a race of hostile 20-foot tall giants.

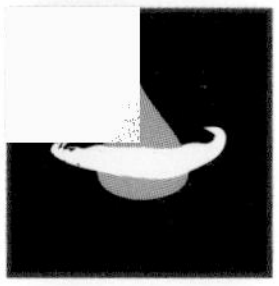

MATA: An aquatic world. Was once home to a great empire and a baroque, almost renaissance-type world, but long ago was flooded and turned into a water-world. The descendants of this monarchy now survive on a floating, mobile kingdom. The ruins of the old cities still lay below the water.

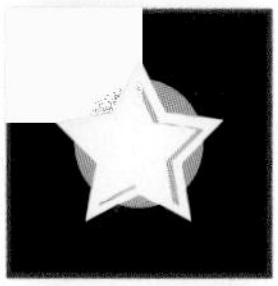

SAMPSON: Home to the original colonists from Old Earth. Sampson is a massive planet and the military center of the Megacosm and home of the largest human cities.

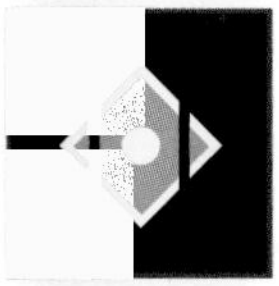

KNOSSOS:
The smallest Core planet in the Megacosm.

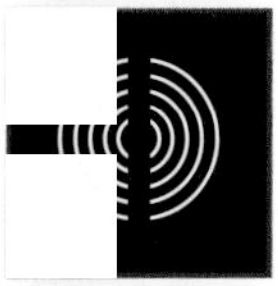

SILENOS: The unique atmosphere on Silenos makes all sound and vibration impossible, creating a totally silent world where the native race communicates by projecting telepathic hieroglyphs into the air.

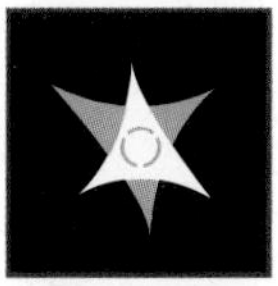

AMUN: The greatest ally of the GNISHIANS.
An insect-like race that live in underground hives.

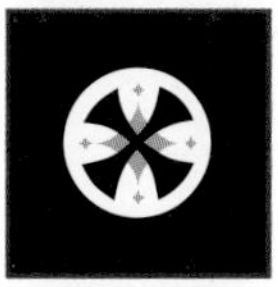

GNISH: The largest planet and the home of the largest military force. Leaders in the anti-robot, anti-technology movement in the wake of the Harvesters. A race ruled by luddite zealots who preach independence and sovereignty for all worlds all the while working for more and more control of Megacosm space. Main funder of the Scrappers. Home to the MELTING PITS, massive gladitorial arenas were Robots are made to fight to the death.

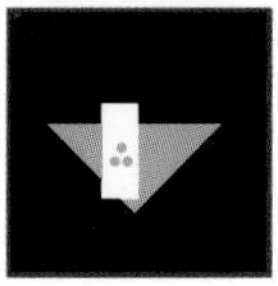

OSTRAKON: A desert wasteland devoid of all life. Contains the ruins of an ancient civilization that has long since gone extinct.

• THE DESCENDER TEAM •

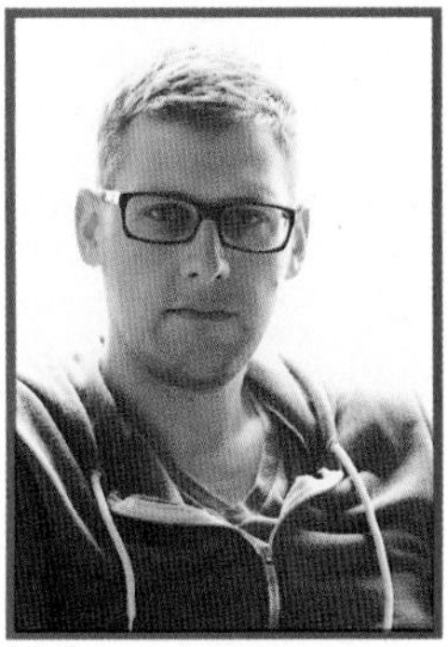

JEFF LEMIRE : *New York Times* bestselling author Jeff Lemire has built a unique career as both the writer and artist of acclaimed literary graphic novels like *Essex County*, *The Underwater Welder*, *Sweet Tooth* and *Trillium* and also as one of the most popular writers of mainstream comics with acclaimed runs on such titles as *Extraordinary X-Men*, *Green Arrow*, *Animal Man* and *Hawkeye* for Marvel and DC Comics.

His next original graphic novel, *ROUGHNECK*, will be published by Simon and Schuster in October 2016.

In 2008 and in 2013 Jeff won the Shuster Award for Best Canadian Cartoonist. He has also received the Doug Wright Award for Best Emerging Talent and the American Library Association's prestigious Alex Award, recognizing books for adults with specific teen appeal. He has also been nominated for eight Eisner Awards, seven Harvey Awards and eight Shuster Awards.

In 2010 *Essex County* became the first graphic novel to be included in the prestigious Canada Reads contest making it to the final five and winning the people's choice vote as best Canadian novel of the decade. *Essex County* is currently in development at CBC as a live action television series with Lemire attached as executive producer.

He lives in Toronto with his wife and son.

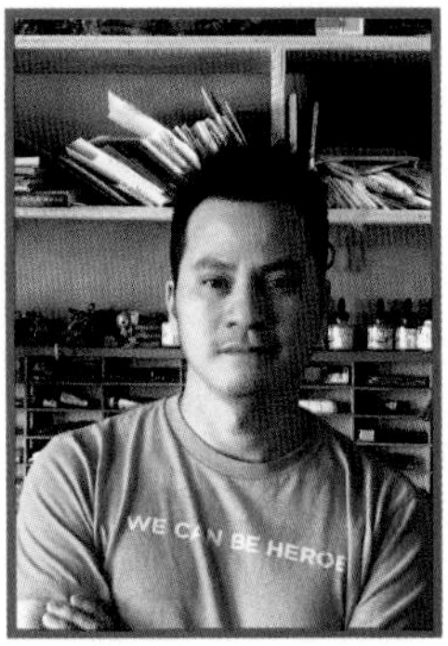
WE CAN BE HEROE

DUSTIN NGUYEN : Dustin is a *New York Times* bestselling American comic artist whose body of work includes – *Wildcats v3.0*, *The Authority Revolution*, *Batman*, *Superman/Batman*, *Detective Comics*, *Batgirl*, and *Batman: Streets of Gotham*. He is also credited as co-writing and illustrating *Justice League Beyond*, illustrating Vertigo's *American Vampire: Lord of Nightmares* with writer Scott Snyder, and co-creator of DC's all ages series, *BATMAN: Lil Gotham* written by himself and Derek Fridolfs. Aside from providing cover illustrations for the majority of his own books, his cover art can also be found on titles ranging from *Batman Beyond* , *Batgirl*, *Justice League: Generation Lost*, *Supernatural* and *Friday the 13th*, to numerous other DC, Marvel, Darkhorse, Boom, IDW, and Image Comics' covers.

Currently, he illustrates *Descender*, a monthly comic published through Image Comics in which he is also co-creator alongside artist/writer Jeff Lemire.

Outside of comics, Dustin also moonlights as a conceptual artist for toys and consumer products, games, and animation.

He enjoys sleeping, driving, and sketching things he cares about.

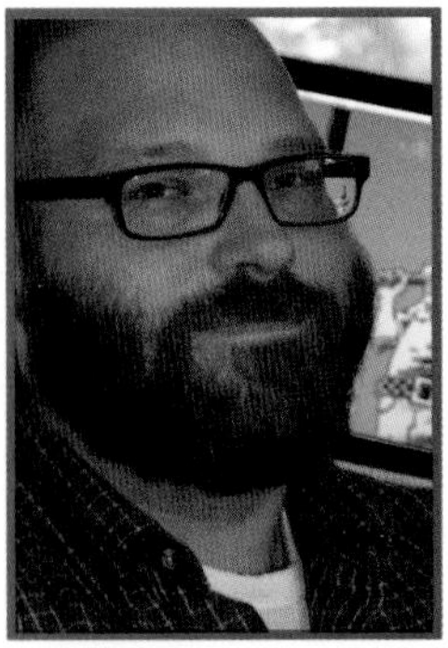

STEVE WANDS : Steve is a comic book letterer. Working on top titles at Image Comics, DC, Vertigo, BOOM! Studios, Archaia, Random House, and Kodansha Comics (to name a few). He also designs, inks, and illustrates for those, and other, companies. When not working like a maniac he spends time with his wife and sons in the greatest state known to man...New Jersey. Oh, and he drinks a lot of coffee.

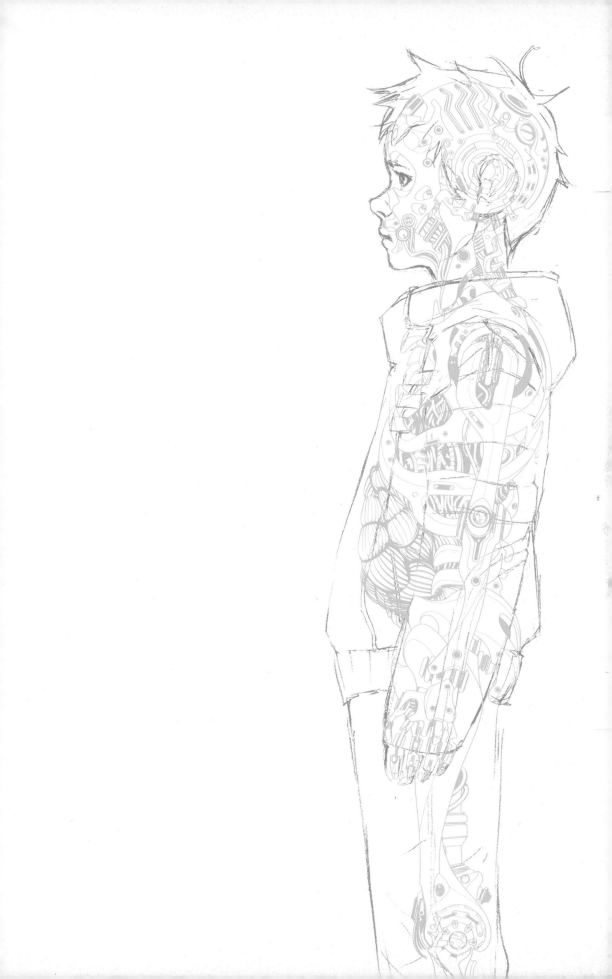

DESCENDER

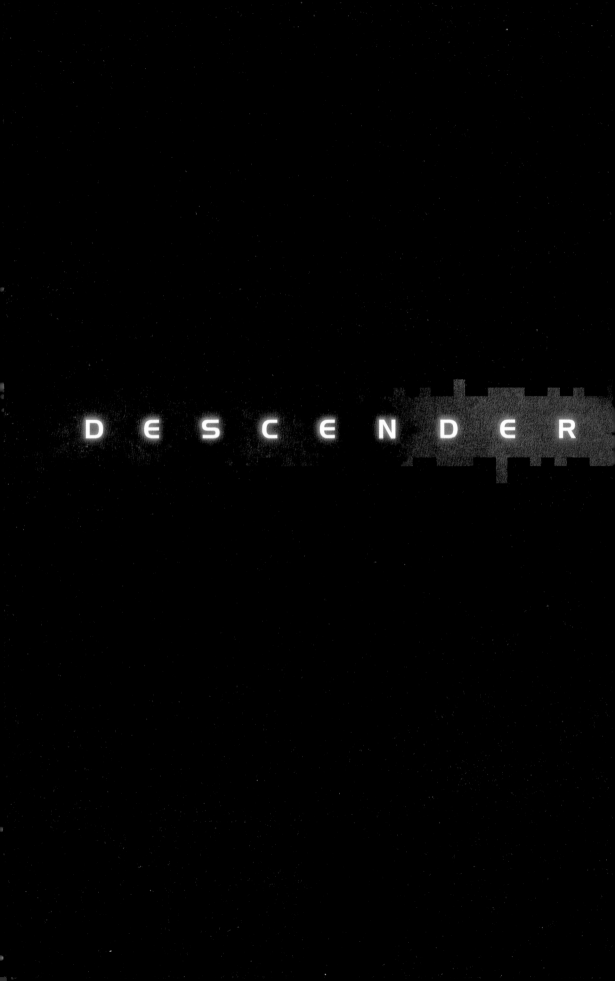